FINE THINGS

DANIELLE STEEL

FINE THINGS

The Delacorte Press Large-Print
Collection

Published by
Delacorte Press
1 Dag Hammarskjold Plaza
New York, N.Y. 10017

MANUFACTURED IN THE UNITED STATES OF AMERICA

LARGE-PRINT EDITION

FIRST PRINTING

Library of Congress Cataloging in Publication Data
Steel, Danielle.
    Fine things.
    I. Title.
PS3569.T33828F5   1987   813'.54   86-13397
ISBN 0-385-29527-8
ISBN 0-385-29542-1 (Large-print edition)

**The Production Review Committee of the
NATIONAL ASSOCIATION
FOR VISUALLY HANDICAPPED
has found this book to meet its criteria
for large type publications.**

To my sweet love, John,
and our children
Beatrix, Trevor, Todd, Nicholas, Samantha,
Victoria, Vanessa, and Maxx
with all my heart,
and love
for all that you are
and do
and mean to me

And in memory of a special lady
and her family, Carola Haller

d.s.

FINE THINGS

Chapter 1

It was almost impossible to get to Lexington and Sixty-third Street. The wind was howling, and the snow drifts had devoured all but the largest cars. The buses had given up somewhere around Twenty-third Street, where they sat huddled like frozen dinosaurs, as one left the flock only very rarely to venture uptown, lumbering down the paths the snowplows left, to pick up a few brave travelers who would rush from doorways frantically waving their arms, sliding wildly to the curb, hurling themselves over the packed snowbanks, to mount the buses with damp eyes and red faces, and in Bernie's case, icicles on his beard.

It had been absolutely impossible to get a taxi. He had given up after fifteen minutes of waiting and started walking south from Seventy-ninth Street. He often walked to work. It was only eighteen blocks from door to door. But today as he walked from Madison to Park and then turned right on Lexington Avenue, he realized that the biting wind was brutal, and he had only gone four more blocks when he gave up. A friendly doorman allowed him to wait in the lobby, as only a few determined souls waited for a bus that had taken hours to come north on Madison Avenue, turned around, and was now heading south on Lexington to carry them to work. The other, more sensible souls had given up when they caught their first glimpse of the blizzard that morning, and had decided not to go to work at all. Bernie was sure the store would be half empty. But he wasn't the type to sit at home twiddling his thumbs or watching the soaps.

And it wasn't that he went to work because he was so compulsive. The truth was that Bernie went to work six days a week, and often when he didn't have to, like today, because he loved the store. He ate, slept, dreamed, and breathed everything that happened from the first to eighth floor of Wolff's. And this year was particularly important. They were introducing seven new lines, four of them by major European designers, and the whole look of American fashion was going to change in men's and women's ready-to-wear markets. He thought about it as he stared into the snowdrifts they passed as they lumbered downtown, but he was no longer seeing the snow, or the stumbling people lurching toward the bus, or even what they wore. In his mind's eye he was seeing the new spring collections just as he had seen them in November, in Paris, Rome, Milan, with gorgeous women wearing the clothes, rolling down the runway like exquisite dolls, showing them to perfection, and suddenly he was glad he had come to work today. He wanted another look at the models they were using the following week for their big fashion show. Having selected and approved the clothing, he wanted to make sure the models chosen were right too. Bernard Fine liked to keep a hand in everything, from department figures to the buying of the clothes, even to the selection of the models, and the design of the invitations that went out to their most exclusive customers. It was all part of the package to him. Everything mattered. It was no different from U.S. Steel as far as he was concerned, or Kodak. They were dealing in a product, in fact a number of them, and the impression that product made rested in his hands.

The crazy thing was that if someone had told him fifteen years before when he was playing football at the University of Michigan that he would be worried about what kind of underwear the models had on, and if the evening gowns would show well, he would have laughed at them . . . or maybe even have busted their jaw. Actually, it struck him funny now, and sometimes he sat in his huge office on the eighth floor, smiling to himself, remembering back then. He had been an all-around jock when he was at Michigan, for the first two years anyway, and after that he had found his niche in Russian literature. Dostoevski had been his hero for the first half of junior year, matched only by Tolstoi, followed almost immediately by Sheila Borden, of slightly less stellar fame. He had met her in Russian I, having decided that he couldn't do the Russian classics justice if he had to read them in translation, so he took a crash course at Berlitz, which taught him to ask for the post office and the rest rooms and find the train in an accent which impressed his teacher enormously. But Russian I had warmed his soul. And so had Sheila Borden. She had sat in the front row, with long straight black hair hanging to her waist romantically, or so he thought, her body very lithe and tight. What had brought her to the Russian class was her fascination with ballet. She had been dancing since she was five, she had explained to him the first time they talked, and you don't understand ballet until you understand the Russians. She had been nervous and intense and wide-eyed, and her body was a poem of symmetry and grace which held him spellbound when he went to watch her dance the next day.

She had been born in Hartford, Connecticut, and her father worked for a bank, which seemed much too plebeian to her. She longed for a history that included greater poignancy, a mother in a wheelchair . . . a father with TB who would have died shortly after she was born. . . . Bernie would have laughed at her the year before, but not in his junior year. At twenty he took her very, very seriously, and she was a fabulous dancer, he explained to his mother when he went home for the holidays.

"Is she Jewish?" his mother asked when she heard her name. Sheila always sounded Irish to her, and Borden was truly frightening. But it could have been Boardman once, or Berkowitz or a lot of other things, which made them cowardly, but at least acceptable. Bernie had been desperately annoyed at her for asking him the question she had plagued him with for most of his life, even before he cared about girls. His mother asked him that about everyone. "Is he Jewish . . . is she . . . what was his mother's maiden name? . . . was he bar mitzvahed last year? . . . . what did you say his father did? She *is* Jewish, isn't she?" Wasn't everyone? Everyone the Fines knew anyway. His parents wanted him to go to Columbia, or even New York University. He could commute, they said. In fact, his mother tried to insist on it. But he had only been accepted at the University of Michigan, which made the decision easy for him. He was saved! And off to Freedomland he went, to date hundreds of blond blue-eyed girls who had never heard of gefilte fish or kreplach or knishes, and had no idea when Passover was. It was a blissful change for him, and by then he had dated all the girls in Scarsdale that his mother was crazy about and he was tired of them. He wanted something new, different, and a trifle forbidden perhaps. And Sheila was all of those. Besides she was so incredibly beautiful with huge black eyes, and shafts of ebony hair. She introduced him to Russian authors he had never heard of before, and they read them all—in translation of course. He tried to discuss the books with his parents over the holidays, to no avail.

"Your grandmother was Russian. You wanted to learn Russian, you could have learned Russian from her."

"That wasn't the same thing. Besides, she spoke Yiddish all the time . . ." His voice had trailed off. He hated arguing with them. His mother loved to argue about everything. It was the mainstay of her life, her greatest joy, her favorite sport. She argued with everyone, and especially with him.

"Don't speak with disrespect about the dead!"

"I wasn't speaking with disrespect. I said that Grandma spoke Yiddish all the time . . ."

"She spoke beautiful Russian too. And what good is that going to do you now? You should be taking science classes, that's what men need in this country today . . . economics . . ." She wanted him to be a doctor like his father, or a lawyer at the very least. His father was a throat surgeon and considered one of the most important men in his field. But it had never appealed to Bernie to follow in his father's footsteps, even as a child. He admired him a great deal. But he would have hated being a doctor. He wanted to do other things, in spite of his mother's dreams.

"Russian? Who talks Russian except Communists?" Sheila Borden . . . that was who. . . . Bernie looked at his mother in despair. She was attractive, she always had been. He had never been embarrassed about the way his mother looked, or his father for that matter. His father was a tall, spare man with dark eyes and gray hair, and a frequently distracted look. He loved what he did, and he was always thinking of his patients. But Bernie always knew he was there, if he needed him. And his mother had been dying her hair blond for years, "Autumn Sun" the color was called, and it looked well on her. She had green eyes, which Bernie had inherited from her, and she had kept her figure well. She wore expensive clothes that one never really noticed. They were navy suits and black dresses and had cost an arm and a leg at Lord and Taylor or Saks. Somehow she just looked like a mother to him. "Why does that girl study Russian anyway? Where are her parents from?"

"Connecticut."

"Where in Connecticut?" He wanted to ask her if she was planning to visit them.

"Hartford. What difference does it make?"

"Don't be rude, Bernard." She looked prim and he folded his napkin and pushed back his chair. Eating dinner with her always gave him stomach pains. "Where are you going? You haven't been excused." As though he were still five years old. He hated coming home sometimes. And then he felt guilty for hating it. And then he got mad at her for making him feel guilty for hating it. . . .

"I have some studying to do before I go back."

"Thank God you're not playing football any-more." She always said things like that that made him want to rebel. It made him want to turn

around and tell her he'd gone back on the team
. . . or that he was studying the ballet with Sheila
now just to shake her up a little bit. . . .

"The decision isn't necessarily permanent,
Mom."

Ruth Fine glared at him. "Talk to your father
about it." Lou knew what he had to do. She had
already talked to him at length. If Bernie ever
wanted to play football again, you offer him a new
car. . . . If Bernie had known, he would have
gone through the roof, and not only refused the
car, but gone back to playing football immediately. He hated being bribed. Hated the way she
thought sometimes, and the overprotective way
she treated him, in spite of his father's more sensible attitudes. It was difficult being an only child,
and when he got back to Ann Arbor and saw
Sheila she agreed with him. The holidays hadn't
been easy for her either. And they hadn't been
able to get together at all, even though Hartford
was certainly not the end of the world, but it might
as well have been. Her parents had had her late in
life, and now they treated her like a piece of glass,
terrified each time she left the house, frightened
that she would get hurt or mugged or raped, or
fall on the ice, or meet the wrong men, or go to
the wrong school. They hadn't been thrilled at the
prospect of the University of Michigan either, but
she had insisted on it. She knew just how to get
what she wanted from them. But it was exhausting
having them hang all over her. She knew just what
Bernie meant, and after their Easter holidays they

devised a plan. They were going to meet in Europe the following summer, and travel for at least a month, without telling anyone. And they had.

It had been blissful seeing Venice and Paris and Rome for the first time together. Sheila had been madly in love, and as they lay naked on a deserted beach in Ischia, with her raven black hair falling over her shoulders, he had known that he had never seen anyone as beautiful. So much so that he was secretly thinking of asking her to marry him. But he kept it to himself. He dreamt of getting engaged to her over the Christmas holidays, and married after they graduated the following June. . . . They went to England and Ireland too, and flew home from London on the same plane.

As usual, his father was in surgery. His mother picked him up, despite his cable not to. Eagerly waving to him, she looked younger than her years in her new beige Ben Zuckerman suit with her hair done just for him. But whatever good feelings he had for her disappeared as she spotted his traveling companion immediately. "Who is that?"

"This is Sheila Borden, Mom." Mrs. Fine looked as though she might faint.

"You've been traveling together all this time?" They had given him enough money for six weeks. It had been his twenty-first birthday present from them. "You've been traveling *together* so . . . so . . . shamelessly . . . ?" He wanted to die as he listened to her, and Sheila was smiling at him as though she didn't give a damn.

"It's okay . . . don't worry, Bernie . . . I have to get the shuttle bus to Hartford anyway . . ." She gave him a private smile, grabbed her duffel bag, and literally disappeared without saying goodbye, as his mother began to dab at her eyes.

"Mom . . . please . . ."

"How could you lie to us like that?"

"I didn't lie to you. I told you I was meeting friends." His face was red and he wanted the floor to open up and swallow him. He wanted never to see his mother again.

"You call *that* a friend?"

He thought instantly of all the times they had made love . . . on beaches, in parks, next to rivers, in tiny hotels. . . . Nothing she ever said could take away that memory and he stared at his mother belligerently.

"She's the best friend I have!" He grabbed his bag and started out of the airport alone, leaving her standing there, but he had made the mistake of turning back to look at her once, and she had been standing there crying openly. He couldn't do it to her. He went back and apologized and hated himself for it afterwards.

Back at school in the fall, the romance had flourished anyway, and this time when they came back for Thanksgiving, he drove up to Hartford to meet her family. They had been cool but polite, obviously surprised by something Sheila hadn't said, and when they flew back to school, Bernie questioned her.

"Were they upset that I'm Jewish?" He was curious. He wondered if her parents were as intense as his own, although that hardly seemed possible. Nobody could be as intense as Ruth Fine, not in his eyes anyway.

"No." Sheila smiled absentmindedly, lighting a joint in the back row of the plane on the way back to Michigan. "Just surprised, I guess. I never thought it was such a big deal I had to mention it." He liked that about her. She took everything in stride. Nothing was ever a big deal, and he took a quick hit with her before they carefully put out the joint and she put the roach in an envelope in her purse. "They thought you were nice."

"I thought they were nice too." He lied. Actually he had thought them boring in the extreme, and was surprised that her mother had so little style. They talked about the weather and world news, and absolutely nothing else. It was like living in a vacuum, or enduring a perennial live commentary of the news. She seemed so unlike them, but then again she said the same thing about him. She had called his mother hysterical after the only time they met, and he hadn't disagreed with her. "Are they coming to graduation?"

"Are you kidding?" She laughed. "My mother already cries talking about it." He was still thinking of marrying her, but he hadn't said anything to her. He surprised her on Valentine's Day with a beautiful little diamond ring he had bought for her, with money his grandparents had left him when they died. It was a small, neat emerald-cut solitaire, it was only two carats but the stone was impeccable. The day he bought it his chest felt tight he was so excited all the way home. He had swept her off her feet, kissed her hard on the mouth, and thrown the red-wrapped box in her lap with a careless toss.

"Try that on for size, kid."

She had thought it was a joke, and laughed until she opened it. And then her mouth fell open and she burst into tears. She had thrown the box back at him and left without a word, as he stood with his mouth open, staring after her. Nothing made any sense to him, until she came back to talk about it late that night. They both had rooms, but more often than not, they both stayed in his. It was larger and more comfortable and he had two desks, and she stared at the ring in the open box on his. "How could you do a thing like that?" He didn't understand. Maybe she thought the ring was too big.

"A thing like what? I want to marry you." His eyes had been gentle as he reached out to her, but she turned away and walked across the room.

"I thought you understood . . . all this time I thought everything was cool."

"What the hell does that mean?"

"It means I thought we had an equal relationship."

"Of course we do. What does that have to do with anything?"

"We don't need marriage . . . we don't need all that traditional garbage." She looked at him disgustedly and he was shocked. "All we need is what we have right now, for as long as it lasts." It was the first time he had heard her talk like that and he was wondering what had happened to her.

"And how long is that?"

"Today . . . next week . . ." She shrugged. "Who cares? What difference does it make? But you can't nail it down with a diamond ring."

"Well, pardon me." But he was suddenly furious. He grabbed the box, snapped it shut, and threw it into one of his desk drawers. "I apologize for doing something so innately bourgeois. I guess my Scarsdale was showing again."

She looked at him as though with brand-new eyes. "I had no idea you were making so much of this." She looked puzzled by him, as though she suddenly couldn't remember his name. "I thought you understood everything . . ." She sat down on the couch and stared at him as he strode to the window, and then turned to look back at her.

"No. You know something? I don't understand anything. We've been sleeping with each other for over a year. We basically live together, we went to Europe together last year. What did you think this was? A casual affair?" Not for him. He wasn't that kind of man, even at twenty-one.

"Don't use such old-fashioned words." She stood up and stretched, as though she were bored, and he noticed she wasn't wearing a bra, which only made things worse. He could suddenly feel his desire mounting for her.

"Maybe it's just too soon." He looked at her hopefully, led by what he felt between his legs as much as what he felt in his heart, and hating himself for it. "Maybe we just need more time."

But she was shaking her head. And she didn't kiss him good night as she walked to the door. "I don't ever want to get married, Bern. It's not my bag. I want to go to California when we graduate and just hang out for a while." He could suddenly just imagine her there . . . in a commune.

"What kind of life is 'hanging out'? It's a dead end!"

She shrugged with a smile. "That's all I want right now, Bern." Their eyes held for a long time. "Thanks anyway for the ring." She closed the door softly as she left, and he sat alone in the dark for a long, long time, thinking about her. He loved her so much, or at least he thought he did. But he had never seen this side of her, this casual indifference to what someone else felt, and then suddenly he remembered how she had treated her parents when he had visited them. She didn't really seem to care a whole lot about what they felt, and she always thought he was crazy when he called his folks, or bought his mother a gift before he went home. He had sent her flowers on her birthday and Sheila had made fun of him, and now it all came rushing back to him. Maybe she didn't give a damn about anyone, not even him. She was just having a good time, and doing what felt good at the time. And up until then he had been what had felt good to her, but the engagement ring did not. He put it back in the drawer when he went to bed, and his heart felt like a rock as he lay in the dark thinking of her.

And things hadn't improved much after that. She had joined a consciousness-raising group, and one of the subjects they seemed to love to discuss most was her relationship with Bernie. She came home and attacked him almost constantly about his values, his goals, his way of talking to her.

"Don't talk to me like a child. I'm a woman, goddammit, and don't you forget that those balls of yours are only decorative, and not too much so at that. I'm just as smart as you are, I've got just as much guts . . . . my grades are just as good . . . . the only thing I don't have is that piece of skin hanging between your legs and who gives a damn anyway?" He was horrified, and even more so when she gave up ballet. She kept up with the Russian, but she talked a lot about Che Guevara now, and she had taken to wearing combat boots, and accessories she bought at the army surplus store. She was particularly fond of men's undershirts, worn without a bra, with her dark nipples showing through easily. He was beginning to be embarrassed to walk down the street with her.

"You're not serious?" she asked when they talked a lot about the senior prom, and they both agreed that it was corny as hell, but he had admitted to her that he wanted to go anyway. It was a memory to save for another time, and finally she had agreed with him. But she had shown up at his apartment wearing army fatigues open to her waist and a torn red T-shirt underneath. And her boots weren't genuine military but they might as well have been. They were perfect replicas sprayed with gold paint, and she laughingly called them her "new party shoes" as he stared at her. He was wearing the white dinner jacket he had worn to a wedding the year before. His father had gotten it at Brooks Brothers for him and it fit him perfectly, and with his auburn hair and green eyes and the beginnings of a summer tan, he looked very handsome standing there. But she looked ridiculous and he told her so. "That's a rude thing to do to the kids who take it seriously. If we do go, we owe it to them to dress with respect."

"Oh for chrissake." She threw herself on his couch with a look of total disdain. "You look like Lord Fauntleroy. Christ, wait till I tell my group about this."

"I don't give a damn about your group!" It was the first time he had lost his temper with her over that and she looked surprised as he advanced on her and stood towering over her as she lay on the couch, swinging her long graceful legs in the fatigues and gold combat boots. "Now get off your ass and go back to your room and change."

"Screw you." She smiled up at him.

"I'm serious, Sheila. You're not going in that outfit."

"Yes, I am."

"No, you're not."

"Then we won't go."

He hesitated for a fraction of an instant and strode to the door of his room. "You. Not me. *You* won't go. I'm going by myself."

"Have a good time." She waved, and he walked outside fuming silently. And he had gone to the dance alone and had a lousy time. He didn't dance with anyone, but he stayed there purposely to prove a point. But she had ruined the evening for him. And she ruined graduation with the same kind of stunt, only worse, because his mother was in the audience. When she came up on the stage, and once she had the diploma in her hand, Sheila turned and made a little speech about how meaningless the token gestures of the establishment were, that there were oppressed women everywhere in the world. And on their behalf, and her own, she was rejecting the chauvinism of the University of Michigan. She then proceeded to tear the diploma in half while the entire audience gasped, and Bernie wanted to cry. There was absolutely nothing he could say to his mother after that. And even less he could say to Sheila that night, before they both began packing up their things. He didn't even tell her how he felt about what she had done. He didn't trust himself to say anything. They said very little, in fact, as she got her things out of his drawers. His parents were having dinner with friends at the hotel, and he was joining them the next day for a luncheon to celebrate his graduation before they all went back to New York. But he looked at Sheila now with an air of despair. The last year and a half seemed about to go down the drain. They had stayed together the last few weeks out of convenience and habit. But he still couldn't accept their separation. Although he had made plans to go to Europe with his parents, he couldn't believe they were through. It was odd how passionate she could be in bed, and how cool everywhere else. It had confused him since the first day they met. But he found himself completely unable to be objective about her. She broke the silence first. "I'm leaving tomorrow night for California."

He looked stunned. "I thought your parents wanted you to come home."

She smiled and tossed a handful of socks into her duffel bag. "I guess they do." She shrugged again and he suddenly felt an overwhelming urge to slap her. He had been genuinely in love with her . . . had wanted to marry her . . . and all she cared about was what she wanted. She was the most egocentric human being he had ever met. "I'm flying standby to Los Angeles. And I guess I'll hitch a ride to San Francisco from there."

"And then?"

"Who knows?" She held out her hands, looking at him as though they had just met, not like the friends and lovers they had been. She had been the most important part of his life during his last two years at the University of Michigan, and now he felt like a damn fool. Two years wasted with her.

"Why don't you come to San Francisco after

you get back from Europe? I wouldn't mind seeing you there." Wouldn't *mind?* After two years?

"I don't think so." He smiled for the first time
in hours, but his eyes were still sad. "I have to look
for a job." He knew she wasn't burdened with
that. Her parents had given her twenty thousand
dollars when she graduated, and he noticed that
she hadn't torn that up. She had enough money to
live in California for several years. And he hadn't
done enough about finding work because he
wasn't sure what she would do. He felt like an
even bigger fool. And what he wanted most was to
find a job in a small New England school, teaching
Russian literature. He had applied and was waiting for answers.

"Isn't it kind of stupid to get suckered in by the
establishment, Bern, to work at a job you hate, for
money you don't need?"

"Speak for yourself. My parents aren't planning
to support me for the rest of my life."

"Neither are mine." She spat the words at him.

"Planning to look for a job on the West Coast?"

"Eventually."

"Doing what? Modeling those?" He pointed at
her cut-offs and boots and she looked annoyed.

"You'll be just like your parents one day." It
was the worst thing she could say as she zipped up
her duffel bag and then stuck a hand out at him.
"So long, Bernie."

It was ridiculous, he thought to himself as he
stared at her. "That's it? After almost two years,
'so long'?" There were tears in his eyes and he

didn't care what she thought now. "That's hard to believe . . . we were going to get married . . . have kids."

She didn't look amused. "That wasn't what we set out to do."

"What did we set out to do, Sheila? Just screw each other for two years? I was in love with you, difficult to believe as that may seem now." He suddenly couldn't imagine what he saw in her, and hated to admit that his mother was right. But she had been. This time.

"I guess I loved you too . . ." Her lip trembled in spite of her efforts at control, and suddenly she went to him and he clung to her in the barren little room that had once been home to them. "I'm sorry, Bernie . . . I guess everything changed . . ." They were both crying and he nodded his head.

"I know . . . it's not your fault . . ." His voice was hoarse as he wondered whose fault it was then. He kissed her, and she looked up at him.

"Come to San Francisco if you can."

"I'll try." But he never did.

Sheila spent the next three years in a commune near Stinson Beach, and he completely lost track of her, until he got a Christmas card finally with a picture of her. He would never have recognized her. She lived in an old school bus, parked near the coast, with nine other people and six little kids. She had two of her own, both girls apparently, and by the time he heard from her, he didn't care anymore, although he had for a long time, and he had been grateful that his parents hadn't made too much of it. He was just relieved when his mother didn't mention her for a while, and she was relieved that Sheila had disappeared.

She was the first girl he had loved, and the dreams had died hard. But Europe had been good for him. There had been dozens of girls he had met in Paris, London, the south of France, Switzerland, Italy, and he was surprised that traveling with his parents could be so much fun, and eventually they went on to meet friends, and so did he.

He met three guys from school in Berlin and they had a ball, before they all went back to real life again. Two of them were going to law school, and one was getting married in the fall and having a last fling, but he was in great part doing it to avoid the draft, which was something Bernie didn't have to worry about, much to his embarrassment. He had had asthma as a child, and his father had documented it carefully. He had been classified 4-F when he registered for the draft at eighteen, although he hadn't admitted it to any of his friends for two years. But in some ways it was convenient now. He didn't have that to worry about. Unfortunately he was turned down at the schools he applied to, because he didn't have a master's yet. So he applied to Columbia and planned to start taking courses there. All the prep schools had told him to come back again in a year, when he had his degree. But it still seemed a lifetime away, and the general courses he'd signed up for at Columbia didn't fascinate him.

He was living at home and his mother was driving him nuts, and everyone he knew was away. Either in the army or in school, or they had gotten jobs somewhere else. He felt like the only one left at home, and in desperation he applied for a job at Wolff's in the Christmas rush, and didn't even mind when they assigned him to the men's department and had him selling shoes. Anything would have been better than sitting home by then, and he had always liked the store. It was one of those large elegant halls that smelled good and where the people were well dressed, even the sales personnel had a certain amount of style, and the Christmas rush was a hair more polite than it was everywhere else. Wolff's had once been a store which set the styles for everyone, and to some extent it still did, although it lacked the pizzazz of a store like Bloomingdale's, only three blocks away.

But Bernie was fascinated by that, and he kept telling the buyer what he thought they could do to compete with Bloomingdale's, and the buyer only smiled. Wolff's didn't compete with anyone. At least that was what he thought. But Paul Berman, the head of the store, was intrigued when he read a memo from Bernard. The buyer apologized profusely to him when he heard about it, he promised that Bernie would be fired at once, but that wasn't what Berman wanted at all. He wanted to meet the kid with the interesting ideas, so they met, and Paul Berman saw the promise in him. He took him to lunch more than once, and he was amused at how brazen he was, but he was smart too, and Berman laughed when Bernie told him he wanted to teach Russian literature, and was going to night school at Columbia toward that end.

"That's a hell of a waste of time."

Bernie was shocked, although he liked the man. He was quiet, elegant, a sharp businessman, and he was interested in what everyone said. He was the grandson of the original Mr. Wolff.

"Russian literature was my major, sir," he said respectfully.

"You should have gone to business school."

Bernie smiled. "You sound like my mother."

"What does your father do?"

"He's a doctor. A throat surgeon, but I've always hated medicine. The thought of some of that stuff makes me sick."

Berman nodded. He understood perfectly. "My brother-in-law was a doctor. I couldn't stand the thought of it either." He frowned as he looked at Bernard Fine. "What about you? What are you really going to do with yourself?"

Bernie was honest with the man. He felt he owed him that, and he cared enough about the store to have written the memo that had brought him here. He liked Wolff's. He thought it was a terrific place. But it wasn't for him. Not permanently anyway. "I'll get my master's, apply for the same jobs again next year, and with luck, the year after that I'll be teaching at some boarding school." He smiled hopefully and looked terribly young. His innocence was touching in a way, and Paul Berman liked him a great deal.

"What if the army grabs you first?" Bernie told him about being 4-F. "You're damn lucky, young man. That little unpleasantness in Vietnam could get damn serious one of these days. Look what happened to the French over there. Lost their shirts. It'll happen to us if we don't watch out." Bernie agreed with him. "Why don't you drop out of night school?"

"And do what?"

"I have a proposal for you. You stay with the store for the next year, and we'll train you in different areas, give you a taste of what's here, and if you want to stay with us, and if you can get in, we'll send you to business school. And in the meantime, you can do a sort of training on the job. How does that sound?" They had never offered anything like it to anyone, but he liked this kid with the wide honest green eyes, and the intelligent face. He wasn't a handsome boy, but he was a nice-looking man, and there was something bright and kind and decent in his face which Paul Berman liked a great deal and he said as much to Bernie before he left his office that day. Bernie had asked to think about his proposal for a day or two, but admitted to being very flattered and very touched. It was just a big decision to make. He wasn't sure he wanted to go to business school, and he hated to give up the dream of the country school in the sleepy little town, teaching eager ears about Dostoevski and Tolstoi. But maybe that was only a dream. Even now, it was growing dim.

He spoke to his parents that night, and even his father had been impressed. It was a marvelous opportunity, if that was what he wanted to do. And the year of training at the store beforehand would give him plenty of time to see if he liked Wolff's. It sounded as though he couldn't lose, and his father congratulated him, as his mother inquired how many children Berman had . . . how many sons . . . how much competition there was in other words . . . or daughters . . . imagine if he married one of them!

"Leave him alone, Ruth!" Lou had been firm when they were alone that night, and with great effort she had restrained herself, and Bernie had given Mr. Berman his answer the following day. He was delighted to accept, and Berman recommended that he apply to several business schools at once. He chose Columbia and New York University because they were in town, and Wharton and Harvard because of who they were. It would be a long time before he heard if he was accepted or not, but in the meantime he had lots to do.

And the year of training flew. He was accepted at three of the business schools where he had applied. Only Wharton turned him down, but said they might have room for him the following year, if he wished to wait, which he did not. And he chose Columbia, and began there while still working at the store a few hours a week. He wanted to keep his hand in, and he found he was particularly interested in the designer aspects of men's wear. He did a study on it for his first paper, and not only got high grades, but made some suggestions which actually worked in the store, when Berman let him try them on a small scale. His business school career was a considerable success, and when he finished, he wound up working for Berman for six months, and then moving back to men's wear after that, and then women's wear. He began to make changes which could be felt throughout the store, and within five years to the day he began at Wolff's, he was their rising star. So it came as a blow when Paul Berman announced on a sunny spring afternoon that they were moving him to the Chicago store for two years.

"But why?" It sounded like Siberia to him. He didn't want to go anywhere. He loved New York, and he was doing splendidly at the store.

"For one thing, you know most of the Midwest. For another"—Berman sighed and lit a cigar—"we need you out there. The store isn't doing as well as we'd like. It needs a shot in the arm, and you're it." He smiled at his young friend. They shared enormous respect, but Bernie wanted to fight him on this. But he didn't win. Berman wouldn't relent, and two months later Bernie flew to Chicago and a year later he was made manager, which kept him there for another two years, even though he hated it. Chicago seemed like a depressing town to him, and the weather really got to him.

His parents came to visit him frequently, and it

was obvious that his position carried with it considerable prestige. To be manager of Wolff's Chicago at thirty years of age was no small thing, but nonetheless he was dying to get back to New York, and his mother threw a huge party for him when he told her the good news. He was thirty-one years old when he came home, and Berman let him write his own ticket when he came back. Nonetheless when Bernie thought of upgrading the level of women's wear, Berman was not convinced. He wanted to introduce a dozen big couture lines, and put Wolff's back on the map as trendsetters for the whole United States.

"Do you realize how much those dresses sell for?" Berman looked genuinely distressed, as Bernie smiled at him.

"Yes. But they can pare them down a little for us. It won't actually be couture after all."

"Damn close. Or the prices will be anyway. Who's going to buy those goods here?" It sounded too extreme to him, but at the same time he was intrigued.

"I think our customers will leap at what we'll offer them, Paul. Especially in cities like Chicago and Boston and Washington and even Los Angeles, where they don't have every store in New York spread out at their feet. We're going to bring Paris and Milan to them."

"Or ourselves to the poorhouse trying, is that it?" But Berman didn't disagree. He looked at Paul thoughtfully. It was an interesting idea. He wanted to leap right into the highest-priced merchandise, selling dresses for as much as five or six or seven thousand dollars, which were after all only ready-to-wear technically, but the designs would be couture.

"We don't even have to buy the stock. We don't have to overload the inventory. We can have each designer put together a show, and the women can order directly through us, which makes even more sense economically." Berman was thrilled with that idea. It took all the danger out of it for him.

"Now you've got it, Bernard."

"I think we need to do some reconstruction first though. Our designer department isn't European enough." They had gone on talking for hours as the idea was born, and when they had roughed out what they were going to do, Berman shook his hand. Bernard had grown up a lot in recent years. He was mature and self-confident, and his business decisions were sound. He even looked grown-up now, Berman teased, pointing at the beard he had grown before returning to New York. He was thirty-one years old and a very nice-looking man.

"I think you've done a fine job thinking this out." The two men exchanged a smile. They were both pleased. It was going to be a very exciting time for Wolff's. "What are you going to do first?"

"I want to speak to some architects this week, and I'll have them do some plans up to show you, and then I want to leave for Paris. We have to see what the designers think about the idea."

"Think they'll balk?"

He frowned pensively but shook his head. "They shouldn't. There's big money in it for them."

And Bernie had been right. They hadn't balked. They had leapt at the idea, and he had signed contracts with twenty of them. He had gone to Paris fully prepared to close the deal, and he returned to New York three weeks later, victorious. The new program was to be launched in nine months, with a fabulous series of fashion shows in June, where the ladies could order their wardrobes for the fall. It was not unlike going to Paris and ordering from the couture lines. And Bernie was going to kick it all off with a party and one fabulous black-tie show which would combine a few pieces from each designer they would be working with. None of it could be bought, it would only be a teaser for the shows that would come next, and all of the models were coming from Paris, along with the designers. And three American designers had been added since the project began. It gave Bernie a huge amount of work to do in the next several months, but it also made him a senior vice president at thirty-two.

The opening-night fashion show was the most beautiful thing anyone had ever seen. The clothes were absolutely staggering and the audience oohed and aahed and applauded constantly. It was absolutely fabulous and one sensed easily that fashion history was being made. It was extraordinary the way he combined good business principles with strong merchandising, and somehow he had an innate sense for fashion. And it all combined to make Wolff's stronger than any other store in New York, or the country for that matter. And Bernie was on top of the world when he sat in the back row watching the first full designer show, as the women watched it avidly. He had seen Paul Berman pass by a short while before. Everyone was happy these days, and Bernie began to relax a little bit as he watched the models coming down the runway in evening gowns, and he particularly noticed one slender blonde, a beautiful catlike creature with chiseled features and enormous blue eyes. She almost seemed to glide above the ground, and he found himself waiting for her as each new series of gowns came out, and he was disappointed when the show finally came to an end and he knew he wouldn't see her again.

And instead of hurrying back to his office, as he had meant to do, he lingered for a moment, and then slipped backstage to congratulate the department manager, a Frenchwoman they had hired, who had worked for years for Dior.

"You did a great job, Marianne." He smiled at her and she eyed him hungrily. She was in her late forties, impeccably turned out and tremendously chic, and she had had her eye on him since she'd come to the store.

"The clothes showed well, don't you think, Bernard?" She said it like a French name, and she was enormously cool and yet sexy at the same time. Like fire and ice. And he found himself looking over her shoulder as girls rushed past in blue jeans and their own simple street clothes with the fabulous gowns over their arms. Salesladies were dashing back and forth, grabbing armfuls of the exquisite clothes to take them to their customers to try on so they could order them. And it was all going extremely well, and then Bernard saw her, with the wedding dress from the finale over her arm.

"Who's that girl, Marianne? Is she one of ours, or did we hire her for the show?" Marianne followed his eyes, and was not taken in by the casual tone of his voice. She felt her heart sink as she looked at her. She couldn't have been a day over twenty-one and she was a beautiful girl.

"She free-lances for us from time to time. She's French." But she didn't need to say more. The girl wandered right over to them, and held up the wedding dress as she glanced first at Bernard, and then at Marianne. She asked her in French what to do with it, as she was afraid to set it down, and Marianne told her who to give it to, as Bernie stood almost gaping at her. And then the department manager knew what her duty was.

She introduced Bernie to her, title and all, and even explained that the new concept was all his plan. She hated to put them together like that but she had no choice. She watched Bernie's eyes as he looked at the girl. It amused her somehow, he was always so aloof. It was obvious that he liked girls, but he never got deeply involved with anyone, from what people said. And unlike the merchandise he selected for Wolff's, in women he pre-

ferred quantity to quality every time . . .
"volume" as they said in the trade . . . but
maybe not this time. . . .

Her name was Isabelle Martin and she was
twenty-four years old. She had grown up in the
south of France and gone to Paris at eighteen to
work for Saint Laurent and then Givenchy. She
was absolutely tops, and she had been a huge
success in Paris. It was no surprise when she had
been asked to come to the States and had done
extremely well in New York for the past four years.
He couldn't imagine why they hadn't met before.
"Usually I do only photography, Monsieur
Fine." She had an accent that enchanted him.
"But for your show . . ." She smiled in a way that
melted the seat of his pants and he would have
done anything for her. And suddenly he remembered her. He had seen her on the cover of *Vogue*
more than once, and *Bazaar* and *Women's Wear*
. . . she just looked very different in real life,
more beautiful actually. It was rare for models to
cross over between runway modeling and photography, but she was skilled at both, and she had
done beautifully in their show and he congratulated her lavishly.

"You were marvelous, Miss . . . uh . . ." His
mind suddenly went blank and she smiled at him
again.

"Isabelle." He thought he would die just looking at her, and he took her to dinner that night at
La Caravelle. Everyone in the room turned to look
at her. And they went dancing afterwards at "Raf-

fles" and Bernie never wanted to go home again. He never wanted to give her up, to let her out of his arms. He had never met anyone like her before, he had never been as swept off his feet by anyone. And the armor he had built after Sheila walked out of his life melted at her hands. Her hair was so blond it was almost white, and more extraordinary, it was natural. He thought her the most beautiful creature on earth, and it would have been difficult for anyone to disagree with him.

They had an enchanted summer in East Hampton that year. He had rented a small house, and she spent every weekend with him. When she had arrived in the U.S. she had immediately become involved with a well-known fashion photographer and after two years she had left him for a real-estate mogul. But all men seemed to fade from her life when Bernie appeared. It seemed like a magical time to him as he took her with him everywhere, showing her off, being photographed, dancing till dawn. It all seemed very jet set, and he laughed when he took his mother to lunch, and she leveled her most motherly gaze at him.

"Don't you think she's a little rich for your blood?"

"What's that supposed to mean?"

"It means that she reeks of 'jet set,' and when all is said and done, how do you fit in, Bernie?"

"You're never a hero in your own home town, isn't that what they say? I can't say it's very flattering though." He was admiring his mother's navy blue Dior suit. He had bought it for her the last time he was abroad and it looked lovely on her. But he didn't particularly want to discuss Isabelle with her. He hadn't taken her home to meet his parents, and he wasn't planning to. The two worlds would never have met successfully, although he knew that his father would have loved seeing her. Any man would have. She was spectacular.

"What's she like?" His mother wouldn't let go, as usual.

"She's a nice girl, Mom."

His mother smiled at him. "Somehow that doesn't seem the right description for her. She's certainly beautiful." She saw her photographs everywhere, and she told all her friends. At the hairdresser she showed everyone "that girl . . . no, the one on the cover . . . she goes out with my son . . ." "Are you in love with her?" She was never afraid to ask what she wanted to know, but Bernie quailed when he heard the words. He wasn't ready for that, although he was crazy about her, but he still remembered all too well his foolishness when he was in Michigan . . . the engagement ring he had given Sheila on Valentine's Day, that she had thrown back at him . . . the wedding plans he had made . . . the day she walked out of his life, carrying her duffel bag and his heart. He never wanted to be in the same position again, and he had guarded himself carefully. But not from Isabelle Martin.

"We're good friends." It was all he could think of to say, and his mother stared at him.

"I hope it's more than that." She looked horrified, as though she suddenly suspected him of being a homosexual, and all he could do was laugh at her.

"It is, okay? It's more than that . . . but nobody is getting married. All right? Satisfied? Now, what do you want for lunch?" He ordered steak and she ordered filet of sole and she pressed him about everything he was doing for the store. They were almost friends now, and he saw his parents less than he had when he first came back to New York. He didn't have much time, particularly with the arrival of Isabelle in his life.

He took her to Europe with him when he went on business that fall and they made a sensation everywhere they went. They were inseparable, and just before Christmas she moved in with him, and Bernie finally had to give in and take her to Scarsdale, much as he dreaded it. She was perfectly pleasant to his parents, although she didn't gush over them, and she made it clear to him that she wasn't interested in seeing a lot of them.

"We have so little time alone . . ." She pouted so perfectly, and he loved making love to her. She was the most exquisite woman he had ever seen, and sometimes he just stood staring at her as she put her makeup on or dried her hair or got out of the shower, or walked in the door carrying her portfolio. Somehow she made one want to freeze-frame and just stand there gazing at her.

His mother had even been subdued when they met. Isabelle had a way of making one feel very small, standing next to her, except Bernie, who had never felt more of a man with anyone. Her sexual prowess was remarkable, and their relationship was based on passion more than love. They made love almost everywhere, the bathtub, the shower, the floor, the back of his car one Sunday afternoon when they took a drive to Connecticut. They almost did it in the elevator once, and then came to their senses as they approached their floor and knew the doors were about to open. It was as though they couldn't stop, and he could never get quite enough of her. For that reason, he took her to France again in the spring, and then back out to East Hampton again, but this time they saw more people than they had before, and there was a movie producer who snagged her eye one night at a party on the beach at Quogue, and the next day Bernie couldn't find her anywhere. He found her on a yacht, moored nearby, making love to the producer from Hollywood on the deck, as Bernie stood for an instant staring at them, and then hurried away with tears in his eyes, realizing something he had hidden from for a long time. She wasn't just a great lay and a beautiful girl, she was the woman he loved, and losing her was going to hurt him.

She apologized when she got back to their house, but it wasn't for several hours. She and the producer had talked for a long time afterwards, about her goals, what she wanted out of her life, and what her relationship with Bernie meant, what he offered her. The producer had been fascinated by her and had told her as much. And when she got back, she tried to tell Bernie what she felt, much to his dismay.

"I can't live in a cage for the rest of my life, Bernard . . . I must be free to fly where I need to be." He had heard it all before, in another life, with combat boots and a duffel bag, instead of a Pucci dress and Chanel shoes, and a Louis Vuitton suitcase standing open in the next room.

"I take it I represent a cage to you?" His eyes were cold as he looked at her. He wasn't going to tolerate her sleeping with someone else. It was as simple as that, and he wondered if she had done it before, and with whom.

"You are not a cage, *mon amour,* but a very fine man. But this life of pretending to be married . . . one can only do this for so long . . ." For them it had been eight months since she had moved in with him, hardly an eternity.

"I think I've misunderstood our relationship, Isabelle."

She nodded at him, looking even more beautiful, and for an instant he hated her. "I think you have, Bernard." And then, the knife to his heart. "I want to go to California for a while." She was totally candid with him. "Dick says he can arrange a screen test at a studio"—she spoke with an accent that melted his heart—"and I would like very much to do a film there with him."

"I see." He lit a cigarette although he seldom

smoked. "You've never mentioned that before." But it made sense. It was a shame not to put that face on film. Magazine covers weren't enough for her.

"I didn't think it was important to tell you that."

"Or was it that you wanted what you could get out of Wolff's first?" It was the nastiest thing he had said and he was ashamed of himself. She didn't need him, and actually he was sorry about that. "I'm sorry, Isabelle . . ." He walked across the room and stood looking at her through the smoke. "Don't do anything hasty yet." He wanted to beg but she was tougher than that. She had already made up her mind.

"I'm going to Los Angeles next week."

He nodded and strode back across the room, looking out at the sea, and then he turned to smile at her bitterly. "There must be something magical about the place. They all seem to head west eventually." He was thinking of Sheila again. He had told Isabelle about her a long time before. "Maybe I should go out there too sometime."

Isabelle smiled. "You belong in New York, Bernard. You are everything vital and exciting and alive that is happening here."

His voice was sad when he answered her. "But that doesn't seem to be enough for you."

Her eyes met his with regret. "It is not that . . . it is not you . . . if I wanted someone serious . . . if I wanted to be married . . . I would want you very much."

"I never suggested that." But they both knew

he would have in time. He was that kind of man, and he was almost sorry he was as he looked at her. He wanted to be racier, more decadent . . . to be able to put her in films himself.

"I just don't see myself staying here, Bernard." She saw herself as a movie star and she left with the producer she had met exactly when she said she would. She left with him three days after she came home from East Hampton with Bernard. She packed all her things, more neatly than Sheila had, and she took all the gorgeous clothes Bernie had given her. She packed them in her Louis Vuitton bags and left him a note that afternoon. She even packed the four thousand dollars in cash he kept hidden in his desk drawer. She called it a "little loan," and was sure he would "understand." She had her screen test, and exactly a year later she appeared in a film. And by then, Bernie didn't give a damn. He was a hardened case. There were models and secretaries and executives. He met women in Rome, there was a very pretty stewardess in Milan, an artist, a socialite . . . but there was no one he gave a damn about, and he wondered if it would ever happen to him again. He still felt like a damn fool when someone mentioned her. She never sent the money back, of course, or the Piaget watch he'd discovered was gone long afterwards. She never even sent a Christmas card. She had used him and moved on to someone else, just as there had been others before him. And in Hollywood she did exactly the same, disposing of the producer who had gotten her her first film and turning him in for a bigger one, and a better part. Isabelle Martin would go far, there was no doubt of that, and his parents knew the subject was taboo with him. They never mentioned her to him again, after one inappropriate remark that sent him out of the house in Scarsdale in blind fury. He didn't come back for two months and his mother was frightened by what she had seen in him. The subject was closed permanently after that.

And a year and a half after she left, he was back in control of his life again. There were more women on his calendar than he could handle almost, business was booming, the store was in fine shape, and when he had woken up to see the blizzard that morning, he had decided to go in anyway. He had a lot of work to do, and he wanted to talk to Paul Berman about the store's summer plans. He had some exciting things in mind, and as he stepped off the bus at Lexington and Sixty-third, wearing a heavy English overcoat and a Russian fur cap, he walked into the store with his head bent against the wind, and then looked up at the store with pride. He was married to Wolff's, and he didn't mind a bit. She was a great old broad, and he was a success in every way. He had a lot to be thankful for, as he pressed the button for the eighth floor and shook the snow off his coat.

"Morning, Mr. Fine," a voice said as the door closed, and he smiled. He closed his eyes for an instant before the doors opened again, thinking

Chapter 2

"Hell of a day." Paul Berman glanced out his
window at the snow still swirling outside, and
knew he'd have to spend another night in town.
There was no way he'd get back to Connecticut.
He had spent the night before at the Pierre, and
had promised his wife he wouldn't even attempt
to come home in the snow. "Is there anyone in the
store?" He was always amazed at the volume of
their business in horrendous weather conditions.
People always found a way to spend money.

Bernie nodded at him.

"Surprisingly, quite a few. And we set up two
stations serving mugs of tea, coffee, and hot chocolate. It's a nice touch, whoever thought that one
up. They deserve a reward for coming out in
weather like this."

"Actually, they're smart. It's a nice way to shop,
with hardly anyone in the store. I prefer it myself." The two men exchanged a smile. They had

of all the work he had to do that day, and w
wanted to say to Paul. But he was in no way
pared for what Paul Berman was going to sa
him later that morning.

been friends for twelve years, and Bernard never lost sight of the fact that Paul had really given him his career. He had encouraged him to go to business school, and opened countless doors at Wolff's to him. More than that, he had trusted him, and given him a vote of confidence at times when no one else would have dared attempt some of Bernie's schemes, and it was no secret that, with no sons of his own, he had been grooming Bernie to be number one for years. He offered Bernie a cigar as the younger man waited to hear what he had to say. "How do you feel about the store these days?"

It was a good day for one of their talks, and Bernie smiled at him. They chatted informally like this from time to time, and their impromptu talks never failed to give birth to some marvelous ideas for Wolff's. The decision to hire a new fashion director for the store had come from their last session like this, and she was doing a fabulous job for them. They had stolen her from Saks. "I think everything is pretty much in control. Don't you, Paul?"

The older man nodded his head, not quite sure how to begin, but he had to start somewhere, he told himself. "I do. Which is why the board and I feel we can afford a somewhat unusual move."

"Oh?" Had someone taken Bernie's pulse just then, they would have felt it escalate. Paul Berman never mentioned the board unless something pretty serious was going on.

"You know we'll be opening the San Francisco

store in June." It was still five months away and construction was in full swing. Paul and Bernie had already gone out several times and everything seemed to be moving on schedule, for the moment at least. "And we just haven't been able to come up with anyone to head the store."

Bernie heaved a silent sigh of relief. For a moment he had thought something was going to happen to him. But he knew how important Paul felt the San Francisco market was. There was a lot of money there, and women bought high fashion as though it were pretzels being sold on the street. It was definitely time for Wolff's to get a share of that. They were well entrenched in Los Angeles, and they all agreed it was time to move north. "I keep thinking that Jane Wilson would be fabulous, but I don't think she'd leave New York."

Paul Berman frowned. This was going to be even harder than he thought. "I don't think she'd be right. She's not strong enough. And a new store needs someone powerful, someone in control, someone who thinks on their feet and has innovative ideas. She's better suited to what's happening here."

"Which leaves us back where we started again. What about hiring someone from outside the store? Maybe even someone from another store?"

It was time to move in for the kill. There was no avoiding it. Paul looked him squarely in the eye. "We want you, Bernard." Their eyes met and Bernie blanched. He couldn't be serious. But the look on his face . . . my God . . . he was. But he had done his time. Three years in Chicago was enough. Wasn't it?

"Paul, I can't . . . I couldn't . . . San Francisco?" He looked genuinely shocked. "Why me?"

"Because you have all of the qualities I just described, and we need you out there. No matter how hard we look, we'll never find anyone as good as you are, and that store is important to us. You know it yourself. There's a tremendous market out there, but a touchy one, high class, high fashion, high style, and if we open our doors wrong, we'll never recover from it. Bernie"—Paul looked at him pleadingly—"you've got to help us out." He looked at him piercingly and Bernie sank back in his chair.

"But, Paul . . . *San Francisco?* . . . What about my job here?" He hated to leave New York again, he was so happy where he was, doing what he did. It was really a hardship leaving now, although he didn't want to let Paul down.

"You can fly back and forth. And I can pitch in for you here. Where we need you is there."

"For how long?"

"A year. Maybe two." Maybe more.

Bernie was afraid of that. "That's what you said when I went to Chicago, Paul. Only I was younger then . . . I've earned my stripes now. I don't want to live in the boondocks again. I've been out there. I know what it's like. It's a pretty town, but it's provincial as hell."

"So go to Los Angeles to play. Do whatever you

have to do to survive out there. But please . . . I wouldn't ask you to do it if we had any other choice, but we just don't have anyone else. And I've got to get someone out there fast, before things start going wrong for us. Someone has got to supervise the last of the construction, make sure everything is running smoothly for the opening, set the tone of the advertising, check the promotion . . ." He waved an impatient hand. "I don't need to tell you what needs to be done. It's an enormous responsibility, Bernard. It's a brand-new store, and the finest one we have, aside from New York." In a way, it was a feather in his cap, but it was one he didn't want. Not at all.

He stood up with a quiet sigh. It hadn't been such a great morning after all, and he was almost sorry he had come in now, even though it would have been handed to him eventually anyway. There was no avoiding it once Paul made up his mind, and it wouldn't be easy talking him out of it now. "I'll have to give it some thought."

"Do that." Their eyes met and held again. And Paul was afraid of what he saw this time.

"Maybe if I had a firm commitment that it wouldn't be for more than a year, I could live with it." He smiled ruefully, but Paul couldn't promise him that. If the store wasn't ready to be handed over yet, then Bernard couldn't leave that soon, and it was unlikely he could, they both knew. It would take two to three years of tender loving care to get a new store settled anywhere, and Bernie just wasn't willing to commit to that long.

And San Francisco didn't look all that great to him.

Paul Berman stood up and looked at him. "You give it some thought. But I want you to know my bottom line." He wasn't going to jeopardize loosing Bernie, no matter what the board said. "I don't want to lose you, Bernard." And it was obvious that he meant every word as Bernie smiled fondly at him.

"And my bottom line is that I don't want to let you down."

"Then we'll both make the right decision, whatever it is." Paul Berman stretched a hand out to Bernard and they shook hands. "Give it some very serious thought."

"You know I will." And he sat alone in his office after that, with the door closed, staring out at the snow, feeling as though he had been hit by a truck. He couldn't even imagine living in San Francisco now. He loved his life in New York. It would be like starting all over again, and he didn't look forward to the prospect of opening a new branch store, no matter how elite and elaborate it was. It still wasn't New York. Even with the blizzards and the filth and the intolerable heat of July, he loved it here, and the pretty little postcard town by the bay had no lure for him. It never had. He thought of Sheila with a grim smile. It was more her style than his, and he wondered if he would have to buy his own combat boots to move out there. The whole thought of it depressed him horribly, and he sounded it when his mother called.

"What's wrong, Bernard?"

"Nothing, Mom. It's just been a long day."

"Are you sick?"

He closed his eyes, trying to sound cheerful for her. "No. I'm fine. How are you and Dad?"

"Depressed. Mrs. Goodman died. Remember her? She used to bake cookies for you when you were a little boy." She had already been ancient then, and that was thirty years ago. It was hardly surprising that she had finally died, but his mother loved reporting things like that. And now she moved back onto him. "So what's wrong?"

"Nothing's wrong, Mom. I told you. I'm fine."

"You don't sound fine. You sound tired and depressed."

"I had a long day." He said it through clenched teeth . . . and they're moving me to Siberia again. . . . "Never mind. Are we still on for dinner for your anniversary next week? Where do you want to go?"

"I don't know. Your father thought you should come here." He knew that was a lie. His father loved to go out. He found it refreshing after the intensity of the work he did. It was his mother who always thought he should come home, as though to prove something to him.

"How about '21'? Would you like that? Or something French? *Côte Basque . . . Grenouille? . . .*"

"All right." She sounded resigned. " '21.' "

"Great. Why don't you come to my place first

for a drink, at seven o'clock? And then we'll have dinner at eight."

"Are you bringing a girl?" She sounded pained, as though it were something he did all the time, although the truth was they had met none of his lady friends since Isabelle. None of them had lasted long enough to bother with.

"Why should I bring a girl?"

"Why wouldn't you? You never introduce us to your friends. Are you ashamed of us?"

He almost groaned into the phone. "Of course not, Mom. Look, I've got to go. I'll see you next week. Seven o'clock, my place." But he knew that repeating it wouldn't keep her from calling four more times just to make sure they were still on, that he hadn't changed the plans, that the reservation had been made, that he didn't want to bring a girl. "Give Dad my love."

"Call him sometime . . . You never call anymore . . ." She sounded like one of those jokes, and he smiled to himself as he hung up, wondering if he would be like her one day if he ever had kids, not that there seemed to be a danger of that anyway. There had been a girl the year before who had thought she was pregnant for several days, and for a moment he had considered letting her have the child, just so that he'd have a baby after all. But it turned out she'd been wrong anyway, and they were both relieved. But it had been an interesting thought for a day or two. He didn't want children desperately anyway. He was too involved in his career, and it always seemed a shame to him not to have a baby born of love. He was still idealistic about that, and there was certainly no likely candidate at the moment to fill that bill. He sat staring at the snow, thinking of what it would be like to give up his entire social life, to stop seeing all his favorite girls. It almost made him want to cry as he left the office that night, on a night that was as cold and clear as an icy crystal bell. He didn't try to catch a bus this time, and the wind had finally died down. He walked straight to Madison Avenue, and then walked uptown, glancing at the shops as he strode past rapidly. It wasn't snowing anymore, and it looked like a fairyland, as a few people skied past, and children threw snowballs. There hadn't even been any rush hour traffic to mess it all up, and he felt better as he walked into his house and rode the elevator upstairs. It was a hideous thought leaving New York now. He couldn't even imagine it. But he couldn't think of a way out. Unless he quit, and he didn't want to do that. There was no way out for him, he realized, as his heart seemed to fall against his ribs. No way out at all for him.

Chapter 3

"You're going where?" His mother stared at him over her vichyssoise, and she seemed not to understand, as though he had said something truly ridiculous. Like he was joining a nudist colony, or having a sex change. "Are they firing you, or just demoting you?"

He appreciated the vote of confidence, but that was typical. "Neither one, Mom. They're asking me to manage the new San Francisco store. It's the most important store we have, aside from New York." He wondered why he was trying to sell it to her, except that he was still trying to sell it to himself. He had told Paul after two days, and he had been depressed about it ever since. They had given him a phenomenal raise, and Berman had reminded him that he would be running Wolff's himself one day. Perhaps not long after he returned to New York. And more important, he knew that Paul Berman was grateful to him, but still it was hard to take, and he wasn't looking forward to it. He had decided to keep his apartment anyway and sublet it for a year or two and just take something temporary in San Francisco. He had already told Paul that he wanted to try to be back in New York in a year. And they hadn't promised him anything, but he knew they would try. And even if it was eighteen months, he'd survive. Anything more than that was questionable, but he didn't say that to his mother now.

"But San Francisco? They're all hippies out there. Do they even wear clothes?"

He smiled. "They do. Very expensive ones in fact. You'll have to come and see for yourself." He smiled at both of them. "Do you want to come to the opening?"

She looked as though he had invited her to a funeral. "We might. When is it?"

"In June." He knew they had nothing to do then. They were going to Europe in July, but they had plenty of time to come out before that.

"I don't know. We'll have to see. Your father's schedule . . ." He was always the fall guy for her moods, but he never seemed to mind, although he looked at his son with concern as they sat at "21." It was one of the rare moments his father seemed relaxed and not preoccupied by his work.

"Is it really a step up for you, son?"

"It is, Dad." He answered him honestly. "It's a very prestigious job and Paul Berman and the board asked me to do it personally. But I have to admit"—he smiled ruefully—"I'd rather be in New York."

"Are you involved with someone?" His mother leaned across the table, as though asking him something intensely personal, and Bernie laughed.

"No, Mom. I'm not. I just like New York. I love it in fact. But I'm hoping to get back in less than eighteen months. I can live with that. And there are worse cities than San Francisco, I guess." Although, at the moment, he couldn't think of one. He finished his drink and decided to be philosophical. "Hell, it could be Cleveland for chrissake, or Miami, or Detroit . . . not that there's anything wrong with them, but they ain't New York." He smiled at them ruefully.

"They say San Francisco is crawling with homosexuals." The Voice of Doom spoke up with an anguished look at her only son.

"I think I can take care of myself, Mom." And then he looked at both of them. "I'm going to miss you both."

"Won't you come back here at all?" There were tears in her eyes and he almost felt sorry for her, except that she cried so much when it was useful to her that he was less moved than he might have been otherwise.

He patted her hand. "I'll be back and forth a lot. But the fact is I'll be living there. You'll just have to come out. And I really want you to come to the opening. It's going to be a beautiful store."

He kept telling himself that as he packed his

things in early February, and said goodbye to his friends, and had a last dinner with Paul in New York. And on Valentine's Day, only three weeks after they'd offered him the job, he was on a plane flying to San Francisco, wondering what he had done to himself, and thinking that maybe he should have quit after all. But as they left New York, a fresh blizzard began, and as they landed in San Francisco at two in the afternoon, the sun was shining, the air was warm, and the breezes were gentle. There were flowers in bloom, and it felt like New York in May or June. And he was suddenly glad he'd come, for a while anyway. At least the weather was nice, that was something to be pleased about. And his room at the Huntington was extremely pleasant too.

But more important than that, even in its unfinished state, the store was fabulous. And when he called Paul the next day, Paul sounded relieved just knowing he was there. And everything was moving on schedule. The construction was going well, the decoration was all lined up and ready to be installed as soon as construction would allow. He met with the ad agency, talked to the public relations people about how they were starting to warm up, and had an interview with the *Chronicle*. Everything was exactly the way they had hoped it would be. And Bernie was in charge.

All that remained to do was to open the store, and find an apartment for himself, hardly two minor tasks, and he was far more concerned about the store. He rapidly rented a furnished apartment in a modern high-rise on Nob Hill; it had none of the charm of the houses he saw everywhere, but it was convenient for him, and it was close to the store.

The opening was fabulous. It was everything they had all wanted it to be. The press had been favorable beforehand. There had been a beautiful party at the store, with models wearing spectacular clothes, while impeccably dressed waiters served caviar, hors d'oeuvres, and champagne. There was dancing, entertainment, and the freedom to roam around the store with no one else there. And Bernie was proud of it. It was really beautiful, with a light airy feeling combined with enormous style. It had all the chic of New York, with the ease of the West Coast. And Paul Berman was thrilled, too, when he flew out.

The crowds that came the day of the opening required police cordons and hordes of smiling PR people just to hold them back. But it was all worth it when they saw the record sales for the first week, and even his mother had been proud of him. She had said it was the most beautiful store she'd ever seen, and she had told every salesgirl who helped her for the next five days of shopping there that the manager was her son, and one day, when he went back to New York, he would run the entire chain. She was sure of it.

When they finally left San Francisco, they went to Los Angeles, and Bernie was surprised to realize how lonely he felt once they were gone, as well as the rest of the contingent from New York. All the board members went back the day after the opening, and Paul had flown on to Detroit that night. And suddenly he was all alone, in the town he had been transplanted in, without a single friend, and an apartment that looked sterile and ugly to him. It was all done in brown and beige, and seemed much too dreary for the gentle northern California sun. He was sorry he hadn't rented a pretty little Victorian flat. But it didn't matter too much anyway. He was always at the store, seven days a week now, since in California they were open every day. He didn't have to come in on weekends at all, but he had nothing else to do anyway, so he did, and everyone noticed it. Bernie Fine worked like a dog, they said, and they all agreed that he was a nice man. He expected a lot of them, but he expected more of himself, and it was difficult to argue with someone like that. He also seemed to have an infallible sense of what was right for the store, and what merchandise they should have, and no one dared quibble with him about that. He was definite, and from what they could see, most of the time, he was right. He had an innate sense of what worked and what didn't, even in this town he barely knew, and he was constantly shifting things, and adjusting to the new information he found out. He kept things moving constantly, shipping things to other branches when they were wrong for San Francisco after all, moving things in, having buyers reorder constantly. But it worked. It was extraordinary, and they all liked him in the store. They didn't even mind the habit he had of roaming the store every day for several hours. He wanted to see what people wore, what they did, how they shopped, what they liked. He would talk to housewives and young girls and single men, he even took a personal interest in their children's wear. He wanted to know everything, and the only way to do that, he said, was to be in the front lines.

He was frequently being handed things to ring up and items to return, and he did what he could, and found a salesperson as quickly as possible, but he was happy to meet the customer every time, and the store personnel were getting used to him. They were used to seeing him everywhere, with his auburn hair, the well-trimmed beard, warm green eyes, and well-tailored English suits. He never said an unkind word, and when he wanted things done differently, he spoke calmly and quietly, explaining what he wanted done so that the employee understood. And as a result, they all had enormous respect for him. In New York, just looking at the sales figures, Paul Berman knew they had done the right thing, and he wasn't surprised at all. Bernie was going to turn Wolff's San Francisco into the finest store in the chain. He was their man all right, and one day he would step into Berman's shoes very successfully. Paul was sure of it.

Chapter 4

The first month was hectic for all of them, but by July they had things fairly well in control, and the autumn merchandise coming in. Bernie had several fashion shows scheduled the following month, and the big event in July was the opera show, which meant a great deal. The opening of the opera was the hottest event of the San Francisco social season, and women were going to be spending five and seven and ten thousand dollars on a single dress.

The racks of exquisite opera gowns were already hanging in a locked room downstairs with a security guard outside at all times, to be sure that no one pirated what they had, took unauthorized photographs, or worse yet, stole the merchandise, which was worth a small fortune. And it was the opera collection he was thinking about in mid-July as he made his way upstairs. He got off the escalator at the children's floor, just to make sure that all was well there. He knew they had had a problem getting some of their back-to-school merchandise the week before and he wanted to be sure that everything was in order again. He met the buyer behind the cash register, instructing some of the saleswomen, who all smiled at him, and he glanced around casually at the racks, and then ventured further into the department on his own, until he found himself facing a rack of bright-colored bathing suits that would be going on sale the following week, and looking into the big blue eyes of a very little girl. She seemed to look at him for a long time, neither smiling nor afraid of him, just watching, as though to see what he would do next, and he smiled down at her.

"Hi. How are you?" It seemed an odd line for a child who couldn't have been more than five years old, but he never had any idea what to say to children like that. And his best line—"How do you like school?"—seemed hopelessly out of date, particularly at this time of year. "Do you like the store?"

"It's okay." She shrugged. She was clearly more interested in him. "I hate beards."

"I'm sorry to hear that." She was the cutest thing he had ever seen, and someone had braided her hair into two long blond braids, and she had pink hair ribbons on, and a little pink dress, with a doll she dragged along in one hand. The doll looked well loved and was obviously a serious favorite of hers.

"Beards scratch." She said it matter-of-factly as

though it were something he should know, and he nodded seriously, stroking it. It seemed reasonably soft to him, but he was used to it, and he hadn't been testing it on five-year-olds. In fact, since coming to San Francisco, he hadn't tested it on anyone at all. And she was the best-looking girl he had seen since he'd arrived. So far the women of San Francisco weren't his type. They wore their hair long and loose, their feet bare in ugly sandals which were obviously comfortable, and they all seemed to favor T-shirts and jeans. He missed the pulled-together look of New York . . . the high heels . . . the hats . . . the accessories, the perfectly groomed hair, the earrings that seemed to frame a face . . . the furs . . . They were frivolous details but they made a difference to him and one saw none of it here.

"My name is Bernie, by the way." He was enjoying his conversation with her and he held out a hand to her, which she shook soberly as she stared at him.

"My name is Jane. Do you work here?"

"I do."

"Are they nice?"

"Very nice." He couldn't possibly tell her that "they" in this case was he.

"That's good. They're not always nice to my mom where she works. Sometimes they're really mean to her." She was extremely serious with him, and he had to fight not to smile at her, while wondering increasingly where her mother was. He wondered if the child was lost but didn't know it yet, which seemed like an excellent possibility. But he didn't want to frighten her by mentioning it. "Sometimes they won't even let her stay home from work when I'm sick." She went on, obviously shocked by the callousness of her mother's employers, as she looked up at him. But the comment brought her mother to mind. And suddenly her eyes grew very wide. "Where is my Mom?"

"I don't know, Jane." He smiled very gently at her, glancing around. There was no one else in sight, except the saleswomen who had been talking to the buyer a few moments before. They were still standing near the cash register, but there was no one else there. Jane's mother was clearly nowhere around. "Do you remember where you saw her last?"

She squinted at him, thinking back. "She was buying pink pantyhose downstairs . . ." She looked up at him a little sheepishly. "I wanted to see the bathing suits." She glanced around where they stood. They were everywhere, and she had obviously come upstairs by herself, to look at them. "We're going to the beach next week . . ." Her voice trailed off and she looked at him. "The bathing suits are very nice." She had been standing next to a rack of tiny little bikinis when he first noticed her. But now he saw her lower lip trembling and he reached a hand out to her.

"Why don't we see if we can find your Mom." But she shook her head and took a step back from him.

"I'm not supposed to go with anyone." He gestured to one of the women, who approached cautiously as Bernie saw tears bulging in the child's eyes, but she was still fighting them, which he thought valiant of her.

"What about if we go to the restaurant and have an ice cream or something, while this lady looks for your Mom?" Jane looked at them both cautiously as the woman smiled. Bernie explained that her mother had been buying pantyhose on the main floor when Jane came upstairs, and then he turned to the woman quietly. "Why don't you activate the P.A. system in this case?" They had it for use in case of fire, or bomb threats, or some other emergency, but it would be simple to use it now to page Jane's mother for her. "Call my office and they'll take care of it." He looked down at Jane again as she used the dolly to wipe her eyes. "What's your Mom's name? Her last name I mean." He smiled and she looked up at him trustingly, despite her unwillingness to go anywhere with him. Her mother had drummed that into her well and he respected that.

"Same as mine." Jane almost smiled again.

"And what's that?"

"O'Reilly." This time she grinned. "It's Irish. And I'm Catholic. Are you?" She seemed fascinated by him, and he was equally so with her. He smiled to himself, thinking that this may have been the woman he had been waiting for, for thirty-four years. She was certainly the best one he had met in a very long time.

"I'm Jewish," he explained as the woman went

off to put the message on the hidden loudspeakers.

"What's that?" She looked intrigued.

"It means we have Chanukah instead of Christmas."

"Does Santa Claus come to your house?" She looked concerned and that was a difficult one.

"We exchange gifts for seven days." He avoided her question with an explanation of his own, and she looked impressed.

"Seven days? That's pretty good." And then suddenly, she grew more serious, forgetting her mother again. "Do you believe in God?"

He nodded, surprised at the depth of her thought. He himself hadn't thought of God in a long time, and he was ashamed to admit it to her. She had obviously been put in his path to straighten up his act. "Yes, I do."

"Me too." She nodded and then looked at him searchingly again. "Do you think my Mommy will come back soon?" The tears were threatening again, but she was in better shape now.

"I'm sure of it. Can I interest you in that ice cream now? The restaurant is right over there." He pointed to it, and she looked in the direction of his hand, greatly intrigued. The ice cream sounded good to her, and she quietly slid her hand into his, and her braids bobbed as they walked along, holding hands.

He helped her up onto a stool at the bar and asked for a banana split, which was not on their menu but he felt certain they could come up with

one, and for him, they did. Jane dove into it with a
blissful smile and worried eyes. She hadn't forgotten her mother totally, but she was well occupied
as she chatted with Bernie about their apartment,
the beach, and school. She wanted a dog, but their
landlord wouldn't let her have one.

"He's real mean," she said with chocolate and
marshmallow all over her face and her mouth full.
"So's his wife . . . and she's real fat too." She
shoved in a mouthful of nuts, banana, and
whipped cream as Bernie nodded seriously, wondering how he had lived without her for this long.
"Your bathing suits are very good." She dabbed at
her mouth and dove in again as he smiled.

"Which ones do you like best?"

"The little ones with the bottom and the top.
My Mom says I don't have to wear a top if I don't
want . . . but I always do." She looked prim as
the chocolate enveloped her nose as well. "I like
the blue and the pink and the red . . . and the
orange . . ." The last of the banana disappeared,
followed by the cherry and more whipped cream,
and suddenly there was a flurry in the door and a
woman appeared with a long shaft of golden hair
that looked like a sheet of gold as she flew across
the room.

"Jane!" She was a very pretty girl, not unlike
Jane. There were tearstains on her face and her
eyes were wild as she juggled her handbag and
three packages and what was obviously Jane's
jacket and another doll. "Where did you go?"
Jane blushed as she looked at her sheepishly.

"I just wanted to see . . ."

"Don't you *ever* do that again!" Her mother cut her off and grabbed her arm, shaking her a little bit, and then she quickly took the child in her arms and held her close as she fought back tears of her own. She had obviously been terrified. And it took her a long time to notice Bernard standing by, admiring them both. "I'm so sorry." She looked at him and he liked the way she looked. She was wearing sandals, a T-shirt, and jeans. But she was prettier than most, more delicate, and terribly frail and blond with the same huge blue eyes as Jane. "I apologize for all the trouble we've caused." The whole store had been looking for mother and child, and the entire main floor was in an uproar by then. Jane's mother had been afraid that she had been kidnapped, and she'd been desperate as she asked a salesperson to help, and then an assistant manager, and a buyer who happened by. Everyone did all they could, and finally the announcement that she was in the restaurant was made on the P.A.

"It's quite all right. We can use a little excitement around here. We had a very good time." He and Jane exchanged a knowing look and Jane suddenly piped up, grinning at him.

"You know, you'd really be a mess if you ate a banana split . . . see! That's why I don't like beards!" They both laughed and her mother looked horrified.

"Jane!"

"Well he would!"

"She's right," he admitted happily. He had enjoyed her so much, and hated to see her leave. He smiled and the pretty young woman blushed.

"I really apologize." And then suddenly she remembered that she hadn't introduced herself. "I'm sorry, I'm Elizabeth O'Reilly."

"And you're Catholic." He was remembering Jane's remark and her mother looked stunned, and then he attempted to explain. "I'm sorry . . . Jane and I had a very serious conversation about that."

Jane nodded sagely and popped another maraschino cherry into her mouth as she watched them talk. "And he's something else . . ." She squinted as she looked up at him again. "What was it again?"

"Jewish," he supplied, as Elizabeth O'Reilly grinned. She was used to Jane, but there were times . . .

"And he has seven Christmases . . ." She looked enormously impressed and the two adults laughed. "Honest, he does. That's what he said. Right?" She looked to Bernie for confirmation and he grinned and nodded at her.

"Chanukah. Actually, she even makes it sound good to me." He hadn't been in temple in years. His parents were Reformed and he didn't practice at all. But he was thinking of someone else. He was wondering just how Catholic Mrs. O'Reilly was, if there was a Mr. O'Reilly around, or not. He hadn't thought to ask Jane, and she hadn't mentioned it.

"I can't thank you enough." Elizabeth pretended to glare at Jane, who looked much happier now. She wasn't clutching her doll quite as hard, and she seemed to be enjoying the last of the ice cream.

"They have good bathing suits too."

Elizabeth shook her head and held out her hand to Bernie again. "Thank you again for rescuing her. Come on, old girl, let's go home. We have some other things to do."

"Can't we just look at the bathing suits before we go?"

"No." Her mother was firm, and she thanked Bernie profusely as they left. Jane shook his hand and thanked him very formally and then looked up at him with a sunny smile.

"You were nice, and the ice cream was very good. Thank you very much." She had obviously had a lovely time, and Bernie was actually sorry to see her go. He stood at the top of the escalator, watching the hair ribbons disappear, and feeling as though he had lost his only friend in California.

He went back to the cash register to thank the employees for their help, and as he left again, the little bikinis caught his eye, and he pulled out three in a size six. The orange, the pink, and the blue—the red one was sold out in her size—and he even picked out two hats to match and a little terry beach robe for her. It all looked perfect for her and he dumped it at the cash register.

"Have we got an Elizabeth O'Reilly on the computer here? I don't know if she's a charge customer or not, or what her husband's name is." He was suddenly hoping that she didn't have one, and the verdict was good when they checked. Two minutes later they confirmed that she had a new account and lived on Vallejo Street in Pacific Heights. "Great." He jotted down the phone number and address and tried to make it look as though he needed it for his files . . . instead of his empty little address book. . . . And he told them to send the stack of beachwear to "Miss Jane . . ." and charge it to his account. He wrote out a card that said only, "Thank you for a very nice time. Hope to see you again soon. Your friend, Bernie Fine," and handed that to the woman as well. And then with a lighter step he went back to his office with a mysterious little smile, convinced that there was a blessing in everything.

Chapter 5

The bathing suits arrived on Wednesday afternoon, and Liz called him the next day to thank him for his generosity to her daughter.

"You really shouldn't have. She's still talking about the banana split, and what a good time she had." Elizabeth O'Reilly had a young voice and he could see her shining blond hair in his mind's eye as he talked to her on the phone.

"I thought she was very brave actually. When she realized she was lost, she was terrified, but she kept her composure the entire time. That's quite something for a five-year-old."

Elizabeth smiled. "She's a pretty good kid."

He was dying to say "So's her mom," but he didn't. "Did the bathing suits fit?"

"Every one of them. She paraded around in them all last night, and she's wearing one under her dress now . . . she's at the park with some friends. I had a lot to do today . . . someone lent us a house in Stinson Beach, so Jane has her whole wardrobe set now.'' Liz laughed. ''Thank you so much . . .'' She didn't know what else to say, and he was groping for words too. Suddenly it all seemed new to him, as though they spoke a different language here. It was like starting all over again.

''Could I . . . could I see you again?'' He felt like a complete fool as he said the words into the phone . . . like a heavy breather on an anonymous call, but he was amazed when she said yes.

''I'd like that very much.''

''You would?'' He sounded stunned and she laughed.

''Yes, I would. Would you like to come to Stinson Beach for an afternoon?'' She sounded so easy and natural that he was grateful to her. She didn't make it sound as though he had his tongue hanging out and was annoying her. It sounded as though she wasn't surprised at all, and would enjoy seeing him.

''I'd love it. How long will you be there?''

''Two weeks.''

He made a rapid calculation in his head. There was no reason why he couldn't take Saturday off for once. There was no rule that said he had to be there. He just had nothing else to do. ''How about this Saturday?'' It was only two days away and his palms grew damp thinking of it.

She paused, trying to remember who she'd invited when. Stinson Beach always gave her a chance to see all her friends, and invite everyone

out for a day. But Saturday was still free. "That
sounds fine . . . great, in fact . . ." She smiled,
thinking of him. He was a nice-looking man, and
he had been nice to Jane, and he didn't appear to
be gay, and he didn't wear a wedding band. . . .
"By the way, you're not married, are you?" It
never hurt to ask. It would have been a bit of a
shock to find out afterwards. But it had happened
before. Not this time though.

"Good God no! What a thought!"

Aha. One of those. "Allergic to marriage, are
you?"

"No. I just work very hard."

"What does that have to do with it?" She was
open and direct and suddenly curious about him.
She had her own reasons for not getting married
again. Once burned, twice smart, but at least
she'd tried it once. But then again maybe he had
too. "Are you divorced?"

He smiled to himself at his end, wondering why
she asked. "No, I'm not divorced. And yes, I like
girls. And I have lived with two women in my life,
and I'm very comfortable the way things are. I
haven't had a lot of time to give to anyone. I've
spent the last ten years concentrating on my career."

"That can be empty sometimes." She sounded
as though she knew and he wondered what she
did. "I'm lucky I've got Jane."

"Yes, you are." He fell silent as he thought of
the little girl, and decided to save the rest of his
questions for Stinson Beach when he could see

her face and her eyes and her hands. He had never been crazy about getting to know someone over the telephone. "I'll see you both on Saturday then. Anything I can bring? A picnic? Wine? Anything from the store?"

"Sure. A mink coat would be nice."

He laughed and they hung up and for a whole hour afterwards he felt good. She had that kind of voice, easy and warm, and she didn't seem to have an ax to grind. She wasn't one of those women who hated men, or at least she didn't seem to be, and she didn't seem out to prove anything. He was really looking forward to their afternoon in Stinson Beach, and on Friday night before he went home, he went to their gourmet shop and bought two shopping bags of goodies to take to her. A chocolate teddy bear for Jane, and a box of chocolate truffles for Liz, two kinds of Brie, a *baguette* bread they flew in from France, a tiny tin of caviar, and another of pâté, two bottles of wine, one red and one white, and another tin of marrons glacés.

He put the bags in his car and drove home, and the next morning at ten o'clock he showered and shaved and put on blue jeans and an old blue shirt, slipped his feet into a beaten-up pair of sneakers, and grabbed a warm jacket from the closet in the hall. He had brought comfortable old clothes with him from New York for when the construction was going on, and now they were useful for the beach, and just as he picked up the two shopping bags, the phone rang. He wasn't going to answer it and then wondered if it was Elizabeth, changing their plans, or asking him to pick something up on the way, so he picked it up, still juggling his jacket and the bags.

"Yeah?"

"That's no way to answer the phone, Bernard."

"Hi, Mom. I'm just on my way out."

"To the store?" The interrogation began.

"No . . . to the beach. I'm visiting some friends today."

"Anyone I know?" Which, roughly translated, meant: Would I approve of them?

"I don't think so, Mom. Is everything okay?"

"Fine."

"Good. Then I'll call you tonight, or tomorrow from the store. I've got to run."

"Must be someone important if you can't talk to your mother for five minutes. Is it a girl?" No. A woman. And then of course there was Jane.

"No, just some friends."

"You're not hanging out with those boys out there, are you, Bernard?"

Oh for chrissake. He was dying to say he was, just to irritate her. "No, I'm not. Look, I'll talk to you soon."

"All right, all right . . . don't forget to wear a hat in the sun."

"Give my love to Dad."

He hung up and hurried out of his apartment before she could call back to warn him to be careful of sharks. And her favorite was warning him about hot items she saw in the *Daily News*. She was always warning him not to use some product that had gone bad and killed two people in Des Moines . . . botulism . . . Legionnaire's disease . . . heart attack . . . hemorrhoids . . . toxic shock. The possibilities were unlimited. It was nice having someone to worry about your health, but not with the passion of his mother.

He put the two shopping bags in the back of his car and got in, and ten minutes later he was on the Golden Gate Bridge, heading north. He had never been to Stinson Beach before, and he loved the intricate, winding road which rode the crest of the hills, looking down on the cliffs that jutted out over the sea. It was a miniature Big Sur, and he enjoyed the ride. He drove through the tiny town, and went to the address she had given him. She was in a private community called Seadrift, and he had to give the guard at the tollgate his name. But other than the security, it didn't look like a fancy place. The houses were on a very human scale, and the people who wandered by were barefoot and in shorts. It looked like the kind of place where families went, like Long Island or Cape Cod, and it looked wholesome and nice, as he pulled into the driveway of the house number she had given him. There was a tricycle outside, and a washed-out rocking horse who looked as though he had been out in the elements for years, and Bernard clanked an old school bell at the front gate, and then opened it. And then suddenly there was Jane, wearing one of the bikinis he had sent, and the little terry cloth robe he had picked out to go with it.

"Hi, Bernie." She beamed up at him, as they both remembered the banana split and their conversation about Christmas and God. "I love my new bathing suit."

"It looks great on you." He walked over to her, and she smiled up at him. "We could use you as a model at the store. Where's your mom? Don't tell me she's lost again." He put on a disapproving frown and Jane laughed a deep belly laugh that touched his heart. "Does she do that a lot?"

Jane shook her head. "Only in stores . . . sometimes . . ."

"What do I do in stores?" Elizabeth stuck her head out the door and smiled at Bernard. "Hello there. How was the drive?"

"Beautiful." He looked as though he had really enjoyed the trip as they exchanged a warm, expressive glance.

"Not everyone says that when they arrive. It's an awfully winding road."

"I always throw up," Jane supplied with a grin. "But I like it once we're here."

"Do you sit in the front seat with the windows down?" He looked concerned.

"Yup."

"Do you eat saltines before you go? . . . Nah . . . I'll bet you eat banana splits all the time." And then he remembered the chocolate teddy bear, and pulled it out of the bag for her before handing the rest to Liz. "For both of you, a few goodies from the store."

Elizabeth looked surprised and touched and Jane let out a squeal of delight as she held the chocolate teddy bear. It was even bigger than her doll, and she almost drooled looking at it. "Can I eat it now, Mommy? . . . Please? . . ." She turned pleading eyes to Liz, who gave a small groan of defeat. "Please, Mommy? . . . Please? . . . Just an ear?"

"All right, all right. I give up. But don't eat too much. Lunch will be ready pretty soon."

"Okay." She scampered off, holding the bear, like a puppy with a bone, and Bernard smiled at Liz.

"She's the greatest little kid." Someone like Jane reminded him that there were empty spots in his life, and children were one of them.

"She's crazy about you." Liz smiled.

"Banana splits and chocolate bears always help. For all she knows I'm the Boston Strangler with a great source for chocolate teddy bears." As he said it, he followed Elizabeth into the kitchen, where she unpacked the bags he had brought, and she gasped when she saw the caviar and the pâté and all the expensive goodies.

"Bernie, you shouldn't have done all that! My God . . . look at that . . ." She looked at the box of chocolate truffles in her hand, and then with a guilty look, she did exactly what Jane would have done. She offered them to him and then popped one in her mouth, closing her eyes with

the ecstasy of it. "Hmm . . . oh . . . sooo good
. . ." She made it sound like a sexual experience,
and it gave him a chance to admire her again. She
was delicate and graceful and really beautiful in a
clean-cut American way. She was wearing her
long blond hair in one long braid today, and her
eyes were as blue as the faded denim shirt she
wore and the white shorts showed off her shapely
legs. And he noticed that she wore carefully applied red polish on her toenails, which showed a
little vanity at least. But she wore nothing on her
eyes, and no lipstick at all, and the nails on her
hands were cut short. She was a pretty girl, more
than that in fact, but she wasn't frivolous, and he
liked that about her. She didn't take your breath
away, but she warmed your heart . . . in fact, she
warmed more than that as she bent over to put the
two bottles of wine away, and then turned to him
with a smile much like Jane's. "You've spoiled us
terribly, Bernard . . . I don't know what to say."

"Listen . . . it's nice to make new friends . . .
I don't have very many out here."

"How long have you been out here?"

"Five months."

"From New York?"

He nodded. "I've lived in New York all my life,
except three years in Chicago a long time ago."

She looked intrigued as she got two beers out of
the fridge and offered him one. "That's where I'm
from. Why did you go out there?"

"My trial by fire. I went out there to run the
store . . ." His voice trailed off, thinking of it.

"And now I'm here." It still felt like a punishment to him, although slightly less so as he looked at her, and then followed her into the comfortable living room. The house was small, and the floor was covered with straw mats. The furniture was covered in faded denim and there was driftwood and shells everywhere. The house could have been anywhere, East Hampton, Fire Island, Malibu . . . it had a nondescript quality, but outside the picture window was the view, a spectacular beach, a vast expanse of sea, and off to one side San Francisco, clustered on the hills sparkling in the sun. It was a beautiful view . . . and more than that, she was a beautiful girl. She waved him to a comfortable chair, and sat down on the couch herself, pretzeling her legs under her.

"Do you like it out here? In San Francisco, I mean."

"Sometimes." He was honest with her. "I haven't seen much of it, I must admit. I've been busy with the store. I like the climate. When I left New York, it was snowing, and when I got here five hours later, it was spring. There's something to be said for that."

"But?" She smiled invitingly at him. She had a nice way about her, a way that made one want to talk to her endlessly, and share one's private thoughts. He had a sudden insight that she must be a nice woman to have as a friend, and he wasn't sure if that was all he wanted from her or not. There was something about her which appealed to him a lot, something subtly sexy he couldn't define, like the curve of her breast in the old blue shirt she wore, and the way she bent her head . . . and the way little wisps of her hair curled softly around her face. He wanted to touch her, to hold her hand . . . to kiss the full lips as she smiled . . . it was difficult even concentrating on what she said. "It must be lonely for you here without friends. I hated it here for the first year."

"But you stayed anyway?" He looked intrigued. He wanted to hear about her, wanted to know everything she had to say.

"Yes. For a while I didn't have any choice. I didn't have any folks to go home to by then. My parents died in a car accident during my sopho- more year at Northwestern." Her eyes clouded thinking about it, and he winced on her behalf. "I think that made me a lot more vulnerable, and I fell madly in love with the star of the play I was in, in junior year."

Her eyes were sad as she thought back. It was funny, she didn't usually tell people about that, but it was easy to talk to him. And they were watching Jane through the picture window as she played in the sand outside, her doll sitting next to her as she waved at them from time to time. And something about Bernie made her want to be hon- est with him right from the beginning. She figured she had nothing to lose. If he didn't like what he heard, he wouldn't call again, but at least every- thing would be straight between them if he did. There was something to be said for that. She was tired of the games people played, and the pretense between people from the moment they met. It wasn't her style. And she looked at him with wide, honest blue eyes. "I was at Northwestern . . . studying drama of course." She smiled at him, thinking back. "And we'd been in summer stock together the summer right after my parents died. I felt like a zombie I was so numb, and I didn't have anyone in the world anymore. I fell head over heels in love with him. He was a gorgeous man and a nice guy, I thought, and I got pregnant just before we graduated. He said he wanted to get married out here. Someone had offered him a part in a movie in Hollywood. So he came out here first, and I followed him. I had nowhere else to go anymore, and I couldn't accept having an abortion. So I followed Chandler out here, even though things were a little less rosy by then. He wasn't too thrilled about the pregnancy, to say the least. But I was still desperately in love with him, and I thought things would work out." She glanced out the window at Jane, as though to reassure herself that they had.

"So I hitchhiked to Los Angeles, and met up with Chandler again. Chandler Scott . . . turned out later his name was really Charlie Schiavo, but he had changed his name . . . anyway, the part had fallen through for him . . . and he was busy chasing starlets and jobs while I worked as a waitress and got bigger every day. And we finally did get married, three days before Jane was born. I thought the justice of the peace was going to faint . . . and then Chandler disappeared. He called to say he had gotten a job doing repertory in Oregon when she was five months old, and afterwards I found out he'd been in jail. It was as if just the act of getting married scared him so much, he had to disappear. Although actually I figured out later that he must have been doing all kinds of strange stuff all along. He got busted for passing stolen goods, then he got arrested again for burglary. Anyway, he came back when Jane was nine months old and lived with us for a few months, and when she was a year old, he disappeared again, and when I found out he was in jail that time, I filed for divorce and that was it. I moved to San Francisco, and I've never heard from him again. He was a con man from beginning to end, and you've never met anyone so convincing in your life. If I met him today, I don't think I'd fall for it all again, but you know, he was so damn smooth, I don't know. . . . Isn't that depressing to realize? Anyway, I took back my maiden name when I got divorced and here we are." She looked matter-of-fact about her history, and he was amazed, anyone else would have been wringing their hankie just thinking about it. But she had survived and survived well. She looked wholesome and happy and she had a wonderful little girl. "And Jane is my family now. I think I got lucky in the end." His heart went out to her at the words.

"What does Jane think of all that?" He was curious about what Liz would have told the child.

"Nothing. She thinks he's dead. I told her he

was a beautiful actor and we got married after school and came out here, and then she came along and he died when she was a year old. She doesn't know the rest, and we'll never see him again, so what difference does it make? God only knows where he is. He'll probably wind up in jail for the rest of his life, and he's not interested in either of us. He never was. I'd rather she have a few illusions about how she came to be at least until later."

"I guess you're right." He admired her. He admired her a great deal. She was a brave girl and she'd made the best of it, and the child seemed to have suffered not at all, thanks to her mother loving her so much. And there was nothing tragic about this girl, she was all guts and heart and beautiful silky blond hair. And she had made a new life for herself.

California was a good place for that. It was a good place to start a new life. And she had.

"I teach school here now. I used my parents' insurance money and went to school at night for a year and got the credits I needed for a teaching credential out here, and I love my job. I teach second grade, and my kids are just great!" She grinned happily. "Jane goes to my school too, and the tuition is less that way. That was one of the reasons I decided to teach. I wanted her to go to a decent school, and I knew I'd have a hell of a time paying for private school, so everything worked out." She made it sound like a success story instead of an agony, and it was. It was remarkable.

She had snatched victory from the jaws of defeat and he could easily understand how it had happened. "Chandler Scott," or whatever his real name was, sounded like a male version of Isabelle, although he was certainly less of a pro than she, and she had never wound up in jail.

"I got myself involved with someone like that a few years ago." Her honesty deserved his. "A beautiful French girl, a model I met at the store. She had me in the palm of her hand for over a year, and I didn't get a wonderful little girl out of it." He smiled at Jane, playing outside, and then Liz, sitting across from him. "I wound up feeling used, and minus several thousand dollars and a watch my parents had given me. She was very slick. Someone offered her a movie career, and I found them making love on the deck of his yacht. I guess they come in all sexes and nationalities, that breed. But it kind of makes you cautious about who you get involved with after that, doesn't it? I've never been that close to anyone again, and that was three years ago." He paused. "People like that make you question your own judgment afterwards. You find yourself wondering how you could have been such a fool."

She laughed at him. "You can say that again! I didn't have a date for two years . . . and even now, I'm cautious . . . I love my work, my friends. The rest"—she shrugged and threw up both hands—"I can do without." He smiled at her. He was sorry to hear that.

"Should I leave now?"

They both laughed and she got up to check on the quiche she had made, and when she opened the oven door, the aroma of it wafted into the room.

"Boy, that smells good."

"Thank you. I love to cook." She whipped up a Caesar salad for both of them, handling the dressing as expertly as his favorite waiter at "21" in New York, and she poured out a Bloody Mary for him. Then she went to knock on the picture window and signaled to Jane to come in. She had a peanut butter and bacon sandwich for her, and she arrived at the lunch table carrying the chocolate teddy bear, minus one ear.

"Can he still hear you, Jane?"

"What?" She looked confused when Bernie asked.

"The bear . . . without his ear . . ."

"Oh." She grinned. "Yes. Next I'm going to eat his nose."

"Poor thing. He's going to be in terrible shape by tonight. I'll have to get you another one."

"You will?" Jane looked thrilled, and Liz served lunch. There were straw mats on the table and a vase filled with bright orange flowers, bright orange napkins, and pretty china and silverware.

"We love being here," Liz explained. "It's such a nice holiday for us. This belongs to one of the teachers at the school where I teach. Her husband is an architect and they built it years ago. And they go east to Martha's Vineyard to visit her parents every year, so they lend it to us, and it's the best part of our year, isn't it, Jane?" The child nodded and smiled up at Bernie.

"Do you like it here too?" Jane questioned him.

"Very much."

"Did you throw up on the way?" She seemed fascinated and he laughed at her choice of lunch conversation. But he loved her ingenuousness and her honesty. She was a lot like Liz, and she even looked like her. She was a miniature version of her mother.

"No, I didn't throw up. But it helps when you drive."

"That's what Mom says. She never throws up."

"Jane . . ." Liz warned her with her eyes, and Bernie watched them happily. It was an easy, comfortable afternoon, and he and Liz went for a walk on the beach afterwards, as Jane scampered ahead, looking for shells. He suspected that it wasn't always easy for them. It was difficult to be alone with a small child, but Liz didn't complain about it. She seemed to love it.

He told her what his job was like, and how much he loved Wolff's, how he had wanted to teach himself, but for him the dream had become something else. He even told her about Sheila and how heartbroken he had been over her, and as they walked back to the house, he looked down at her. She was considerably smaller than he and he liked that too. "You know, I feel as though I've known you for years. It's funny, isn't it?" He had never felt that way about anyone before.

She smiled up at him. "You're a nice man. I knew it the minute I met you at the store."

"That's a nice thing to say." He was pleased. He cared about what she thought.

"I could see it in the way you talked to Jane, and she talked about you all the way home. It sounded like you were one of her best friends."

"I'd like to be." He looked into Liz' eyes and she smiled at him.

"Look what I found!" Jane came bounding up to them, hurtling herself between them as she spoke. "It's a perfect silver dollar! It's not broken or anything!"

"Let me see that." He bent down to her and held out a flat hand and she placed the perfectly round white shell on his palm carefully as they inspected it. "By George, you're right!"

"Who's George?"

Bernie laughed. "That's just a dumb expression grown-ups use."

"Oh." She seemed satisfied.

"Your silver dollar is beautiful." He handed it back to her as carefully as she had given it to him, and as he stood up, he met her mother's eyes again. "I guess I should be getting back." Not that he wanted to.

"Would you like to stay for potluck tonight? We're having hamburgers." She had to watch their budget carefully, but they always did all right. It had been rough in the beginning, but she was good at juggling things now. She made a lot of Jane's clothes, had learned to cook everything herself, she even baked bread, and with friends like the ones who lent them the house in Stinson Beach, they had everything they needed . . . even Bernie and his bathing suits. . . . She had been planning to buy Jane one, or maybe two. And instead she had a whole stack of them, thanks to him.

"I have a better idea." He had seen the restaurant as he drove through town on the way. "What if I take you ladies out tonight?" And then suddenly he remembered what he had worn. "Will the Sand Dollar let me in like this?" He extended his arms as the ladies inspected him and Liz laughed.

"You look fine to me."

"Then what about it?"

"Come on, Mommy, please . . . can we go? . . . please!" she clamored instantly, and the idea appealed to Liz too. She accepted happily and sent Jane to her room to change, while she offered Bernie a beer in the living room. But he declined.

"I'm not much of a drinker," he admitted to her.

Elizabeth looked relieved. She hated going out with men who expected her to drink a lot. Chandler had always drunk too much, and that had made her nervous about him, but she hadn't been as brave about speaking up about it then. Now she was. "It's funny how annoyed some people get when you don't drink."

"I guess it threatens them, particularly if they drink too much."

It was so easy being with him, she couldn't get over it. And they had a marvelous time that night. The Sand Dollar had the aura of an old saloon, as people poured through the swinging doors all night long, to stand at the bar, or eat the enormous steak and lobster dinners they served. It was the only show in town, Liz explained, but fortunately the food was very good, and even Jane dove into her plate and attacked a small steak with glee. It wasn't often they ate so extravagantly. And she fell asleep in the car on the way back, and Bernie carried her inside and laid her gently on her bed. She was sleeping in the house's tiny guest room, right next to the room where Liz slept, and they tiptoed back to the living room.

"I think I'm falling in love with her." His eyes met Liz', and she smiled.

"It's entirely mutual. We had a wonderful time."

"So did I." He walked slowly to the door, wanting to kiss her, but afraid it was too soon. He didn't want to scare her away, he liked her too much. It was like being in high school again. "When will you be back in town?"

"Two weeks from today. But why don't you come back next week? It's an easy drive from town. You can do it in forty minutes or so, if you can stand the winding road. We'll have an early dinner and you can go back afterwards. Or you can even stay here if you want. You can have Jane's room, and she can sleep with me." He would have preferred to sleep with her himself, but he didn't dare say it to her, even jokingly. It was much too soon to suggest anything like that, and he didn't want to jeopardize anything. It was also going to be delicate with Jane so much a part of her mother's life. She was always there with them, and he had to consider that. He didn't want to do anything to harm her.

"I'd love to come out, if I can get out of the store at a decent hour."

"What time do you usually leave work?" They were whispering in the living room so as not to wake Jane, and he laughed.

"Between nine and ten o'clock at night, but that's just the way I am. That's no one's fault. I work seven days a week," he confessed, and she looked shocked.

"That's no way to live."

"I have nothing better to do." It was a terrible admission, and even to him it sounded awful. And now maybe he would have something better to do . . . with them. . . . "I'll try to reform by next week. I'll give you a call." She nodded, hoping he would. The beginning was always so difficult, establishing the contact, laying out one's hopes and dreams. But it had been easier with him. He was the nicest man she had met in a long, long time. And she followed him outside to his car.

She thought she had never seen as many stars as hung over them that night, and she looked up at them and then at him as he stood looking at her for a long time. "Today was wonderful, Liz." She had been so honest with him, and so warm. She had even told him the truth about how she had had Jane, and her disastrous marriage to Chandler Scott. It was nice to know those things right from the first sometimes. "I'll look forward to seeing you again." He reached out and touched her hand, and she held his for a moment before he slipped into his car.

"So will I. Drive home carefully."

He grinned at her, peering out from the open window as he laughed. "I'll try not to throw up on the way back."

They both laughed, and he waved as he backed down the driveway and then drove off, thinking of her, and Jane, talking and laughing over dinner.

Chapter 6

Bernie made it back to Stinson Beach to dinner twice the following week. Once Liz cooked for him, and the second time he took them out to the Sand Dollar again, and then he came back on Saturday again too. And this time he brought a new beach ball for Jane, and several games, including a ring toss they played on the beach, and all kinds of sand equipment Jane loved. And he even brought a new bathing suit for Liz. It was a pale blue, almost the color of her eyes, and she looked spectacular in it.

"Good Lord, Bernie . . . this has to stop."

"Why? That bathing suit was just sitting there on a mannequin this week, and it looked so much like you, I had to bring it out." He was pleased. He loved spoiling her, and he knew no one ever had before, which made it even more fun to do.

"You can't spoil us like this!"

"Why not?"

"Oh"—she looked sad for a minute and then smiled again—"we might get used to it, and then what would we do? We'd be banging on your door at the store every day, begging for bathing suits and chocolate teddy bears and caviar and pâté . . ." He grinned at the image she conjured up.

"I'll just have to see to it that you keep supplied then, won't I?" But he understood what she meant. It would be difficult if he faded from their lives, but he couldn't envision that yet. On the contrary he couldn't envision it at all.

He came back two more times the following week, and this time on the second night Liz got a teenager from another house to babysit for Jane and they went out alone, to the Sand Dollar again, of course—there was nowhere else to go—but they both liked the food and the atmosphere there.

"You've been an awfully good sport about taking both of us out." Liz smiled across the table at him.

"I haven't figured out which of you I like best actually. So it works out pretty well for now."

She laughed. He always made her feel so good. He was such a nice easygoing happy man. And she told him so.

"God only knows why." He smiled. "With a mother like mine I should have grown up with a twitch and several tics, at least."

"She can't be that bad." Liz smiled and he groaned.

"You have no idea. Just wait . . . if she ever

comes out here again, which I doubt. She hated it in June. At least she liked the store. You have no idea of how difficult she is though." He had been avoiding her calls for the last two weeks. He didn't want to have to explain to her where he had been spending his time, and if she'd been calling him, she would know that he'd been out a lot. "Just cruising the bars, Mom." He could just imagine what she would have to say to that. Of course going out with a girl called "O'Reilly" would take the cake. But he couldn't tell Liz that yet. He didn't want to scare her off.

"How long have they been married?"

"Thirty-eight years. My father is up for a Purple Heart." She laughed at the thought. "I'm serious. You don't know what she's like."

"I'd like to meet her sometime."

"Oh my God! Shhh . . ." He looked over his shoulder, as though expecting to see his mother standing there, with an ax in her hand. "Don't say a thing like that, Liz! It could be dangerous!" He teased and she laughed and they talked halfway through the night. He had kissed her the second time he had come to the beach, and Jane had even caught them at it once or twice, but the romance had gone no further than that. He was nervous about Jane, and it was more comfortable courting Liz in an old-fashioned way for now. There would be plenty of time for other things when they moved back to town, and Jane wasn't asleep in the next room, with only a paper-thin wall between them.

He came back that Sunday to help Liz pack up. Her friends had told her she could stay one extra day, and she and Jane were obviously unhappy to go home. It was the end of the vacation for them, and they wouldn't be going anywhere else that year. Liz couldn't afford to take any trips, with or without Jane, and their mood was so gloomy on the way home that Bernie felt sorry for them.

"Listen, you two, why don't we go somewhere else sometime soon? Maybe Carmel . . . Lake Tahoe? How does that sound? I haven't been anywhere yet, and you ladies could show me around. In fact, we could do both!" Liz and Jane let out a whoop of glee and the next day he told his secretary to make reservations for them somewhere. She got a condominium in Lake Tahoe for the three of them, he had specified three bedrooms to her, and she was able to get it for the following weekend, as well as Labor Day, and when he told them that night they were thrilled. Jane blew him a kiss as Liz tucked her into bed, but Liz looked concerned as she came out to sit in her tiny living room with him. She had a one-bedroom flat, and Jane slept in the single bedroom, while Liz slept in the living room on a convertible couch. It became rapidly obvious to him that their love life would not improve here.

She looked worried as she looked up at him apologetically. "Bernie . . . I don't want you to misunderstand . . . but I don't think we should go to Lake Tahoe with you."

He looked like a disappointed child as he stared at her unhappily. "Why not?"

"Because this is all so wonderful . . . and I'm sure it sounds crazy to you . . . but I can't do these things with Jane. And if I let you do them for us, what are we going to do afterwards?"

"After what?" But he knew what she meant. He didn't want to, but he did.

"After you go back to New York." Her voice was as soft as silk, and she held his hand as they sat on the couch and talked. "Or after you get tired of me. We're grown-ups, and it all feels wonderful to us now . . . but who knows what will happen next month, or next week or next year . . ."

"I want you to marry me." His voice was small and hard and she stared at him. But she wasn't nearly as surprised as he. The words had just come to his lips of their own, but now that they were there, he knew that they were right as he looked at her.

"You what? You're not serious." She leapt to her feet and paced the small room nervously. "You don't even know me yet."

"Yes, I do. All my life I've been going out with women whom I knew on the first date I never wanted to see again, but I figured what the hell, give it a try, you never know . . . and two months later, or three or six, I threw in the towel and never called them again. Now I find you, and I knew the first time I laid eyes on you that I was in love with you, and the second time I saw you I knew you were right for me and that you were the best woman I'd ever meet, and if I was very, very lucky, you'd let me shine your shoes for the rest of my life . . . so what am I supposed to do now? Play games for six months and pretend that I need to figure it out? I don't need to figure out anything. I love you. I want to marry you." He was beaming at her, and he suddenly knew that the best thing possible had just happened to him. "Will you marry me, Liz?"

She was grinning at him and she looked even younger than her twenty-seven years. "You're nuts. Do you know that? You're crazy." But she knew the same things. She was wild about him. "I can't marry you after three weeks. What are people going to say? What will your mother say?" She said the magic words and he groaned, but he still looked happier than he ever had in his life.

"Listen, as long as your name is not Rachel Nussbaum and your mother's maiden name wasn't Greenberg or Schwartz, she's going to have a nervous breakdown anyway, so what difference does it make?"

"It'll make a big difference to her if you tell her you met me three weeks ago."

She walked back to where he stood, and he pulled her back down on the couch next to him and took her hands in his. "I'm in love with you, Elizabeth O'Reilly, and I don't care if you're related to the Pope and I met you yesterday. Life is too short to waste time playing games. I never have and I never will. Let's not waste what we've got." And then he had an idea. "Tell you what.

We'll do this properly. We'll get engaged. Today is August first, we'll get married at Christmastime, that's almost five months away. If you can tell me by then that that isn't what you want to do, we'll cancel everything. How does that sound?" He was already thinking of the ring he would buy . . . five carats . . . seven . . . eight . . . ten . . . anything she wanted. He put an arm around her shoulders and she was laughing with tears in her eyes.

"Do you realize you haven't even slept with me yet?"

"An oversight on my part." He looked unimpressed, and then looked at her thoughtfully. "As a matter of fact, I meant to discuss that with you. Do you suppose you could find a babysitter one of these days? It's not that I don't love our little girl" —she was already his, too—"I do, but I have this wicked, lewd, lecherous idea that involves your coming up to my place for a few hours . . . ."

"I'll see what I can arrange." She was still laughing at him. It was the craziest thing that had ever happened to her. But he was such a good man, and she knew he would be wonderful to her and Jane for the rest of their lives, but much more important, she knew she was in love with him. It was just so damn difficult to explain that she had fallen in love with him and knew it was right in just three weeks. She couldn't wait to tell Tracy, her best friend at school, a substitute teacher, who was due back from a cruise. She left Liz a lonely woman and when she came back she would find

Liz engaged to the general manager of Wolff's. It was absolutely nuts. "All right, all right, I'll get a babysitter." He was pressing her.

"Does this mean we're engaged?" He was beaming and so was she.

"I guess it does." She still couldn't believe what they'd done, and he was squinting now, trying to figure something out.

"How about having the wedding on December twenty-ninth? That's a Saturday." He already knew that from plans they'd made at the store. "That way we'll have Christmas with Jane, and we can go to Hawaii or something for our honeymoon." Liz was completely bowled over by him and as she laughed he leaned over and kissed her and suddenly it all made sense to both of them. It was a dream come true, a perfect match . . . a match made over a banana split with Jane watching over them, like a guardian angel.

Bernie leaned over and kissed Liz, and she could feel his heart pounding as he held her close to him. And they both knew with absolute certainty, this was forever.

Chapter 7

It took her two days to find a babysitter, and she announced it to Bernie over the phone that afternoon, and blushed when she mentioned it. She knew exactly what he had in mind, and it was embarrassing to be so unspontaneous about it. But with Jane in the only bedroom she had, there wasn't much else they could do. The woman was coming at seven o'clock and was willing to stay until one.

"It's a bit like Cinderella, but it'll do," she said with a smile.

"That's all right. Don't worry about it." He had a fifty-dollar bill just begging to fall into the woman's hands when Liz went to kiss Jane good night. "Wear something a little dressy tonight."

"Like a garter belt?" She was as nervous as a bride, and he laughed at what she said.

"Sounds great. But wear a dress over it. Let's have dinner out."

She was surprised. She had visions of going to his apartment straight from hers, and getting the "first time" over with. It seemed almost like a surgical procedure to her. First times were so awkward anyway, and the idea of going to dinner instead appealed to her enormously.

And when he picked her up that night, they went to L'Étoile, where he had reserved a table for two, and she began to relax as they talked the way they always did. He told her what was happening in the store, about the plans they'd made for the fall, the promotions, the fashion shows. The opera show had come and gone and been a great success and the others were under way now. She was fascinated by what he did, and even more so because he was so much a businessman. He simply applied the principles of good economics to whatever he touched in the store, that and his extraordinary sense for upcoming trends, and everything he touched turned to gold, as Paul Berman said. And lately, Bernie didn't even mind having been sent to San Francisco to open the store. The way he figured it, he had one more year in California at best, and that would give them time to get married and spend a few months alone, before they went back to New York and Liz would have to deal with his mother at close range. They might even have a baby on the way by then . . . and he had to think of schools for Jane . . . but he didn't tell all that to Liz. He had warned her that they were going back to New York eventually, but he didn't want to worry her with the details of the move yet. It was a year away after all, and they had their wedding to think of first.

"Are you going to wear a real wedding dress?" He loved the thought of it, and had seen one in a show at the store only two days before that would have been fabulous on her, but she blushed at the thought as she smiled at him.

"You really mean it, don't you?"

He nodded, holding her hand under the table as they sat side by side on the banquette. He loved the feel of her leg next to his, and she had worn a pretty white silk dress that showed off her tan, and her hair was swept up in a bun high on her head. He noticed that she had worn nail polish, which was unusual for her, and he was glad, but he didn't tell her why as he leaned over and kissed her gently on the neck. "Yes, I do mean it. I don't know . . . somehow one knows when one is doing the right thing, and when one isn't. I've always known, and the only mistakes I've made have been when I didn't trust my instincts. I've never gone wrong when I have." She understood him perfectly, but it seemed amazing to move into marriage so quickly, and yet she knew they weren't wrong, and she suspected that she'd never regret it. "I hope one day you feel as sure as I do right now, Liz." His eyes were gentle on hers, and her heart went out to him as they sat side by side. He loved the feel of her thigh next to his, and it thrilled him to his very core as he thought of lying next to her, but it was too soon to think about that now. He had the whole evening planned to perfection.

"You know, the crazy thing is that I do feel sure. . . . I just don't know yet how I'll explain it to anyone."

"I think real life happens this way, Liz. You always hear about people who live together for ten years, and then one of them meets someone else and they get married in five days . . . because the first relationship was never really right, but in the twinkling of an eye that person knew the second relationship was."

"I know, I've often thought of things like that. I just never thought it would happen to me." She smiled at him, and they ate duck and salad and soufflé, and then they moved into the bar, where he ordered champagne, and they sat listening to the piano and chatting as they had for weeks now, sharing opinions and ideas and hopes and dreams. It was the most beautiful evening she had had in a long, long time, and being with him made up for everything bad that had ever happened to her, her parents' death, the nightmare with Chandler Scott, and the long lonely years alone since Jane's birth, with no one to help her out or be there for her. And suddenly none of it mattered now that she was with him. It was as though all her life had been in preparation for this man who was so good to her now, and absolutely nothing else mattered.

After their champagne, when he had paid the check, they walked slowly upstairs hand in hand,

and she was about to stroll outside when he directed her through the hotel instead, guiding her gently by the arm, but she didn't think anything of it, until he walked her to the elevators and looked down at her with a small, boyish smile, barely concealed by his beard.

"Want to come upstairs for a drink?" She knew what he was up to, and that he didn't live there, but it seemed romantic somehow, and a little mischievous at the same time. He had whispered the words to her and she answered him with a smile.

"As long as you promise not to tell my mother." It was only ten o'clock and she knew they still had three hours.

The elevator rose to the top floor, and Liz followed him to a door directly across the hall without saying a word. He took a key from his pocket and let her inside. It was the most beautiful suite she had ever seen, in a movie or real life, or ever even dreamed of. Everything was white and gold, and done in delicate silks, with fine antiques everywhere, and a chandelier which sparkled over them. The lights were dim, and there were candles burning on a table with a platter of cheese and fruit, and a bottle of champagne chilling in a silver bucket.

Liz looked over at him with a smile, bereft of words at first. He did everything with such style, and he was always so thoughtful. "You're amazing, Mr. Fine . . . do you know that?"

"I thought if this was going to be our honeymoon, we ought to do it right." And he had. One couldn't possibly have done it better. The lights were dim in the other room as well. He had rented the suite himself at lunchtime, and he had come upstairs before picking her up to make sure that everything looked right. He had the maid open the bed for them, and there was a beautiful pink peignoir laid out, trimmed in marabou with pink satin slippers to match, and a pink satin night-gown. She discovered it as she walked into the other room, and she gave a little gasp as she saw the beautiful things laid out on the bed, as though they were waiting for a movie star, and not just little old Liz O'Reilly from Chicago.

She said as much to him and he took her in his arms. "Is that who you are? Little old Liz O'Reilly from Chicago? Well, what do you know . . . and pretty soon you'll be little old Liz Fine from San Francisco." He kissed her hungrily, and his kisses were answered as he laid her gently on the bed and pushed the peignoir aside. It was the first chance they had had to sate their hunger for each other, and three weeks of desire swept over them like a tidal wave as their clothes melted into a heap on the floor, covered by the pink satin peignoir trimmed in marabou, as their bodies intertwined and her mouth covered every inch of his body. She made every dream he'd ever had come true, and he dazzled her with the heights of passion they reached as they gasped for each other, want-ing more and more and more until they lay spent at last, sleepy-eyed, in the dim room, her head on his shoulder, as he played with the long blond hair that hung over her like a satin curtain.

"You are the most beautiful woman I've ever seen . . . do you know that?"

"You're a beautiful man, Bernie Fine . . . inside and out." Her voice was suddenly husky, and she looked into his eyes lovingly and then suddenly burst out laughing when she saw what he had left under her pillow. It was a black lace garter belt with a red rosette and she held it aloft now like a trophy, and then kissed him and they began all over again once she put it on for him. It was the most beautiful night either of them had ever spent, and it was long after one o'clock when they sat in the bathtub in the hotel, and he played with her nipples amidst the soap suds.

"We're never going to get out of here if you start that again." She smiled sleepily, leaning her head against the luxurious pink marble. She had wanted to call the sitter to tell her they would be late, but Bernie had finally told her he had taken care of it, and Liz had actually blushed when he told her. "You paid her off?" She giggled at the thought.

"I did." He looked pleased and Liz kissed him.

"I love you so much, Bernie Fine." He smiled and more than ever he wanted to spend the night with her, but he knew they couldn't, and he was already sorry that he had suggested they get married after Christmas. He couldn't imagine waiting that long, but thinking of it reminded him of the one thing he had forgotten.

"Where are you going?" She looked up in surprise as he climbed out of the tub with soap all
over him.

"I'll be right back." She watched him go. He
had a powerful body with broad shoulders and
long, graceful legs. It was a body that appealed to
her, and she could feel desire gnawing at the pit of
her stomach as she watched him, and she lay back
in the tub with her eyes closed, waiting for him to
return again. He was back only a moment later,
and he slid a hand down low over her stomach as
he slid back into the water, and before he had a
chance to give her what he had brought from the
other room, his fingers traveled to where her legs
joined and he was exploring her again, his mouth
hungry on her lips as, with his other hand, he
touched her. They made love this time in the tub,
and the sounds of their lovemaking echoed in the
pink marble bathroom.

"Shh," she whispered afterwards, giggling.
"They're going to throw us out of here."

"Either that or sell tickets." He hadn't felt this
good in years and he didn't want it to end. Ever.
He had never known another woman like her.
And neither of them had made love to anyone in a
long, long time, so their hunger was well spent on
each other. "By the way, I brought you something
before you attacked me."

"*I* attacked *you* . . . ha!" But she glanced over
her shoulder in the direction he was looking. Being with him was like celebrating Christmas every
day and she wondered what he was going to sur-

prise her with now . . . peignoirs . . . and garter belts and . . . He had left a shoe box on the
side of the tub, and when she opened it, there was
a pair of gaudy gold slippers inside with large
rhinestones all over them. She laughed, not sure if
he was serious or not. "Are these hand-me-downs
from Cinderella?" They were actually very tacky
and she wasn't quite sure why he had given them
to her, but he was looking amused as he watched
her. They had huge cube-shaped hunks of glass
glued on all over them, and one of them even had
a huge rhinestone dangling from the gold bow.
"My God!" she gasped, suddenly realizing what
he had done. "My God!" She stood straight up in
the tub and stared down at him. "Bernie . . .
No! You can't do this!" But he had, and she had
seen it. He had carefully pinned a huge diamond
engagement ring to one of the gaudy gold bows,
and at first it just appeared to be one more ghastly
rhinestone like the others. But she had seen the
ring, and she was crying as she held the slipper,
and he stood up quietly and unpinned it for her.
Her hands were shaking too badly, and there were
tears pouring down her cheeks as he slipped it on
her finger. It was more than eight carats, a simple
emerald-cut stone, and the most beautiful ring he
had ever seen when he bought it. "Oh, Bernie
. . ." She clung to him as they stood in the bathroom, and he stroked her hair and kissed her, and
after he had gently washed the soap off her, and
himself, he carried her to the bed in the other
room, and made love to her again . . . this time

more gently . . . slowly . . . . it was like singing in a whisper . . . or doing a slow delicate dance, moving gracefully together until they could no more, and then he held her close to him as she shuddered with delight and he rose to his own heights beside her.

It was five o'clock in the morning when she got home that night, looking neat and clean, and as though she had been at a teacher's meeting all night. It would have been difficult to believe what she'd been doing. And she apologized profusely to the babysitter for coming home so late, but the woman said she didn't mind, and they both knew why. She'd been asleep for hours anyway, and she closed the door quietly when she left, as Liz sat alone in her living room, looking out at the summer fog, thinking with infinite tenderness of the man she was going to marry, and of how lucky she was to have found him. The huge diamond sparkled on her hand, as tears shimmered in her eyes, and she called him as soon as she got into her bed and they spoke in hushed, romantic whispers for another hour. She couldn't bear to be without him.

Chapter 8

After the trip to Tahoe with Jane, where they all slept in separate bedrooms, and Liz had mentioned several times how great it would be if they could be together all the time, Bernie insisted that she pick out a dress from the store for the opening of the opera. They would be sitting in a box, and it was the most important event of the San Francisco social season. He knew she didn't have anything dressy enough of her own, and he wanted her to pick out something spectacular for the opening.

"You might as well start taking advantage of the store now, sweetheart. There have to be some advantages to working seven days a week." Although nothing was free, he always enjoyed an enormous discount. And for the first time he enjoyed using it on her.

She went to the store, and after trying on dozens of dresses, she selected one from an Italian designer he loved, a dress which hung in rich vel-

vet folds, in a cognac-colored velvet, encrusted
with gold beads and little stones all of which appeared to be semiprecious. At first Liz thought it
far too elaborate and wondered if it looked too
much like the outlandish slippers he had given her
with her engagement ring, but the moment she
put it on she realized how magnificent it was. It
was cut in a style reminiscent of the Renaissance,
with a generous décolleté and big full sleeves, and
a long sweeping skirt with a small train she could
hook to her finger. As she moved around the large
fitting room in the designer salon, she felt like a
queen, and she giggled as she preened, and then
suddenly she was startled as she saw the fitting
room door open and heard a familiar voice behind her.

"Find anything?" His eyes danced above the
beard when he saw the gown she had on. He had
seen it when it arrived from Italy, it had caused
quite a stir in the designer salon and was one of
the most expensive ones they had, but he didn't
look disturbed about it as he watched her. He was
mesmerized by how exquisite she looked in the
dress, and with his discount it wouldn't be too
painful for him. "Wow! The designer should see
you in that dress, Liz!" The saleslady smiled at
him as well, it was a pleasure seeing someone as
pretty as Liz so perfectly molded into a dress
which enhanced everything from her golden
bronze skin to her eyes to her figure. Bernie
strode to where she stood and kissed her as he felt
the soft fabric beneath his hands, and the door to

the dressing room closed discreetly behind the vendeuse as she left, murmuring something about "look for something else . . . perhaps some shoes to go with . . ." She knew her job well, and always performed it with skill and discretion.

"Do you really like it?" Liz' eyes sparkled like one of the gems on the dress as she twirled gracefully for him and her laughter rang out like silver bells in the dressing room. He could almost feel his heart expand with delight just looking at her, and he could hardly wait to show her off at the opera.

"I love it. It was made for you, Liz. Do you see anything else you like?"

She laughed and her tan heightened with a rosy blush. She didn't want to take advantage of him. "I should say not. They wouldn't let me see the price tag on this yet . . . but I don't think I should even buy this one." She knew just from the feel of the fabric that she couldn't afford it, but it was fun to dress up, not unlike something Jane would have done in the same circumstances, and she knew Bernie would let her use his discount. But still . . .

He was smiling at her. She was an amazing girl, and he was suddenly reminded of Isabelle Martin of the distant past, and how different they were. The one who couldn't take enough, the other who wouldn't take at all. He was a lucky man. "You're not buying anything, Mrs. O'Reilly. The dress is a gift from your future husband, along with anything else you see here that you like."

"Bernie . . . I . . ."

He sealed her lips with a kiss and then walked to the door of the dressing room with a last look over his shoulder. "Go look at some shoes to go with it, sweetheart. And come up to the office when you're all through. We'll go to lunch afterwards." He smiled at her and then disappeared as the saleslady reappeared with an armload of other dresses she thought Liz might like, but Liz absolutely refused to try them. She consented only to try on a pair of shoes to go with the dress and found a beautiful brandy-colored pair of satin evening shoes encrusted with stones that were almost identical. They were the perfect match and Liz looked victorious when she picked Bernie up upstairs, and as they left the store she was chatting happily, telling him about the shoes, how much she loved the dress, and how overwhelmed she was by how much he spoiled her. They walked to Trader Vic's arm in arm, and had a long lazy lunch, teasing and laughing and enjoying the afternoon, and it was with regret that he left her at almost three o'clock. She had to pick up Jane at a friend's. They were both enjoying their liberty before they started school again. They only had a few days left before they went back to school the following Monday.

But the opera was foremost on Liz' mind, and on Friday afternoon she had her hair done and a manicure, and at six o'clock she slipped into the magical dress that he had bought her. She zipped it up carefully, and stood staring at herself for a moment in amazement. Her hair was swept up and caught in a thickly woven gold net she had found during another foray at Wolff's and the shoes peeked out from beneath the heavy velvet folds of her dress, and she heard the doorbell faintly in the distance, and then suddenly Bernie was standing in the doorway of her bedroom looking like a vision himself in white tie and tails and the starched bibfront of an impeccably made English shirt and the diamond studs that had been his grandfather's.

"My God, Liz . . ." He couldn't say more as he looked at her, and he kissed her carefully so as not to disturb her makeup. "You look so lovely," he whispered, as Jane watched them from the doorway, forgotten for the moment. "Ready?"

She nodded and then spotted her daughter. Jane looked less than pleased as she watched them. In a way, it pleased her to see her mother looking so pretty, and in another, it troubled her to see them so close. It had been worrying her since Lake Tahoe, and Liz knew they had to say something to her soon about their plans, but in a way she was frightened to tell her. What if she objected to their getting married? Liz knew she liked Bernie, but liking him wasn't enough. And in some ways, Jane considered Bernie her friend, more than her mother's.

"Good night, sweetheart." Liz stooped to kiss her, and Jane turned away, with angry eyes, and this time she said nothing to Bernie. And as they left the house, for a moment Liz looked worried, but she said nothing to Bernie. She didn't want anything to spoil their magical evening.

They went to the dinner at the Museum of Modern Art first, in the Rolls Bernie had rented for the occasion, and they were rapidly swept into the throng of women in dazzling gowns and ornate jewels, and photographers fighting to take their picture. But Liz felt perfectly at home in their midst and proud on Bernie's arm as she clung tightly to him and the flashbulbs went off all around them. She knew they had taken their photograph too, and Bernie was already becoming known around town as the manager of the city's most elegant store, and many of the expensively dressed women seemed to know him. The museum had been decorated by the local socialites, and was filled with silver and gold balloons and trees that had been sprayed gold. There were beautifully wrapped gifts at each seat, cologne for the men, and a handsome bottle of perfume for the ladies, from Wolff's, of course, and it was easy to recognize their distinctive wrapping on every table.

The crowd pressed them close as they walked into the huge hall where the tables were, and Liz looked up at Bernie with a smile as he squeezed her arm and another photographer took their picture.

"Having fun?" She nodded but it was difficult to call it that. It was a crush of bodies in exquisite evening gowns, and enough jewelry to fill several wheelbarrows had anyone wanted to try. But there was an aura of excitement too. Everyone knew that they were part of an important evening.

Bernie and Liz took their seats at the same table with a couple from Texas, the curator of the museum and his wife, an important customer of Wolff's and her fifth husband, and the mayor and her husband. It was an interesting table, and conversation was rapid and light as the dinner was served and the wines poured, and everyone chatted about their summer, their children, their most recent trips, and the last time they had seen Placido Domingo. He was flying to San Francisco especially to sing *Traviata* this evening with Renata Scotto, and it would be a treat for the real opera lovers in the crowd, although there were few of those. Opera in San Francisco had more to do with social standing and fashion than it did with any real passion for music. Bernie had heard it said for months, but he didn't care. He was having a good time, and it was fun being out with Liz for such an elegant evening. And Domingo and Scotto were only additional treats as far as he was concerned. He knew very little about opera.

But as they walked across the horseshoe driveway a little later on, to the War Memorial Opera House, even Bernie felt the intensity of the moment. The photographers appeared en masse this time, to photograph everyone going into the opera house, and there was a crowd held back by cordons and police. They had come just to ogle the elegantly dressed crowd on opening night, and Bernie suddenly felt as though he were attending the Academy Awards, only the crowd was staring at him and not at Gregory Peck or Kirk Douglas. It was a heady feeling as he shielded Liz from the eddying movements of the crowd and ushered her into the building and up the stairs to where he knew their box was. They found their seats easily, and he recognized familiar faces all around him, the women anyway. They were all clients of Wolff's. In fact, he was pleased at how many of their gowns he had seen since the evening began. But Liz was by far the most beautiful in her magnificent Renaissance gown, with her hair caught up in the woven threads of gold. He found himself aching to kiss her as others looked at them admiringly, and he pressed her hand gently as the light dimmed, and they held hands through the whole first act. And Domingo and Scotto were extraordinary together. It was a breathtaking evening in every way, and they followed the others to the bar, where the champagne poured like water and the photographers were hard at work again. He knew they had taken Liz' photograph at least fifteen times since the evening began, but she didn't seem to mind it. She looked shy and demure and she felt safe at his side. Everything about her made him want to protect her.

He handed her a glass of champagne, and they stood sipping it and watching the crowd, and suddenly Liz giggled as she looked up at him. "It's funny, isn't it?"

He grinned. It was funny. It was so overwhelmingly elegant, and they all took themselves so seriously that it was difficult to believe that they hadn't been cast backwards into another time when moments like this were infinitely more important. "It's kind of a nice change from one's daily routine though, isn't it, Liz?"

She smiled again and nodded. The next morning she would be at Safeway buying groceries for herself and Jane for the week, and on Monday she would be writing simple additions on a chalkboard. "It makes everything else seem unreal."

"That should be part of the magic of opera, I think." He liked the importance of the event in San Francisco, and he liked being part of it. And most of all, he liked sharing it with her. It was a first time for both of them and he wanted to share a lifetime of firsts with her. The lights dimmed then before he could say anything, and then rose again, as a discreet bell sounded in the distance. "We have to go back." He put down his glass, as did Liz, but he noticed rapidly that no one else did, and when they finally left the bar at the insistence of the bell, most of the crowd from the boxes remained at the bar, talking and laughing and drinking. That was part of the San Francisco tradition too. The bar and its intrigues being, in most instances, far more important than the music.

The boxes were half empty during the second act, theirs as well, but the bar was in full swing when they returned to it during the second intermission. Liz stifled a yawn, with a sheepish glance at Bernie.

"Tired, sweetheart?"

"A little . . . it's such a big evening." And they both knew there was more. They were having supper at Trader Vic's afterwards, in the Captain's Cabin. Bernie was already a regular there, and after that they were going to make a quick stop at the opera ball at City Hall. He suspected they wouldn't get home until three or four in the morning, but it was the event that launched San Francisco's social season every year, and it stood out like the largest diamond in the tiara.

Their car was waiting for them in the driveway after the last act, and they climbed into it cozily, and then sped toward Trader Vic's. Even that seemed better than usual tonight as they drank champagne and ate caviar and Bongo Bongo soup and mushroom crepes. And Liz laughed with delight at the message in her fortune cookie. "He will always love you as much as you love him."

"I like that one." She beamed happily at him. It had been an incredible evening, and Domingo and Scotto and their entourage had just come in and been seated at a long table in the corner with a great flurry. Numerous people asked for autographs and both artists looked pleased. It had been a remarkable performance. "Thank you for a beautiful evening, sweetheart."

"It's not over yet." He patted her hand on the table, and poured her another glass of champagne as she giggled in protest.

"You'll have to carry me out if you give me much more of that."

"I can manage that." He put a gentle arm around her and toasted her with his eyes. It was after one when they left Trader Vic's and went on to the opera ball, which was almost anticlimactical after all the earlier events of the evening. Liz was beginning to recognize the faces she had seen earlier, at the museum, the opera, the bar, Trader Vic's, and everyone seemed to be having fun. Even the press had begun to relax and enjoy themselves. By then they had gotten most of the photographs they needed. Although they took another of Liz and Bernie as they circled the floor easily in a graceful waltz that made her dress look even more lovely.

And it was that photograph which ran the next morning. A large photograph of Liz in Bernie's arms, as they circled the floor at the opera ball at City Hall. You could see some of the detail of the dress, but more than that, you could see Liz beaming up into Bernie's face as he held her.

"You really like him, huh, Mom?" Jane had her chin propped up in both hands, and Liz had a terrific headache as they read the newspaper over breakfast the next morning. She had come home at four-thirty and had realized, as the room spun slowly around her as she tried to get to sleep, that they must have consumed at least four or five bottles of champagne that evening. It had been the most beautiful night of her life, but now just the thought of the sparkling wine made her nauseous. And she was in no shape whatsoever to spar with her daughter.

"He's a very nice man, and he likes you a lot, Jane." It seemed the smartest thing to say and the only thing she could think of.

"I like him too." But her eyes said she wasn't quite as sure as she had once been. Things had gotten complicated over the summer. And she instinctively sensed the seriousness of their involvement. "How come you go out with him so much?"

Liz' head pounded ominously as she stared at her daughter silently over her coffee. "I like him." To hell with it. She decided to say it. "Actually I love him." The woman and the girl stared at each other over the table. She wasn't telling Jane anything she didn't know, but it was the first time Jane had heard the words and she didn't think she liked them. "I love him." Liz' voice wobbled on the last word and she hated herself for it.

"So? . . . So what?" Jane got up and flounced away from the table as her mother's eyes grabbed her back.

"What's wrong with that?"

"Who said there was something wrong?"

"You did, by the way you're acting. He loves you, too, you know."

"Yeah? How do you know?" There were tears in Jane's eyes now, and Liz' head was throbbing.

"I know because he told me." She stood up and walked slowly to her child, wondering just how much she should tell her and tempted to say it all. She had to tell her eventually, and maybe it was better sooner than later. She sat down on the couch and pulled Jane onto her lap. The little body was stiff, but she didn't fight her. "He wants to marry us." Her mother's voice was soft in the quiet room, and Jane couldn't fight back the tears any longer. She buried her face as she sobbed and clung to her mother. There were tears in Liz' eyes, too, as she held the little girl that had once been her baby, and in some ways always would be. "I love him, sweetheart. . . ."

"Why? . . . I mean why do we have to marry him? We were okay just us."

"Were we? Didn't you ever wish we had a daddy?"

The sobbing stopped, but only for a moment. "Sometimes. But we did okay without one." And she still had the illusion of the father she had never known, the "handsome actor" who had died when she was a baby.

"Maybe we'd do better with a daddy. Did you ever think of that?"

Jane sniffed as Liz held her. "You'd have to sleep in his bed and I couldn't get into bed with you anymore on Saturday and Sunday mornings."

"Sure you could." But they both knew it would be different, and in some ways it was sad and in other ways it was happy. "Think of all the good stuff we could do with him . . . go to the beach, and go for drives, and go sailing, and . . . think of what a nice man he is, baby."

Jane nodded. She couldn't deny that. She was too fair to ever try maligning him. "I guess I kind of like him . . . even with the beard . . . ." She smiled up at her mother through her tears and then asked what she really wanted to know. "Will you still love me if you have him?"

"Always." The tears spilled onto Liz' cheeks as she held her. "Always and always and always."

Chapter 9

Jane and Liz started buying all the bride magazines, and when they finally went to Wolff's together to pick out their dresses for the wedding, Jane was not only resigned, she was beginning to enjoy it. They spent an hour in the children's department, looking for just the right dress for Jane and they finally found it. It was white velvet with a pink satin sash, and a tiny pink rosebud at the neck, and it was exactly what Jane wanted. And they were equally successful finding a dress for Liz. And afterwards Bernie took them to lunch at the Saint Francis.

And the following week in New York, Berman had already heard the news. News traveled fast in retail circles, and Bernie was an important man at Wolff's. Berman called him with curiosity and amusement.

"Holding out on me, are you?" There was a smile in Berman's voice and Bernie felt sheepish replying.

"Not really."

"I hear Cupid has struck a blow on the West Coast. Is it rumor or truth?" He was pleased for his longtime friend and he wished him well. Whoever she was, he was sure Bernie had made a wise choice, and he hoped to meet her.

"It's true, but I wanted to tell you myself, Paul."

"Then go ahead. Who is she? All I know is that she bought a wedding dress on the fourth floor." He laughed. They lived in a tiny world run by rumors and gossip.

"Her name is Liz, and she's a second-grade teacher. She's originally from Chicago, went to Northwestern, is twenty-seven years old, and has a delicious little girl named Jane who is five years old. And we're getting married right after Christmas."

"It all sounds very wholesome. What's her last name?"

"O'Reilly."

Paul roared. He had met Mrs. Fine several times. "What did your mother say?"

Bernie smiled too. "I haven't told her yet."

"Let us know when you do. We should be hearing the sonic boom over here, or has she mellowed in recent years?"

"Not exactly."

Berman smiled again. "Well, I wish you the best of luck. Will I be seeing Liz with you when you come east next month?" Bernie had to go to New York, and then Europe, but Liz was not planning to go along. She had to work, and take care of

Jane, and they were looking for a house to rent for the next year. There was no point buying if they were going back to New York so soon.

"I think she'll be busy here. But we'd love to see you at the wedding." They had already ordered the invitations, at Wolff's, of course. But the wedding was going to be small. They didn't want more than fifty or sixty people. It was going to be a simple lunch somewhere, and then they were leaving for Hawaii. Tracy, Liz' friend from school, had already promised to stay with Jane at the new house while they were away, which was helpful.

"When is it?" Bernie told him. "I'll try to come. And I imagine now you may not be in such a hurry to get back to New York." Bernie's heart sank at the words.

"That's not necessarily true. I'm going to be looking for schools for Jane in New York when I'm there, and Liz will look at them with me next spring." He wanted Berman to feel pressured to bring him home, but there was no sound at the other end as Bernie frowned. "We want to have her enrolled for next September."

"Right. . . . Well, I'll see you in New York in a few weeks. And congratulations." Bernie sat staring into space afterwards and that night he said something to Liz. He was worried.

"Christ, I'll be damned if I'll let them stick me here for three years like they did in Chicago."

"Can you talk to him when you go east?"

"I intend to."

But when he did, when he was in New York,

Paul Berman wouldn't commit himself to a sure return date.

"You've only been there for a few months. You have to get the branch on its feet for us, Bernard. That was always our understanding."

"It's doing beautifully, and I've been there for eight months."

"But the store has only been open for less than five. Give it another year. You know how badly we need you. The tone of that store will be set for years by what you're doing there right now, and you're the best man we have."

"Another year is an awfully long time." To Bernie it felt like a lifetime.

"Let's talk about it in six months." Paul was putting Bernie off, and he was depressed when he left the store that night. It was the wrong frame of mind to meet with his parents. He had made a date with them at La Côte Basque, because he explained that he didn't have time to go out to Scarsdale. And he knew how anxious his mother was to see him. He had bought her a beautiful handbag that afternoon, a beige lizard with a tiger's eye clasp that was the latest from Gucci. It was a work of art more than a handbag and he hoped she'd like it. But his heart was heavy as he walked from his hotel to the restaurant. It was one of those beautiful October nights, when the weather is perfect for exactly two minutes, and the way it is in San Francisco all year round. But because it's so rare, in New York, it always seems much more special.

But everything seemed alive as the taxis swirled past, and the horns honked, and even the sky looked clear as elegantly dressed women darted from cabs to restaurants, and in and out of limousines wearing fabulous suits and brilliantly hued coats, on their way to plays and concerts and dinner parties. And it suddenly reminded him of everything he had been missing for the past eight months, and he wished that Liz were there with him, and he promised himself that the next time he would bring her. With luck, he could plan his spring business trip while she had Easter vacation.

He went quickly through the revolving door at La Côte Basque and took a deep breath of the elite ambience of his favorite restaurant. The murals were even prettier than he remembered and the light was soft as beautifully bejeweled women in black dresses lined the banquettes watching passersby and chatting with dozens of men, all in gray suits, as though in uniform, but they all had the same air of money and power.

He looked around and said a word to the maître d'hôtel. His parents were already there, seated at a table for four in the rear, and when he reached them his mother reached out to him with a look of anguish and clung to his neck as though she were drowning.

It was a style of greeting which embarrassed him profoundly, and then made him hate himself for not being happier to see her.

"Hi, Mom."

"That's all you have to say after eight months?

'Hi, Mom'?" She looked shocked, as she relegated her husband to a chair so she could sit next to Bernie on the banquette. He felt as though everyone in the room were staring at them as she scolded him for being so unfeeling.

"It's a restaurant, Mom. You can't make a scene here, that's all."

"You call that a scene? You don't see your mother for eight months, and you barely say hello to her, and that's a *scene?*" He wanted to crawl under the table. Everyone within fifty feet could hear her talking.

"I saw you in June." His voice was deliberately low, but he should have known better than to argue with her.

"That was in San Francisco."

"That counts too."

"Not when you're so busy you can't even see me." It had been when the store opened, but he had still managed to spend time with them, not that she would admit it.

"You look great." It was definitely time to change the subject. His father was ordering a bourbon on the rocks for himself and a Rob Roy for his mother, and Bernie ordered a kir.

"What kind of a drink is that?" His mother looked suspicious.

"I'll let you try it when it comes. It's very light. You look wonderful, Mom." He tried again, sorry that the conversations were always between himself and his mother. He couldn't remember the last time he and his father had had a serious talk, and he was surprised he hadn't brought his medical journals to Côte Basque with him.

The drinks arrived and he took a sip of the kir, held it out to her, and she refused it. He was trying to decide if he should tell her about Liz before or after they ate. If he told her after, she would always accuse him of being dishonest with her all night by not telling her first. If he told her before, she might make a scene and embarrass him further. After was safer in some ways, before was more honest. He took a big swallow of the kir and decided on before. "I have some good news for you, Mom." He could actually hear his voice tremble, and she looked at him with hawklike eyes, sensing that this was important.

"You're moving back to New York?" Her words turned the knife in his heart.

"Not yet. But one of these days. No, better than that."

"You got a promotion?"

He held his breath. He had to end the guessing game. "I'm getting married." Everything stopped. It was as though someone had pulled her plug as she stared silently at him. It felt like a full five minutes before she spoke again, and as usual, his father said nothing.

"Would you care to explain that?"

He felt as though he had just told them he had been arrested for selling drugs and something way deep down inside him began to get angry. "She's a wonderful girl, Mom. You'll love her. She's twenty-seven years old, and the most beautiful girl you've ever seen. She teaches second grade," which proved that she was wholesome at least. She was not a go-go dancer or a cocktail waitress or a stripper. "And she has a little girl named Jane."

"She's divorced."

"Yes, she is. Jane is five."

His mother searched his eyes, wanting to know what the hitch was. "How long have you known her?"

"Since I moved to San Francisco," he lied, feeling ten years old again, and fumbling for the photographs he had brought. They were pictures of Liz and Jane at Stinson Beach, and they were very endearing. He handed them to his mother, who passed them on to his father, who admired the pretty young woman and the little girl, as Ruth Fine stared at her son, wanting to know the truth.

"Why didn't you introduce her to us in June?" Obviously, that meant she had a limp, a cleft palate, or a husband she still lived with.

"I didn't know her then."

"You mean you've only known her a few weeks, and you're getting married?" She made it impossible to explain anything to her and then she moved in for the coup de grace. She went straight to the heart of the matter. And maybe it was just as well. "Is she Jewish?"

"No, she's not." He thought she was going to faint, and he couldn't suppress a smile at the look on her face. "Don't look like that for chrissake. Not everyone is, you know."

"Enough people are so you could find one. What is she?" Not that it mattered. She was just torturing herself now, but he decided to get it all over with at once.

"She's Catholic. Her name is O'Reilly."

"Oh my God." She closed her eyes and slumped in her chair, and for a moment he thought she had really fainted. In sudden fright he turned to his father, who calmly waved a hand, indicating that it was nothing. She opened her eyes a moment later and looked at her husband. "Did you hear what he said? Do you know what he's doing? He's killing me. And does he care? No, he doesn't care." She started to cry, and made a great show of opening her bag, taking out her handkerchief, and dabbing at her eyes, while the people at the next table watched and the waiter hovered, wondering if they were going to order dinner.

"I think we should order." Bernie spoke in a calm voice and she snapped at him.

"You . . . you can eat. Me, I would have a heart attack at the table."

"Order some soup," her husband suggested.

"It would choke me." Bernie would have liked to choke her himself.

"She is a wonderful girl, Mom. You're going to love her."

"You've made up your mind?" He nodded. "When is the wedding?"

"December twenty-ninth." He purposely didn't

say the words "after Christmas." But she began to cry again anyway.

"Everything is planned, everything is arranged . . . the date . . . the girl . . . nobody tells me anything. When did you decide all this? Is this why you went to California?" It was endless. It was going to be a very long evening.

"I met her once I moved out there."

"How? Who introduced you? Who did this to me?" She was dabbing at her eyes again as the soup arrived.

"I met her through the store."

"How? On the escalator?"

"For chrissake, Mom, stop it!" He pounded the table and his mother jumped, as did the people at the tables next to them. "I'm getting married. Period. I am thirty-five years old. I am marrying a lovely woman. And frankly, I don't give a damn if she's Buddhist. She's a good woman, a good person, and a good mother, and that is good enough for me." He dug into his own soup with a vengeance as his mother stared at him.

"Is she pregnant?"

"No."

"Then why do you have to get married so soon? Wait a while."

"I've waited thirty-five years, that's long enough."

She sighed, and looked at him mournfully. "Have you met her parents?"

"No. They're dead." For a moment, Ruth almost looked sorry for her, but she would never have admitted it to Bernie. Instead, she sat and suffered in silence, and it was only when coffee was served that he remembered the gift he had brought her. He handed it across the table, and she shook her head and refused to take it.

"This is not a night I want to remember."

"Take it anyway. You'll like it." He felt like throwing it at her, and reluctantly she took the box and put it on the seat next to her, like a bomb rigged to go off within the hour.

"I don't understand how you can do this."

"Because it's the best thing I've ever done." It suddenly depressed him to think of how difficult his mother was. It would have been so much simpler if she could be happy for him, and congratulate him. He sighed and sat back against the banquette after he took a sip of coffee. "I take it you don't want to come to the wedding."

She started to cry again, using her napkin to dab at her eyes instead of her hankie. She looked at her husband as though Bernie weren't there. "He doesn't even want us at his wedding." She cried harder and louder and Bernie thought he had never been as exhausted.

"Mom, I didn't say that. I just assumed . . ."

"Don't assume anything!" she snapped at him, recovering momentarily and then lapsing back into playing Camille for her husband. "I just can't believe this has happened." Lou patted her hand and looked at his son.

"It's difficult for her, but she'll get used to it eventually."

"What about you, Dad?" Bernie looked at him directly. "Is it all right with you?" It was crazy, but in a way he wanted his father's blessing. "She's a wonderful girl."

"I hope she makes you happy." His father smiled at him, and patted Ruth's hand again. "I think I'll take your mother home now. She's had a hard night." She glared at both of them, and began to open the package Bernie had brought her. She had the box open and the handbag out of the tissue paper a moment later.

"It's very nice." Her lack of enthusiasm was easily discerned as she looked at her son, attempting to convey the extent of the emotional damage he had caused her. If she could have sued him, she would have. "I never wear beige." Except every other day, but Bernie did not point that out to her. He knew that the next time he saw her she would be wearing the bag.

"I'm sorry. I thought you'd like it."

She nodded, as though humoring him, and Bernie insisted on picking up the check, and as they all walked out of the restaurant, she grabbed his arm. "When are you coming back to New York?"

"Not until spring. I leave for Europe tomorrow, and I'm flying back to San Francisco from Paris." He felt less than pleased with her after what she had just put him through, and he was not warm toward her.

"You can't stop in New York for one night?" She looked crushed.

"I don't have time. I have to be back at the store for an important meeting. I'll see you at the wedding, if you come."

She didn't answer at first, and then she looked at him just before she entered the revolving door. "I want you to come home for Thanksgiving. This will be the last time." And with those words, she passed through the revolving door and emerged again on the street, where she waited for Bernie.

"I'm not going to prison, Mother. I'm getting married, so this is not the last anything. And hopefully, next year, I'll be living in New York again, and we can all have Thanksgiving together."

"You and that girl? What's her name again?" She looked at him mournfully, pretending to have a memory lapse, when he knew perfectly well that she could have recited every single detail she'd heard about "that girl," and probably described the photographs in detail too.

"Her name is Liz. And she's going to be my wife. Try to remember that." He kissed her and hailed a cab. He didn't want to delay their departure a moment longer. And they had to pick up their car, which they'd parked near his father's office.

"You won't come for Thanksgiving?" She hung out of the cab, crying at him again as he shook his head, and physically pushed her inside to her seat, in the guise of assistance.

"I can't. I'll talk to you when I get back from Paris."

"I have to talk to you about the wedding." She was hanging out the window and the driver was starting to snarl.

"There's nothing left to say. It's on December twenty-ninth, at Temple Emanuel, and the reception is at a little hotel she loves in Sausalito." His mother would have asked him if she was a hippie but she didn't have time as Lou gave the driver the address of his office.

"I don't have anything to wear."

"Go to the store and pick something you like. I'll take care of it for you."

And then she suddenly realized what he had said. They were getting married at the temple. "She's willing to get married in temple?" She looked surprised. She didn't think Catholics did things like that, but she was divorced anyway. Maybe she'd been excommunicated or something like that.

"Yes. She's willing to get married in temple. You'll like her, Mom." He touched his mother's hand, and she smiled at him, her eyes still damp.

"Mazel tov." And with that, she pulled back into the cab, and they roared off thundering over the potholes, as he heaved a huge sigh of relief. He had done it.

Chapter 10

They spent Thanksgiving at Liz' apartment with Jane, and Liz' friend, Tracy. She was a pleasant woman in her early forties. Her children were grown and gone. One was at Yale and wasn't coming home for the holidays, the other, a daughter, was married and lived in Philadelphia. Her husband had died fourteen years before, and she was one of those cheerful, strong people whom misfortune had struck often and hard, and yet managed not to be a downer. She grew plants and loved to cook, she had cats, and a large Labrador, and she lived in a tiny apartment in Sausalito. She and Liz had become friends when Liz had first begun to teach, and she had helped her with Jane frequently during those first difficult years when Liz was saddled with a very young child and no money. Sometimes she babysat for her just so she could scrape a few dollars together and go to a movie. And there was nobody happier than Tracy over Liz' sudden good fortune. She had already agreed to be matron of honor at the wedding, and Bernie was surprised at how much he liked her.

She was tall and spare and wore Birkenstock shoes, and she came from Washington State, and had never been to New York. She was a warm earthy person, totally foreign to his more sophisticated ways, and she thought he was the best thing to have ever happened to Liz. And he was perfect for her. Perfect in the way her husband had been before he died. Like two people carved from the same piece of wood, made to fit, made to blend, made to be together. She had never found anyone like him again, and she had stopped trying a long time since. She was content with her simple life in Sausalito, a few good friends, and the children she taught. And she was saving money to go to Philadelphia to see her grandchild.

"Can't we help her, Liz?" Bernie asked her once. It embarrassed him to drive an expensive car, buy expensive clothes, give Liz an eight-carat diamond ring and Jane a four hundred dollar antique doll for her birthday when Tracy was literally saving pennies to see a grandchild she had never seen in Philadelphia. "It's just not right."

"I don't think she'd take anything from us." It still amazed her to no longer have to worry, although she was adamant with Bernie that she would take no money from him before the wedding. But he was burying her in extravagant presents.

"Won't she at least take a loan?" And finally,

unable to stand it any longer, he had broached the subject with Tracy after they cleared the table on Thanksgiving. It was a quiet moment while Liz put Jane to bed, and he looked at her as they sat by the fire.

"I don't know how to ask you this, Tracy." In some ways, it was worse than battling his mother, because he knew how proud Tracy was. But he liked her enough to at least try it.

"You want to go to bed with me, Bernie? I'd be delighted." She had a wonderful sense of humor and her face was still that of a very young girl. She had one of those fresh, clear-skinned, blue-eyed faces that never grew old, like old nuns, and certain women in England. And like them, she always had dirt under her nails from her garden. She often brought them roses, and lettuce and carrots, and tomatoes.

"Actually, I was thinking of something else." He took a deep breath and plunged in, and a moment later she was in tears and silently reached out to him and held his hand tight in her own. She had strong cool hands that had held two children and a husband she loved, and she was the kind of woman one wished had been one's mother.

"You know, if it were something else . . . like a dress, or a car, or a house, I'd turn you down flat . . . but I want to see that baby so much . . . I'd only take it as a loan." And she insisted on traveling standby to save him money. And finally, unable to stand it any longer, he went to the airlines himself, bought her a business-class ticket on a flight to Philadelphia, and they saw her off the week before Christmas. It was their wedding gift to her, and it meant everything to her. And she promised to be home on the twenty-seventh, two days before the wedding.

Christmas was hectic for all of them. He managed to take Jane to see Santa Claus at the store, and they celebrated Chanukah too that year. But they were so busy moving into the new house that everything seemed doubly hectic. Bernie moved into it on the twenty-third, and Jane on the twenty-seventh. Tracy came back that night and they picked her up at the airport, and she just beamed, and cried as she hugged all three of them and told them about the baby.

"He's got two teeth! Can you beat that at five months!" She was so proud that they teased her all the way home, and took her to their new house to show her their progress. It was a cute little Victorian on Buchanan, teetering on a hill, right near a park where Liz could take Jane after school. It was exactly what they wanted, and they had rented it for a year. Bernie was hoping they'd be gone before that, but the store could buy out his lease if they had to.

"When are your parents coming in, Bernie?"

"Tomorrow night." He sighed. "It's like waiting for a visitation from Attila the Hun." Tracy laughed. She would be grateful to him for a lifetime for the trip he had given her, and he had absolutely refused to make it a loan.

"Can I call her Grandma?" Jane asked with a yawn, as they sat in their new living room. It felt good to be living under one roof finally, and not running around between three places.

"Sure you can call her Grandma," Bernie answered casually, silently praying that his mother would let her. And a little while later, Tracy took her car out of their garage and drove home to Sausalito, and Liz climbed into their new bed in their new house and put her arms around Bernie's neck. She was snuggling up next to him when they heard a small voice next to the bed and Bernie jumped a foot as Jane tapped him on the shoulder.

"I'm scared."

"Of what?" He was attempting to look very proper as Liz lay under the covers and giggled.

"I think there's a monster under my bed."

"No, there's not. I checked the whole house before we moved in. Honest." He tried to look sincere, but he was still embarrassed to be caught in bed with her mother.

"Then it got in afterwards. . . . The moving men brought it." She sounded genuinely upset and Liz emerged from the sheets to look at her daughter with a raised eyebrow.

"Jane O'Reilly, you go right back to bed."

But she started to cry instead and clung to Bernie. "I'm too scared."

"What if I go upstairs and we check for monsters together?" Bernie felt sorry for her.

"You go first." And then suddenly she looked from him to her mother and then back to Bernie. "How come you're sleeping in Mommy's bed if you're not married yet? Isn't that against the law?"

"Well, no . . . sort of . . . actually, it's just not usually done, but in some cases it's . . . it's more convenient . . . you see . . ." Liz was laughing at him, and Jane was staring at him with interest. "Why don't we go look for the monster?" He put his legs over the side of the bed, grateful that he had worn the bottoms of an old pair of pajamas. Actually, he had worn them in Jane's honor, and he was glad he had now.

"Can I get into bed with you?" She glanced from him to her mother, and Liz groaned. She had been that route with her before, and whenever she gave in, it meant three weeks of arguments afterwards.

"I'll take her up to bed." Liz started to get up but he stopped her with a pleading look.

"Just this once . . . it's a new house . . ." Bernie intervened and Jane beamed at him and slipped a hand into his. They had an enormous king-size bed, and there was room for all of them, although it certainly curtailed Liz' plans for the evening.

"I give up." She threw herself back on her pillow, and Jane climbed over Bernie like a friendly mountain, and hurled herself into the small gap between them.

"This is fun." She grinned at her benefactor and then her mother, and Bernie told her funny stories about when he'd been a little boy, and when Liz fell asleep they were both still talking.

Chapter 11

The plane touched down twenty minutes late because of bad weather when they left New York, but Bernie was waiting at the airport. He had decided to come alone, he wanted to get his parents settled at the Huntington first, and then Liz was going to join them for cocktails. They were going to have dinner at L'Étoile, which brought back happy memories for them, of the night they'd spent at the hotel, making love for the first time and when he'd given her the engagement ring. And he had ordered a special dinner beforehand. His parents were going on to Mexico afterwards, and he and Liz were leaving for Hawaii after the wedding. So this was their only chance to spend a quiet evening together. His mother had wanted to come out the week before, but with Christmas at the store, sales to plan, and moving into the new house, there just wasn't time to spend with her, and Bernie had told her not to.

He stood watching the first passengers disembark, and then he saw a familiar face in a fur hat and a new mink coat. She was carrying a Louis Vuitton traveling bag he had given her the year before, and his father was wearing a fur-trimmed overcoat, and his mother was actually smiling when she threw her arms around him.

"Hello, darling." She clung to him briefly but in an airport he expected it as he smiled down at her, and then glanced at his father.

"Hi, Dad." They shook hands and he turned his attention to his mother again. "You're looking wonderful, Mom."

"So are you." She scrutinized his face. "A little tired maybe, the rest in Hawaii will do you good."

"I can hardly wait." They were planning to stay for three weeks. Liz had gotten a leave of absence from school, and they were both looking forward to it. And then he saw his mother glancing around curiously.

"Where is she?"

"Liz didn't come. I thought I'd get you settled at your hotel first, and then she'll meet us for dinner." It was four o'clock, and it would be five before they got to the hotel. He had told Liz to meet them at the bar at six, and their dinner reservation was for seven o'clock, which would be ten o'clock for them. With the time change, they would be tired that night, and there was a lot going on the next day. The ceremony at Temple Emanuel, the luncheon at the Alta Mira Hotel, and then their flight to Hawaii . . . and his parents' flight to Acapulco.

"Why didn't she come?" His mother looked prepared to be annoyed, and Bernie smiled, hoping to head her off at the pass. She never changed, but somehow he always thought that she might. It was as though he had expected someone else to get off the plane with his father.

"We've had so much to do, Mom. With the new house and everything . . ."

"She couldn't come to meet her mother-in-law?"

"She's meeting us at the hotel."

His mother smiled at him bravely, and then tucked her hand into his arm as they walked to the baggage claim. But she seemed in fairly good spirits for once. There were no reports of neighbors who had died, relatives getting divorced, products that had gone amuck and killed dozens of innocent people. And she didn't even complain when one of her suitcases almost didn't turn up. It was the last one off the plane, and Bernie grabbed it with a sigh of relief and then went to get the car to drive them into town. He chatted about the wedding plans all the way in, and his mother loved the dress she had picked out at Wolff's a few weeks before. She said it was light green and it suited her very well, but she wouldn't tell him more than that. And then he chatted with his father for a little while, and they arrived at the hotel and he dropped them off and promised to return in an hour.

"I'll be back in a little while," he assured them, like children he was leaving somewhere, and he hopped in his car and went home again, to shower and change himself and pick Liz up. She was still in the shower when he got in, and Jane was in her room, playing with a new doll. But she was looking wistful these days and he wondered if the new house was bothering her. She had spent the previous night with them, and he had promised Liz it wouldn't happen again.

"Hi, there. . . . How's your friend?" He stopped in the door of her room and looked down at her. And she looked up at him with a small wintry smile as he walked into the room and sat down next to her. And then suddenly she laughed at him.

"You look just like Goldilocks." She giggled and he grinned.

"With a beard? What kind of books do you read?"

"I mean 'cause you're too big for the chair." He was sitting on one of her little chairs.

"Oh." He put an arm around her. "You okay?"

"Yeah." She shrugged. "Pretty much."

"What does that mean? You worried about the monster under the bed again? We can check it out, if you like. But there's nothing there, you know."

"I know that." She looked at him haughtily as though she could never have said such a thing. Only babies did that. Or kids who wanted to spend the night in their mothers' beds.

"Then what's up?"

She looked him squarely in the eye. "You're taking my mom away . . . and for such a long time . . ." There were suddenly tears in her eyes and she looked bereft as she looked at him. And he was overwhelmed with guilt at the pain he had caused her.

"It's . . . well, it's our honeymoon . . . and Aunt Tracy will take good care of you." But he didn't sound convinced and Jane looked positively morbid.

"I don't want to stay with her."

"Why not?"

"She makes me eat vegetables."

"What if I tell her not to?"

"She will anyway. That's all she eats. She says dead animals are bad for you."

He winced, thinking of the dead animals he was about to eat at L'Étoile, and had been looking forward to. "I wouldn't put it quite like that."

"She never lets me eat hot dogs or hamburgers or any of the good stuff I like . . ." Her voice trailed off miserably.

"What if I told her she had to let you eat what you want?"

"What's this all about?" Liz was standing in the doorway, wrapped in a towel, looking down at them, her blond hair cascading over her damp shoulders, as Bernie looked up at her with passion.

"We were just discussing something." They both looked guilty when they looked at her.

"Are you still hungry, Jane? There are some

apples and bananas in the kitchen." Liz had already given her dinner, and a huge dessert.

"No, I'm okay." She looked wistful again and Liz beckoned to him.

"We're going to be late if you don't hurry up. She's okay, sweetheart." But once the bathroom door was closed, he whispered to her.

"She's upset that we're going away for three weeks."

"Did she tell you that?" Liz looked surprised as he nodded at her. "She hasn't said anything to me." And then she smiled at him. "I think she's figured out that you're a softie." She slid her arms around his neck with a smile. "And she's right." The towel fell and he groaned as he felt her body against his.

"If you do that, I'll never get dressed." He slowly took off his clothes, intending to get into the shower, but he couldn't take his eyes off of her, and his interest was obvious as he stood naked in front of her. She fondled him with lingering caresses, and he pressed her against the stack of towels next to the sink, and moments later he was kissing her and she was stroking him. He reached over and locked the door and turned the water on, and the bathroom filled with steam as they made love, and she had to fight not to scream, as she always did when she made love with him. It had never been like that for her before, but it was now, and they both looked pleased afterwards, as he stepped into the shower with a boyish grin. "That was nice. . . . First course . . . or hors d'oeuvres?"

She looked at him mischievously. "Wait till you get dessert tonight . . ." He turned the shower on and sang to himself as he lathered up, and she stepped into it with him, and he was tempted to start all over again, but they had to get ready in a hurry. He didn't want to be late, or his mother would be annoyed when she met Liz, and he wanted to avoid that at all costs.

They kissed Jane good night, told the babysitter where everything was, and hurried out to the car. Liz was wearing a dress Bernie had bought for her, a pretty gray flannel with a white satin collar, and she wore it with a rope of pearls he had picked up at Chanel for her, and gray flannel Chanel shoes with black satin toes, and her huge engagement ring, her golden hair swept up, her makeup faint but impeccable, and pearl and diamond earrings on her ears. She looked alluring and demure and very beautiful and he could see that his mother was impressed when they met her in the hotel lobby. She looked at Liz searchingly, as though wanting to find something wrong, but as they walked downstairs to the bar, and Liz took his father's arm, she whispered to her son.

"She's a nice-looking girl." From her, that was high praise.

"Bullshit," he whispered back. "She's gorgeous."

"She has nice hair," his mother conceded. "Is it natural?"

"Of course," he whispered back again, as they took a table and they ordered drinks. His parents ordered their usual, and he and Liz each ordered a glass of white wine, and he knew she wouldn't take more than a few sips of hers before they went into the other room for dinner.

"So." Ruth Fine looked at her, as though she was going to pronounce sentence or tell her something terrible. "How did you two meet?"

"I already told you that, Mom." Bernie interrupted her.

"You told me you met in the store." His mother remembered everything just as he knew she would. "But you never explained."

Liz laughed nervously. "Actually, my daughter picked him up. She got lost, and Bernie found her and took her for a banana split while they looked for me."

"You weren't looking for her?" Liz almost laughed again. His description had been accurate. He had warned her what it would be like. The Spanish Inquisition in a mink hat, he had said, and he was right, but she was prepared for it.

"Yes, I was. We met upstairs. And that was that. He sent her some bathing suits, I invited him to the beach . . . a chocolate teddy bear or two"— she and Bernie smiled at the memory—"and that was it. Love at first sight, I guess." She looked blissfully at Bernie and Mrs. Fine smiled at her. Maybe she was all right. Maybe. It was too soon to tell. And of course, she wasn't Jewish.

"And you expect it to last?" She looked search-

ingly at Liz, as Bernie almost groaned at the rudeness of the question.

"I do, Mrs. Fine." Liz saw his mother staring at
her enormous engagement ring, and she was suddenly embarrassed. His mother's was a third the
size of the one he had bought her, and his mother
had registered that fact with a practiced eye, like
an appraiser.

"Did my son buy you that?"

"Yes." Liz' voice was soft. She was still embarrassed about it herself but it was so beautiful, and
she was deeply grateful for it.

"You're a very lucky girl."

"Yes, I am," Liz agreed as Bernie blushed beneath the beard.

"I'm the lucky one." His voice was gruff, but his
eyes were gentle.

"I hope you are." His mother stared at him
pointedly, and then back at Liz as the Inquisition
continued. "Bernie says you teach school."

She nodded. "Yes, I do. I teach second grade."

"Are you going to continue doing that now?"
Bernie wanted to ask her what business it was of
hers, but he knew his mother too well to even try
and stop her. She was in all her glory, interrogat-
ing Liz, the future wife of her only son. Looking at
Liz, so sweet and blond and young, he suddenly
pitied her and reached out and squeezed her hand
with a warm smile, telling her with his eyes how
much he loved her. His father was looking at her
too, and thought she looked like a lovely girl. But

Ruth wasn't quite as sure. "You'll go on working afterwards?" She pressed on.

"Yes, I will. I finish at two o'clock, I'll be home when Bernie comes home at night, and all afternoon with Jane." It was hard to find fault with that, and the maître d' came to lead them to their table then. When they sat down, she questioned them about the wisdom of living together before their wedding. She didn't think it was good for Jane, she said primly, as Liz blushed. He had told her it was only for two days and she was somewhat mollified, but everything was cause for comment that night. Not that the night was so different from any other. Ruth Fine always made comment on anything she chose to.

"Christ, and she wonders why I hate seeing her," he said to Liz afterwards. Even his father's efforts to make the evening go more smoothly hadn't appeased him.

"She can't help it, sweetheart. You're her only child."

"That's the best argument I've heard for having twelve of them. She drives me nuts sometimes. No, make that all the time." He looked less than amused and Liz smiled at him.

"She'll relax. Or at least I hope she will. Did I pass the test?"

"Brilliantly." He reached over and slid a hand up her dress. "My father was drooling over your legs all night. Every time you moved, I saw him look down at them."

"He's very sweet. And he's a very interesting

man. He was explaining several complicated surgical techniques to me and I think I actually understood them. I had some very nice talks with him while you talked to your mother."

"He loves talking about his work." Bernie looked at her tenderly. But he was still annoyed at his mother. She had been such a pain in the ass all night, but she always was. She loved torturing him. And now she had Liz to torture too, and maybe even Jane. The very thought depressed him.

He poured himself a drink before they went to bed that night, and they sat in front of the fire, talking of their wedding plans. He was going to dress at a friend's the next day. And Liz would dress at the house with Jane, and Tracy was coming, and she would go to the temple with them. Bernie was picking his parents up separately in a limousine. Bill Robbins, Liz' architect friend with the house at Stinson Beach, was giving her away. They had been friends for years, and although they didn't see much of each other, he was a serious man, and she liked him. And he seemed the appropriate choice for that role in her wedding.

They were both feeling mellow and happy as they stared at the fire and talked.

"I still feel badly about leaving Jane for three weeks," he confessed to her.

"Don't," she said, laying her head back against him. "We have a right to it. We've hardly had any time alone." She was right of course but he still remembered how sad Jane had looked earlier that night when she had objected to staying with Tracy.

"She's so little though . . . she's only five . . . what does she know from honeymoons?"

Liz smiled at him with a sigh. She was sorry to leave her too. She seldom had before. But this time she felt she had to for their sakes, and she had come to terms with that. She was comfortable about it now, but it pleased her that he was so concerned about how Jane felt. He was going to be a wonderful father. "You're a big softie, you know that. A giant marshmallow." She loved that about him. He was the sweetest man in the world, and when Jane turned up in their bed again that night, he lifted her in gently so they wouldn't wake her mother up, and he cuddled her close to him. She was beginning to feel like his own child, and he was surprised himself at the love he had for her. They tiptoed out of bed the next day, brushed their teeth side by side, and made breakfast for Liz, and brought it to her on a tray with a rose in a vase that Bernie put there for her.

"Happy wedding day!" they intoned simultaneously, and she looked up with a sleepy smile.

"Happy wedding day, you guys . . . when did you get up?" She looked at Bernie, then at Jane, and suspected there was a conspiracy she didn't know about, but neither of them would confess and she sat up to eat the breakfast they had made.

Bernie disappeared after that, and went to his friend's to dress. The wedding was at noon, and they had plenty of time, as Liz carefully braided

Jane's hair with thin white satin ribbons. She put on the beautiful white velvet dress they had chosen together at Wolff's, and Liz put a little crown of baby's breath in her hair. She wore little white socks, and brand-new black patent leather Mary Janes, and a navy blue wool coat Bernie had bought in Paris for her. She looked like a little angel as she stood at the door, waiting for Liz, who took her hand and walked outside to the waiting limousine Bernie had ordered for her. She wore a white satin Dior dress, with big bell sleeves and a skirt that stopped at her ankles, so one could see the equally exquisite Dior shoes. Everything she wore was the color of antique ivory, including the matching headpiece that held back her hair as it cascaded down her back like a young girl's. She looked incredible and Tracy looked at her with tears in her eyes.

"May you always be as happy as you are right now, Liz." She brushed away her tears and smiled down at Jane. "Your mom sure looks good, doesn't she?"

"She does." Jane gazed at her mother admiringly. She was the prettiest lady she had ever seen.

"And so do you." Tracy gently touched the braids, remembering her own little girl, and they got into the car and drove to Arguello Boulevard and got out at Temple Emanuel. It was beautiful, and there was something awesome about it as they walked inside. Liz felt her breath catch and her heart pound as she squeezed Jane's hand tight, and the little girl looked up at her as they exchanged a smile. It was a big day for both of them.

Bill Robbins was waiting for her in a dark blue suit, his sober gray beard and kind eyes making him look like a church elder, and the guests were already sitting in the pews as the music began, and suddenly Liz realized what was happening. It had all been like a dream up till then, and now suddenly it was real, and as she looked down the aisle, she saw Bernie standing there, with Paul Berman next to him, and the Fines in the front pew. But it was only Bernie she saw now, bearded, handsome, dignified, waiting for her, as she walked slowly down the aisle to him, to begin her new life.

Chapter 12

The reception at the Alta Mira was a great success, and everyone seemed to have a good time as they stood on the terrace and looked at the view. It wasn't as elaborate as one of the big hotels might have been but it had more charm and Liz had always loved the quaintness of it, and Bernie agreed with her. Even his mother couldn't find fault with anything. Bernie danced with her for the first dance, and his father with Liz and then they switched, and after a little while, Paul Berman cut in on him, and Bernie danced with Tracy while Paul danced with Liz. And after that Bernie danced with Jane, who was thrilled to be included in the ritual.

"So what do you think, old girl? Is everything okay?"

"Yup." She looked happier again, but he was still worried about leaving her when they went away. He was taking his brand-new parental responsibilities to heart and Liz had teased him about it again the night before. She worried about Jane too, and she had hardly ever left her in the past five years, but she knew that she'd be safe with Tracy, and they had a right to their honeymoon after all.

"I'm Jewish, what do you expect?" He had claimed finally. "Guilt is important to me."

"Use it on something else. She'll be fine." And after his dance with her, he led her to the buffet and helped her collect everything she wanted there, and he deposited her next to her new grandmother and went off to dance with his wife again.

"Hello." Jane looked up at Ruth, who was staring carefully at her. "I like your hat. What kind of fur is it?" Ruth was somewhat taken aback at the question, but she thought her a pretty child, and fairly polite from what she'd seen of her so far.

"It's mink."

"It looks nice with your dress . . . the dress is the same color as your eyes. Did you know that?" She was fascinated by her as she looked at every detail, and in spite of herself Ruth smiled at her.

"You have beautiful blue eyes."

"Thank you. They're like my mom's. My father is dead, you know." She said it matter-of-factly, with her mouth half full of roast beef, and suddenly Ruth felt sorry for her. It couldn't have been an easy life for Liz or the girl before Bernie came along. She saw Bernie in the light of a savior now, but so did Liz, so there was no harm in that. Neither Liz nor Jane would have disagreed with her. Only Bernie might.

"I'm sorry to hear about your dad." She didn't know what else to say.

"Me too. But I have a new daddy now." She looked proudly at Bernard, and Ruth's eyes filled with tears. And then Jane looked unexpectedly at Ruth. "You're the only grandmother I have, you know."

"Oh." She was embarrassed for the child to see her cry. And she reached out and touched her little hand. "That's very nice. You're my only grandchild too." Jane smiled up at her adoringly and squeezed her hand.

"I'm glad you're so nice to me. I was scared before we met." Bernie had introduced them that morning at the temple, very carefully. "I thought maybe you'd be real old, or mean or something."

Ruth looked horrified. "Did Bernie say that to you?"

"No." She shook her head. "He said you were wonderful." Ruth beamed at her. The child was adorable, and she patted her hand and caught a cookie off a passing tray and handed it to her. Jane broke the cookie in two, and handed her the remaining half, which Ruth ate, still holding her hand. The two were fast friends by the time Liz went to change out of her wedding gown. And as Jane saw her mother disappear and realized what time it was, she suddenly began to cry silently, as Bernie caught a glimpse of her from across the room, and came hurrying to her side.

"What's the matter, sweetheart?" His mother had gone for a last dance with the father of the groom. Bernie bent and put an arm around her.

"I don't want you and Mommy to go." Her voice was a tiny wail, and he felt his heart breaking in half.

"We won't be gone that long." But three weeks seemed an eternity to her, and he wasn't sure he disagreed with her. It seemed like a hell of a long time to leave her with someone else, and as Tracy approached, Jane only cried more, and a moment later Ruth had returned, and Jane clung to her as though she'd always known her.

"Good lord, what's happening?" Bernie explained and Ruth looked sorry for her. "Why don't you take her along?" She whispered to her son.

"I'm not sure Liz would think that's such a great idea. . . . It is our honeymoon. . . ."

His mother looked at him reproachfully and then down at the crying child. "Could you forgive yourself for that? Could you really have a good time thinking about her?" He grinned at her.

"I love you, Mom." Guilt did it every time. And a moment later he went to find Liz and told her what he thought.

"You can't take her with us. We don't have anything packed, we don't even have a room for her at the hotel."

"So we'll get one. . . . We'll stay somewhere else if we have to. . . ."

"What if we can't get another room?"

"Then she'll sleep with us." He grinned. "And we'll take another honeymoon."

"Bernard Fine . . . what's happened to you?" But she was smiling at him, grateful to have found a man who loved her child so much. She had had qualms about leaving her anyway, and in some ways this was easier. "Okay. Now what? Do we run home and pack?"

"As fast as we can." He glanced at his watch, and then ran out to the reception again, kissed his mother hastily, shook hands with Paul Berman, and his father, and swept Jane into his arms as Liz appeared and the rice began to fly. Jane looked frightened suddenly, as though she didn't understand and thought he was saying goodbye, but he tightened his arms around her and whispered in her ear. "You're coming with us. Just close your eyes so you don't get rice in them." She squeezed them tightly shut and grinned happily as he held her in one powerful arm, and grabbed Liz' hand with his free hand, and they raced for the door as rose petals and rice flew, and a moment later they were in the limousine, speeding back to San Francisco.

It took them ten minutes to pack Jane's things, including all the bathing suits he'd bought her the summer before, and they made the plane on time. There was one seat left in first class, and he bought it for Jane, hoping they would be as lucky at the hotel, and Jane grinned at them as she boarded the plane. Sweet victory! She was going with them. She bounced happily on Bernie's lap, and then slept peacefully in her mother's arms as they flew west. They had all gotten married. And Bernie leaned over and kissed Liz gently on the lips as the lights in the plane went down so the movie could come on.

"I love you, Mrs. Fine."

"I love you," she mouthed so as not to wake the sleeping child. And she nestled her head gently against his and dozed until they reached Hawaii. They spent the night in Waikiki and the next day flew on to Kona on the island of Hawaii. They had reservations at the Mauna Kea Resort Hotel, and the gods were smiling on them. They were able to get one room adjoining theirs by turning in the suite Bernie had reserved for them, but at least they didn't have to share a room with the child, not that it mattered in the end. There was a monster under her bed at Mauna Kea too, and she spent most nights sleeping between them in the big bed, as the sun came up over the palm trees. It was a honeymoon they shared, all three of them, and a story Bernie knew they would tell for years as he grinned sheepishly over her head at Liz at night, and sometimes they just lay in bed and laughed at how funny it was.

"Paris, in the spring, I swear!" He held up a hand like a good boy scout and she laughed at him.

"Until she cries again."

"No, this time, I promise . . . no guilt!"

"Ha!" But she didn't mind. She was glad. She leaned over Jane's sleeping form and kissed him

again. This was their life after all, and they shared
it with Jane. It was a heavenly three weeks and the
three of them returned from "their" honeymoon
brown and happy and relaxed and Jane bragged
to everyone that she had gone on her Mommy's
honeymoon. It was a memory the three of them
would cherish forever.

Chapter 13

The months after Hawaii seemed to fly, and they were busy all the time. Bernie was scheduling all the summer and fall shows for the store, planning for new merchandise, having meetings with people from New York. Liz was busy with the house, and she always seemed to be cooking, baking, or sewing for him. There was absolutely nothing the woman didn't do. She also entertained for him, and did everything herself. She even grew roses in the little garden on Buchanan Street, and she and Jane had a vegetable garden on the deck which Tracy had helped them start. Life seemed very full these days, and April came along almost immediately. It was time for him to go to New York on a trip for the store, and then on to Europe as he did every year at that time. Liz had never been to New York or Europe before and he could hardly wait to take her. In some ways, he was tempted to take Jane too, but he had promised Liz this would be

their real honeymoon, and an excellent solution
had come along. He had planned the trip so that
Liz would be on vacation from school for two
weeks, and Jane was, too, of course, so they were
taking her to stay with Grandma and Grandpa
Fine, and she was so excited about that, she hardly
seemed to mind that she wasn't going to Europe
with them.

"And . . ." she announced on the plane,
"we're going to Radio City Music Hall!" It was to
be a triumphant tour. The Museum of Natural
History to see the dinosaurs, which she was studying in school, the Empire State, the Statue of Liberty. She could hardly wait, and neither could
Ruth, from what Bernie could gather on the
phone. Their phone calls were much easier these
days. Liz was constantly calling Ruth just to say
hello and give her the news, which took the pressure off him, and all his mother wanted to do was
talk to Jane anyway. It was amazing that she liked
the child so much, but Jane doted on her. She
loved the idea of having a grandmother now, and
she had asked Bernie very solemnly one day if she
could use his name in school.

"Of course." He had been stunned when she
asked, but she had been serious. And she had
become Jane Fine officially in school the next day.
She had come home beaming at him. "Now I'm
married to you too," she said. But Liz seemed
pleased as well, and she was relieved to know that
Jane would be in good hands while they were
away. Tracy would have been her first choice at

home, but she and Jane didn't always get along these days. Jane was becoming more sophisticated than their old friend, which made Tracy laugh. She was relaxed about it, and happy that the threesome were as happy as they obviously were.

And in New York, "Grandma Ruth" was waiting for the plane at Kennedy.

"How's my little sweetheart?" For the first time in his life, Bernie felt no one hanging on his neck with those words and for a moment it felt strange to him, and then he watched Jane fly into his mother's arms and it brought tears to his eyes as he shook his father's hand and Liz kissed them hello, and then he gave his mother a hug, and Liz kissed her too, and the five of them went home to Scarsdale chattering and talking all at once. It was as though suddenly they had become a family instead of enemies, and he realized that Liz had done that for them. She had a remarkable way of touching everyone, and he saw her smiling at his mother in the car as the two women exchanged a knowing look about something Jane had said, and then they smiled. It was a relief to know that his parents had accepted her. He had been afraid they never would, but he hadn't realized the impact that being grandparents would have on them.

"And now my name is just like yours," she announced proudly in the car, and then got serious. "It's a lot easier to spell. I never could spell the other one." She grinned toothlessly. She had just lost her first tooth that week, and told her grand-mother how much the tooth fairy had brought.

"Fifty cents?" Ruth was clearly impressed. "It used to be only ten cents."

"That was in the olden days," Jane said with disgust, and then kissing her grandmother's cheek, she whispered to her. "I'll buy you an ice cream cone, Grandma." As her heart melted in the child's small hands.

"We're going to do a lot of fun things while your mommy and daddy are away." She called him Daddy now too, and he had asked Liz once if he should adopt her formally.

"You could," she had replied. "Officially, her father has abandoned us, so we can do anything we want. But I don't see why you have to go to all that trouble, sweetheart. If she uses your name, it becomes legal by usage over the years, and she decided to call you Daddy all by herself anyway." He had agreed with her. It didn't seem appropri-ate somehow to drag Jane through court unneces-sarily.

It was the first time in years he had stayed at his parents' house, and he was surprised at how pleasant it was with Liz and Jane there with him. Liz helped his mother cook dinner, and then clean up afterwards. Their maid was sick, which was the only dismal bulletin she gave that night. But since all Hattie had were bunions she'd had operated, even that wasn't up to her usual gruesome stan-dards of strokes and heart attacks. And everyone was in a good mood. The only problem was that he felt desperately uncomfortable when Liz wanted to make love to him that night.

"What if my mother comes in?" he whispered in the dark and she giggled naughtily.

"I could climb out the window and wait on the lawn until the coast is clear."

"Sounds good to me, sweetheart . . ." He rolled over and slid a hand into the satin nightgown she wore, and they giggled and wrestled and kissed and made love, whispering, feeling like wicked kids, and afterwards as they talked in the dark, he told her what a change she had brought to his entire family. "You can't imagine what my mother was like before you came along. I swear, sometimes I hated her." It seemed a sacrilege to say it under her own roof, but sometimes it was true.

"I think Jane is the one who cast the spell."

"I think it's both of you." And as he looked at her in the moonlight, his heart was full. "You're the most remarkable woman I've ever met."

"Better than Isabelle?" she teased, and he tweaked her boob.

"At least you haven't taken my best watch . . . only my heart. . . ."

"That's all?" She pouted prettily, which made him want her again as he slipped a hand between her thighs. "I had something else in mind, monsieur." She put on an accent for him and he attacked her again, and they both felt as though the honeymoon had begun, and Jane didn't come in to sleep with them that night, which was just as well, because Liz' nightgown seemed to have disappeared somewhere underneath the bed, and Bernie had forgotten to bring pajamas with him.

But they looked very respectable at breakfast the next day in their dressing gowns, and his mother made an announcement as she and Jane made orange juice. "We won't have time to take you to the airport today." They exchanged a meaningful look, and Jane didn't look upset at all. "We are going to Radio City Music Hall. We already have the tickets."

"And it's the first day of the Easter Show!" Jane was so excited she could hardly control herself, and Bernie smiled as he glanced at Liz. His mother was a smart one. She had set it up so Jane wouldn't have to go to the airport with them, and cry when they left. It was perfect, and instead they waved goodbye to her as she and Grandma got on the train, which was an excitement in itself, and Grampa was going to pick them up at the Plaza Hotel! "Imagine that!" Jane had said. "And we're going to ride in a hansom cab, that's a carriage with a horse! Right into Central Park . . ." There had been just a moment when they hugged her goodbye that her lip had trembled just a little bit, but a moment later she was gone, and chatting happily with Ruth as Bernie and Liz went back to the house and made love again. They carefully locked the door when they left, and a cab took them to the airport, and the honeymoon began.

"Ready for Paris, Madame Fine?"

"*Oui, monsieur.*" She giggled and they both

laughed. She still hadn't seen New York. But they had decided to spend three days in New York on the way back. It was easier for Jane this way, to get the hard part over with, with them gone, and then they could spend time with her in New York on the way home. And it worked better for his meetings anyway.

They flew to Paris on Air France, and landed in Orly bright and early the next day. It was eight o'clock in the morning local time, and they arrived at the Ritz two hours after that, after finding their bags, going through Customs and then getting into town. Wolff's had arranged for a limousine for him, and Liz was awestruck at the hotel. She had never seen anything as beautiful as the lobby of the Ritz, with elegant women, and well-dressed men, and porters walking poodles and Pekingese, and the shops on the Faubourg St.-Honoré were even more wonderful than she'd imagined. It was all like something in a dream, and he took her everywhere. Fouquet's, Maxim's, the Tour d'Argent, the top of the Eiffel Tower and the Arc de Triomphe, the Bateaux-Mouche, the Galeries Lafayette, the Louvre, the Jeu de Paume, even the Rodin Museum. The week they spent in Paris was the happiest of her life and she never wanted it to end, as they flew on to Rome and Milan for the fashion shows he had to see for the store. He was still in charge of determining all of Wolff's important import lines, and it was an awesome job selecting them. She was impressed at the work he did and she went everywhere with him, taking notes for him, trying on clothes for him once or twice, to see how they moved on an "ordinary mortal" and not someone who was trained to show them off. She told him how they felt, if they were comfortable, how she thought they could be improved, and she was learning a lot about his business as they went from place to place. He also noticed the shows' effect on her. She was suddenly much more aware of fashion, and much more chic. She looked suddenly sleeker and she was more careful about selecting her accessories. She had had a natural flair when they met, and with greater resources she had quickly shown how well dressed she could be. But she wasn't just chic now, she was striking suddenly. And she was happier than she'd ever been, traveling at his side, working with him every day, going back to their hotel room to make love in the afternoon and then stay out half the night, strolling on the Via Veneto or tossing coins into the Fontana di Trevi with him.

"What are you wishing for, little love?" He had never loved her more than he did right then.

"You'll see." She smiled up at him.

"Will I? How?" But he thought he knew. He wanted the same thing, and they were trying. "Will your wish make you big and fat?" He loved the thought of her that way, carrying his child, but they hadn't been trying for very long, and she smiled at him.

"If I tell you what I wished, it won't come true." She wagged a finger at him, and they went back to the Excelsior and made love again. It was a lovely thought, thinking of a baby conceived on this second honeymoon of theirs. But when they got to London for the last two days of the trip, it was obvious that that was not the case and she was so disappointed she cried when she told him the news.

"Never mind." He put an arm around her and held her close. "We'll try again." They did an hour later, knowing it would do them no good, in terms of conceiving a child, but they had fun anyway. And it was obvious how happy they were, when they flew back to New York, after the best two weeks they'd ever shared. And it was obvious they weren't the only ones who'd had a good time. It took Jane two hours to tell them everything she'd done while they were gone. And it looked as though Grandma Ruth had bought out Schwarz for her.

"It's going to take a truck to take all this stuff home." Bernie stared at the dolls, the toys, a life-sized dog, a tiny horse, a doll house, and a miniature stove. Ruth looked faintly embarrassed and then stuck out her chin.

"She had nothing to play with here. All I have are your old trucks and cars," she said almost accusingly. And she'd loved buying all the new toys.

"Oh." Bernie grinned, and handed his mother the box from Bulgari. He had bought her a beautiful pair of earrings made from old gold coins, surrounded by tiny diamonds in a hexagonal shape. He had bought similar ones for Liz and she was crazy about them. And so was Ruth. She clipped them on instantly and hugged them both, and then ran to show Lou, as Liz held Jane close to her. She had missed her terribly, but the trip to Europe had been so wonderful. And it had done them good to be alone together.

The days they spent together in New York were almost as good. Dinners at Côte Basque and "21" and Grenouille, his three favorite restaurants, and he shared their specialties with her. They had drinks at the Oak Room in the Plaza Hotel, and the Sherry Netherland, went to listen to Bobby Short play at the Carlyle at night and she fell in love with him. She shopped at Bergdorf's, Saks, Bendel's and the legendary Bloomingdale's, but she insisted she still preferred Wolff's, and Bernie took her everywhere with him. She stood giggling with him one day at the bar at P. J. Clark's, watching all the characters come in.

"I'm having such a good time with you. Do you know that? You make my life so much fun, Bernie. I never knew it could be like this. I was so busy just surviving before, it seems incredible. It was all so small and intense, and now everything is so lavish. It's like a giant painting . . . like the Chagall murals at Lincoln Center." He had taken her there too. "It's all reds and greens and sunny yellows and bright blues now . . . and before it was all kind of gray and white." She looked up at him adoringly and he bent to kiss her again, tasting the Pimm's cup on her lips.

"I love you, Liz."

"I love you too." She whispered and then hic-cuped so loudly the man in front of them turned around to look at her and she looked at Bernie again. "What did you say your name was?"

"George. George Murphy. I'm married and I have seven children in the Bronx. Want to go to a hotel with me?"

The man next to them at the bar stared in fasci-nation. The place was full of men looking for a quick lay, but most of them didn't talk about their wives and kids.

"Why don't we go home and make another one?" She suggested brightly.

"Great idea."

He hailed a cab on Third Avenue that took them to Scarsdale by the quickest route, and they got home before his mother came home with Jane. His father was still at the hospital. It was nice being home alone with her. It was nice being any-where with her, especially in bed, he decided as they slipped between cool sheets. He hated to get up again when his mother and Jane got home. And he hated even more leaving New York and going back to California again. But he had spoken to Paul about it again, to no avail.

"Come on, Paul. I've been there a year. Four-teen months in fact."

"But the store's only been open for ten. And what's your hurry now? You have a lovely wife, a nice house, San Francisco is a good place for Jane."

"We want to put her in school here." But they wouldn't take her application, they'd discovered, unless it was definite that they were coming back. "We can't just hang in limbo out there for years."

"Not years . . . but let's say just one more. There's just no one else as competent for the job."

"All right." He sighed. "But then, that's it. Is that a deal?"

"All right, all right . . . you'd think we'd left you in Armpit, West Virginia, for chrissake. San Francisco is hardly a hardship post."

"I know. But this is where I belong, and you know it too."

"I can't deny that, Bernard. But we need you out there right now too. We'll do our best to bring you back in a year."

"I'm counting on it."

He hated leaving New York when they did, but he admitted that getting back to San Francisco wasn't so terrible. Their little house was nicer than he remembered it, and the store looked good to him on his first day back. Not as good as the New York store did, but good just the same. The only thing he hated about being back was not being with Liz all day long, and he turned up in the cafeteria at her school at lunchtime their first day back to share a sandwich with her. He looked very citified and grown-up and elegant in a dark gray English suit, and she was wearing a plaid skirt and a red sweater they had bought together at Trois Quartiers, with shoes she'd bought in Italy, and she looked very pretty and young to him, and Jane was very proud to see him there.

"That's my daddy over there, with my mom." She pointed him out to several friends and then went to stand next to him, to show that he belonged to her.

"Hi there, short stuff," he said, tossing her up in the air, and then doing the same to three of her friends. He was a big hit in the cafeteria, and Tracy came over to say hello to him. She gave him a big hug and announced that her daughter was pregnant again. And he saw the hungry look in Liz' eyes and squeezed her hand. She was beginning to worry that something was wrong with her, and he had suggested that maybe it was he, since she had had a child before. And they had finally both decided to relax about it for a while, and they were trying to, but it still came to mind a lot. They both desperately wanted a baby.

And in June he had a surprise for her. He had rented a house in Stinson Beach for two months, and she was thrilled. It was the perfect place for them. A bedroom for them, one for Jane, a guest room for friends, a huge spacious living room with a dining area, a sunny kitchen, and a sheltered deck where they could even sunbathe nude if they wanted to, not that they would have if Jane were at home. It was perfect for them, and Liz couldn't have been happier. They decided to move there for the two months, and he would commute every day. But they had scarcely been there for two weeks, when Liz came down with the flu, and it took her weeks to get over it. He mentioned it to his father when he called, and Lou thought it was probably her sinuses and she should see someone about starting antibiotics right away. Her head felt heavy all the time and she was nauseous at the end of the day. She was exhausted and depressed and she couldn't remember ever feeling that terrible. It was a little better the second month they were there, but not much, and she hardly enjoyed the place, although Jane was having a ball with all her friends, and she ran on the beach with Bernie every night, but Liz could hardly walk down the street without feeling sick. She didn't even feel up to going into town to try on her dress for the opening of the opera. She had selected a slinky black satin Galanos that year, with one shoulder and a ruffled cape of its own, and she was shocked when she finally tried it on right after Labor Day.

"What size is this?" She was stunned. She was generally a six, but she couldn't even close the dress they had sent her. She looked amazed as the salesgirl glanced at the tag and looked up at her.

"It's an eight, Mrs. Fine."

"How's it look?" He poked his head in the door and she glared at him.

"Terrible." She couldn't have gained weight. She'd been sick since July. She'd finally made an appointment to see the doctor the next day. She had to start school in a week and she needed her energy back. She was even ready to take the antibiotics her father-in-law thought she should try.

"They must have sent the wrong size. It has to be a four. I just don't understand it." She had tried the sample on when she ordered it, and it had swum on her. And that had been a six, and this was larger than that was.

"Did you gain weight at the beach?" He came into the fitting room to look. And she was right. The zipper wouldn't come near to closing at her waist and down the side. There were a good three or four inches of her suntanned flesh separating it. He glanced at the fitter standing by quietly. "Can it be let out?" He knew how expensive the dress was and it was a sacrilege to alter it very much. It was better to order it in another size and let that one go, except that now they didn't have time. She'd have to wear something else to the opening if it couldn't be let out. The fitter took a look and shook her head, and then felt Liz' waist and glanced at her questioningly.

"Madame has gained weight at the beach this summer?" She was French and Bernie had brought her from New York. She had worked for Wolff's for years, and Patou before that.

"I don't know, Marguerite." She had worked with Liz before, on her wedding dress and last year's opera gown, and other things she had bought. "I didn't think I had." But all she'd been wearing were loose old clothes, jogging suits, sweatshirts, baggy old shirts, and she had even worn a shapeless cotton dress into the store, and suddenly she looked at Bernie and grinned at him. "Oh my God."

"You okay?" He looked worried, but she was smiling at him. Her face had gone white, and now it was bright pink, and she started to laugh at him. She threw her arms around his neck and kissed him and he smiled, as the salesgirl and fitter discreetly disappeared from the fitting room. They liked working with her. She was always so pleasant to them, and they were so much in love. It was nice to be around people like them. "What's up, Liz?" He looked puzzled as he glanced at her, she was still smiling blissfully, in spite of the lost dress, or because of it.

"I don't think I'll take those antibiotics after all."

"Why not?"

"I think he's wrong."

"A lot you know." He smiled at her.

"You can say that again." She had missed all the signs. Every one of them. "I don't think this is a sinus infection after all." She sat down on a chair and looked up at him with a broad grin and suddenly he understood. He stared at the dress and then back at her, amazed.

"Are you sure?"

"No . . . I didn't even think of it till just now . . . but I'm almost sure . . . I just kind of forgot while we were at the beach." But she suddenly realized that she had skipped a period while they were there. She was four weeks late. But she'd been so sick she hadn't even noticed. And the doctor confirmed it to her the next day. She was six weeks pregnant, he said, and she rushed to the store to tell Bernie the news. She found him in his office, looking at some reports from New York and he looked up the minute she walked through the door.

"Well?" He held his breath and she grinned, pulling a bottle of champagne from behind her back.

"Congratulations, Dad." She set the champagne down on his desk and he threw his arms around her with a whoop of glee.

"We did it! We did it! Ha ha . . . you're knocked up!" And she laughed and they kissed and he picked her up off her feet, as his secretary wondered what they were doing in there. They didn't come out for a long time, and when they did, Mr. Fine looked extremely pleased with himself.

Chapter 14

He went to New York alone on his usual fall business trip. He had to go to Paris after that and he thought the trip would be too much for her. He wanted her to rest, keep her feet up, eat healthy food, watch TV and relax after school, he said. And before he left, he told Jane to take care of her. She was stunned when they told her about the baby at first, but after a little bit she was pleased.

"Kind of like a big doll," Bernie explained. And she was equally pleased that he wanted a little boy, and said she would always be his favorite little girl. She promised to take care of Liz while he was gone, and he called them from New York when he arrived. He was staying at the Regency because it was close to the store, and he had dinner with his parents the first night he was there. They met at Le Cirque, and Bernie walked in with a quiet smile, and saw them sitting at a table waiting for him.

He kissed his mother, sat down, ordered a kir, and his mother looked at him suspiciously.

"Something's wrong."

"Not at all."

"You got fired."

This time he laughed at her, and ordered a bottle of Dom Perignon as his mother stared at him.

"What happened?"

"Something very nice."

She didn't believe a word he said, and then observing him cautiously: "You're coming back to New York?"

"Not yet." Though he wished that he would, but even that was eclipsed now. "Better than that."

"You're moving somewhere else?" She still looked suspicious and his father was smiling. He had guessed their news and the two men exchanged a knowing look as the waiter poured the champagne, and Bernie raised his glass to them.

"To Grandma and Grampa . . . mazel tov."

"So?" Ruth looked at him, confused, and then suddenly, like a bolt of lightning striking her, she fell back in her seat, staring at him with open, startled eyes. "No! Is Liz . . . she's . . . ?" For once in her life she couldn't find the words, and tears sprang to her eyes as he nodded with a broad smile and touched her hand.

"We're having a baby, Mom." He was so pleased he could hardly control himself and his father congratulated him as his mother jabbered incoherently and they sipped their champagne.

"I just can't imagine . . . Is everything all right? . . . Is she eating all right? . . . How does she feel? . . . I have to call her when we get home." And then she suddenly thought of Jane, and looked at Bernie with worried eyes. "How is Jane taking it?"

"I think she was a little shocked at first. I don't think it dawned on her that we might do something like that to her, but we've been spending a lot of time explaining it to her, telling her how important she is to us, stuff like that, and Liz is going to get her some books to deal with whatever negative feelings she has."

His mother scowled at him. "You're beginning to talk like one of them. . . . Californians don't speak English anymore. Watch out you don't become one of them and stay out there." She had been worrying about that since he left, but now all she could think of was her grandchild on the way. "Is Liz taking vitamins?" She turned to Lou, without waiting for her son to respond. "You should talk to her when we call tonight. Explain to her what she should eat, what vitamins to take."

"I'm sure she has an obstetrician, Ruth. He'll tell her what to do."

"What does he know? For all you know she's going to one of those hippies in the pie plate shoes, rubbing herbs on her head and telling her to sleep naked on the beach." She looked at her son ferociously. "You should be back here when the baby is born. He should be born in New York

Hospital, safe and sound, where he belongs and your father can look into everything."

"They have very good hospitals out there, Ruth." The two men were smiling at her. She was beside herself. "I'm sure Bernie is keeping a good eye on everything." And he was of course. He had already been to the doctor with her, and he liked the obstetrician she had found through a friend. They were going to do Lamaze training eventually, and Liz was determined to have the baby naturally, with Bernie helping her and holding her hand. It still made him nervous thinking about it, but he didn't want to let her down and he had every intention of being there.

"Everything's fine, Mom. I went to the doctor with her before I left. He seems very competent, and he's even from New York." He knew that would reassure her but she wasn't listening. She was listening to something he had said first.

"What do you mean, you went to the doctor with her? You stayed in the waiting room, I hope."

Bernie poured her another glass of champagne and smiled at her. "No. It doesn't work like that anymore. The father is part of everything."

"You're not going to be there for the birth, are you?" She looked horrified. She thought it was a disgusting trend. They were doing it in New York too, and she couldn't think of anything worse than a man watching his wife give birth to a baby.

"I plan to be there, Mom."

She made a face. "That's the most disgusting thing I ever heard." She then lowered her voice conspiratorially. "You know, you'll never feel the same way about her again if you see the baby being born. Take my word for it. I've heard stories that would make you sick. . . . Besides"—she sat up again with a dignified sniff—"a decent woman wouldn't want you there. That's a horrible thing for a man to see."

"Mom, it's a miracle. . . . There's nothing horrible or indecent about seeing your wife giving birth." He was so proud of her, and he wanted to see their baby coming into the world, he wanted to be there to welcome him or her. They were going to see a movie of a baby being born, so they both knew what to expect. None of it seemed disgusting to him, just a little frightening sometimes. And he knew Liz was a little nervous about it too, even though she'd had one child, but that had been six years before. But it all still seemed so far away to both of them. They still had another six months to go, and they could hardly wait. And by the end of the meal Ruth had not only planned the entire layette and suggested the best nursery schools in Westchester, she was urging him to make his son go to law school when he grew up. They drank a lot of champagne and she was a little tipsy when they left, but it was the nicest dinner he had had with her in a long time, and he conveyed Liz' invitation to them. And he was just drunk enough himself that the prospect of having them stay with them didn't even frighten him.

"Liz wants you to come out for the holidays." He looked at both of them.

"And you don't?"

"Of course I do, Mom. And she wants you to stay with us."

"Where?"

"Jane can sleep in the baby's room."

"Never mind. We'll stay at the Huntington like we did before. That way we won't bother you. When does she want us for?"

"Her Christmas vacation starts on December twenty-first, I think. Something like that. Why don't you come out then?"

"She won't still be working, will she, Bernard?"

He smiled at her. "I've been surrounded by stubborn women all my life. She's going to work right up until the Easter holidays, and then take a leave from school after that. Her friend Tracy will substitute for her. They already have it all worked out between them."

"Meshuggeneh. She should be home in bed by then."

He shrugged. "She won't, and the doctor says she can work right till the end . . . so will you come?"

There was a twinkle in her eyes as she smiled at him. "What do you think? You think I'm not going to come and visit my only son, in the godforsaken place he lives?"

He laughed at her. "I wouldn't exactly call it that, Mom."

"It's not New York." He glanced around them wistfully at the cabs flying past, the people walking by, the little shops on Madison Avenue only a few feet from them as they waited for the doorman to find them a cab. There were times when he felt his romance with New York would never end, and San Francisco still felt like an exile to him. "San Francisco's not so bad." He was still trying to convince himself of that, in spite of how happy he was there with Liz, but he would have been happier with her in New York. His mother shrugged, and looked at him ruefully.

"Just so you come home soon. Especially now." They were all thinking of Liz and the child she was to bear. His mother acted as though it were a gift especially for them. "Take care of yourself." She hugged him tight as a taxi finally stopped for them, and there were tears in her eyes as she took a step back from him. "Mazel tov, to both of you."

"Thank you, Mom." He squeezed her hand and he and his father exchanged a warm look, and then they waved and were gone and he walked slowly back to his hotel, thinking of them, and Liz, and Jane, thinking how lucky he was . . . no matter where he lived. Maybe it didn't matter so much for now . . . San Francisco would be easier for Liz this year, better than slipping on ice, and battling the snow and the elements. It was just as well, he convinced himself. . . . And the next day when he left it was pouring rain. And the city still looked beautiful to him. It was blanketed in gray, and as the plane rose in the sky, he thought of his parents again. It must have been hard for them, having him so far away. He suddenly understood it differently now that he was having his own child. He would have hated his son to live so far away. And then he leaned his head back against the seat and smiled to himself, thinking of Liz and the baby they would have. . . . He hoped it would look like her, and he wouldn't have minded a little girl . . . a little girl. . . . He drifted off to sleep, and slept most of the way to Europe.

The week in Paris went too fast, and from there he went to Rome and Milan, as he always did. This time he went to Denmark and Berlin, as well, with a round of meetings in London before he left. It was a very successful trip and he was away for almost three weeks, and when he saw Liz again he laughed at her. Her stomach had suddenly exploded while he was gone, and she couldn't wear her clothes anymore. And when she lay in bed, she looked as though she'd swallowed a cantaloupe.

"What's that?" He grinned at her after the first time they made love again.

"I dunno." She threw out her hands in ignorance as she lay naked on their bed, her hair in pigtails and their clothes strewn across the floor. They hadn't waited very long, and they were in a hurry before Tracy brought Jane home from an excursion they'd been on.

But when Liz got up and walked across the room, and saw Bernie watching her, she felt self-conscious suddenly, and she pulled his shirt on and covered herself. "Don't look at me . . . I'm so fat I hate myself."

"Fat? Are you crazy? You've never looked better. You're gorgeous!" He came over and gently fondled her behind, and then let his hand drift over the cantaloupe with fascination.

"Any idea what it is?" He was curious.

She shrugged with a smile. "It's bigger than Jane was at this point, but that doesn't mean anything." And then, hopefully, "Maybe it's a boy. That's what you want, isn't it?"

He cocked his head to one side, looking at her. "I don't really think I care. Just so it's okay. When do we go back to the doctor again?"

"Are you really sure you want to do that?" She looked at him worriedly and he was stunned.

"What's happened to you?" And then he understood perfectly. "Has my darling mother been talking to you?" She blushed and then shrugged again, trying to brush it off and explain it at the same time, and he held her close to him. "You're beautiful to me. And I want to share this with you . . . all of it . . . the good, the bad, the scary part, the wonder of it all. We both made this child, and now we're both going to share it as much as we can. Is that okay with you?"

She looked relieved and her eyes were bright as she looked at him. "You're sure it won't turn you off forever?" She looked so worried and he laughed, remembering their antics in bed only moments before. He waved at the bed and then kissed her tenderly.

"Did I seem turned off to you?" She giggled happily and hugged him tight.

"Okay . . . I'm sorry . . ." And with that, the

doorbell rang, and they jumped back into their clothes again as quickly as they could, in time to welcome Tracy and Jane. He tossed the child into the air and showed her all the goodies he'd brought her from France, and it was hours later before Liz and Bernie were alone again.

She curled into bed next to him, and they chatted for a while, about his work, the store, the trip, and the child she was carrying. She seemed more interested in that than anything these days and he didn't mind. It was his baby too, and he was so proud of her. He pulled her into his arms, and they went to sleep, as she purred contentedly beside him.

Chapter 15

Bernie's parents arrived the day after Christmas vacation began, and Liz and Jane drove out to the airport to pick them up. She was five and a half months pregnant by then. And Ruth had brought everything from a layette from Bergdorf's to pamphlets about her health that she had forced Lou to bring her from the hospital. She had advice for her that dated back to her own grandmother, and after a close look at Liz' profile in the baggage claim she announced that it was a boy, which delighted everyone.

They stayed for a week, and then went to Disneyland with Jane, to leave Bernie and Liz alone for their anniversary. They celebrated three nights in a row. On their anniversary they went to L'Étoile, and came home and made love until all hours, the following night they went to a huge charity affair given at the store, and on New Year's Eve they went out with friends, and wound up in the bar at L'Étoile again. They had a wonderful few days, but when Ruth and Lou came back, Ruth told Bernie she thought Liz looked terrible. Pale and tired and worn out. And she'd been complaining of pains in her hips and back for the last month.

"Why don't you take her somewhere?"

"I guess I should." He'd been working so hard, he hadn't really thought of it, and it was going to be difficult for him this year. The baby was due exactly when he made his usual trip to New York and Europe. He was going to have to put it off until after the baby came, and somehow he had much more to do at the store just then. "I'll see if I can."

His mother wagged an angry finger at him. "Don't overlook your responsibilities, Bernard."

And he laughed at her. "Whose mother are you, anyway? Hers or mine?" He felt sorry for Liz sometimes, she had absolutely no family at all, except him, and Jane, and his parents in New York. As aggravating as his mother was at times, it was still nice to know that someone gave a damn about him.

"Don't be so smart. It might do her good to get away before the baby comes." And for once, he took his mother's advice and took Liz away to Hawaii for a few days, and this time they didn't take Jane, although she pouted at them for several weeks because of it. But he came home from the store with stacks of tropical maternity clothes for her, and the reservations already made. He faced her with a fait accompli and three days later they left. And when they returned, she was brown and healthy and relaxed, and she felt like her old self again. Or almost, except for heartburn, insomnia, back pains, swollen legs, and increasing fatigue, all of which were normal the doctor said. The pains in her back and hips were the worst, but that was normal too.

"God, Bernie, sometimes I feel like I'm never going to be my old self again." She had gained more than thirty pounds, and she had two months to go, but she still looked cute to him. Her face had filled out a little bit, but it didn't spoil her looks, she just looked younger than she usually did. And she always looked neat and well dressed. He thought she looked sweet that way, although he was aware that his desire for her was waning. But it didn't seem to be a time for that, although she complained sometimes. He was afraid he would hurt the child, especially if they got too enthusiastic, which they often did. And eventually, Liz didn't care about making love anyway. By the end of March she was so uncomfortable, she could barely move, and she was grateful that she didn't have to go to work anymore. She couldn't have stood another day of trying to stand on her feet, keeping the kids in line, or teaching them simple math or their ABC's.

Her class gave a baby shower for her, and everyone brought something they'd made. She had booties, sweaters, hats, an ashtray, three drawings, a cradle someone's father had built for them, and a tiny pair of wooden shoes, along with all the gifts the other teachers had given her. And of course Bernie brought home more baby clothes from the store every few days. Between what he brought home, and what his mother sent from New York, she had enough for quintuplets at least. But it was fun seeing it all, and now she could hardly wait to get it over with. She was getting nervous about the birth, and she could hardly sleep at night. Instead, she would roam the halls, sit in the living room and knit, watching late-night TV, or go and sit in the baby's room, thinking about what it would be like when the baby was born.

She was there one afternoon, waiting for Jane to come home from school, sitting in the rocking chair Bernie had painted for her only two weeks before, when the telephone rang. She thought about not answering it. But she always hated to do that when Jane was out. You never knew when something would go wrong, or they needed her, or she got hurt coming home from school, or it might have been Bernie and she loved talking to him. She pushed herself out of the chair with a groan, rubbed her back, and lumbered slowly into the living room.

"Hello?"

"Good afternoon." There was something familiar about the voice, but she wasn't sure what. It was probably someone trying to sell something to her.

"Yes?"

"How've you been?" Something about the voice gave her the creeps.

"Who's this?" She tried to sound casual, but she felt breathless as she stood there, holding the phone. There was something ominous about the voice, but she wasn't sure what.

"You don't remember me?"

"No, I don't." She started to hang up, hoping it was just a prank, but the voice was quick to grab her back.

"Liz, wait!" It was a command, and the voice suddenly lost its fluidity. It was sharp and brusque, and suddenly she knew, but it couldn't be . . . it only sounded like him. She stood very still holding the phone, and said nothing at all to him. "I want to talk to you."

"I don't know who you are."

"The hell you don't." He laughed, and it was an evil, raucous sound. She had never liked his laugh, and now she knew exactly who it was. What she didn't know was how he had found her again, or why. And she wasn't sure she wanted to know. "Where's my kid?"

"What difference does it make?" It was Chandler Scott, the man who had fathered Jane, which was different from being a father to her. What he had done had to do with Liz, but nothing to do with the child. The man who was a father to her was Bernie Fine, and Liz wanted nothing more to do with this man. Her voice told him so when she answered him.

"What do you mean?"

"You haven't seen her in five years, Chan. She doesn't even know who you are." Or that you're alive, but she didn't tell him that. "We don't want to see you anymore."

"I hear you're married again." She looked down at her belly and smiled. "I'll bet the new hubby has bucks." It was a disgusting thing to say and it angered her.

"What difference does that make?"

"I want to know my kid's all right, that's why. In fact, I think I ought to see her. I mean, after all, she ought to know she has a real father who cares about her."

"Really? If you were so interested in that, you should have let her know a long time ago."

"How was I supposed to know where you were? You disappeared."

That brought something else to mind she couldn't figure out as she listened to him, her heart pounding angrily. There was a lot she would have liked to say to him once upon a time, but now it was so long ago. Jane was seven years old. "How'd you find me now?"

"You're not too hard to find. You were listed in an old phone book. And your old landlady told me your married name. How's Jane?"

Her jaw clenched as he said her name. "Fine."

"I thought I'd drop in to say hi one of these days." He tried to sound casual.

"Don't waste your time. I'm not going to let you see her." She thought he was dead, and Liz wished he were.

"You can't keep her from me, Liz." His voice had a nasty ring to it.

"Oh no? Why not?"

"Try explaining to a judge that you're keeping a natural father from his daughter."

"Try telling him you abandoned her six years ago. I'm sure he'll be very sympathetic to you after that." The doorbell rang, and Liz felt her heart pound. It was Jane, and she didn't want her to hear her talking to him. "Anyway, get lost, Chan. Or to put it a little more clearly for you, go screw yourself."

"I think you just did. I'm seeing a lawyer this afternoon."

"What for?"

"I want to see my kid."

The doorbell rang again and she shouted out to wait just a minute.

"Why?"

"Because it's my right."

"And then what? You disappear for another six years? Why don't you just leave her alone?"

"If that's what you want, you'll have to talk to me." So that was it. Another scam. He wanted money from them. She should have known.

"Where are you staying? I'll call you back." He gave her a number in Marin, and she jotted it down.

"I want to hear from you by tonight."

"You will." Sonofabitch, she said through clenched teeth as she hung up and she went to the door, looking pale, and let Jane in. She had been banging her lunch box against the door and there was a big chip on the black paint and Liz yelled at her, which made her cry, and she slammed into her room, as Liz went in and sat down on the bed, close to tears herself.

"I'm sorry, sweetheart. I had a rough afternoon."

"So did I. I lost my belt." She was wearing a pink skirt with a white belt she loved. Bernie had brought it from the store, and she treasured it, like everything else he gave her, and most of all himself.

"Daddy'll bring you another one."

She looked slightly mollified as she sniffed and Liz held out her arms, as Jane came to her reluctantly. It was a hard time for all of them. Liz was tired. Bernie was on edge, thinking she was going to have the baby every night when they went to bed. And Jane wasn't sure just how the newcomer would affect her life. It was natural that they were snapping at each other a little bit. And this sudden reappearance of Chandler Scott didn't help. Liz brushed the hair back from Jane's face, and gave her a plate of the cookies she'd made for her that day, and a glass of milk, and when Jane sat down at her desk to do the homework she'd been given in school, Liz went quietly back to the living room. She sat down with a sigh, and dialed Bernie's private line. He picked it up himself, but he sounded busy when he did.

"Hi, sweetheart, bad time to talk?" She was so damn tired, and she was having contractions all the time, especially when she was upset, like now, after talking to Chandler.

"No, no, it's okay." And then suddenly he realized with a start. "Is it time?"

"No." She laughed. She wasn't due for two more weeks. And it could be late, the doctor always reminded her.

"You okay?"

"I'm fine . . . more or less . . ." She really wanted to talk to him before he came home. She didn't want Jane to overhear her telling him about Chandler Scott. "Something very disagreeable happened today."

"Did you get hurt?" He was beginning to sound like Grandma Ruth and Liz smiled, but not for long.

"No. I got a call from an old friend. Or an old enemy, I should say."

He looked puzzled as he frowned. What enemies did she have? None she'd ever mentioned to him. Not that he could remember anyway. "Who was that?"

"Chandler Scott." The name electrified them both, and there was a long silence from his end.

"Is that who I think it is? Your ex-husband, right?"

"If you can call him that. I think we lived together for a total of about four months, and legally a lot less than that."

"Where did he come from?"

"Jail probably."

"How the hell did he find you?"

"My old landlady. Apparently she gave him my married name and told him we were living here, and it was easy after that."

"You'd think she'd ask before she gave the information out."

"I guess she saw no harm in it." She stretched uncomfortably on the couch. Everything was uncomfortable. Sitting, standing, lying down. Even breathing was difficult now, and the baby felt huge, and moved constantly.

"What did he want?"

"He claimed he wanted to see Jane."

"Why?" Bernie sounded horrified.

"Honestly, I don't really think he does. He said he wanted to 'discuss it' with us. He said he'd go to an attorney about visiting rights unless we talked to him."

"That sounds like blackmail to me."

"It is. But I think we ought to talk to him. I said we'd call him back tonight. He gave me a number in Marin."

"I'll talk to him. You stay out of it." He looked worried as he stared at his desk. The timing was just terrible. Liz didn't need a headache like that at a time like this.

"I think we ought to talk to an attorney ourselves. Maybe he has no rights by now."

"That's not a bad idea, Liz. I'll check it out before I come home."

"Do you know who to call?"

"We have counsel for the store. I'll see who they suggest." He hung up after that, and Liz went back to see if Jane had finished her math home-work. She was just closing her books and she looked up at Liz expectantly.

"Is Daddy bringing me a new belt tonight?" She looked hopeful and Liz sat down with a sigh.

"Oh sweetheart . . . I forgot to ask . . . we'll ask him tonight."

"Mommy . . ." She started to cry, and Liz felt like crying herself. Everything seemed so difficult suddenly. It was hard enough just moving around and putting one foot in front of the other these days, and she wanted to make things easier for Jane, not more difficult. Poor Jane was all shook up about the baby coming into her life and chang-ing everything. She climbed onto her mother's lap, still wanting to be the baby herself, and Liz held her while she cried. It made them both feel better afterwards and they went for a long walk, and bought some magazines. Jane wanted to buy some flowers to give to Bernie when he came home, and Liz let her pick a bouquet of iris and daffodils, and they walked slowly home again.

"Do you think the baby will come soon?" She looked at her mother half hopeful and half afraid, and half wishing it would never come at all. Al-though the pediatrician had told Liz that Jane was a good age to deal with this sort of thing. He thought she'd adjust very quickly once the baby was born, but Liz was beginning to wonder about it.

"I don't know, sweetheart. I hope so. I'm getting pretty tired of being fat." They exchanged a smile as they walked hand in hand.

"You don't look so bad. Kathy's mom looked terrible. Her face got all fat like a pig"—she distorted her face and Liz laughed—"and she got all these blue things in her legs."

"Varicose veins." She was lucky, she had never gotten them.

"It must be horrible, having a baby, huh?"

"No, it's not. It's beautiful. I don't know, afterwards it's all worth it. You forget all this yucky stuff, and it's really not so bad. If you have a baby with a man you love, then it's the nicest thing in the world."

"Did you love my daddy too?" She looked worried and it was odd that she should ask the question today, when Chandler Scott had called after all these years, and Liz was reminded of how much she had hated him. But she couldn't tell Jane that now, and wondered if she ever would. It might affect the way she saw herself, Liz thought.

"Yes, I did. Very much, in fact."

"How did he die?" It was the first time Jane had asked her that, and she wondered if she had heard something that afternoon. Liz fervently hoped not.

"He died in an accident."

"A car accident?"

It seemed as reasonable as anything else. "Yes. He was killed instantly. He didn't suffer at all." She thought that might be important to her and it was.

"I'm glad. It must have been very sad for you."

"It was," Liz lied.

"How old was I?" They were almost home and Liz was so out of breath she could hardly talk.

"Just a few months old, sweetheart." They swung up the front steps and she unlocked the door with her key, and inside she sat down at the kitchen table, while Jane put the flowers in a vase for Bernie and looked at her mother with a happy smile.

"I'm so glad you married Daddy. Now I have a daddy again."

"I'm glad too." And he's a hell of a lot better than the other one.

Jane took the flowers into the other room, and Liz started cooking dinner for them. She still insisted on making dinner every night, baking bread, making everyone's favorite desserts. She wasn't sure what she'd feel like after the baby came, or how busy she would be, and it was easier to spoil them now. She made a point of it every day, and Bernie looked forward to coming home and eating the treats that she had made for them. He had gained ten pounds himself, and laughingly blamed it on the pregnancy.

He came home early that night, made a big fuss over them both, thanked Jane for the flowers, and only appeared as worried as he was when he and Liz were alone after Jane had gone to bed. He had refused to discuss the subject before, for fear the child would overhear what they said. And now he closed their bedroom door, and Jane's, and turned their television on, so she couldn't hear them talk, and then he turned to Liz with troubled eyes.

"Peabody, our attorney for the store, recommended a guy to me. His name is Grossman, and I talked to him this afternoon." He also trusted him because he was from New York and had gone to Columbia Law School. "He says this thing's not good. The guy has rights."

"He does?" Liz looked shocked as she sat uncomfortably at the foot of their bed. She felt out of breath again. She was really miserable. "After all these years? How is that possible?"

"Because the laws are very liberal in this state, that's why." He was sorrier than ever that Berman hadn't moved him home to New York before this. "Apparently, if I'd adopted her by now it would be too late for him. But I didn't. That was my mistake. I didn't think we had to bother with the legalities, as long as she was using my name anyway." And now he could have kicked himself, after what the attorney had said.

"But what about the fact that he abandoned her . . . abandoned us, for chrissake?"

"That might actually win the case for us, but the problem is, that isn't automatic. That depends on the judge, and it would have to become a 'case' and the judge would have to decide how he felt about the abandonment. If we win, great. And if we don't, we can appeal his decision. But in the interim, and even before this thing would get to court for the first round, which could take a while, they would give him temporary visitation, just to be 'fair' to him.''

"The man's a jailbird, for chrissake, a con man, a snake.'' He had never seen Liz so worked up before. She looked as though she hated the man, and he knew she had good reason to. He was beginning to hate him himself. "They'd expose a child to him?''

"Apparently, yes. The assumption is that the natural father is a good guy until proven otherwise. So first they'd let him visit Jane, then we'd go to court to fight it out, and then we win or lose. But in the meantime, we'd have to explain to her who he is, why he's visiting her, and how we feel about it.'' They both looked horrified, as horrified as he had felt when he spoke to the attorney that afternoon. He decided to tell her all of it. "And Grossman says that there's a good chance we wouldn't win. This state is extremely in favor of father's rights, and the judge could be sympathetic to him, no matter how big a sonofabitch we think he is. The theory seems to be that fathers have rights, no matter what, unless maybe they beat their kids or something like that. And even if they do that, apparently provisions are made to protect the child but still allow the abusive parent to see the child. Isn't that encouraging?'' He was so angry he had gone at it full force, and suddenly as Liz started to cry, he realized how foolish he had been. She was in no condition to face the possibility of all that. "Oh baby, I'm sorry. . . . I never should have told you all that.''

"I have to know it if it's true," she sobbed. "Isn't there anything we can do to get rid of him?"

"Yes and no. Grossman was honest with me. It's against the law to buy this guy off, but it's been done before. And he suspects that's all he wants. After seven years, it's not very likely that he's interested in teaching Jane to ride a bicycle. I think probably he just wants a few bucks to tide him over till he winds up in jail again. The only trouble is, if we do that, he may turn up again, and again, and again. It could be a bottomless pit." But for the moment, he was tempted to try it at least once, and maybe that would get rid of him for good. He had thought about it on the way home, and was willing to give him ten thousand bucks to get out of their lives. He would have given him more than that, but he was afraid if he gave him too much, it would whet his appetite. He said as much to Liz and she agreed with him.

"Shall we give him a call?" She wanted to get it over with, and the contractions were driving her nuts tonight. She could feel her heart race as she handed Bernie the paper she'd written Chandler's number on.

"I want to talk to him myself. And I want you to stay out of it. For all you know, this is just a ploy to catch your attention again, and the less satisfaction he gets, the better off you'll be." It made sense to her, and she was happy to let Bernie handle all of it.

The phone rang at the other end, and Bernard asked for Chandler Scott. They waited for what seemed a long time, and he held the receiver so Liz could listen too, as a male voice came on. He wanted to know if he had the right man, and she nodded at him and signaled that it was. Bernie took it from there.

"Mr. Scott? My name is Fine."

"Oh?" And then he understood. "Right. You're married to Liz."

"Correct. I understand you called this afternoon, about a business deal." Grossman told him not to mention the child or what the money was for, in case Scott was recording him. "I have the results on that for you now."

Scott was quick to understand. He liked a man who didn't mess around, although it had been fun talking to Liz again. "Do you think we should all meet to talk it out?" He was talking in the same veiled terms as Bernard, afraid of the police perhaps. God only knew what he was into now, Liz thought.

"I don't think that's necessary. My client has come up with a price for you. Ten thousand, for the whole package. One time only, for your previous services. I believe they want to buy you out." The meaning of that was clear to all three of them, and there was a long silence at the other end.

"Do I have to sign anything?" He sounded cautious.

"That won't be necessary." Bernie would have liked that but Grossman had already told him it wouldn't be worth the paper it was written on.

He came right to the point, and he sounded

hungry to Bernie. "How do I get it?" In a brown paper bag at the bus station, Bernie almost laughed, except it wasn't funny. And he wanted to get rid of the sonofabitch as soon as he could, for all their sakes, especially Liz, who did not need the heartache right before the birth of their baby.

"I'll be happy to meet you with it."

"In cash?"

"Of course." Bastard. All he wanted was the money. He didn't give a damn about Jane. He never had, just as Liz had told Bernie.

"I'll be happy to give it to you tomorrow."

"Where do you live?" At least their address was not listed in the phone directory, and Bernie was suddenly glad they had done that. And he was equally reluctant to meet him at his office. He wanted to meet him in a bar, or a restaurant, or a doorway. It was beginning to feel like a sleazy movie. But he was trying to think of where to tell him he would meet him.

"I'll meet you at Harry's, on Union Street, at lunchtime. Noon." His bank was only half a block away, and he could give him the money and then come home to check on Liz.

"Great." Chandler Scott sounded delighted and as though he didn't have a care in the world. "See you tomorrow." He hung up quickly and Bernie turned to Liz.

"He'll take it."

"Do you think that's all he wants?"

"For now. I think to him that's a hell of a lot of money, and right now he can't see beyond it. The only problem with this, as Grossman says, is that he can come back at us again, but we'll just have to face that when he does." He couldn't afford to have it become a monthly arrangement. "With any luck, we'll be living in New York when he gets hungry again, and he'll never find us. I think next time we'll skip informing your ex-landlady when we move, or maybe you should just tell her not to give out any information." Liz nodded. And Bernie was right, once they were in New York, Chandler probably wouldn't be able to find them. "I didn't want to meet him at the store, because then he'd always know how to find us." She looked up at him with grateful eyes and shook her head.

"I'm so sorry I got you into this, sweetheart. I promise I'll pay you back when I save up the money."

"Don't be ridiculous." He put an arm around her. "This is just one of those things and we'll get it all cleaned up tomorrow."

She looked at him with sad, serious eyes, re-membering the pain Chandler Scott had caused her, and then she felt a tremor run through her and she reached a hand out to Bernie. "Will you promise me something?"

"Anything you like." He had never loved her more, as he sat looking down at her with her enor-mous belly.

"If anything ever happens to me, will you pro-tect Jane from him?" Her eyes were huge in her face and he frowned at her.

"Don't say things like that." He was Jewish enough to be superstitious, not as much so as his mother, but enough. "Nothing's going to happen to you." Although the doctor had warned him that women sometimes got unusually fearful, or even morbid just before they gave birth. Maybe that meant the baby would come soon.

"But will you promise? I never want him to get near her. Swear to me . . ." She was getting agitated and he promised.

"I love her like my own, you know that. You don't ever have to worry." But she had nightmares as she lay in his arms that night, and he was nervous himself as he went to Harry's to meet Scott with an envelope with one hundred hundred-dollar bills in it. Liz had told him to look for a tall, thin, golden-haired man. She warned him that he might not look like anyone he might expect to meet for this purpose.

"He looks more like you'd expect to see him on a yacht or as though you'd love to introduce him to your baby sister."

"That's terrific. I'll probably walk up to some normal guy, hand him the envelope and he'll punch me . . . or worse yet, take it and run."

But as he stood at the bar at Harry's, feeling faintly like a Russian spy on a mission, watching the lunch crowd arrive, he saw him immediately as he walked in. As Liz had said, he looked handsome and jaunty. He was wearing a blazer and gray slacks, but when one looked more closely, the blazer was cheap, the shirt cuffs were frayed, and his shoes were all but worn out. His con man suit was in serious disrepair, and he looked like an aging preppie down on his luck as he walked to the bar and ordered a Scotch straight up, and held it with a trembling hand, eyeing the crowd. Bernie had not told him what he looked like, so he had the advantage. And he was almost certain this was his man. He watched Scott chat with the bartender. He said he had just returned from Arizona, and after a few more minutes and half his drink, he heard him admit that he'd been in prison there. He shrugged with a boyish smile.

"Screw 'em if they can't take a joke. . . . Hell, I passed a few bad checks, and the judge went nuts. It's good to be back in California." It was a sad commentary on the state's laws, and once again Bernie was sorry they weren't back in New York, as he finally decided to approach him.

"Mr. Scott?" He spoke in a quiet voice, and slid discreetly next to Chandler as he stood with his second drink in his hand. And he was obviously very nervous. At close range, he had the same blue eyes as Jane, but so did Liz, so it was difficult to say whose eyes Jane had inherited. He had a handsome face, but he looked older than his twenty-nine years. He had thick blond hair which fell over one eye, and he could easily see how Liz might have fallen for him. He had that innocent boyish air, which had made it easy for him to rip people off, and convince them to invest in his bunko schemes. He had been kidding people ever since he was eighteen, and his frequent arrests didn't seem to stop him. But he still had the naive look of a midwestern kid, and one could see how he might have tried to give himself the aura of the country club at one time, though he appeared to be down on his luck now, and he looked at Bernie with nervous, hungry eyes the moment he spoke.

"Yes?" He smiled, but only his mouth moved. His eyes were as cold as ice as they slid over Bernie.

"My name is Fine." He knew that was all he had to say.

"Great." Chandler beamed. "Got something for me?"

Bernie nodded, but did not rush to hand him the envelope, as Chandler Scott's eyes took in every detail of the clothes he was wearing. "Yes, I do." The eyes then took in his watch, but he had been careful not to wear a Patek Philippe, or even his Rolex. He was wearing a watch his father had given him years before, when he was in business school, but even that wasn't cheap, and Scott knew it. He suspected that he had hit a live one.

"Looks like little Liz found herself a nice husband this time around."

Bernie did not comment. He silently pulled the envelope from his inside breast pocket. "I believe this is what you want. You can count it. It's all there."

He glanced at Bernie for the flicker of an instant. "How do I know it's real?"

"Are you serious?" Bernie was shocked.

"Where the hell do you think I would get counterfeit money?"

"It's been done before."

"Take it to the bank, have them take a look. I'll wait here." Bernie refused to look worried, and Scott didn't look as though he was going anywhere as he thumbed through the hundred-dollar bills in the envelope. It was all there. Ten thousand dollars. "I want to make one thing very clear before you go. Don't come back again. We won't give you a dime next time. Is that clear?"

His eyes bore into Chandler's and the handsome blond smiled. "I get the message." He drained his drink, set down the glass, slipped the envelope into his blazer, and looked at Bernie one last time. "Give Liz my love. Sorry not to have seen her." Bernie wanted to kick him in the gut, but he sat very still. It was interesting he hadn't mentioned Jane once since they'd met. He had sold her for ten thousand dollars, and with a casual wave at the bartender, he strolled out of the restaurant and sauntered around the corner, as Bernie sat shaking at the bar. He didn't even want his drink. He just wanted to go home to Liz, and make sure she was all right. He was faintly afraid that he might show up to bother Liz, or try to see Jane in spite of the arrangement. But Bernie found it difficult to believe that he cared about the child. He had shown absolutely no interest in her.

He hurried outside, got back in his car, and drove to Buchanan and Vallejo. He left the car in front of their garage and hurried up the steep steps. He felt shaken by the encounter and he wasn't sure why, but all he knew was he had to see Liz. He struggled with the key, and at first he thought there was no one home, but as he looked into the kitchen he saw her. She was brushing the hair out of her eyes and baking more cookies for him and Jane.

"Hi there." His face broke into a slow smile. He was so relieved to see her he could have cried, and she sat down heavily on a kitchen chair, and smiled up at him. She looked like a princess in a fairy tale, except for the enormous tummy. "Hello, sweetheart." He went to gently touch her face and she leaned her head against him. She had been worried about him all morning, and feeling guilty because of the trouble and expense she had caused him.

"Did everything go all right?"

"Perfectly. And he looked exactly the way you said he would. I suspect he's very hard up for money."

"If that's true, he'll wind up in jail again pretty soon. That man has pulled off more scams and con jobs than anyone can imagine."

"What does he need the money for?"

"To survive, I guess. He's just never known how to earn a living any other way. I used to think that if he put as much effort into something honest, he could have been the head of General Motors by now." He smiled at her. "Did he say anything about Jane?"

"Not a word. He just took the money and ran, as the saying goes."

"Good. And I hope he never comes back again." She heaved a sigh of relief and smiled at Bernie. She was so grateful to have him, especially after the tough times she'd been through before him. She never lost sight of how lucky she was now.

"I hope so too, Liz." But he wasn't convinced they had seen the last of Chandler Scott. He was just too slick, and a little too cheerful. But he didn't tell her that. She had enough to think about. He wanted to suggest adopting Jane to her now too, but he didn't want to burden her with anything until after the baby was born. She was so tired and so uncomfortable most of the time. "Anyway, just put it out of your mind. It's all over, finished, goodbye. How's our little friend?" He rubbed her tummy like a Buddha and she laughed.

"He sure kicks a lot. He feels like he's going to come any minute." Her baby was getting so heavy and she was carrying it so low that she could barely walk now, and he wouldn't have dared try to make love to her. You could feel the baby's head pressing down on her pelvis, and she said she felt it constantly, pressing on her bladder. In fact, that night she had several sharp pains, and he made her call the doctor. But the doctor wasn't impressed by what she said, and they went back to bed for the rest of the night, although she couldn't sleep.

The next three weeks crawled by at a snail's pace, and ten days past her due date she was so exhausted she sat down and cried when Jane wouldn't eat her dinner.

"It's all right, sweetheart." He had offered to take them out but Jane had a cold and Liz was too tired. She didn't want to get dressed up anymore and her hips hurt constantly. Bernie read Jane a story that night and took her to school the next day himself, eliminating the need for the carpool. And he had just walked into his office when his secretary buzzed him on the intercom, as he glanced over some reports from New York about their sales figures for March, which were outstanding.

"Yes?"

"It's Mrs. Fine on four."

"Thanks, Irene." He picked up the line, still perusing the reports and wondering why she had called. "What's up, sweetheart?" He didn't think he'd forgotten anything at home. He wondered if Jane's cold had gotten worse and she wanted him to pick her up at school now. "Everything okay?"

She giggled, which was a major change from her mood when he'd left that morning. She had been distracted and grumpy and she had snapped at him when he suggested they go out to dinner that night. But he understood how jumpy she was and how lousy she felt and he didn't get upset when she barked at him. "Everything's just fine." She suddenly sounded excited and happy.

"Well, you certainly sound cheerful. Anything special happen?"

"Maybe."

"What does that mean?" His antenna suddenly went up.

"My water just broke."

"Hallelujah! I'll be right home."

"You don't have to, nothing major has started yet, just a few little cramps." But she sounded so victorious and he couldn't have stayed away. They had waited nine and a half months for this and he wanted to be there with her.

"Did you call the doctor yet?"

"I did. He said to call him when things start to happen."

"How long does he think that will take?"

"You remember what they said in class. It could get going half an hour from now, or maybe not till tomorrow morning. It should be soon though."

"I'll be right there. Do you want anything?"

She smiled at the phone. "Just my sweetheart. . . . I'm sorry I've been such a bitch these past few weeks. . . . I just felt so rotten." She hadn't even told him how badly her back and hips hurt all the time.

"I know you did. Don't you worry about that, baby. It's almost over."

"I can hardly wait to see the baby." But suddenly, she was scared too, and when he got home he found her very tense, so he rubbed her back, and talked to her while she took a shower. And the shower seemed to get things started. She sat down afterwards with a serious look, and she winced as she got the first strong contractions. He made her breathe, and got out his favorite watch while he timed them. "Do you have to wear that thing?" She was getting grouchy again, but they both knew why from what they learned in the class they had taken. She was probably going into transition. "Why do you have to wear that watch? It's so gaudy." He smiled to himself, knowing that she was getting closer. Her irritability meant this was the real thing.

He called Tracy at school and asked her to take Jane home with her that afternoon. She was excited to hear that Liz was in labor, and by one o'clock the pains were coming hard and fast, and Liz could barely catch her breath between them. It was definitely time to go, and the doctor was waiting at the hospital when they got there. Bernie was pushing Liz in a wheelchair as a nurse walked behind them, and Liz signaled to him to stop each time she had a contraction. And suddenly she began to wave frantically, unable to catch her breath as one contraction became two and then three and four without letting up, and she started to cry as they helped her out of the wheelchair in the labor room, and up onto the bed where Bernie helped her take her clothes off.

"It's okay, baby. . . . It's okay. . . ." He suddenly wasn't scared anymore. He couldn't imagine anyplace else to be, except with her, as their baby came. She let out a hideous scream as the next contraction came, and a worse one as the doctor examined her. Bernie held her hands and told her to breathe but she was having a difficult time concentrating and she was losing control, as the doctor looked down at her, satisfied with her progress.

"You're doing fine, Liz." He was a warmhearted man with gray hair and blue eyes, and Bernie had liked him from the first, as had Liz. He exuded competence and warmth, as he did now, but Liz wasn't listening. She was clutching Bernie's arm, and screaming with each contraction. "You're eight centimeters dilated . . . two more to go . . . and you can start pushing."

"I don't want to push . . . I want to go home. . . ." Bernie smiled at the doctor, and urged her to pant. And the next two centimeters went faster than the doctor expected. She was in the delivery room pushing by four o'clock, and it was eight hours since labor had begun, which didn't seem long to Bernie as he talked to Liz and quieted her over and over, but it seemed like an eternity to her as the pains continued to roar through her.

"I can't take anymore!" She suddenly screamed, refusing to pant anymore. But they were putting her legs in the stirrups now, and the doctor was talking about doing an episiotomy. "I don't care what you do. . . . Just get that baby out of me. . . ." She was sobbing now like a child, and Bernie felt a lump rise in his throat as he watched her. He couldn't stand watching her continue to writhe in pain and the breathing didn't seem to help her at all, but the doctor didn't look worried.

"Can't you give her something?" Bernie whispered and the doctor shook his head as the nurses began to run around everywhere and two women in green surgical suits came in pushing a bassinet with a heat lamp, and suddenly it all became real. The bassinet was there for their baby. The baby was coming, and he bent low next to Liz' ear and encouraged her to breathe, and then push when the doctor told her.

"I can't . . . can't . . . hurts too much . . ." She couldn't take much more, and Bernie was stunned when he looked at his watch and saw that it was after six o'clock. She had been pushing for more than two hours.

"Come on." The doctor was intent now. "Push harder . . . come on, Liz! Again . . . Now! . . . that's it . . . that's it . . . come on . . . the baby's head is crowning . . . he's coming through . . . come *on!*" And then suddenly along with Liz' howl of anguish, there was another smaller one, and Bernie stared as the baby's head came from between her legs into the doctor's hands, and he propped up Liz' shoulders so she could watch and push again, and suddenly he was there. Their son. She was crying and laughing and Bernie was kissing her and crying too. It was a celebration of life, and just as they had promised, the pain was almost forgotten. The doctor cut the cord once the placenta was out, and he handed Bernie his son as Liz watched, trembling on the delivery table as she smiled, and the nurse assured her that the trembling was a normal reaction too. They cleaned her up as Bernie held the baby's face next to hers, and she kissed the satin cheek of their baby.

"What's his name?" The doctor smiled at them both as Bernie beamed and Liz continued to touch the baby with wonder.

They exchanged a look, and Liz said her son's name for the first time. "Alexander Arthur Fine."

"Arthur was my grandfather," Bernie explained. Neither of them was crazy about the baby's middle name, but Bernie had promised his mother. "Alexander A. Fine," he repeated, and bent to kiss his wife, with the baby in his arms, their tears mixing as they kissed, and the baby slept happily as Bernie held him.

Chapter 16

The arrival of Alexander Arthur Fine created a stir like no other that had occurred in the recent history of his family. Bernie's parents arrived, carrying shopping bags full of gifts and toys, for Jane, and Liz, and the baby. Grandma Ruth was especially careful about not neglecting Jane. She made an enormous fuss over her, for which Bernie and Liz were grateful.

"You know, sometimes just when I decide I can't stand her, my mother does something so nice, I can't believe she's the same woman who's always driven me crazy."

Liz smiled at him. They were even closer now that they had shared Alexander's birth. They were both still awed by the experience. "Maybe Jane will say that about me one day."

"I don't think so."

"I wish I were sure of that." Liz laughed at him again. "I'm not so sure I'm exempt. . . . I think a mother is a mother is a mother. . . ."

"Never fear. I won't let you . . ." He patted Alexander's behind as he lay sleeping on his mother's chest after she had nursed him. "Don't worry, kid, if she shows any early signs, I'll beat the hell out of her for you." But he bent to kiss her, as she sat comfortably in their bed, in an ice blue satin bed jacket his mother had brought her.

"She spoils me rotten, you know."

"She should. You're her only daughter." And she had given Liz the ring that Lou had given her when Bernie was born thirty-six years before. It was an emerald surrounded by small, perfect diamonds. And they had both been touched by the importance of the gesture.

They stayed for three weeks, at the Huntington again, and Ruth helped her with the baby every day while Jane was in school, and then in the afternoon she took Jane out for special treats and private adventures. It was a huge help to Liz, who had no one to help her and refused to let Bernie hire anyone. She wanted to take care of the baby herself, and she had always cleaned her own house and done her own cooking. "I couldn't stand having someone else do it for me." And she was so adamant about it, that he let her. But he noticed that she wasn't really getting her strength back. And his mother said as much to him before she left for New York.

"I don't think she should nurse the baby. It takes too much out of her. She's just exhausted." The doctor had warned her that that would happen, and Liz wasn't impressed when Bernie told her he thought she'd recover more quickly if she gave up nursing.

"You sound just like your mother." She scowled at him from her bed. After four weeks, she was still in bed most of the day. "Nursing makes all the difference in the world to the baby. They get all the immunities they need . . ." She gave him the party line of the nursing enthusiasts, but he still wasn't convinced. His mother had worried him about how tired Liz was, and whether or not it was normal.

"Don't be so California."

"Mind your own business." She laughed at him and wouldn't hear of giving up nursing the baby. The only thing that really bothered her was that her hips still hurt, which surprised her.

He went to New York and Europe in May, after his parents left, and Liz was still too tired to go with him, and wouldn't consider weaning the baby. But he was upset when he found her just as tired when he got back, and even more so at Stinson Beach that summer. And he thought she was having trouble walking, but she wouldn't admit it to him or the doctor.

"I think you should go back to the doctor, Liz." He was beginning to insist. Alexander was four months old, and a strapping baby with his father's green eyes, and his mother's golden curls. But Liz was looking pale and wan, even after two months at the beach, and the final straw came when she refused to go to the opening of the opera with him. She said it was too much trouble to go in and pick out a dress, and she didn't have time anyway. She had to start teaching again in September. But he knew just how exhausted she was when he heard her make arrangements with Tracy to sub for her part-time until she felt better.

"What was that all about? You won't go downtown to pick out a dress, and you won't go to Europe with me next month"—she had turned that down too even though he knew how much she had loved Paris when she went with him before—"and now you only want to work part-time. What the hell is going on?" He was frightened, and that night he called his father. "What do you think it is, Dad?"

"I don't know. Has she been to her doctor?"

"She won't go. She says it's normal for nursing mothers to be tired. But he's nearly five months old for chrissake, and she refuses to wean him."

"She may have to. She might just be anemic." It was a simple solution to the problem, and Bernie felt relieved after he had spoken to him but he insisted that she go to the doctor anyway and he was secretly beginning to wonder if she was pregnant.

Pretending to grumble all the way, she made an appointment the following week, but her obstetrician couldn't find anything wrong with her gynecologically. She wasn't pregnant again at any rate, and he sent her to an internist for some simple tests. An EKG, some blood tests, an X ray, and whatever else he thought was indicated. She had an appointment with the internist at three o'clock in the afternoon, and Bernie was enormously relieved that she was doing it. He was leaving for Europe in a few weeks, and he wanted to know what was going on before he left, and if the doctors in San Francisco couldn't figure it out, he was going to take her to New York and leave her with his father, and see if he couldn't find someone to figure out what was wrong with her.

The internist who checked her out seemed to think she was all right. He did several ordinary tests. Her blood pressure was fine, the electrocardiogram looked good, her blood count was low, so he ran a few more elaborate tests, and when he listened to her chest, he suspected she might have a mild case of pleurisy.

"And that's probably what's been wearing you out." He smiled. He was a tall Nordic man with large hands and a big voice and she felt comfortable with him. He sent her to a lab for a chest X ray and at five-thirty she got home, and kissed Bernie, who was reading Jane a story as they waited for her. She had left both children with a sitter that afternoon, which was rare for her.

"See . . . I'm fine . . . I told you so."

"Then how come you're so tired?"

"Pleurisy. He sent me for a chest X ray just to be sure I don't have some weird disease, and other than that I'm great."

"And too tired to go to Europe with me." He still wasn't convinced. "What's this guy's name anyway?"

"Why?" She looked at him suspiciously. What

was he going to do now? What else did he expect her to do?

"I want my father to check him out."

"Oh, for chrissake . . ." The baby was crying to be nursed and she went to his room to pick him up while Bernie wrote the check for the babysitter. Alexander was fat and blond and green-eyed and beautiful and he squealed with delight the minute she approached and burrowed happily at her breast, patting her with one hand as she held him close to her. And later when she set him down to sleep again, she tiptoed out of his room, and found her husband standing there waiting for her. She smiled at him and touched his cheek, looking up at him. "Don't worry so much, sweetheart," she whispered to him. "Everything is fine."

He pulled her into his arms and held her tight. "That's how I want it to be." Jane was playing in her room, the baby was asleep, and he looked down at his wife, but she looked too pale to him, and there were circles under her eyes that never went away anymore, and she was much, much too thin. He wanted to believe that everything was fine, but a gnawing fear inside him kept saying that it was not, and he held her for a long time, and then she went to cook dinner, and he played with Jane. And that night, as Liz slept he looked down at her fearfully. And when the baby woke at four o'clock, Bernie didn't wake her up, but made up one of the bottles with the supplement he took, and held the baby close to him.

Alexander was satisfied with the bottle and

cooed happily in Bernie's arms as he smiled at the child, changed his diapers eventually, and then set him down again. He was becoming an expert at that sort of thing, and that morning it was Bernie who answered the phone when Dr. Johanssen called. Liz was still sleeping.

"Hello?"

"Mrs. Fine, please." The voice was not rude, but curt, and Bernie went to wake her up.

"It's for you."

"Who is it?" She looked at him sleepily. It was nine o'clock, on Saturday morning.

"I don't know. He didn't say." But he suspected it was the doctor, and it frightened him as Liz read the fear in his eyes.

"A man? For me?"

The caller identified himself as quickly to her and asked her to come in at ten o'clock. It was Dr. Johanssen.

"Is something wrong?" she asked him, glancing at her husband.

But the doctor took too long to answer. It couldn't be. She was tired, but not that tired. She glanced at Bernie involuntarily, and could have kicked herself.

"Can it wait?" But Bernie was shaking his head no.

"I don't think it should, Mrs. Fine. Why don't you and your husband come in to see me in a little while?" He sounded much too calm and it frightened her. She hung up the phone and tried to make light of it for Bernie's sake.

"Christ, he acts like I have syphilis."

"What did he say it is?"

"He didn't say. He just said to come in an hour from now."

"Okay, we will." He looked terrified while trying to pretend that he was not, and he called Tracy for her while she got dressed. Tracy said she'd be over in half an hour. She'd been doing some gardening and she was a mess but she'd be happy to sit with the kids for an hour or two. She sounded as concerned as he felt, but she didn't ask any questions when she arrived. She was cheerful and businesslike and sped them on their way.

They barely spoke at all on the way to the hospital where they were meeting the doctor, and they found his office there easily. He had two X rays clipped to a light box when they walked into the room, and he smiled at them, but the smile wasn't cheerful enough somehow, and suddenly, feeling a hand of terror at her throat, Liz wanted to run away and not hear what he had to say to them.

Bernie introduced himself and Dr. Johanssen asked them to sit down. He hesitated for only an instant, and then did not mince words with them. It was serious. Liz was terrified.

"Yesterday when I saw you, Mrs. Fine, I thought that you had pleurisy. A mild case perhaps. Today, I want to discuss it with you." He swiveled in his chair and pointed the tip of his pen at two spots on her lungs: "I don't like the looks of these." He was honest with her.

"What do they mean?" She could hardly catch her breath.

"I'm not sure. But I'd like to reconsider another symptom you mentioned yesterday. The pain in your hips."

"What does that have to do with my lungs?"

"I think a bone scan may tell us more of what we want to know." He explained the procedure to them, and he had already made arrangements for her at the hospital. It was a simple test, involving an injection of radioactive isotopes to show lesions in the skeleton.

"What do you think it is?" She was feeling panicked and confused, and she wasn't sure she wanted to know. But she had to.

"I'm not sure. The spots on your lungs may indicate a problem elsewhere in your system."

She could barely think all the way to the hospital, absentmindedly clutching Bernie's hand. All he wanted was to get away from her to call his father and there was no way he could leave her. He was with her when they administered the injection. She looked gray and terrified and it was only moderately painful. But it was terrifying as they sat and waited for the doctor to talk to them about his findings.

And his findings were profoundly depressing. They believed that Liz had osteosarcoma, cancer of the bone, and it had already metastasized to her lungs. It explained the pain she had had in her back and hips for the past year, and the frequent breathlessness. But all of it had been attributed to her pregnancy. And instead, she had cancer. A biopsy would have to confirm it, the doctors explained, as Liz and Bernie held hands tightly, and tears rolled down their cheeks. She was still wearing the green hospital gown, as Bernie reached out and took her into his arms, and held her with a feeling of desperation.

Chapter 17

"I don't give a damn! I *won't!*" She was almost hysterical.

"*Listen to me!*" He was shaking her, and they were both crying as they walked along. "I want you to come to New York with me . . ." He tried to fight for calm, for air . . . they had to be sensible . . . cancer didn't always have to mean the end . . . what the hell did this guy know anyway? . . . He himself had recommended them to four other specialists. A bone man, a lung man, a surgeon, and an oncologist. He recommended a biopsy, perhaps followed by surgery, and then radiation or chemotherapy, depending on the advice of the other doctors. He admitted that he himself knew too little about it.

"I won't have chemotherapy. It's horrible. Your hair falls out, I'm going to die . . . I'm going to die . . ." She was sobbing in his arms and he felt as though his guts were going to fall out. They both had to calm down. They *had* to.

"You're not going to die. We're going to fight this thing. Now calm down, dammit, and listen to me! We'll take the kids to New York when I go, and you can see the best men there."

"What'll they do to me? I don't want chemotherapy."

"Just listen to them. No one said you had to do that. This guy isn't sure what you need. For all you know, you have arthritis and he thinks it's cancer." It would have been nice to believe that anyway.

But that wasn't what the lung man said, or the bone man. Or the surgeon. They wanted to do a biopsy. And when Bernie had his father call them, he said to go ahead. The doctors in New York would want that information anyway. And the biopsy told them that Johanssen was right. It was osteosarcoma. But the news was even worse than that. Given the nature of the cells they'd found, and the extent of it, metastasized in both lungs they discovered now, it made no sense to operate. They suggested brief and intense radiation, followed by chemotherapy as soon as possible. And Liz felt as though she had fallen into a nightmare and could not wake up. They had said nothing to Jane, except that Mommy wasn't feeling so great after the baby and they wanted to do some tests. They had no idea how to tell her what had been discovered.

Bernie sat up late at night talking to Liz after the biopsy came back, and she sat in her hospital bed with patches over both breasts where the biopsies had been done. And she had no choice now, she had to wean the baby. He was crying at home, and she was in the hospital, crying in Bernie's arms, trying to express the sorrow she felt, the guilt, the regret, and the terror.

"I feel . . . I feel as though I would poison him if I would nurse him now . . . isn't that terrible? Think of what I've been giving him all this time."

He told her what they both knew anyway. "Cancer isn't contagious."

"How do you know? How do you know I didn't catch it from someone on the street . . . some crazy goddamn germ that flew into me . . . like in the hospital when I had the baby . . ." She blew her nose and looked at him and neither of them could believe the gravity of the situation. It was something that happened to someone else, not to people like them, with a seven-year-old and a baby.

He was calling his father five times a day these days, and he already had everything lined up for her in New York. Bernie talked to him again the following morning before he went to pick her up at the hospital.

"They'll see her as soon as you get in." His father sounded grave, and Ruth was crying beside him.

"Great." Bernie tried to pretend to himself they'd have good news, but he was frightened. "Are they the best?"

"Yes, they are." His father sounded very quiet.

His heart was grieving for his only son and the girl he loved. "Bernie . . . this isn't going to be easy . . . I talked to Johanssen myself yesterday. It seems to be pretty well metastasized." It was a word he hated. But it was new to Bernie. "Is she in pain?"

"No. She just feels very tired."

"Give her our love." She needed that. And their prayers. And when he hung up the phone, Bernie found Jane standing in the bedroom doorway.

"What's wrong with Mommy?"

"She's . . . she's just real tired, sweetheart. Like we told you yesterday. Having the baby just made her get pooped." He smiled, choking on a lump in his throat the size of her elbow, but he put an arm around her anyway. "She'll be okay."

"People don't go to the hospital because they're tired."

"Sometimes they do." He gave her a sunny smile, and a kiss on the tip of her nose. "Mommy's coming home today." He took a breath. It was time to prepare her. "And next week we're all going to see Grandma and Grampa in New York. Won't that be fun?"

"Will Mommy go to the hospital again?" She knew too much. She'd been listening. He could feel it, but he couldn't face it.

"Maybe. Just for a day or two."

"Why?" Her lip trembled and tears filled her eyes. "What does she have?" It was a plaintive wail, as though she knew, as though some spirit in the depths of her knew just how badly her mommy was ailing.

"We just have to love her very much," Bernie said through his own tears as he held the child. The tears fell into his beard as he held her. "Very, very much, sweetheart. . . ."

"I do."

"I know you do. So do I." She saw him crying and dried his eyes with her little hand. They felt like butterflies on his beard.

"You're a wonderful daddy." It brought the tears back to his eyes again and he held her for a long, long time. It was good for both of them, and they had a special secret that afternoon when he picked her up. The secret of a special kind of closeness and love and courage. She was waiting in the car with a bouquet of pink sweetheart roses, and Liz clung to her all the way home, as she and Bernie told her all the funny things Alexander had done that morning. It was as though they both knew that they had to help her now, that they had to keep her alive with their love and their jokes and their funny stories. It was a bond that laced them even tighter than before, and it was an awesome burden.

Liz walked into the baby's room and Alexander woke up and let out a squeal of ecstasy when he saw her. His little legs shot out, and he waved his arms, and Liz picked him up and winced as he hit the spots where the biopsies were.

"Are you going to nurse him, Mommy?" Jane

was standing in the doorway, watching her, the big blue eyes wide and worried.

"No." Liz shook her head sadly. She still had the milk he wanted but she didn't dare feed him anymore, no matter what they said. "He's a big boy now. Aren't you, Alex?" She tried to fight back the tears that came anyway as she held him and turned her back to Jane so she wouldn't see them. Jane walked back to her room quietly and sat holding her doll, staring out the window.

And Bernie was in the kitchen cooking dinner with Tracy. The door was closed. The water was on. And he was crying into a kitchen towel. Tracy patted his shoulder from time to time. She had cried herself when Liz had told her but now she felt she had to have strength for Bernie and the children.

"Can I get you a drink?" He shook his head and she touched his shoulder again as he took a deep breath and looked up at their friend.

"What are we going to do for her?" He felt so helpless, as the tears rolled down his cheeks.

"Everything we can," Tracy answered. "And maybe a miracle will happen. Sometimes it does." The oncologist had said as much, maybe because he didn't have much else to offer. He had talked to them about God and miracles and chemotherapy, and Liz had insisted again that she didn't want it.

"She doesn't want chemotherapy." He was in despair, and he knew he had to pull himself together. It was just the shock of it. The incredible brutality of the blow that had been dealt them.

"Can you blame her for not wanting it?" Tracy looked at him as she made the salad.

"No . . . but sometimes it works . . . for a while anyway." What they wanted, Johanssen had said, was a remission. A long one. Like fifty years maybe, or ten or twenty . . . or five . . . or two . . . or one. . . .

"When are you going to New York?"

"Later this week. My father has everything arranged. And I told Paul Berman, my boss, that I couldn't go to Europe. He understood perfectly. Everyone's been wonderful." He hadn't been to the store for two days and he didn't know how long he'd be gone, but his managers had promised to take care of everything for him.

"Maybe they'll suggest something different in New York."

But they didn't. The doctors there said exactly the same thing. Chemotherapy. And prayers. And miracles. Bernie sat looking at her in the hospital bed, and she already seemed to be shrinking. The dark circles had darkened and she was losing weight. It seemed incredible, like an evil spell that had been cast on them, and he reached out and took her hand. Her lip was trembling terribly and they were both frightened. He didn't hide his tears from her this time. They sat and held hands and cried, and talked about what they felt. It helped that they had each other.

"It's like a bad dream, isn't it?" She tossed her hair back over her shoulder and then realized that it wouldn't be there soon. She had agreed to start chemotherapy when they went back to San Francisco. He had been talking about leaving Wolff's and coming back to New York if they wouldn't bring him back, so she could get care in New York. But his father told him that in truth it didn't make any difference. The doctors were just as good in San Francisco, and it was familiar to her. There was a lot to be said for that. She didn't need to worry about finding an apartment, or a new house, or putting Jane in a new school. And right now they needed to cling to what they had . . . their house . . . their friends . . . even her job. She had talked about that with Bernie too. She was going to keep on working. And the doctor hadn't objected. She was going to get the chemotherapy once a week at first, for a month, and after that once every two weeks, then once every three. The first month would be horrible, but after that she would only be sick for a day or two, and Tracy could substitute for her. The school was willing to let her do that. And they both thought she'd feel better if she didn't sit home moping.

"Do you want to go to Europe with me, when you start feeling better?" She smiled at him. He was so good to her. And the crazy thing was that she didn't feel bad now. All she felt was tired. And she was dying.

"I'm so sorry to do this to you . . . to put you through all this. . . ."

He smiled through his tears. "Now I know you're my wife." He laughed. "You're beginning to sound Jewish."

Chapter 18

"Grandma Ruth?" Her voice was very little in the darkened room as Ruth held her hand. They had just said a prayer for her mommy. Bernie was spending the night at the hospital, and Hattie, Ruth's old housekeeper, was helping with the baby. "Do you think Mommy will be okay?" Her eyes filled and she squeezed Ruth's hand. "You don't think God will take her away, do you?" She let out a horrible gulp as she sobbed, and Ruth bent down to hold her, her own tears falling onto the pillow beside the child's head. It was so wrong, so unfair . . . she was sixty-four years old, and she would so gladly have gone instead of her . . . so young, so beautiful, so much in love with Bernie . . . with these two children who needed her so badly.

"We just have to ask Him to leave her here with us, don't we?"

Jane nodded, hoping that would do the trick,

and then she looked at Grandma Ruth again. "Can I go to temple with you tomorrow?" She knew that their day was Saturday, but Ruth only went once a year, for Yom Kippur. But for this she would make an exception.

"Grampa and I will take you." And the next day, the three of them went to the Westchester Reform Temple in Scarsdale. They left the baby at home with Hattie, and when Bernie came home that night, Jane told him solemnly that she and Grandma and Grampa had gone to temple. It brought tears to his eyes again, but everything did now, everything was so sweet and sad and tender. He held the baby in his arms and he looked so much like Liz, Bernie almost couldn't stand it.

And yet, when she was back with them again, things didn't seem so tragic. She came back from the hospital two days later, and suddenly there were the same bad jokes, the throaty voice he loved, the laughs, the sense of humor. Nothing seemed quite as terrible, and she wouldn't let him get maudlin. She was dreading the chemotherapy, but she was determined not to think about it before she had to.

They went into New York for dinner once, and went to La Grenouille in a limousine he had rented for them, but he could see halfway through dinner that she was absolutely exhausted. And his mother urged him to cut the dinner short and take her home. They were quiet on the way back, and that night in bed she apologized again, and then slowly, gently, she began touching him, and fearfully, he reached out and held her, wanting to make love to her, but afraid to do her any harm. "It's okay . . . the doctors say we can . . ." She whispered to him, and he was horrified at himself when he took her with force and passion, but he was so hungry for her, so hungry to hang onto her, to pull her back to him, as though she were slipping away slowly. And afterwards he cried and clung to her, and then hated himself for it. He wanted to be brave and strong and manly and instead he felt like a little boy, nestled at her breast, needing her so badly. Like Jane, he wanted to cling to her, to make her stay, to beg for a miracle. Maybe the chemotherapy would do that for them.

Grandma took Jane to Schwarz once before they left and bought her an enormous teddy bear and a doll, and she had her pick out something she thought Alexander would like. Jane selected a big clown that rolled and made music. And when they got home, he loved it.

Their last night together was warm and comfortable and touching. Liz insisted on helping Ruth make dinner, and she seemed in better shape than she'd been in a long time, calm, and quiet, and stronger. And afterwards, she touched Ruth's hand and looked into her eyes.

"Thank you for everything. . . ."

Ruth shook her head, wanting not to cry with her, but it was so difficult. After a lifetime of crying for everything, how could one stop for what was really important? But this time, she knew she had to hold back. "Don't thank me, Liz. Just do everything you have to."

"I will." She seemed to have grown older in the last weeks, more mature somehow. "I feel better about it now. I think Bernie does too. It won't be easy, but we'll make it." Ruth nodded, unable to say more, and the next day she and Lou took them to the airport. Bernie carried the baby, and Liz held Jane's hand, and she walked onto the plane unaided, as the elder Fines struggled not to cry. But once the plane was gone, Ruth fell sobbing into her husband's arms, unable to believe their courage, and the evil fate that had befallen people she loved so much. Suddenly it wasn't the Rosengarden's grandson . . . or Mr. Fishbein's father . . . it was her daughter-in-law . . . and Alex and Jane . . . and Bernie. It was so wrong and so unfair and so unkind, and as she cried in her husband's arms she thought her heart would break. She couldn't bear it.

"Come on, Ruth. Let's go home, sweetheart." He took her gently by the hand and they went back to their car, and suddenly she looked at him, realizing that it would be them one day.

"I love you, Lou. I love you very much. . . ." She began to cry again and he touched her cheek as he held open the door for her. It was a terrible time for all of them, and he was so damn sorry for Liz and Bernie.

When they arrived in San Francisco, Tracy was waiting for them with their car, and she drove into the city with them, chatting and laughing and holding the baby close to her.

"Well, it's good to have you guys back." She smiled at her friends but she saw easily that Liz was exhausted. She was to go into the hospital the next day to begin the chemotherapy.

And that night, as she lay in bed, after Tracy went home, Liz rolled over, propped her head up on her elbow, and looked at Bernie. "I wish I were normal again." She said it like a teenager wanting to wish away pimples.

"So do I." He smiled at her. "But you will be one of these days." They were both putting a lot of faith in the chemotherapy. "And if that doesn't work, there's always Christian Science."

"Listen, don't knock it," she said seriously to him. "One of the teachers at school is a Christian Scientist, and it really works sometimes . . ." Her voice trailed off, thinking about it.

"Let's try this first." He was, after all, Jewish and the son of a doctor.

"You think it'll be really horrible?" She looked scared, and he remembered how frightened she had been, and in how much pain, when Alexander was born, but this was very different. This was forever.

"It won't be great." He didn't want to lie to her. "But they said they were going to give you stuff to knock you out. Valium or something. I'll be right there with you." She leaned over and kissed his cheek.

"You know, you're one of the last great husbands."

"Oh yeah? . . ." He rolled over and slid a hand under her bed jacket. She was always cold these days, and she wore his socks to bed. And he made love to her gently this time, feeling all his strength and love go into her, wanting to give her a gift of himself, and she smiled sleepily afterwards. "I wish I could get pregnant again. . . ."

"Maybe you will one day." But that was too much to ask. He would have settled for her life in place of another one, and it made Alexander even more precious to them now. She held him in her arms for a long time that next morning before she went to the hospital, and she had made Jane's breakfast herself and packed her favorite lunch for her. In a way, it was crueler to be doing so much for them. They would miss her more, if something happened.

Bernie drove her to the hospital, and they put her in a wheelchair when she checked in. A student nurse pushed her upstairs as Bernie walked along, holding Liz' hand, and Doctor Johanssen was waiting for them. Liz undressed and put on a hospital gown, and the world looked so sunny outside. It was a beautiful November morning, and she turned to Bernie.

"I wish I didn't have to do this."

"So do I." It was like helping her to the electric chair as she lay down, and he held her hand, and a nurse in what looked like asbestos gloves appeared. The stuff they used was so powerful that it would have burned the nurse's hands, and they were going to put that inside the woman he loved. It was almost more than he could bear but they gave her the IV of Valium first, and she was half asleep when the chemotherapy began. And Johanssen stayed to supervise the treatment. When it was over she lay sleeping peacefully, but by midnight, she was throwing up and desperately ill, and for the next five days her life was a nightmare.

The rest of the month was just as bad, and Thanksgiving was no holiday for them that year. It was almost Christmas before she felt halfway human again, and by then she had no hair and she was rail-thin. But she was home again, and she only had to face the nightmare once every three weeks now, and the oncologist promised it would only make her sick for a day or two. After Christmas vacation she could go back to school to teach again, and Jane was like a different child once she was home, and Alexander was crawling.

The last two months had taken their toll on all of them. Jane cried a lot in school, the teacher said, and Bernie was barking at everyone at the store, and constantly distracted. He was using babysitters to help take care of the baby all day long, but even that wasn't working out. One of them got lost with the baby, another never showed up, and he had to take the baby to a meeting, none of them knew how to cook, and nobody seemed to be eating except Alexander. But as Christmas approached and Liz felt better again, things slowly returned to normal.

"My parents want to come out." He looked at her one night, as they sat in bed. She was wearing a kerchief on her head to cover her baldness and she glanced at him with a sigh and a smile. "Do you feel up to it, sweetheart?" She didn't, but she wanted to see them, and she knew how much it would mean to Jane, and even though he wouldn't admit it, to Bernie. She thought of only a year before, when they had taken Jane to Disneyland and given them a chance to celebrate their anniversary. She had been pregnant then . . . and their whole life had been directed to living, not dying.

She said as much to him and he looked at her angrily. "It is now too."

"Not exactly."

"Bullshit!" All his impotent rage was suddenly directed at her and he couldn't stop it. "What do you think all this chemotherapy is about, or are you giving up now? Christ, I never thought you were a quitter." His eyes filled with tears and he slammed the door as he walked into the bathroom. And he came out twenty minutes later, as she lay quietly in their bed, waiting for him. He looked sheepish as he came to sit next to her and took her hand in his. "I'm sorry I was an asshole."

"You're not. And I love you. I know it's hard on you too." She touched the kerchief on her head without thinking. She hated feeling so ugly, and her head was so round and bumpy. She felt like something in a science fiction movie. "This is awful for everyone. If I was going to die, I should have been hit by a truck, or drowned in the bathtub." She tried to smile, but neither of them thought it was funny, and then suddenly her eyes filled with tears. "I hate being bald." But more than that, she hated knowing she was dying.

He reached for the kerchief and she ducked away from him. "I love you with or without hair." There were tears in his eyes, and hers as well.

"Don't."

"There is no part of you I don't love, or that's ugly." He had discovered that when she gave birth to their son. His mother had been wrong. He hadn't been shocked or disgusted. He was touched, and he loved her more, as he did now. "It's no big deal. So you're bald. One day I will be too. I'm just making up for it now." He stroked the beard and she smiled.

"I love you."

"I love you too . . . and this is about living too." They exchanged a smile. They both felt better again. It was an hourly battle to keep their heads above water. "What'll I tell my parents?"

"Tell them to come out. They can stay at the Huntington again."

"My mother thought Jane might like to go away with them again. What do you think?"

"I don't think she'll want to. Tell them not to be hurt." She was clinging to Liz for dear life, and sometimes cried when she left the room now.

"She'll understand." His mother, who had been

a tower of guilt all his life was suddenly wearing a
halo. He talked to her several times a week and
she had a depth of understanding he had never
found in her before. Instead of torturing him, she
was a source of comfort.

And she was once again when they arrived just
before Christmas and brought mountains of toys
for both the children, and his mother touched Liz
to tears when she brought her the one thing she
wanted. In fact, she brought half a dozen of them.
She closed the door to their room, and advanced
on her, carrying two huge hat boxes.

"What's that?" Liz had been resting, and as
always, tears had slid from her eyes to her pillow,
but she wiped them away quickly as she sat up and
Ruth looked at her nervously, afraid that she
might be offended.

"I brought you a present."

"A hat?"

Ruth shook her head. "No. Something else. I
hope you won't get angry." She had tried to
match the lovely golden hair she remembered but
it hadn't been easy, and as she took the tops off
the boxes, Liz suddenly saw a profusion of wigs, in
different cuts and styles, and all in the same familiar color. She started to laugh and cry all at once,
and Ruth looked at her cautiously. "You're not
mad?"

"How could I be?" She stretched her arms out
to her mother-in-law, and then pulled out the
wigs. There was everything from a short boyish
cut to a long page boy. They were beautifully

made, and Liz was touched beyond words. "I've been wanting to buy one, but I was afraid to go into the store."

"I thought you might be . . . and I thought this might be more fun." Fun . . . what could be fun about losing your hair from chemo? . . . But Ruth had made it better.

Liz went to the mirror and slowly pulled off her kerchief as Ruth looked away. She was such a beautiful girl and so young. It wasn't fair. Nothing was anymore. But she looked up at Liz now, as she stared into the mirror in one of the blond wigs. She had tried the page boy on first and it suited her to perfection.

"It looks wonderful!" Ruth clapped her hands and laughed. "Do you like it?"

Liz nodded and her eyes danced as she looked in the mirror. She looked decent again . . . better than decent. Maybe even pretty. In fact, she felt gorgeous—female again. She suddenly laughed, feeling healthy and young, and Ruth handed her another. "You know, my grandmother was bald. All orthodox women are. They shaved their heads. This just makes you a good Jewish wife." She gently touched Liz' arm then. "I want you to know . . . how much we love you. . . ." If love could have cured her, she would have had the remission they wanted so badly. Ruth had been shocked to see how much weight she'd lost, how thin her face was, how deeply sunk her eyes, and yet she said she was going back to teach after Christmas.

She tried on the rest of the wigs, and they decided on the page boy for her first entrance. She put it on, and changed her blouse. It required something more sophisticated than what she'd been wearing and she walked into the living room, trying to look casual, as Bernie did a double take and stared at her in amazement.

"Where did you get that?" He was smiling. He liked it.

"Grandma Ruth. What do you think?" She asked in an undertone.

"You look great." And he meant it.

"Wait till you see the others." It was a gift that had boosted her morale immeasurably and Bernie was grateful to his mother, even more so as Jane came bounding into the room and stopped dead.

"You got your hair back!" She clapped her hands with delight, and Liz smiled and looked at her mother-in-law.

"Not exactly, sweetheart. Grandma brought me some new hair from New York." She laughed and suddenly Jane giggled.

"She did? Can I see?" Liz nodded and took her in to look in the boxes, and Jane tried on two or three of them herself. They looked funny on her and she and Liz laughed. Suddenly it felt like a party.

They all went out to dinner that night, and like a gift from God, Liz felt better over the holidays. They managed to go out two more times, she even went downtown to see the Christmas trees at Wolff's with Jane and Bernie, and Ruth pretended to disapprove, but Liz knew she really didn't. They had celebrated Chanukah, too, and on Friday they lit the candles before dinner. And her father-in-law's solemn voice as he intoned the prayers seemed right to all of them. Liz closed her eyes and prayed to their God and her own that something would save her.

Chapter 19

Their second anniversary was very different from the first. Tracy invited Jane and Alexander to spend the night with her, and Bernie's parents went to dinner on their own. Liz and Bernie were alone for once, and they spent a quiet evening. He had wanted to take her out, but in the end she had admitted she was too tired. He uncorked a bottle of champagne for her instead, and poured her a glass which she barely sipped as they sat by the fire and talked.

It was almost as if they had made a silent vow not to talk about her sickness. She didn't want to think about that tonight, or the chemotherapy she had to go back for in a week. It was hard enough doing it without talking about it all the time, and she longed to be like everyone else, complaining about her job, laughing over her kids, planning a dinner for friends, and worrying if the dry cleaner could fix her zipper. She longed for simple prob-

lems, and they held hands quietly as they stared
into the fire, moving carefully through the obsta-
cles of all the difficult subjects to avoid . . . it
even hurt to talk about their honeymoon two
years before, although once Bernie reminded her
of how cute Jane had been on the beach. She was
only five then. And now suddenly she was nearly
eight. And Liz surprised him by mentioning
Chandler Scott again.

"You won't forget your promise to me, will
you?"

"What promise was that?" He was pouring
more champagne, even though he knew she
wouldn't drink it.

"I don't ever want that bastard to see Jane. You
promise?"

"I promised you, didn't I?"

"I meant it." She looked worried, and he kissed
her cheek and smoothed away the frown on her
brow with gentle fingers.

"So did I." He had been thinking a lot recently
about adopting Jane, but he was afraid that Liz
wasn't well enough to go through all the legal
hassle. He decided to put it off until she was in
remission and feeling stronger.

They didn't make love that night, but she fell
asleep in his arms by the fire and he carried her to
bed ever so gently, and then lay looking down at
her, feeling his heart break as he thought of the
months to come. They were still praying for a
remission.

On January fifth his parents went back to New

York. His mother offered to stay, but Liz said she was going back to teaching anyway, and even if it was only for three mornings a week, it was going to keep her very busy. She had already had her chemotherapy right after the holidays and she had done well this time. It was a relief to all of them, and she could hardly wait to get back to teaching.

"Are you sure she should?" his mother asked him when she came to see him at the store the day before they left.

"That's what she wants." He wasn't crazy about it either, but Tracy said it would do her good, and maybe she was right. It couldn't do any harm at least and if it was too much for her, she'd have to give it up. But Liz was very insistent.

"What does the doctor say?"

"That it won't hurt her."

"She should rest more." He nodded, he told Liz the same thing himself, and she would look at him with angry eyes, knowing how little time she had left. She wanted to do everything, not sleep her life away.

"We have to let her do what she needs to, Mom. I promised her that." She was extracting a lot of promises from him these days. And he walked his mother downstairs quietly. There wasn't much left to say, and they were both afraid of the words they had to say. It was all so terrible, so incredibly painful.

"I don't know what to say to you, sweetheart." She looked up at her only son with tears in her eyes as they stood in the doorway to Wolff's, with people eddying around them.

"I know, Mom. . . . I know . . ." His eyes were damp and his mother nodded as the tears came and she couldn't control them. A few people glanced at them, wondering what drama they were playing out, but they had their own lives to lead and they hurried on as Ruth looked up at him.

"I'm so sorry. . . ."

He nodded, unable to answer her, touched her arm, and went back upstairs silently with his head bent. His life was a nightmare suddenly and it wouldn't go away no matter what he did to stop it.

It was even worse that night when he took his parents back to the hotel after Liz had insisted on cooking dinner. They were leaving the next morning, and she wanted to cook for them. The food had been wonderful, as it always was, but it was a ghastly strain watching her struggle to do all she had done so effortlessly before. Nothing was effortless for her anymore, not even breathing.

He kissed his mother good night at the hotel. They were going to the airport on their own the next day, and then he turned to shake his father's hand, and their eyes met, and suddenly Bernie couldn't take it a moment longer. He remembered when he had been a little boy and had loved this man . . . when he had looked up to him in his white doctor's coat . . . when they had gone fishing in New England in the summer. . . . Suddenly it all came rushing back to him and he was five years old again . . . and his father, sensing that, put his arms around him as Bernie began to sob, and his mother turned away, almost unable to stand it.

His father walked him slowly outside, and they stood there in the night air for a long, long time, as his father held him.

"It's all right, son, it's all right to cry . . ." And as he said the words, tears slid down his own face onto his son's shoulders.

There was nothing anyone could do for him. And at last they both kissed him goodbye and he thanked them, and when he got back to the house, Liz was already in bed, waiting for him, wearing one of the wigs his mother had brought her. She wore them all the time now and Bernie teased her about them sometimes, secretly disappointed that he hadn't thought of buying them for her himself. She loved them. Not as much as her own hair of course, but they saved her vanity, and it was a subject of constant conversation between her and Jane. "No, Mommy, I like the other one . . . the long one. . . . This one's pretty good." Jane would grin. "You look funny with curly hair." But at least she was no longer scary.

"Were your mom and dad okay, sweetheart?" She looked at Bernie questioningly when he got back. "It took you a long time to take them back to the hotel."

"We had a drink." He smiled, pretending to look guilty instead of sad. "You know how my mother is, she never wants to let go of her baby."

He patted her hand and went to change, and slipped into bed beside her a moment later. But she had already drifted off to sleep, and he listened to the labored breathing beside him. It had been three months since they'd found out that she had cancer, and she was fighting valiantly and the doctor thought the chemotherapy was helping. But in spite of all of that, Bernie thought that she was getting worse. Her eyes grew larger every day, they sunk deeper, her features grew sharper and she lost more weight, and there was no denying now that she was having trouble breathing. But he wanted to hang onto her anyway, for as long as he could, doing whatever they had to do, no matter how difficult it was for her. She had to fight, he told her constantly . . . he wouldn't ever let her leave him.

And that night he slept fitfully, dreaming that she was going on a trip, and he was trying to stop her.

Her teaching seemed to bring some life back to her. She loved "her" children, as she called them. She was only teaching them reading this year. Tracy was teaching them math and another sub was handling the rest of the curriculum. The school had been incredibly flexible about letting Liz reduce her schedule. They cared about her a great deal, and they had been stunned at the news she had told them so bluntly and quietly. And word had traveled around the school fairly rapidly, but it was still being spoken in hushed whispers. Liz didn't want Jane to know yet, and she prayed that none of the children would hear it from their teachers. It was no secret to her colleagues, but she didn't want the children to know yet. She knew she wouldn't be able to come back next year. It was too hard getting up and down stairs, but she was determined to finish out the year, no matter what, and had promised the principal she would, but in March word got out and one of her students looked at her sadly, with tears bright in her eyes, and her clothes disheveled.

"What's up, Nance?" She had four brothers and loved a good fight. Liz looked at her with a special smile and smoothed down her blouse for her. She was a year younger than Jane, who was in third grade now. "You get in a fight with someone?"

The child nodded and stared at her. "I punched Billy Hitchcock in the nose."

Liz laughed. They gave life back to her every day she was there with them. "Why'd you do a thing like that?"

She hesitated, and then jutted out her chin, ready to take the whole world on. "He said that you were dying . . . and I told him he was a big, fat liar!" She started to cry again and used two fists to wipe her eyes as she mixed tears and dirt and left two giant streaks down her cheeks as she looked up at Liz, begging for a denial. "You aren't, are you, Mrs. Fine?"

"Come here, let's talk about this." She pulled up a chair in the empty classroom. It was lunchtime, and Liz had been looking over some papers.

She sat the little girl down next to her, and held her hand. She had wanted this to come much later. "You know, we all have to die sometime. You know that, don't you?" The little hand in hers held fast to her, as though trying to be sure she'd never leave them. She had been the first to make her a present for Alexander the year before. She had knitted him a little blue scarf with holes and knots and dropped stitches everywhere, and Liz had loved it.

Nancy nodded, crying again. "Our dog died last year, but he was real old. My daddy said that if he were a person, he'd have been a hundred and nineteen years old. And you're not that old." She looked worried for a minute. "Are you?"

Liz laughed. "Not quite. I'm thirty. And that's not very old . . . but sometimes . . . sometimes things just happen differently. We all have to go up to God at different times . . . some people even go when they're babies. And a long, long time from now, when you're very old and go up to God, I'll be waiting for you there." She started to choke, and fought back tears of her own. She didn't want to cry, but it was so hard not to. She didn't want to be waiting for anyone. She wanted to be there with them, with Bernie and Jane and Alexander.

And Nancy understood that perfectly. She cried harder and threw her arms around Liz' neck, holding her tight. "I don't want you to go away from us . . . I don't want you to . . ." Her mother drank, and her father traveled a lot. Since kindergarten she had had a passion for Liz, and now she was going to lose her. It wasn't fair. Nothing was anymore. And Liz gave her some cookies she had made as she tried to explain about the chemotherapy and that it was supposed to help her.

"And it might, Nance. I might stick around for a real long time that way. Some people do that for years." And some don't, she thought to herself. She saw the same things Bernie did. And now she hated looking in the mirror. "And I'm going to be here at school all this year, and that's a pretty long time, you know. Why don't you not worry about it for a while? Okay?" Little Nancy Farrell nodded, and eventually went outside to think over what Liz had said, with a handful of her chocolate peanut cookies.

But on the way home in the car that afternoon, Liz felt drained and Jane was staring silently out the window. It was almost as though she were angry at her mother, and just before they got to the house, she snapped her head around and glared at her, her eyes filled with accusation.

"You're going to die, aren't you, Mom?"

Liz was shocked by the suddenness and vehemence of what she said but she knew instantly where it had come from. Nancy Farrell. "Everyone will someday, sweetheart." But it wasn't as easy to put her off as Nancy. They had more at stake between them.

"You know what I mean . . . that stuff . . . it

isn't working, is it? The chemo." She said it like a dirty word as Liz watched her.

"It's helping a little bit." But not enough. They all knew that. And it was making her so damn sick. Sometimes she thought it was killing her more quickly.

"No, it's not." Her eyes said that she thought her mother wasn't trying.

Liz sighed as she parked the car in front of the house. She still drove the same old Ford she'd had when she married Bernie, and she parked it on the street. He used the garage for his BMW. "Baby, this is hard for all of us. And I'm trying very, very hard to get better."

"Then why aren't you?" The enormous blue eyes in the child's face filled with tears and suddenly she crumpled on the seat beside her mother. "Why aren't you better yet? . . . Why? . . ." And then she looked up at her, terrified. "Nancy Farrell says you're dying. . . ."

"I know, sweetheart, I know." Her own tears rolled down her face as she held Jane close to her. And Jane could hear the labored breathing. "I don't know what to say to you. One day everyone has to die, and maybe it won't happen to me for a long time. But it could. It could happen to anyone. Someone could drop a bomb on us while we're sitting here."

She looked up at her mother and sobbed raggedly. "I'd like that better. . . . I want to die with you. . . ."

Liz squeezed her so tight it hurt. "No, you

don't. . . . Don't ever say a thing like that. . . . You have a long, long life to live. . . ." But Liz was only thirty.

"Why did this have to happen to us?" She echoed the question they all asked themselves, but there was no answer.

"I don't know . . ." Her voice was barely more than a whisper, as they sat in the car, together, holding each other tight, waiting for the answer.

Chapter 20

In April, Bernie had to decide whether or not he would go to Europe. He had hoped to take Liz along, but it was obvious she couldn't go with him. She didn't have the strength to go anywhere now. It was a major venture to go to Sausalito to visit Tracy. She was still going to school, but only twice a week now.

And he called Paul Berman to tell him. "I hate to let you down, Paul. I just don't want to go away right now."

"I understand perfectly." He sounded bereft for him. It was a tragedy beyond words, and it hurt him each time he spoke to Bernie. "We'll send someone else this time." It was the second time he had had to skip Europe, but they were being very supportive of him. And in spite of the trauma he was going through, he was doing a fine job at the San Francisco store, as Paul said gratefully. "I don't know how you do it, Bernard. If you need a leave of absence, tell us."

"I will. Maybe in a few months, but not now." He didn't want to be working when she neared the end, if it came that soon, although it was hard to predict that sometimes. Sometimes she seemed better for a few days, or she would be markedly more cheerful, and then suddenly she'd be much worse again, and then just as he began to panic, she would fool him by appearing almost normal. It was torture dealing with it, because he could never figure out if the chemo was working and she was finally in remission and would be with them for a long, long time, or if she wouldn't last more than a few weeks or months. And the doctor couldn't tell him that either.

"How do you feel about being out there now? I don't want to press to keep you there under these circumstances, Bernard." He had to be fair to them, and Bernie had been like his son for years. He had no right to force them to stay in California if his wife was terminal. But Bernie surprised him. He had been open with him from the first, and had told him when they found out Liz had cancer. It had been a terrible shock for everyone. It was impossible to believe that the beautiful little blonde he had danced with at her wedding only two years before was dying.

"To be honest with you, Paul, I don't want to go anywhere right now. If you can have someone else keep an eye on the import lines for me, and go over there twice a year, that would be great. But right now we don't want to go anywhere. This is home to Liz, and I don't want to uproot her. I don't think it would be fair to her." They had thought about it a lot, and that was their conclusion. Liz had told him point-blank she didn't want to leave San Francisco. She didn't want to be a burden on his parents, or him, didn't want Jane to have to face a new school, new friends, and it was comforting to Liz to be near the people she knew right now, and especially Tracy. She even took comfort in seeing Bill and Marjorie Robbins more than she used to.

"I understand that perfectly." He had been in California exactly three years, twice the length of time Bernie had hoped to spend in California, but it didn't matter to him now.

"I just can't go anywhere right now, Paul."

"That's fine. Let me know if you change your mind, and I'll start looking for someone to take on the San Francisco store. We miss you in New York. In fact"—he glanced at his calendar, hoping Bernie could make it—"is there any chance you could come to the board meeting next week?"

Bernie frowned. "I'll have to talk to Liz." She didn't have chemo that week, but still, he hated to leave her. "I'll see. When is it?" Paul gave him the dates and he jotted them down.

"You don't have to stay in town for more than three days. You can fly in Monday, and go home Wednesday night, or Thursday if you can stay that long. But I understand, whatever you decide."

"Thank you, Paul." As usual, Paul Berman was being wonderful to him. It just frustrated everyone that there was so little they could do. And that night he asked Liz how she felt about his going to New York for a few days. He even asked if she would come, but she shook her head with a tired smile.

"I can't, sweetheart. I've got too much to do at school." But it wasn't that, and they both knew it. And in two weeks it was Alexander's birthday, and she would see his mother then anyway. His father couldn't leave his practice again, but Ruth had promised to come out. She was coming out for the Big Event, and to see Liz.

But when Bernie came back from New York, he saw the same thing she saw when she arrived. How rapidly Liz was changing. By leaving her for only a few days, he got enough distance to realize just how bad it was. And the night he got home, he locked himself in the bathroom and cried into the big white towels she kept so immaculate for him. He was terrified she would hear him, but he just couldn't stand it. She looked pale and weak, and she had lost more weight. He begged her to eat, and brought home every possible treat he could think of, from strawberry tarts to smoked salmon, from the gourmet shop at Wolff's, but to no avail. She was losing her appetite, and she had dropped to less than ninety pounds by the time Alexander's birthday came. Ruth was shocked when she saw her when she came out, and she had to pretend that she didn't notice. But the tiny shoulders felt even more frail than they had before as the two women kissed at the airport, and Bernie had to get a motorized cart to get her to the baggage claim. She could never have walked that far, and she refused to be pushed in a wheelchair.

They chatted about everything except what really mattered on the drive home, and Ruth felt as though she were desperately treading water. She had brought an enormous rocking horse on springs for Alexander and another doll for Jane, both from Schwarz, and she could hardly wait to see the children, but she was deeply troubled by Liz, and amazed as she watched her cook dinner that night. She was still cooking and cleaning house, and teaching school, she was the most remarkable woman Ruth had ever seen, and it broke her heart to see the struggle Liz engaged in daily, just to stay alive. Ruth was still there when she had her next chemo treatment, and she stayed with the children while Bernie stayed at the hospital with Liz overnight. They rolled a cot into the room, and he slept beside her.

Alexander looked a lot the way Bernie had as a little boy, and he was a chubby, happy child. It seemed impossible to believe that he had arrived only a year before, and now this tragedy had struck him. And as Ruth put him to bed that night, she left the room with tears streaming from her eyes, thinking that he would never know his mother.

"When are you coming to New York to visit us again?" Ruth asked Jane as they sat down to a game of Parcheesi. Jane smiled at her hesitantly. She loved Grandma Ruth. But she couldn't imagine going anywhere for a while. "Not until

Mommy is better" was the party line, but Jane didn't say that. "I don't know, Grandma. We're going to Stinson Beach as soon as school gets out. Mommy wants to go there to rest. She's tired from teaching." They both knew she was tired from dying, but it was too frightening to say that.

Bernie had rented the same house they'd had before, and the plan was to go for three months this year, to help Liz regain whatever strength she could. The doctor had suggested that she not renew her contract at school, because it was too much for her. And she didn't argue with him. She just told Bernie she thought it was a good idea. It would give her more time to spend with him and Jane and the baby. And Bernie went along with it. But they were all anxious to go to the beach. It was as though they could turn the clock back by going there. And at the hospital, Bernie watched her as she slept, and he touched her face, and then gently held her hand as she stirred sleepily and smiled up at him, and for a moment his heart gave a leap, she looked as though she were dying.

"Something wrong?" She frowned at him as she raised her head, and he fought back tears as he smiled casually.

"You doing okay, sweetheart?"

"I'm fine." She dropped her head onto her pillow again, but they both knew that the chemicals they were using were so powerful that she could sustain a fatal heart attack just from the treatment. They had been warned of that from the beginning. But there was no choice. She had to do it.

She went back to sleep, and he went out to the hall and called home. He didn't want to do it from the room, for fear that he would wake her. And he had left her with a nurse watching her. He was used to the hospital by now. Too much so. It almost seemed normal to him. Things didn't shock him as they once had. And he longed to be on the floor they had been on only a year before, downstairs on two, having another baby . . . not here among the dying.

"Hi, Mom. How's it going?"

"Everything's fine, dear." She glanced across the room at Jane. "Your daughter is beating me at Parcheesi. Alexander just went to sleep. He's so cute. He drank the whole bottle, gave me a big smile, and went right to sleep in my arms. He didn't even move when I put him down." It was all so normal, except that Liz should have been telling him that and not his mother. He should have been at the store for a meeting, and she should have been telling him that all was well at home. Instead, she was in the hospital being poisoned by chemotherapy, and his mother was watching the children. "How does she feel?" She lowered her voice so Jane wouldn't be as aware of the conversation, but she was listening intently anyway, so much so that she moved Ruth's man on the Parcheesi board instead of her own. Later she would tease her about it and accuse her of cheating. She knew why it had happened, but she needed a little levity in her life. There wasn't much of that these days. And she was only eight years old. But there was a profound sadness about the child, just under the surface, and it was almost impossible to cheer her.

"She's all right. She's asleep now. We should be home by lunchtime tomorrow."

"We'll be here. Bernie, is there anything you need? Are you hungry?" It was odd seeing his mother so domestic. In Scarsdale she left everything to Hattie. But these were unusual times, for all of them. Especially Liz and Bernie.

"I'm fine. Give Jane a kiss for me, and I'll see you tomorrow, Mom."

"Good night, darling. Give Liz our love when she wakes up."

"Is Mommy okay?" Jane turned to Ruth with terror in her eyes as Ruth crossed the room to give her a hug.

"She's fine, darling, and she sent you her love. And she'll be home in the morning." She thought it would be more reassuring if the love came from Liz and not Bernie.

But in the morning, Liz awoke with a new pain. Suddenly she felt as though all of the ribs on one side were breaking. It was a sudden sharp pain that had never happened before, and she reported it to Dr. Johanssen, who called the oncologist in and the bone man. And they sent her upstairs for an X ray and another bone scan before she went home.

The news was not good when they got it a few hours later. The chemotherapy wasn't working. She had metastasized further. They let her go home, but Johanssen told Bernie that it was the beginning of the end. From now on, the pain would increase and they would do what they could to help her control the pain, but eventually very little would help her. Johanssen told him this in a little office down the hall from her room, and Bernie pounded his fist on the desk right under the doctor's nose.

"What the hell do you mean, there's very little you can do to help her? What is that supposed to mean, dammit!?" The doctor understood perfectly. He had every right to be angry, at the fates that had struck her down and the doctors who couldn't help her. "What do you goddamn guys do all day long? Take out splinters and lance boils on people's asses? The woman is dying of cancer and you're telling me there's very little you can do for the pain?" He began to sob as he sat across the desk staring at Johanssen. "What are we going to do for her . . . Oh God . . . somebody help her . . ." It was all over. And he knew it. And they were telling him there was very little they could do for her. She was going to die a death of agonizing pain. It wasn't right. It was the worst travesty of everything he believed that he had ever known. He wanted to shake someone until they told him that something could be changed, that Liz could be helped, that she would live, that it was all a terrible mistake and she didn't have cancer.

He laid his head down on the desk and cried, and feeling desperately sorry for him and totally helpless, Dr. Johanssen waited, and in a moment, he went to get him a glass of water. He handed it to Bernie with sad Nordic eyes and shook his head. "I know how terrible it is, and I'm so sorry, Mr. Fine. We'll do everything we can. I just wanted you to understand our limitations."

"What does that mean?" Bernie's eyes were those of a dying man. He felt as though his heart was being torn from him.

"We'll start her on Demerol pills, or Percodan if she prefers. And eventually, we'll move her to injections. Dilaudid, Demerol, morphine if that works better for her. She'll get increasingly large doses and we'll keep her as comfortable as we can."

"Can I give her the shots myself?" He'd do anything to ease the pain.

"If you like, or you may want a nurse for her eventually. I know you have two small children."

He suddenly thought of their summer plans. "Do you think we'd be able to go to Stinson Beach, or do you think we should stay closer to the city?"

"I see no harm in going to the beach. It might do you all good to have a change of scene, especially Liz, and you're only half an hour away. I go there myself sometimes. It's good for the soul."

Bernie nodded grimly, and set down the glass of water the doctor had given him. "She loves it."

"Then by all means take her."

"What about her teaching?" Suddenly their whole life had to be thought out again. And it was still spring. She had weeks more of school. "Should she quit now?"

"That's entirely up to her. It won't do her any harm, if that's what you're afraid of. But she may not feel up to it if the pain bothers her too much. Why don't you let her set her own pace." He stood up, and Bernie sighed.

"What are you going to tell her? Are you going to tell her that it's in her bones?"

"I don't think I have to. I think she knows from the pain that the disease is advancing. I don't think we need to demoralize her with these reports"—he looked at Bernie questioningly—"unless you feel we should tell her." Bernie was quick to shake his head, wondering how much more bad news they could take, or if they were doing the wrong thing. Maybe he should take her to Mexico for laetrile, or put her on a macrobiotic diet, or go to Lourdes, or the Christian Science Church. He kept hearing remarkable tales of people who had been healed of cancer through outlandish diets, or hypnosis or faith, and what they were trying was obviously not working. But he also knew that Liz didn't want to try the other stuff. She didn't want to go haywire and run all over the world on a wild-goose chase. She wanted to be home with her husband and her kids, teaching at the school where she had taught for years. She only wanted to go so far, and she wanted her life to remain as close as possible to what it had been when it was normal.

"Hi, sweetheart, all set?" She was dressed and

waiting in her room, in a new wig his mother had brought out. This one looked so real he couldn't even tell it wasn't her hair, and other than the dark circles under her eyes and the fact that she was so thin, she looked very pretty. She was wearing a light blue shirtwaist dress and matching espadrilles and the blond hair of the wig cascaded over her shoulders much the way her own hair would have.

"What did they tell you?" She looked worried. She knew something was wrong. The ribs hurt too much, and it was a sharp pain like nothing she'd ever had before.

"Nothing much. Nothing new. The chemo seems to be working."

Liz looked up at her doctor. "Then why do my ribs hurt so much?"

"Have you been picking up the baby a lot?" He smiled at her, and she nodded, thinking back. She carried him all the time. He wasn't walking yet, and he always wanted to be carried.

"Yes."

"And how much does he weigh?"

She smiled at the question. "The pediatrician wants to put him on a diet. He weighs twenty-six pounds."

"Does that answer your question?" It didn't, but it was a noble attempt and Bernie was grateful to him.

The nurse wheeled her to the lobby and Liz left with her arm tucked in Bernie's. But she was walking more slowly now, and he noticed that she winced when she got into the car.

"Is the pain very bad, baby?" She hesitated and then nodded. She could barely speak. "Do you think your Lamaze breathing would help?" It was a stroke of genius and they tried it on the way home, and she said it gave her some relief. And she had the pills with her that the doctor had prescribed for her.

"I don't want to take them till I have to. Maybe at night."

"Don't be a hero."

"You're the hero, Mr. Fine." She leaned over and kissed him gently.

"I love you, Liz."

"You're the best man in the world . . . I'm sorry to put you through all this . . ." It was so hard on everyone, and she knew it. It was hard on her, too, and she hated it, but she also hated it for them, and once in a while, she even hated them because they weren't dying.

He drove her home and helped her up the steps, and when they arrived, Jane and his mother were waiting. Jane was looking worried because it was so late and they weren't home yet, but the bone scan and the X rays had taken a long time. And it was four o'clock by the time they got home, and Jane was haranguing Bernie's mother.

"She *always* comes home in the morning, Grandma. Something's wrong, I *know* it." She made Ruth call, but by then Liz was on her way home, and Ruth looked at Jane knowingly as the front door opened.

"See!" But what she saw and Jane didn't was that Liz looked much weaker than she had before and she seemed to be in pain although she didn't admit it.

But she refused to cut down her teaching. She was determined to finish the year, no matter what, and Bernie didn't argue with her about it, although Ruth told him he was crazy when she dropped in on him at the store on her last day in San Francisco.

"She doesn't have the strength. Can't you see that?"

He shouted back at her in his office. "Dammit, Mom, the doctor said it wouldn't hurt her."

"It'll kill her!"

And then suddenly the rage he felt spent itself on his mother.

"No, it won't! The *cancer* is going to kill her! That's what's going to kill her, that goddamn rotten disease that's rotting her whole body . . . that's what's going to kill her and it doesn't make a damn bit of difference if she sits home and waits or goes to school or has chemotherapy or doesn't or goes to Lourdes, it's *still* going to *kill* her." The tears rushed into his throat like a bursting dam and he turned away from his mother and paced the room. He stood with his back to her finally, looking blindly out the window. "I'm sorry." It was the voice of a broken man, and it tore his mother's heart out to hear him. She walked slowly to where he stood and put her hands on his shoulders.

"I'm sorry . . . I'm so sorry, sweetheart . . . this shouldn't happen to anyone, and not to people you love, especially. . . ."

"It shouldn't even happen to people you hate." There was no one he would have visited this on. No one. He turned slowly to face her. "I keep thinking of what's going to happen to Jane and the baby. . . . What are we going to do without her?" The tears filled his eyes again. He felt as though he had been crying for months and he had. It was six months since they'd found out, six months as they slid into the abyss, praying for something to stop them.

"Do you want me to stay out here for a while? I can. Your father would understand perfectly. In fact, he suggested it to me last night when I called him. Or I can take the children home with me, but I don't think that would be fair to them or Liz." She had grown to be such a decent, sensible woman, it amazed him. Gone was the woman who had given him bulletins on Mrs. Finklestein's gallstones all his life, the woman who had threatened to have a heart attack every time he dated a girl who wasn't Jewish. He smiled, thinking back to the night at Côte Basque when he had told her he was marrying a Catholic named Elizabeth O'Reilly.

"Remember that, Mom?" They both smiled. It had been two and a half years before, and it felt like a lifetime.

"I do. I keep hoping you'll forget it." But the memory only made him smile now. "What about my staying out here to give you kids a hand?" He was thirty-seven years old and he didn't feel like a kid. He felt a hundred.

"I appreciate the offer, Mom, but I think it's important to Liz to maintain things as normally as she can. We're going to move to the beach as soon as school lets out, and I'll commute. In fact, I'm taking six weeks off till the middle of July, and I'll take more if I have to. Paul Berman has been very understanding."

"All right." She nodded sensibly. "But if you want me, I'll be on the next plane. Is that clear?"

"Yes, ma'am." He saluted, and then gave her a hug. "Now go do some shopping. And if you have time, maybe you could pick something nice out for Liz. She's down to preteen sizes now." There was nothing left of her. She weighed eighty-five pounds, from a hundred and twenty. "But she'd love something new. She doesn't have the energy to shop for herself now." Or for Jane, but he brought home boxes and boxes of clothes for the children. The manager of the department had a major crush on Jane and hadn't stopped sending Alexander presents since before he was born. And right now Bernie appreciated the attention they were getting. He was so distracted himself that he felt as though he weren't doing either of them justice. He felt as though he had barely looked at the baby since he was six months old, and he snapped at Jane constantly, only because she was there, and he loved her, and they both felt so helpless. It was a hard time for everyone, and Bernie was sorry they hadn't gone to a shrink, as Tracy had suggested. Liz had rejected the idea out of hand, and now he was sorry.

The worst moment of all came the next day when Ruth left for the airport. She stopped at the house first, in the morning before Liz left for school. Tracy picked Jane up every day now, and Bernie had already left for work. But Liz was waiting for the sitter so she could leave for school, and Alexander was down for his morning nap. Liz went to the door, and for a moment the two women stood in the doorway knowing why she had come. There was no pretense as their eyes met, and then Liz reached out and hugged her.

"Thank you for coming. . . ."

"I wanted to say goodbye to you. I'll be praying for you, Liz."

"Thank you." She couldn't say more as the tears filled her eyes and she looked at Ruth. "Take care of them for me, Grandma . . ." It was only a whisper . . . "And take care of Bernie."

"I promise. Take care of yourself. Do everything they tell you." She squeezed the frail shoulders and noticed suddenly that Liz was wearing the dress she had bought her the day before. "We love you, Liz . . . very, very much. . . ."

"I love you too." She held her for one more minute and then turned to leave, with a last wave, as Liz stood in the doorway, watching the cab pull away. Ruth waved for as long as she could see her.

Chapter 21

Liz managed to hang onto her classes until the end of school. Bernie and the doctor were amazed that she could do it. She had to take the Demerol every afternoon now and Jane complained that she slept all the time, but she didn't know how to voice the complaints that she really felt. The real complaint was that her mother was dying.

The last day of school was June ninth, and Liz went in one of the new dresses Ruth had bought her before she left. She talked to them all the time on the phone, and Ruth told her funny stories about the people in Scarsdale.

Liz drove Jane to school herself on the last day, and Jane looked at her happily. Her mother looked wide-eyed and alert and beautiful, just like she had before, only thinner, and they were moving to Stinson Beach the next day. She could hardly wait. And she scampered off to her own classroom in a pink dress and black patent-leather shoes that Grandma Ruth had helped her pick out for the occasion. There was going to be a party with cakes and cookies and milk before dismissal.

And when Liz walked into her classroom, she closed the door quietly and turned to look at her students. They were all there, twenty-one little clean shining faces, bright eyes and expectant smiles, and she knew for certain that they loved her. And she knew just as certainly that she loved them. And she had to say goodbye to them now. She couldn't just leave them, disappear without explaining. She turned and drew a big heart on the blackboard with pink chalk and they giggled.

"Happy Valentine's Day, everybody!" She looked happy today, and she was. She had completed something that meant a great deal to her. It was her gift to them, and herself, and to Jane.

"It's not Valentine's Day!" Bill Hitchcock announced. "It's Christmas!" Ever the wise guy and she laughed.

"Nope. Today is my Valentine's Day to you. This is my chance to tell you how much I love you." She felt a lump rise in her throat and she knew she couldn't let it. "I want everyone to be very quiet for a little while. I have a Valentine for everyone . . . and then we're going to have a party of our own . . . before the other party!" They began to look intrigued and sat as still as they could, considering it was the last day. She called them up, one by one, and handed them each a Valentine she had made, which told them what she loved best about them, their skills, and their best features, and their achievements. She reminded each one of how well they had done, even if it was only at sweeping the playground. She reminded each one of the fun they had had, and each Valentine was covered with cutouts and pictures and funny sayings that were important to each child, and they sat back, a little awed, holding their Valentines like rare gifts, which they were. It had taken her months and the last of her strength to make them.

And then she pulled out two trays of heart-shaped cupcakes and another tray of beautifully decorated cookies. She had made them for everyone, and she hadn't even told Jane. She had just told her that it was for the main party. And she had done some for them, too, but these were special. These were for "her" second graders.

"And the last thing I'm going to say to you is how much I love you, how proud I am of how wonderful you've been all year . . . and how well I know you'll do in third grade next year with Mrs. Rice."

"Won't you be here anymore, Mrs. Fine?" a little voice piped up from the back row, and a little boy with black hair and dark eyes looked at her sadly, clutching his Valentine in one hand, and his cupcake with the other. It was so beautiful he didn't even want to eat it.

"No, Charlie. I won't. I'm going away for a while." The tears came anyway. "And I'm going to miss you all terribly. But I'll see you again one day. Each one of you. Remember that . . ." She took a deep breath and didn't try to hide the tears anymore. "And when you see Jane, my little girl, give her a kiss from me." There was a loud sob in the front row. It was Nancy Farrell, and she ran up and threw her arms around Liz' neck.

"Please don't go, Mrs. Fine . . . We love you. . . ."

"I don't want to, Nancy. I really, really don't . . . but I think I have to . . ." And then, one by one, they came up and she kissed them and held each one of them. "I love you. Each and every one of you." And with that, the bell sounded, and she took a deep breath and looked at them. "I think that means it's time to go to the party." But they were a solemn little group, and Billy Hitchcock asked if she would visit them. "If I can, Billy." He nodded, and they filed into the hall more neatly than they had all year, with their goodies in little bags, and their Valentines. And they looked at her, as she smiled at them. She was a part of them forever. And as she stood watching them, Tracy came by, and sensed what had happened. If nothing else, she knew Liz' last day would be hard on her.

"How'd it go?" She whispered.

"Okay, I guess." She blew her nose and wiped her eyes, and her friend gave her a warm hug.

"Did you tell them?"

"More or less. I said I was leaving. But I think I said it. Some of them understood it."

"That's a nice gift to give them, Liz, instead of just disappearing from their lives."

"I couldn't have done that." She couldn't do it to anyone. Which was why she had appreciated Ruth coming by the house on the way to the airport. It was a time to say goodbyes, and she didn't want to be cheated of the chance to say them. She had a difficult time leaving the teachers when she left the school, and she was exhausted as she and Jane drove home later that morning. Jane was so quiet that it frightened her and she suspected that she might have heard about her "Valentine party" and resented it. She was still trying not to face what was coming.

"Mommy?" It was the most solemn little face Liz had ever seen as she turned off the car and looked at her outside their house.

"Yes, sweetheart?"

"You're still not getting better, are you?"

"Maybe a little." She wanted to pretend, for her sake, but they both knew she was lying.

"Can't they do something special?" After all, she was such a special person. Jane was eight years old and she was losing the mother she loved. Why wouldn't anyone help her?

"I feel okay." Jane nodded, but the tears poured down her cheeks as Liz whispered hoarsely. "I'm so sorry to have to leave you. But I'll always be near you, watching over you and Daddy and Alex." Jane hurled herself into her mother's arms, and it was a long time before they got out of the car and went inside arm in arm. Jane almost looked bigger than her mother.

That afternoon Tracy came to take Jane out for

an ice cream cone and a walk in the park, and she left with a lighter step than Liz had seen in months, and she herself felt better, and closer to the child than she had since it had all begun. It wasn't easier, but it was better.

And that afternoon she sat down with four pieces of paper, and wrote a letter to each of them, not a long one, but she told each of the people she loved how much she loved them, and why, and how much they meant to her, and how sorry she was to leave them. There was a letter for Bernie, and Ruth, and Jane, and Alexander. The one to him was the hardest of all because he would never even have known her.

She slipped the letters into her Bible, which she kept in a dresser drawer, and she felt better after she had done it. It had been on her mind for a long time. And now it was done. And that night, when Bernie came home, they packed for Stinson Beach, and everyone was in a festive mood when they left the next morning.

Chapter 22

It was three weeks later, on the first of July, that she was scheduled to come back to town for another treatment, and for the first time she refused. The day before she told Bernie she didn't want to, and at first he panicked, and then he called Johanssen and asked him what to do about it.

"She says she's happy here and she wants to be left alone. Do you think she's giving up?" He had waited till she had gone for a walk with Jane. They would walk down to the water, and sit looking at the surf, and sometimes Jane carried the baby. Liz hadn't wanted any help at the beach, and she was still cooking and taking care of Alexander as best she could. And Bernie was there to help her all the time, and Jane loved helping with the baby.

"She might be," the doctor answered. "And I can't really tell you that forcing her to come in for chemo is going to make a lot of difference. Maybe it won't do her any harm to take a week off. Why don't we postpone it till next week?"

He suggested it to Liz that afternoon, admitting that he had called the doctor and she scolded him, but she laughed when she did it. "You're getting sneaky in your old age, you know that?" She leaned over and kissed him, and he remembered the happy times and the first time he had come to the beach to see her.

"Remember when you sent me the bathing suits, Daddy? I still have them!" She loved them so much she would never give them away, even though she'd long since outgrown them. She was going on nine. And it was such a difficult time to be losing her mother. Alexander was fourteen months old, and on the day Liz would have been getting chemotherapy, he began walking. He lurched forward on the beach, and teetered toward Liz squealing in the sea breeze as they all laughed. And she looked at Bernie with victory.

"See! I was right not to go today!" But she had agreed to go the following week, "maybe." She was in pain now, much of the time. But she still controlled it with pills. She didn't want to resort to shots yet. She was afraid that if she used the stronger medication too soon, it wouldn't work when she'd need it. She had been honest about it with Bernie.

And that night, after the baby walked, he asked her if she wanted to see Bill and Marjorie Robbins. He called but they were out, and instead she called Tracy, just to chat. They talked for a long time and laughed a lot. And she was smiling when she hung up. She loved Tracy.

On Saturday night she cooked them dinner, their favorite, steak. He did the barbecue, and she made baked potatoes and asparagus and hollandaise, and she made hot fudge sundaes for dessert. And Alexander dove into the fudge and smeared it all over his face while they laughed. She hadn't served his hot so he wouldn't burn himself and Jane reminded Bernie of the banana split he had bought her when she got lost at Wolff's. It seemed to be a time for remembering for all of them . . . Hawaii . . . their joint honeymoon . . . the wedding . . . their first summer at Stinson Beach . . . the first opera opening . . . first trip to Paris. . . . Liz talked to him all night that night, remembering all of it, and the next day she was in too much pain to get up, and he begged Johanssen to come and see her. Remarkably, he did, and Bernie was grateful to him. He gave her a shot of morphine, and she fell asleep with a smile, and woke again late that afternoon. Tracy had come to help him with the kids and she was out running with them on the beach, with Alexander in a backpack she had brought just for the occasion.

The doctor had left more medication for Liz, and Tracy knew how to administer the shots. It was a blessing having her there. And Liz didn't even wake up at dinnertime. The children ate quietly, and went to bed, and Liz suddenly called out to Bernie at midnight.

"Sweetheart? . . . Where's Jane?" He'd been reading and was surprised at how alert Liz looked.

She looked as though she'd been awake all day and hadn't been sleeping or in pain. It was a relief to see her looking so well. She didn't even look as thin to him as she had before, and he suddenly wondered if this was the beginning of remission. But it was the beginning of something else and he didn't know it.

"Jane's in bed, sweetheart. Want something to eat?" She looked so well, he would have brought her the dinner she had missed, but she shook her head with a smile.

"I want to see her."

"Now?"

Liz nodded and looked as though it were urgent, and feeling a little foolish, he put his robe on and tiptoed past Tracy asleep on the couch. She had decided not to go home after all, in case Liz needed a shot during the night, or Bernie needed her to help with the children in the morning.

Jane stirred for a moment as he kissed her hair and then her cheek and then she opened an eye and looked at Bernie. "Hi, Daddy," she whispered sleepily and then sat up quickly. "Is Mommy okay?"

"She's fine. But she misses you. Want to come give her a good-night kiss?" Jane looked pleased to be called for something so important. She got out of bed immediately, and followed him to their room, where Liz looked wide awake and was waiting for her.

"Hi, baby." She spoke in a strong, clear voice, and her eyes were bright as Jane bent to kiss her.

She thought her mother had never looked more beautiful and she looked better to her too.

"Hi, Mommy. Are you feeling better?"

"Much." She didn't even have the pain anymore. For the moment nothing hurt her. "I just wanted to tell you that I love you."

"Can I get into bed with you?" She looked hopeful and Liz smiled and pulled back the covers.

"Sure." It was then that one saw how painfully thin she was, but her face looked as though it were filling out again. At least tonight anyway.

They whispered and chatted for a little while and eventually Jane began to fall asleep, and she opened her eyes one last time and smiled at Liz, who kissed her once more and told her how much she loved her. And then she fell asleep in her mother's arms and Bernie carried her back to her bed, and when he came back, Liz wasn't in bed. He looked in the bathroom and she wasn't there and then he heard her in the room next to theirs, and he found her leaning over Alexander's crib, stroking his soft blond curls. "Good night, pretty one . . ." He was such a beautiful baby, and she tiptoed back to their room quietly as Bernie watched her.

"You ought to get some sleep, sweetheart. You're going to be exhausted tomorrow." But she looked so alert and so alive and she snuggled into his arms as they whispered. And he held her and stroked her breast and she purred and told him how much she loved him. It was as though she needed to reach out to each of them, to hang onto life, or perhaps to let go of it. She was just falling asleep when the sun came up. She and Bernie had talked almost all night, and he drifted off to sleep just as she did, holding her close to him, and feeling her warmth beside him. She opened her eyes once more, and saw him drifting off happily, and she smiled to herself and closed her eyes. And when Bernie awoke the next morning, she was gone. She had died quietly, in her sleep, in his arms. And she had said goodbye to each of them before she left them. He stood looking down at her for a long, long time, as she lay sleeping in the bed. It was difficult to believe that she wasn't sleeping. He had shaken her at first . . . and touched her hand . . . and then her face . . . and he had known, as a great sob wrenched from him and he locked their bedroom door from the inside so no one could come in, and slid open the glass windows that led to the beach. He let himself out and quietly closed the door and ran for a long, long time, feeling her next to him . . . running . . . and running . . . and running . . .

And when he came back, he walked into the kitchen, and found Tracy giving the kids breakfast. He looked at her, and she started chatting, and then suddenly she knew, and she stopped, looking at him, and he nodded. And he looked down at Jane, and sat down next to her, and he took her in his arms and told her the worst thing she would ever hear from him or anyone else. Ever.

"Mommy's gone, sweetheart. . . ."

"Gone where? . . . To the hospital again? . . ." She pulled away from him to see his face and then she took a sharp breath as she understood and she started to cry in his arms. It was a morning they would all remember for a lifetime.

Chapter 23

Tracy took the children home after breakfast and the people from Halsted's funeral parlor came at noon. Bernie sat alone in the house, waiting for them, with the bedroom door still locked, and finally, he went back through the sliding doors, and sat there with her, holding her hand, waiting for them to come. It was the last time they'd be alone, the last time they'd be in bed, the last time they'd be anything, but there was no point hanging onto it, he kept telling himself. She was already gone. But as he looked down at her and kissed her fingers, she didn't feel gone to him. She was part of his soul and his heart, and his life. And he knew she always would be. He heard the car from Halsted's drive up, and he unlocked the door and went out to meet them. He couldn't watch while they covered her up and took her out. He spoke to the man in the living room, and told him what he wanted to arrange. He said he'd be

back in town by the end of the afternoon. He had
to pack up the house and go back to town. The
man said he understood, and he gave Bernie his
card. Everything was going to be made as easy as
possible for him. Easy. What was easy about losing his wife, the woman he loved, the mother of
his children?

Tracy had called Dr. Johanssen for him, and he
called the house owners himself. He was giving up
the house that afternoon. He didn't want to come
back to the beach again. It would have been too
painful for him. There were suddenly so many
details to arrange, and none of it mattered anyway. The man made such a fuss about whether the
box was mahogany or metal or pine, lined in pink,
blue, or green, who gave a damn anyway. She was
gone . . . three years and it was over . . . he
had lost her. His heart felt like a rock in his chest,
as he threw Jane's things into her bag, and Alexander's into another one . . . and yanked open
the drawer where he found Liz' wigs, and suddenly he sat down and began to cry, and he felt as
though he would never stop. He looked out at the
sky and the sea, and shouted "Why, God? *Why?*"
But no one answered him. And the bed was empty
now. She was gone. She had left the night before,
after kissing him and thanking him for the life and
the baby they'd shared, and he hadn't been able to
hold onto her, no matter how hard he'd tried to.

He called his parents once everything was
packed. It was two o'clock by then, and his mother
answered the phone. It was hot as hell in New

York, and even the air conditioning didn't help. They were meeting friends in town, and she thought they were calling to say they'd be late picking them up.

"Hello?"

"Hi, Mom." There was suddenly an enormous letdown, and he wasn't even sure he could get up enough energy to speak to her.

"Sweetheart, is something wrong?"

"I . . ." He nodded no and then yes, and then the tears came again. "I . . . wanted you to know . . ." He couldn't say the words. He was five years old and his world had come to an end. . . . "Liz . . . Oh Mom . . ." He was sobbing like a child and she began to cry just listening to him. "She died . . . last night . . ." He couldn't go on and she signaled to Lou standing beside her with worried eyes.

"We'll come right out." She was looking at her watch and her husband and her dinner dress and crying all at the same time, thinking of the girl he had loved, the mother of their grandson. It was so inconceivable that she was gone, and so wrong, and all she wanted to do was put her arms around Bernie. "We'll catch the next plane." She was gesticulating incoherently at Lou and he understood, and when Ruth let him, he took the phone from her ear.

"We love you, son. We'll get there as soon as we can."

"Good . . . good . . . I . . ." He didn't know how to handle it, what one said, what one did . . . he wanted to cry and scream, and kick his feet and bring her back, and she would never come back to him again. Never. "I can't . . ." But he could. He had to. He had to. He had two children to think about now. And he was alone. They were all he had now.

"Where are you, son?" Lou was desperately worried about him.

"At the beach." Bernie took a deep breath. He wanted to get out of the house where she died. He couldn't wait as he looked around, and he was glad the bags were already in the car. "It happened here."

"Are you alone?"

"Yes . . . I sent Tracy home with the kids, and . . . they took Liz a little while ago." He choked at the thought. They had covered her with a tarp . . . they'd put it over her face and her head . . . he felt sick at the thought. "I have to go in now. To take care of everything."

"We'll try to get there tonight."

"I want to stay with her at the funeral parlor." Just as he had at the hospital. He wasn't leaving her till she was buried.

"All right. We'll be there as soon as we can."

"Thank you, Dad."

He sounded like a little boy again, and it broke his father's heart as he hung up the phone and turned to Ruth. Ruth was sobbing quietly and he took her in his arms, as suddenly the tears rolled down his cheeks, too, crying for his boy, and the tragedy that had struck him. She had been such a lovely girl, and they had all loved her.

They caught a nine P.M. flight, after canceling their dinner with their friends, and arrived in San Francisco at midnight local time. It was three in the morning for them, but Ruth had rested on the plane and she wanted to go straight to the address Bernie had given them.

He was sitting with his wife at the funeral parlor and the casket was closed. He wouldn't have been able to sit, watching her, and it was bad enough like this. He was all alone in the lonely funeral parlor. All the other mourners had gone home hours before and only two solemn men in black suits were there to open the door for the Fines when they arrived at one o'clock in the morning. They had dropped their bags at the hotel on the way. And Ruth was wearing a somber black suit, black blouse, and black shoes she had bought at Wolff's years before. His father was wearing a dark gray suit and a black tie, and Bernie was wearing a charcoal gray suit and a white shirt and black tie, and he looked suddenly older than his thirty-seven years. He had gone home earlier for a few hours to visit the children, and then he had come back here. And now he sent his mother home to stay at the house, so she would be there when they woke up. And his father announced that he wanted to spend the night with him at Halsted's.

They spoke very little, and in the morning Bernie went home to shower and change, while his father went to the hotel to do the same. His mother was already making breakfast for the kids, as Tracy made calls. She had a message that Paul Berman was arriving in town at eleven A.M. to be at the funeral at noon. In the Jewish tradition, they were burying Liz that day.

Ruth had picked out a white dress for Jane, and Alexander was staying home with a sitter Liz used sometimes. He didn't understand what was going on, and staggered around the kitchen table, shouting "Mommm Mommm Mommm Mommm," which was what he called Liz, and it reduced Bernie to tears again. Ruth patted his arm and told him he should lie down for a while, but he sat down at the table next to Jane.

"Hi, sweetheart. You okay?" Who was? But one had to ask. He wasn't okay either and she knew that. None of them were. She shrugged, and slipped her little hand into his. At least they weren't asking each other anymore why it had happened to her, and to them. It had. And they had to live with it. Liz was gone. And she wanted them to go on. Of that, he was sure. But how? That was the bitch of it.

He walked into their bedroom, remembering the Bible she read once in a while, and thought about reading the Twenty-third Psalm at her funeral. And as he reached for it, it was thicker than he expected it to be, and the four letters fell out at his feet. He bent down to pick them up and saw what they were. The tears rolled down his cheeks unabashed as he read his, and he called Jane in to read hers, and then handed his mother the letter

Liz had written to her. The one to Alexander he would keep for him for much, much later. He planned to keep it in a safe, until Alexander was old enough to understand it.

It was a day of constant pain, constant tenderness, constant memories. And Paul Berman stood next to Bernie at the funeral, as he clung to Jane's hand, and his father held Ruth's arm, and they all cried as friends and neighbors and colleagues filed in. She would be missed by everyone, the principal of her school said, and Bernie was touched by how many of Wolff's salespeople had come. There were so many people who had loved her and would miss her now . . . but none as much as he, or the children she had left behind. "I'll see you again one day," she had promised everyone. She had told her schoolchildren that on the last day of school . . . she had promised them . . . on what she had called Valentine's Day. And Bernie hoped she was right . . . he wanted to see her again . . . desperately . . . but first he had two children to bring up. . . . He squeezed Jane's hand as they stood listening to the words of the Twenty-third Psalm, wishing she were there with them . . . wishing she had stayed . . . and blinded by tears as he longed for her. But Elizabeth O'Reilly Fine was gone forever.

Chapter 24

His father had to go back to New York, but his mother stayed for three weeks, and insisted she take the children home with her for a little while when she left. It was almost August by then, and they had nothing else to do. He had to go back to work eventually, and privately Ruth thought it would do him good. They had given up the house in Stinson Beach anyway, so all the children could do was sit in the house with a babysitter while he went to work.

"Besides, you need to get organized, Bernard." She had been wonderful to him, but he was beginning to snarl at her. He was angry at life and the fate it had dealt to him, and he was looking to take it out on everyone, and she was the nearest target.

"What the hell does that mean?" The children were in bed, and she had just called a cab to take her back to her hotel. She was still staying at the Huntington. She knew he needed some time to

himself every day, and so did she. It was a relief to
go back to the hotel after the children were in bed
every night. But he was eyeing her angrily now.
He was spoiling for a fight and she didn't want to
get into it with him.

"You want to know what it means? I think you
should get out of this house and move. This might
be a good time to come back to New York, and if
you can't arrange that yet, then at least get out of
here. It's too full of memories for all of you. Jane
stands in her mother's closet every day, sniffing
her perfume. Everytime you open a drawer
there's a hat or a purse or a wig. You can't do that
to yourself. Get out of here."

"We're not going anywhere." He looked like he
was going to stamp his foot but his mother was
not kidding.

"You're a fool, Bernard. You're torturing them.
And yourself." They were trying to hang on to
Liz, and they couldn't.

"That's ridiculous. This is our house, and we're
not going anywhere."

"All you do is rent it, what's so wonderful about
this house?" The wonderful thing was that Liz
had lived there and he wasn't ready to give that up
yet. No matter what anyone said, or how un-
healthy it was. He didn't want her things touched,
her sewing machine moved. Her cooking pots
were staying right where they were. Tracy had
gone through the same thing, she had explained
to Ruth a few days before when she'd stopped by.
It took her two years to give away her husband's

clothes, but Ruth was upset about it. It wasn't good for any of them. And she was right. But Bernie wasn't about to give in to her. "At least let me take the children to New York for a few weeks. Until school starts for Jane."

"I'll think about that." And he did, and he let them go. They left at the end of the week, still looking shell-shocked, and he worked every night until nine and ten o'clock, and then he would go home to sit in a chair in the living room, staring into space, thinking about her, and only answering the phone on the fourteenth ring when his mother called.

"You have to find a babysitter for them, Bernard." His mother wanted to reorganize his life and he wanted her to leave him alone. If he had been a drinker, he would have been an alcoholic by then, but he didn't even do that, he just sat there, doing nothing, numb, and only climbing into bed at three in the morning. He hated their bed now because she wasn't in it. He barely made it to the office every day, and then he sat there too. He was in shock. Tracy recognized the signs before anyone else did, but there was very little one could do for him. She told him to call whenever he wanted to, but she never heard from him. She reminded him too much of Liz. And now he stood in the closet, as Jane had, smelling her perfume.

"I'll take care of the children myself." He kept telling his mother that, and she kept telling him he was crazy.

"Are you planning to give up your job?" She

was sarcastic with him, hoping to shake him a little bit. It was dangerous letting him sit this way, but his father thought he'd be all right sooner or later. He was more worried about Jane, who had nightmares all the time, and had lost five pounds in three weeks. In California, Bernie had lost twelve. Only Alexander was doing well, although he wore a puzzled look when someone said Liz' name, as though wondering where she was and when she was coming back again. There was no answer to his "Mom . . . Momm . . . Momms" now.

"I don't have to give up my job to take care of the kids, Mom." He was being unreasonable and enjoying it.

"Oh? You're going to take Alexander to the office with you then?"

He had forgotten about that. He'd been thinking about Jane. "I can use the same woman Liz used when she taught school last year." And Tracy would help him.

"And you'll cook dinner every night, and make the beds, and vacuum? Don't be ridiculous, Bernard. You need help. There's no shame in that. You have to hire someone. You want me to come out and interview for you when the children come home?"

"No, no." He sounded annoyed again. "I'll take care of it." He was angry all the time. Angry at everyone, and sometimes even at Liz, for deserting him. It wasn't fair. She had promised him everything. She had done everything for him. For all of them. She cooked, she baked, she sewed, she loved them all so well, she had even taught school right up till the end. How does one replace a woman like that with a maid or an au pair? He hated the idea, as he called the agencies the next day, and explained what he needed.

"You're divorced?" A woman with a brassy voice inquired. Seven rooms, no pets, two children, no wife.

"No. I'm not." I'm a kidnapper, and I need help with two kids. Shit. "The children have . . ." He had been about to say "no mother," but what a terrible thing to say about Liz. "I'm alone. That's all. I have two children. Sixteen months old, and almost nine. Nine years that is. A boy and a girl. The nine-year-old goes to school."

"Obviously. Live-in or live-out?"

"Live-out. She's too young for boarding school."

"Not the child. The nurse."

"Oh . . . I don't know . . . I hadn't thought about it. I suppose she could come in around eight o'clock and then leave after dinner at night."

"Do you have room for an au pair?" He thought about it. She could sleep in the baby's room, if she didn't mind.

"I suppose I could."

"We'll do our best." But their best was not very good. They sent a handful of candidates to Wolff's and Bernie was horrified at the caliber of people they were sending out. Most of them had never taken care of children before, or were in the country illegally, or really didn't give a damn. They were a mess, and some of them weren't even nice. He finally settled on a very unattractive Norwegian girl. She had six brothers and sisters, she looked solid, and she said she wanted to stay in the country for a year or more. She said she could cook, and she went to the airport with him when the children came home. Jane didn't look enthused, and Alexander looked at her curiously and then smiled and clapped his hands, but she let him run loose in the airport as Bernie attempted to find their bags, and set up the stroller for him. He was halfway out the door by himself when Jane brought him back with an angry look at the girl, and Bernie snapped at her.

"Keep an eye on him, Anna, will you please?"

"Sure." She was smiling at a boy with a knapsack and long blond hair as Jane whispered to Bernie.

"Where'd you find her?"

"Never mind. At least we'll eat." And then he smiled down at her. She had thrown herself into his arms when they arrived, squeezing Alexander between them as he roared with delight and Bernie had thrown him into the air, and then done the same to Jane. "I sure missed you guys." He knew about the nightmares from Ruth. They were all about Liz. "You especially."

"Me too." She still looked sad. But so did he. "Grandma was so nice to me."

"She loves you a lot." They smiled and he found a porter to help with the bags, and a few minutes later everything was in the car and they drove off toward the city. Jane sat in the front seat next to him. And Alexander and the au pair sat in the back. She had worn jeans and a purple shirt, and she had long, shaggy blond hair, and Jane didn't seem very impressed with her as they chatted on the way in. She seemed to answer mostly in monosyllables and grunts, and wasn't very interested in making friends with the kids. And when they got home, the dinner she made for them consisted of breakfast cereal and undercooked French toast. In desperation, Bernie sent out for a pizza, which the au pair dove into before they did. And then suddenly Jane glared at her. "Where did you get that blouse?" Jane was staring at her as though she had seen a ghost.

"What? This?" Her face got red. She had changed from a purple blouse to a pretty green silk one, which now had perspiration marks under the arms that hadn't been there before. "I found this in the closet in there." She waved toward Bernie's room, and his eyes grew as wide as Jane's. She was wearing Liz' blouse.

"Don't ever do that again." He spoke through clenched teeth and she shrugged.

"What difference does it make? She's not coming back anyway." Jane got up and left the table and Bernie followed her and apologized.

"I'm sorry, sweetheart. I thought she was nicer than that when I interviewed her. She looked clean and young and I thought it would be more fun for you than some old bat." She smiled unhappily at him. Life was so difficult for them now. And this was only her first night home. But nothing was ever going to be easy for her again. Instinctively, she knew that.

"Shall we give her a try for a few days, and if we don't like her, boot her out?" Jane nodded at him, relieved that nothing was being forced on her. Forever It was difficult for all of them. And Anna drove them nuts in the next few days. She continued to borrow Liz' clothes, and even Bernie's sometimes. She turned up in some of his favorite cashmere sweaters, and once even borrowed his socks. She never washed, the house smelled terrible, and when Jane came home from school in the afternoon, she found Alexander with dirty pants, running around the house in drooping diapers and an undershirt, with dirty feet and lunch all over his face, while Anna talked to her boyfriend on the phone, or listened to rock on the stereo. The food was inedible, the house despicable, and Jane was taking care of Alexander almost full-time herself. She bathed him when she got home from school, and dressed him up before Bernie got home, she fed him and put him to bed at night, and went in to him when he cried. Anna never even woke up. The laundry wasn't done, the beds weren't changed, the children's clothes weren't washed. Anna drove them crazy, and in less than ten days they kicked her out. Bernie announced it to her on a Saturday night, as the steaks burned in a large filthy cooking pot, and she sat on the kitchen floor talking on the phone, and she had left Alexander alone in the tub. Jane found him there, slippery as a fish, attempting to climb over the side, and she rescued him, but he could have drowned, which terrified everyone except Anna. Bernie told her to pack her things and leave, and she did, with barely an apology, and wearing Bernie's favorite red cashmere sweater.

"So much for that." He put the pot full of burnt steaks into the sink and ran hot water over them. "Can I interest you in a pizza tonight?" They had been eating pizza a lot, and they decided to invite Tracy to join them.

When she arrived, she helped Jane put the baby to bed. They all cleaned up the kitchen together. It was almost like the old days, except that someone very important was missing and they all felt it. And to make matters worse, she told them she was moving to Philadelphia. Jane looked stricken. It was like losing her second mother, and she was depressed for weeks after they saw her off at the airport.

And the next nurse didn't help. She was Swiss and had been trained as a baby nurse, which sounded perfect to him in the interview, but what she didn't say was that she must have been trained in the German army. She was rigid and inflexible and unkind. The house was immaculate, the dinners were small, the rules were ironclad and plentiful, and she slapped Alexander all the time. The poor child cried constantly and Jane hated to come home from school and find her there. Milk and cookies were not allowed, nor were treats of any kind, and they were not to speak at meals, except if their father was there. Television was a sin, music was a crime against God. Bernie decided that the woman was half crazy, and when Jane laughed at her inadvertently on a Saturday afternoon two weeks after she'd come, she walked across the room and slapped Jane hard across the face. Jane was so stunned she didn't even cry at first, but Bernie was trembling when he stood up and pointed at her. "Get out of this house, Miss Strauss. *Immediately!*" He took the baby from her, put an arm around Jane to comfort her, and an hour later, with an enormous bang, the front door slammed behind her.

And it was discouraging after that. He felt as though he had interviewed everyone in town, and he wouldn't have trusted any of them. The first thing he did was get a cleaning lady, but even that didn't help. His big problem was Alexander and Jane. He wanted someone to take care of them properly. They were beginning to look unhappy and bedraggled to him, and he was desperate to find someone to help him. He was beside himself as he ran home from work every day to take care of Alex and Jane. He had a daytime sitter temporarily, who could only stay until five o'clock. And his mother was right. It was difficult working all day, and then taking care of the children and the house and the laundry and the groceries and the cooking and the ironing and the backyard all night.

Their luck changed six weeks after school began. The agency called him again and he listened to the usual tale. Mary Poppins had turned up and she was waiting for him. According to the agency, she was perfect for the job.

"Mrs. Pippin is perfect for you, Mr. Fine." He looked bored as he jotted down her name. "She's sixty years old, British, and was ten years in her last job, with two children, a boy and a girl. And" —the woman at the agency sounded victorious— "there was no mother."

"Is that something to be particularly proud of?" It was none of their goddamn business.

"It just means that she is acquainted with this kind of situation."

"Wonderful. What's the hitch?"

"There is none." He had not been an easy client, and they were frankly annoyed at how suspicious he was of everyone they sent him. In fact, the woman made a note to herself as she hung up, if he didn't like Mrs. Pippin, they were not sending anyone else after that.

Mrs. Pippin rang the doorbell at six o'clock on a Thursday evening. Bernie had just gotten home and taken off his coat and tie. He had Alexander in his arms, and Jane was helping him start dinner. They were going to have hamburgers, for the third night in a row, with potato chips and buns and lettuce. But he hadn't had time to go to the store since the weekend, and somehow the rest of the meat had gotten lost on the way home, or they'd never brought it home in the first place.

Bernie opened the door and found himself staring down at a tiny woman with short white hair and bright blue eyes, in a navy hat and coat, and sensible black shoes that looked like golf shoes. And the woman at the agency was right. She did look like Mary Poppins. She was even carrying a tightly furled black umbrella.

"Mr. Fine?"

"Yes."

"I'm from the agency. I'm Mary Pippin." Her accent was Scots and he grinned to himself. It was like a joke. Not Mary Poppins. But Mary Pippin.

"Hello." He stepped back, with a smile, and waved her to a seat in the living room, as Jane walked out of the kitchen, with a roll of hamburger in her hands. She was curious to see what they had sent this time. The woman was hardly taller than she was, but she smiled at Jane and asked her what she was cooking.

"How nice of you to take care of your dad and your little brother. I'm not much of a cook myself, you know." She grinned, and almost instantly, Bernie liked her. And then he suddenly realized what the shoes were. They weren't golf shoes. They were brogues. She was Scottish through and through. Her skirt was tweed, her blouse was white and starched, and when she took her hat off, he saw that she even wore a hatpin.

"That was Jane." Bernie explained as she went back to the kitchen. "She's nine, or will be soon. And Alexander is nearly eighteen months old now." He set him down on the floor as they sat down and he took off at top speed for his sister in the kitchen, as Bernie smiled at Mrs. Pippin. "He doesn't stop all day, he wakes up all night. So does Jane." He lowered his voice. "She has night-mares. And I need someone to help me. We're alone now." This was the part he hated, and usu-ally they just stared at him dumbly, but this woman nodded sensibly, with a sympathetic look. "I need someone to take care of Alexander all day, to be here when Jane gets home from school, to do things with them, to be their friend"—it was the first time he had said that, but somehow she seemed that kind of woman—"to cook for us, to keep their clothes neat . . . to buy their school shoes if I don't have time . . ."

"Mr. Fine"—she smiled gently—"you want a nanny." She seemed to understand completely.

"Yes. That's right." He thought briefly of the sloppy Norwegian who kept taking Liz' clothes and glanced at Mrs. Pippin's starched collar. He decided to be honest with her. "We've had a tough time, or actually, they have." He glanced toward the kitchen. "My wife was sick for almost a year, before . . ." He could never say the words, even now. "And she's been gone for three months. It's a tremendous adjustment for the children." And for me, he didn't add, but her eyes said she knew it, and he suddenly felt like sighing and lying on the couch, letting her take care of everything. Something about her suggested to him that she was absolutely perfect. "The job isn't easy, but it isn't overwhelming either." He told her about the two women he'd had, the others he'd seen, and described exactly what he wanted. Miraculously, she seemed to find it entirely normal.

"It sounds wonderful. When could I start?" She beamed at him and he couldn't believe his ears.

"Immediately if you like. Oh, and I forgot to mention. You'd have to sleep with the baby. Is that a problem?"

"Not at all. I prefer it."

"Eventually, we might move, but I don't have any plans at the moment." He was vague and she nodded. "And actually . . ." There was so much in his head that he was confused now. He wanted to be completely honest with her. "One day, I may go back to New York, but I don't know anything about that right now either."

"Mr. Fine"—she smiled gently at him—"I understand. Right now you don't know if you're coming or going, and neither do the children, and that's perfectly normal. Suddenly all of you have lost the mainstay of your existence. You need time to heal, and someone to watch over you while you do. I would be honored to be that person, thrilled if you would let me take care of your children. And whether you move to another house, an apartment, New York, or Kenya is not a problem. I'm a widow, I have no children, and my home is with the family I work for. Where you go, I go, if you want me." She smiled at him as though speaking to a child and he wanted to giggle.

"That sounds wonderful, Mrs. Poppin . . . I mean Pippin. . . . Sorry. . . ."

"Not at all." She laughed with him and followed him into the kitchen. She was tiny, but there was something powerful about her, and amazingly the children liked her. Jane invited her to stay for dinner, and when Mrs. Pippin accepted, she put another hamburger on, and Alexander sat on her lap until he had his bath, and then Mrs. Pippin went to discuss the financial arrangements with Bernie. She wasn't even very expensive. And she was exactly what he needed.

She promised to return the next day, with her things, "such as they are," she apologized. She had left her previous family in June. The children were grown up and simply didn't need her anymore, and she had gone to Japan on a holiday, and come back through San Francisco. She was actually on her way to Boston, but had decided to check with the agency because she found the city so enchanting, and *voilà.* The match was made in Heaven.

After she had left to go back to her hotel, while Jane was putting the baby to bed that night, Bernie called his mother.

"I found her." He sounded happier than he had in months and he was actually smiling. You could almost hear it, and you could hear something different in his voice. Relief.

"Who did you find?" His mother had been half asleep. It was eleven o'clock in Scarsdale.

"Mary Poppin . . . actually, Mary Pippin."

"Bernie"—she sounded firm and much more awake now—"have you been drinking?" She glanced disapprovingly at her husband, who had been awake on his side of the bed, reading his medical journals. He looked unconcerned. Bernie had a right to drink these days. Who wouldn't?

"No. I found a nurse. A Scottish nanny, and she's fantastic."

"Who is she?" His mother was instantly suspicious, and he told her all the details. "She might be all right. Did you check her references?"

"I will tomorrow." But the references checked out exactly as she had described them, and the family in Boston raved about their beloved "nanny." They told him how lucky he was, and suggested that he keep her forever. And when she arrived the next day, he was inclined to. She tidied up the house, sorted the laundry, read to Alexander, found a brand-new suit for him to wear, and had him clean and combed for his father when he came home. And Jane was wearing a pink dress and pink hair ribbons and a smile in time for dinner, and suddenly he felt a lump in his throat remembering the first time he had seen her, lost at Wolff's with long braids and pink ribbons just like the ones Mrs. Pippin had put on for her that night.

The dinner wasn't wonderful, but it was decent and simple. The table was nicely set, and she played a game with both children afterwards in their room. By eight o'clock the house was neat, the table was set for breakfast, and both children were in bed, brushed, clean, read to, well fed, and cuddled, and as Bernie said good night to each of them, and thanked Mrs. Pippin, Bernie only wished that Liz could have seen them.

Chapter 25

It was the day after Halloween that Bernie came home and sat on the couch, glancing at his mail, and then up at Mrs. Pippin as she emerged from the kitchen wiping flour off her hands to hand him a message.

"Someone just called for you, Mr. Fine." She smiled at him. She was a pleasure to come home to, and the children loved her. "It was a gentleman. I hope I got his name right."

"I'm sure you did. Thank you." He took the slip of paper and glanced at it as she walked away. The name didn't mean anything to him at first, and as he walked into the kitchen to make himself a drink, he questioned Nanny. She was breading fish for dinner, and Jane was helping, while Alexander played on the floor with a pile of small, bright-colored boxes. It was the kind of scene Liz would have created around her as she worked, and it gnawed at his heart to see them. Everything still made him miss her. "Was that the man's first or last name, Mrs. Pippin?"

"I didn't get a chance to write down his first name, although he said it." She was busy breading the fish, and didn't look up at Bernie. "The last name was Scott." It still didn't mean anything to Bernie. "The first was Chandler."

His heart stopped as she said it, and he went back to the living room to look at the number. He thought about it for a long time, and didn't say anything about it at dinner. It was a local number, and Chandler was obviously back for more money. Bernie was thinking of ignoring the message when the phone rang at ten o'clock that night and he had a premonition as he picked it up. And he was right. It was Chandler Scott.

"Hi there." There was the same aura of false cheer about him as before and Bernie was not impressed.

"I thought I made myself clear last time." There was no hospitality in his voice.

"Just passing through town, my friend."

"Don't let us stop you."

Chandler laughed as though Bernie had said something very, very funny.

"How's Liz?" He didn't want to tell him what had happened. It was none of his goddamn business.

"Fine."

"How's my kid?"

"She's not your child. She's mine now." It was

the wrong thing to say and Bernie could hear him
bridle.

"That's not how I remember it."

"Really? How's your memory on the ten thousand dollars?" Bernie's voice sounded hard, but
Chandler sounded slimy.

"My memory's okay, but my investments didn't
turn out so hot."

"Sorry to hear it." Then he was back for more
money.

"Me too. I thought maybe we'd have another
little talk, you know, about my kid." Bernie's jaw
went taut beneath his beard and he remembered
his promise to Liz. He wanted to get rid of the guy
once and for all, and not have him come back once
a year. In fact, it had been a year and a half since
they'd given him the money.

"I thought I told you last time that it was a one-
shot deal, Scott."

"Maybe so, my friend, maybe so." Something in
his voice made Bernie want to smash his face in.
"But maybe we'll have to play this one one more
time."

"I don't think so."

"Are you telling me the pot's run out?" Bernie
hated the way he talked. He sounded like exactly
what he was. A two-bit con man.

"I'm telling you I'm not playing this game with
you again. Got that, buddy?"

"Then how about a little visit with my daughter?" He played a cool hand of poker.

"She's not interested."

"She will be if I take you to court. How old is she now? Seven? Eight?" He wasn't sure.

"What difference does it make?" She was nine, and he didn't even know that.

"Why don't you ask Liz how she feels about it?"

It was blackmail in the purest sense and Bernie was sick of him. He wanted him to know there was no game to play with Liz now. "Liz doesn't feel anything about it, Scott. She died in July." There was a long, long silence.

"Sorry to hear that." For a moment he sounded sober.

"Does that end our conversation?" He was suddenly glad he'd told him. Maybe the bastard would go away now, but he had sorely misjudged him.

"Not quite. The kid didn't die, did she? What did Liz die of anyway?"

"Cancer."

"That's too bad. Anyway, she's still my kid, with or without Liz, and I imagine you'd just as soon see me get lost. And for a price, I will be happy to do that."

"For how long? Another year? Nah, it's not worth it to me, Scott. This time I'm not buying."

"Too bad. I guess I'll just have to go to court and get me some visitation."

Bernie remembered his promise to Liz and decided to bluff him anyway. "You do that, Scott. Do anything you want. I'm not interested."

"I'll get lost for another ten thousand. Tell you what, I'll make you a deal. How about eight?"

Bernie's skin crawled just thinking about him. "Go screw yourself." And with that, he hung up. He would have liked to kick the guy in the guts. But three days later Chandler did it to him instead. A notice arrived in the mail, through a lawyer on Market Street, that Chandler Scott, father of one Jane Scott, ex-husband of Elizabeth O'Reilly Scott Fine, was requesting visitation with his daughter. Bernie's hands trembled when he read the letter. He was ordered to appear in court on November seventeenth, fortunately without the child. But his heart pounded as he read the words, and he dialed Bill Grossman's office.

"What do I do now?" Bernie sounded desperate. Grossman had taken the call immediately. He remembered Bernie's first call on the subject.

"You go to court, it looks like."

"Does he have any rights?"

"Did you ever adopt the child?"

His heart sank at the question. There was always something happening, the baby, Liz getting sick, the last nine months, then their adjustment. . . . "No . . . I haven't. . . . Dammit, I meant to, but there was no reason. Once I bought him off, I figured we'd seen the last of him for a while."

"You bought him off?" The lawyer sounded worried.

"Yeah. I paid him ten thousand bucks to get lost a year and a half ago." It had actually been twenty months. He remembered it perfectly, it was right before Liz had had the baby.

"Can he prove it?"

"No, I remembered what you said about it being against the law." Grossman had said it was considered like buying black-market babies. You could not buy or sell a child to anyone, and in effect, Chandler Scott had sold Jane to Bernie for ten thousand dollars. "I paid him in cash, in an envelope."

"So much for that." Grossman sounded pensive. "The problem is, when you do that kind of thing, they always come back for more sooner or later. Is that what he wants now?"

"That's how this whole thing started. He called me up a few nights ago and asked for another ten thousand to get lost again. In fact, he offered me a cut rate, for eight."

"Christ." Grossman sounded annoyed. "He sounds charming."

"I thought when I told him my wife had died that he'd lose interest. I figured if he thought he was only dealing with me, he'd realize that I wasn't going to take any crap from him."

Grossman was strangely quiet at the other end. "I didn't realize that your wife had passed away in the meantime. I'm sorry to hear that."

"It was in July." Bernie's voice was very quiet, thinking of Liz, and the promise that she had insisted on, that he would keep Jane away from Chandler Scott at all costs. Maybe he should have paid him the ten thousand dollars after all. Maybe it was foolish to call his bluff.

"Did she leave a will regarding the child?" They had talked about it but she had nothing to leave anyone except the things that Bernie had bought her, and she was leaving everything to him and the children.

"No. She really had no estate."

"But what about the guardianship of the child? Did she leave that to you?"

"Of course." Bernie sounded almost offended. Who else would she leave her children to?

"Did she put it in writing?"

"No, she didn't."

Bill Grossman sighed silently at the other end. Bernie had just gotten himself a major problem. "The law is on his side, you know, now that your wife is gone. He is the child's natural father." Bernie almost shuddered.

"Are you serious?" Bernie's blood ran cold.

"I am."

"The guy's a crook, a con man, an ex-con, in fact. He probably just got out of jail again."

"That doesn't make any difference. California feels that natural fathers have rights, no matter what else they are. Even ax murderers have a right to see their children."

"Now what?"

"They may grant him temporary visitation, pending a hearing." He didn't tell him that he could lose custody completely. "Has he ever had a relationship with the child?"

"Never. She doesn't know he's alive, and from what my wife said, the last time he saw her she was a year old. He doesn't have a leg to stand on, Bill."

"Yes, he does. Don't kid yourself. He's the child's natural father. . . . What kind of marital history did they have?"

"Almost nonexistent. They got married a few days before the child was born, and I think he disappeared after that. He came back for a month or two just before Jane was a year old and then disappeared again for good that time. Liz divorced him on the basis of abandonment, without consent or notification, I guess since she didn't know where he was until he turned up last year."

"It's a damn shame you didn't adopt the child before he did."

"This is ridiculous."

"I agree with you, but that doesn't mean the judge will. Do you think he has a genuine interest in the child?"

"Do you, if he sold out for ten thousand dollars and would have again three days ago for eight? He just thinks she's some kind of cash register. When I met him with the money last time, he did not ask or say one thing about Jane. Not one. What does that tell you?"

"That's he's a smart sonofabitch who wants to put the squeeze on you. I suspect you'll hear from him again before we go to court on the seventeenth." And Grossman was right. Scott called three days before they were due to appear in court, and offered to disappear again. But this time the price tag was higher. He wanted fifty thousand dollars.

"Are you crazy?"

"I've been doing a little research on you, old pal."

"Don't call me that, you sonofabitch."

"I hear you're a rich Jew from New York and you run a fancy department store. For all I know, you own it."

"Hardly."

"Anyway, pal. That's my price this time. Fifty thousand bucks or forget it."

"I'll go for ten, but that's it." He would have gone to twenty, but didn't want to tell him. But Scott only laughed at him.

"Fifty or nothing." It was disgusting, bargaining over a child."

"I'm not going to play this game with you, Scott."

"You may have to. With Liz gone, the court is going to give me anything I want. They might even give me custody if I want . . . Come to think of it, I think my price has just gone up to a hundred." Bernie felt his blood run cold, and as soon as Scott hung up, Bernie dialed Grossman.

"Does he know what he's talking about? Is that possible?"

"It could be."

"Oh my God. . . ." He was terrified. What if he lost Jane to him? And he had promised Liz . . . Besides, Jane was like his own flesh and blood now.

"Legally, you have no rights to the child. Even if your wife had left a will, designating you guardian of the person, he might still have the rights to her.

Now if you can show how unsuitable he is, you'll probably win, unless the judge is a complete lunatic. But if you were both bankers, or lawyers, or businessmen, he'd win it. In this case, all he can do is scare you for a while, and put the child through a lot of trauma."

"To spare her that," Bernie said bitterly, "he now wants a hundred thousand dollars."

"Do you have a recording of that?"

"Of course not! What do you think I do? Tape my conversations? I'm not a dope dealer for God's sake, I run a department store." He was getting testy. It was an outrageous situation. "So what do I do now?"

"If you don't want to give him the hundred thousand dollars, and I suggest you don't, because he'll be back for more by next week, then we go to court, and show what an unsuitable parent he is. They may grant temporary visitation pending a hearing, but that's no big deal."

"Not to you maybe. The child doesn't even know him. In fact"—he sounded grim—"she doesn't even know he's alive. Her mother told her he died a long time ago. And she's already had enough shocks this year. She's had nightmares since her mother died."

"If a psychiatrist will testify to that, then it may affect his bid for permanent visitation."

"And the request for temporary visitation?"

"That would go through anyway. The courts figure that even Attila the Hun can do no harm on a temporary basis."

"How do they justify that?"

"They don't have to. They run the show. Mr. Scott has now put you, and himself, at their mercy." And Jane. He had put Jane at the mercy of the courts. The thought made him sick, and he knew how distraught Liz would have been. It would have killed her. And the irony of that did not make him smile. It was a terrible situation.

The day of the first hearing dawned dark and gray, and it suited his mood to perfection. The carpool came for Jane, and Mrs. Pippin was busy with Alexander when Bernie left for court. He hadn't told anyone what he was doing. He was still hoping the whole thing would go away. And as he stood beside Grossman in the courtroom in City Hall, he prayed that the whole situation would vanish. But he noticed Chandler Scott lounging against the wall at the other side of the room, with a different blazer, this time a better one, and new Gucci shoes. His hair was neatly trimmed, and if one didn't know better, one would have thought him totally respectable.

Bernie pointed him out to Bill, who glanced casually in Chandler Scott's direction. "He looks all right." He whispered to Bernie.

"That was what I was afraid of."

Grossman said that the matter would take twenty minutes to be heard, and when the judge heard what they had to say, Grossman explained that the child did not know her natural father, and had undergone a severe, recent shock due to her mother's death. It was felt that it was best not to grant temporary visitation until the entire matter were settled. And the respondent felt that there were certain issues that were crucial to the court's final decision.

"I'm sure there are," the judge intoned, smiling at both fathers and both attorneys. This was something he did every day, and he never got caught up in the emotions. Fortunately, he almost never had to see the children affected by his decisions. "But it wouldn't be fair to deny Mr. Scott the right to see his daughter." He smiled benevolently at Scott, and then sympathetically at Grossman. "I'm sure this is distressing to your client, Mr. Grossman, and we will of course be very interested in hearing all the issues when the matter comes to court for a full hearing. In the meantime, the court would like to grant Mr. Scott a weekly visitation with his daughter." Bernie thought he was going to faint and he immediately whispered in Grossman's ear that Scott was a convicted felon.

"I can't tell them that now," Grossman whispered back, and Bernie wanted to cry. He wished he had paid him the ten thousand the first time. Or even the fifty the second. The hundred was impossible for him. He was out of his league now.

Grossman raised his voice to address the judge. "Where will the visits take place?"

"In the place of Mr. Scott's choosing. The child is . . ." The judge looked at some records, and then glanced at both parties with an understanding smile. "Let's see. . . . She's about nine years old. . . . There's no reason why she can't go out with her father. Mr. Scott could pick her up at her home, and bring her back. I suggest Saturday, say from nine A.M. to seven P.M. Does that sound reasonable to both parties?"

"No!" Bernie whispered in Grossman's ear in a loud stage whisper.

And Grossman whispered back almost immediately. "You have no choice in this. And if you play ball with the judge now, he may give you a better deal later." What about Jane? What kind of deal did she get?

Bernie was furious when they walked out into the hall again. "What kind of crap is that anyway?"

"Keep your voice down." Grossman spoke in low tones to him, his face a mask, as Chandler Scott and his attorney walked past. He had one of the sleaziest attorneys in town, Grossman later told Bernie, and he was sure they were going to try and stick Bernie with the tab, by asking the court to assign fees to him at a later date. But Bill didn't even mention that now. They had enough to worry about. "You just have to go along with it."

"Why? It's wrong. Why do I have to do something I know is wrong for my daughter?" He spoke from the heart without thinking of what he had just said. But Bill Grossman shook his head.

"She's not your daughter, she's his, and that's the whole point of this."

"The real bitch is that all that bastard wants is

money. Only now he wants so much I can't afford it."

"You never could have anyway. People like that just keep raising the ante. You're better off dealing with it here. The hearing is set for December fourteenth anyway. So you have a month of temporary visitation to contend with and then you get a permanent ruling. Do you really think he'd keep up with visitation?"

"He might." But Bernie hoped he wouldn't. "What if he kidnaps her?" It was a thought that had been frightening him ever since Scott had turned up again. It was his own brand of paranoia. And Grossman was quick to squelch it.

"Don't be ridiculous. The man is greedy. He's not crazy. He'd have to be nuts to kidnap her on a visit."

"What would happen if he did?" He wanted to pursue the thought to the end, just so he'd know what his recourse was.

"People only do things like that in movies."

"I hope you're right." Bernie narrowed his eyes and looked at him. "Because I'm telling you right now that if he ever does anything like that to her, I'm going to kill him."

Chapter 26

The visits were to start on Saturday, which didn't give Bernie much time. He took Jane out to dinner after his morning in court, and he took a deep breath before he told her. He had taken her to the Hippo, which had always been a favorite with her, but she seemed quiet that night, and finally she looked at him. She knew something was wrong, and she couldn't imagine what it was. Maybe they were moving to New York, or some fresh disaster was happening. And she was certain of it when he reached for her hand with eyes filled with sorrow.

"Baby, I've got to tell you something." Her heart pounded horribly and she wanted to run away from him. She looked so frightened that it broke his heart. He wondered if she would ever be her old self again. Even though, thanks to Mrs. Pippin, she was getting better. She didn't cry as much now and she even laughed sometimes. "It's not as bad as all that, sweetheart. Don't look so worried."

She looked at him with eyes filled with terror. "I thought you were going to tell me . . ." She couldn't say the words, and he looked at her, still holding her hand.

"Tell you what, sweetheart?"

"That you had cancer." Her voice was so small and sad and he shook his head as tears came to his eyes. That was the worst thing that either of them could imagine.

"It's nothing like that. It's something else entirely. Okay . . . now . . . do you remember that your mommy was married before?" It felt strange saying that to her, but he had to explain from the beginning.

"Yes. She said she was married to a very handsome actor, and he died when I was a baby."

"Something like that." He had never heard that version of the explanation.

"And she said she loved him very much." Jane looked up at him innocently and something turned over in his stomach.

"She did?"

"That's what she told me."

"Okay. She told me something a little different, but it doesn't matter." Suddenly he was wondering if he was poisoning her mind against someone Liz had truly loved. Maybe she really had loved him and hadn't had the courage to tell him. But then suddenly he remembered the solemnity of the promise she had extracted from him. "She told me that that man, your real father, disappeared right after you were born, and disappointed her a lot. I think he did something dumb like steal money from someone or something and he went to jail." Jane looked shocked.

"My father?"

"Mmm . . . yes. . . . Anyway, he disappeared for a while and then came back when you were nine months old and did the same thing again. This time he disappeared when you were a year old. And she never saw him again. End of story."

"Is that when he died?" She was confused by the tale he told her, but he shook his head as the waiter took their plates away, and Jane pensively sipped her soda.

"No. He didn't die, sweetheart. That's what this is all about. He just disappeared and eventually your mommy divorced him. And a few years later, I came along, and we got married." He smiled and squeezed her hand a little tighter, and she smiled in answer.

"That was when we got lucky . . . that's what Mommy used to say." And it was obvious that she shared her mother's opinion in that, as in everything. And by then, she had idolized Liz even more than when she was living. But she still looked startled to hear that her father was alive, according to Bernie.

"That was when *I* got lucky. Anyway, Mr. Chandler Scott vanished and turned up a couple of weeks ago . . . here, in San Francisco. . . ."

"How come he never called me?"

"I don't know." He decided to be blunt with

her. "He did finally call a year or so ago because he wanted money from your mommy. And when she gave it to him, he went away again. But this time he's come back, and I didn't think we should give him any money, so I didn't." It was all simplified, but basically what had happened. He didn't tell her that they'd bought him off so he wouldn't see Jane, or that Liz hated his guts. He decided to let Jane make that decision for herself, when she saw him. But it worried him that she might like him.

"Did he want to see me?" She looked intrigued about the handsome actor.

"Now he does."

"Can he come to dinner?" It all seemed very simple to her, but Bernie was shaking his head and she looked surprised at his reaction.

"It's not as simple as that. He and I went to court today."

"Why?" She looked even more surprised, and a little frightened. Court sounded ominous to her.

"I went to court because I don't think he's a nice person, and I want to protect you from him. And your mommy wanted me to do that." He had promised Liz, and he had done his best to keep his promise.

"Do you think he'd do something bad to me?"

He didn't want to frighten her too much, after all, she had to go out with him in two days, for ten hours. "No. But I think he's a little too interested in money. And we really don't know much about him."

Her eyes looked deep into his. "Why did Mommy tell me he was dead?"

"I think because she thought it was easier to think that than always wonder where he was, or why he had gone away." Jane nodded, it made sense to her, but she looked disappointed.

"I didn't think she ever lied to me."

"I don't think she ever did, except that one time. And she thought it was better for you." Jane nodded, trying to understand.

"So what did they say in court?" She was curious now.

"That we have to go to court again in another month, but in the meantime he has the right to see you. Every Saturday from nine in the morning until dinner."

"But I don't even know him! What will I say to him all day like that?"

It seemed a funny thing to worry about to Bernie and he smiled at her. "You'll think of something." That was the least of their problems.

"What if I don't like him? He couldn't have been too nice if he kept running out on Mommy."

"That's what I always thought." He decided to be honest with her. "And I didn't like him the one time I met him."

"You met him?" She looked even more surprised, as he nodded. "When?"

"That time he came to get money from your

mom. It was right before Alexander was born, and she sent me to give him the money."

"She didn't want to see him?" That told Jane a great deal as Bernie shook his head.

"No, she didn't."

"Maybe she didn't love him so much."

"Maybe not." He didn't want to get into that with her.

"Did he really go to jail?" She looked horrified at that and Bernie nodded. "What if I don't want to go on Saturday?"

That was the hard part. "Baby, I'm afraid you have to."

"Why?" Her eyes suddenly filled with tears. "I don't even know him. What if I don't like him?"

"Then you just kind of pass the time. It's only four times until we go to court again."

"Four times?" The tears started to roll down her cheeks.

"Every Saturday." Bernie felt as though he had sold out his only daughter and he hated Chandler Scott and his attorney and Grossman and the courts and the judge for making him do it. And especially Grossman for telling him so coolly not to rock the boat. Chandler Scott wasn't coming to his house on Saturday to take his daughter.

"Daddy, I don't want to." She wailed, and he told her the ugly truth of it.

"You have to." He handed her his handkerchief and sat on the banquette next to her, and put an arm around her shoulders. She leaned her head against him and cried harder. Everything was so difficult for her now. It wasn't fair to add more. And he hated them all for it. "Look at it this way, it's only four times. And Grandma and Grampa are coming from New York for Thanksgiving. That'll give us plenty to think about." He had put off his trip to Europe again, with all the headaches he'd been having with help at the time, and Berman didn't push him. It had been months since he'd seen his parents. Since August when his mother took the children home with her. And Mrs. Pippin had promised to make the Thanksgiving turkey. She had turned out to be the godsend she had promised to be, and Bernie was in love with her. He only hoped his mother liked her. They were about the same age and as different as night and day. His mother was expensively dressed, well groomed, a little frivolous, difficult as hell when she chose to be. Mrs. Pippin was starched and plain and as unfrivolous as a woman could be, but decent and warm and competent, and wonderful to his children, and very British. It was going to be an interesting combination.

He paid the check at the Hippo then, and walked out to the car with Jane, and when they got home, Mrs. Pippin was waiting to keep Jane company while she took a bath, read her a story, and put her to bed. And the first thing Jane did when she walked in the door, was take one look at Nanny, as they all called her now, throw her arms around her neck, and intone tragically. "Nanny, I have another father." Bernie smiled at the drama of the words, and Nanny sniffed as she led Jane away to the bathtub.

Chapter 27

The "other" father, as Jane had referred to him, appeared almost punctually at nine-fifteen on Saturday morning. It was the Saturday before Thanksgiving. And all of them sat in the living room waiting. Bernie, Jane, Mrs. Pippin, and Alexander.

The clock on the mantel in the living room ticked mercilessly as all of them waited and Bernie began hoping that Chandler Scott wouldn't show up. But they weren't that lucky. The doorbell rang, and Jane jumped, as Bernie went to get it. She still didn't want to go out with him, and she was feeling extremely nervous as she stood close to Nanny and played with Alexander, keeping an eye on the man standing in the doorway talking to Bernie. She couldn't see him yet. But she could hear him. He had a loud voice and he sounded friendly, maybe because he was an actor, or had been.

Then she saw Bernie step aside and the man walked into the living room and looked from her to Alexander, almost as though he didn't know which was which, and then he glanced at Nanny and back at Jane.

"Hello, I'm your dad." It was an awkward thing to say. But it was an extremely awkward moment. He didn't hold out a hand to her, and he didn't approach her, and she wasn't sure she liked his eyes. They were the same color as hers, but they darted around the room a lot, and he seemed more interested in her real daddy, as she called Bernie, than he was in her. He was looking at Bernie's big gold Rolex watch, and he seemed to be taking in the whole room, and the neat woman in the blue uniform and navy brogues who sat watching him with Alexander on her lap. He didn't ask for an introduction. "Are you ready?"

Jane shrank back and Bernie stepped forward. "Why don't you talk here for a little while, and get to know each other before you go out?" Scott didn't look pleased at the suggestion. He looked at his watch, and then at Bernie with annoyance.

"I don't think we have time." Why? Where were they going? Bernie didn't like the sound of it, but he didn't want to say so and make Jane even more nervous than she was.

"Surely, you can spare a few minutes. Would you like a cup of coffee?" Bernie hated being so pleasant to him, but it was all for Jane's sake. Scott declined the coffee, and Jane sat on the arm of Nanny's chair and watched him. He was wearing a turtleneck sweater and blue jeans and he was carrying a brown leather jacket, and he was handsome . . . but not in a way she liked. He looked shiny, instead of warm and cozy like Daddy. And he looked too plain without a beard like Bernie's, she decided.

"What's the little guy's name?" He glanced at the baby, but without much interest, and Nanny told him it was Alexander. She was watching the man's face, and especially his eyes. She didn't like what she saw there, and neither did Bernie. The eyes were darting everywhere and he paid no attention to Jane at all. "Too bad about Liz," he said to Jane, and she almost choked as he said it. "You look a lot like her."

"Thank you," Jane said politely. And with that he stood up and looked at his watch again.

"See you later, folks." He didn't hold a hand out to Jane or tell her where they were going. He just walked to the door and expected her to follow, like a dog, and she looked as though she were about to cry, as Bernie smiled at her encouragingly and gave her a hug before she left, clutching a little pink sweater that matched the dress she wore. She looked as though she were dressed for a party.

"It'll be all right, sweetheart," he whispered. "It's just for a few hours."

"Bye, Daddy." She hung around his neck. "Bye, Nanny . . . bye, Alex." She waved at both of them and blew the baby a kiss as she headed for the door. She suddenly looked like a very little girl again, and Bernie was reminded of the first time he saw her. And something deep inside him made him want to run out and stop her, but he didn't. He watched them instead from the window. Chandler Scott said something to her as he got into a beaten-up old car, and as though with a premonition of doom, he wrote down the license number, as Jane got into the passenger seat gingerly, and the door slammed. And a moment later they drove off and he turned to see Mrs. Pippin frowning at him.

"There's something wrong with that man, Mr. Fine. I don't like him."

"Neither do I, and I agree with you. But the court doesn't want to hear that, not for another month anyway. I just hope to hell nothing happens to her. I'll kill the sonofabitch . . ." He didn't finish the thought, and Nanny went out to the kitchen to pour herself a cup of tea. It was almost time for Alexander's morning nap, and she had work to do, but all day she fretted about Jane, and so did Bernie. He puttered around the house, and he had paperwork and errands to do at home, and other projects waiting for him at the store, but he couldn't concentrate on any of it. He stayed close to home all day in case she called. And at six o'clock he was sitting in the living room, tapping his foot, waiting for her. She was due in an hour, and he was anxious for her to get home.

Nanny brought the baby in to him before he went to bed, but Bernie couldn't even concentrate on him, and she shook her head as she took him to his room. She didn't want to say anything, but she had a terrible feeling in her stomach about the man who had come to take Jane away. And she had the most terrible premonition that something had happened. But she didn't say any of that to Bernie as he waited.

Chapter 28

"Get in the car" was all he said to her as they came down her front steps, and for a moment she was tempted to run back upstairs again. She didn't want to go anywhere with him, and she couldn't imagine how her mother could have loved him. He looked scary to her. He had mean eyes and dirty fingernails, and there was something about the way he talked to her that frightened her. He opened the car door and got in, and as soon as he did he told her again to get in, and with a last look up at the window where Bernie stood, she did.

The car sped away almost immediately, and Jane had to hold onto the door so as not to fall off the seat as he rounded turns and hurried south toward the freeway.

"Where are we going?"

"To pick up a friend at the airport." He had the whole thing worked out, and he wasn't about to discuss it with her. It was none of her goddamn business.

She wanted to ask him not to go so fast, but she was afraid to say anything, and he didn't say anything to her at all. He put the car in the parking lot, and took a small tote bag out of the back seat, and grabbing her arm, he didn't even bother to lock the door, he just pulled her firmly down the path to the terminals.

"Where are we going?" She couldn't fight back the tears anymore. She didn't like him at all, and she wanted to go home. Now. Not later.

"I told you, kid. To the airport."

"Where's your friend going?"

"You're my friend." He turned and looked at her. "And we're going to San Diego."

"For the day?" She knew there was a zoo there, but Daddy had said they would be home by seven. He was the kind of man your parents would have told you not to talk to on the street, but suddenly here she was with him, alone, and going to San Diego.

"Yeah. We'll be home by dinnertime."

"Shouldn't I call Daddy and tell him?"

He laughed at her innocence. "No, sweetheart. I'm Daddy now. And you don't have to call him. I'll call him for you when we get there. Believe me, baby, I'll call him." Everything about him was scary and he took a rough grip on her arm and hurried her along as they crossed the road into the terminal building. She had a sudden urge to run from him, but his grip on her arm was too hard and she sensed easily that he wouldn't have let her go.

"Why are we going to San Diego, Mr. . . . er . . . uh . . . Daddy?" He seemed to want her to call him that, and maybe if she did, he would be nicer to her.

"To visit friends of mine."

"Oh." She wondered why he couldn't have done that another day, and then thought she was stupid not to be enjoying the adventure. It would give her something exciting to talk about that night, but as they got to the security check, he grabbed her arm hard, and his face tightened as he told her to hurry up. And then she had a sudden idea. If she told him she had to go to the bathroom, maybe there would be a phone and she could call Bernie. She had this funny feeling that he would want to know she was going to San Diego with her "other" daddy. She pulled away from Chandler Scott when she saw the door with the familiar sign, and he made a lunge and grabbed her back, as she jumped with surprise. "No, no, cutie pie."

"But I have to go to the bathroom." There were tears in her eyes now. She knew he was doing something wrong. He wouldn't let her out of his sight. Not even to go to the bathroom.

"You can go on the plane."

"I really think I should call Daddy and tell him where we're going."

But he only laughed at her. "Don't worry. I told you. I'll call him." And as he held her arm fast in his hand, he seemed to be looking around, and suddenly a woman with dyed blond hair and dark glasses approached them. She was wearing tight jeans and a purple parka and baseball cap, cowboy boots, and there was something very tough about her. "Got the tickets?" He asked her without a smile and she nodded. She handed them to Chandler without a word and they fell into step side by side, with Jane between them, wondering what was going on. "This her?" She finally asked. Scott only nodded, and Jane was filled with terror. They stopped at the photo machine, took four shots for a dollar, and much to Jane's amazement Chandler Scott pulled out a passport and glued one of the photographs into it. It was a counterfeit passport which would not have borne close inspection, but he knew that children's passports were rarely inspected. And at the gate she suddenly balked and tried to bolt, as Chandler Scott grabbed her arm so hard she almost cried out, and he told her exactly what he was doing.

"If you say one word, or try to run away from us again, your daddy, as you call him, and your baby brother will be dead by five o'clock. Got that, sunshine?" He was smiling evilly at her and speaking in a soft voice, as the woman lit a cigarette and looked around. She appeared to be very nervous.

"Where are you taking me?" She was afraid to speak up after what he had just said. Their lives were in her hands, and she would have done nothing to jeopardize Bernie or the baby. She wondered if they were going to kill her, and her only consolation was that, if they did, she would go to join her mommy. She felt sure of that, and it made it all a little bit less frightening.

"We're going on a little trip."

"Can I go to the bathroom on the plane?"

"Maybe." He looked at her noncommittally, and she wondered again how her mother could have thought him handsome. He looked vicious and dissipated and there was nothing handsome about him. "Whatever you do, sunshine," he snarled at her through clenched teeth, "you're not going anywhere without us. You, my darling daughter, are our little gold mine." She still didn't understand what they were doing and she was convinced they were going to kill her. He then went on to describe to his friend the enormity of Bernie's gold Rolex.

"Maybe he'll give you the watch, if you take me back," she said hopefully as they both laughed and pushed her onto the plane ahead of them. The stewardesses seemed not to notice anything amiss and Jane would never have dared speak up, after the threat they'd made against Bernie and the baby. They never bothered answering her and they both ordered a beer once the plane took off. They got her a Coke but she didn't touch it. She wasn't hungry or thirsty. She just sat very still in her seat, wondering where they were going with the falsified passport, and if she would ever see Bernie or the baby or Mrs. Pippin again. For the moment, it seemed highly unlikely.

Chapter 29

It was after eight o'clock when Bernie finally called Grossman. For an hour he had told himself that maybe they were late. Maybe he'd had a flat tire on the way back, in that ramshackle car of his, maybe anything . . . but by eight o'clock they could have called, and suddenly he knew that something terrible had happened.

Grossman was home, having dinner with friends, and Bernie apologized for bothering him. "That's all right. How'd it go today?" He hoped it had gone without a hitch. It would be easier for all of them if they accepted the inevitable. His experience told him that Chandler Scott was going to be difficult to get rid of.

"That's why I called you, Bill. I'm sorry. They were supposed to be back over an hour ago, and they're not back yet. I'm getting worried. No, I'm getting *very* worried." Grossman thought he was being premature, and he thought he overrated Scott as a villain.

"Maybe he had a flat tire."

"He could have called. And when was the last time you had a flat tire?"

"When I was sixteen years old and stole my father's Mercedes."

"Right. Try again. What do we do now?"

"First of all, you relax. He's probably just trying to be a big shot with her. They'll probably turn up at nine o'clock or something, having gone to a double feature, and had ten ice cream cones." He was still convinced of that, and wouldn't let Bernie drag him into his paranoia. "Just relax for a while."

Bernie looked at his watch. "I'll give him another hour."

"And then what? You hit the streets with your shotgun?"

"I don't find this as amusing as you do, Bill. That's my daughter he's out with."

"I know, I know, I'm sorry. But it's also his daughter. And he'd have to be a raving maniac to do something crazy, particularly the first time out. The man may be unpleasant, but I don't think he's stupid."

"I hope you're right."

"Look. Give it till nine o'clock, then call me back, and we'll see what comes to mind then."

Bernie called him back at five minutes to nine, unwilling to be put off again. "I'm calling the police."

"And what are you going to tell them?"

"For one thing, I wrote down his license plate,

for another, I'm going to tell them I think he's kidnapped my child."

"Let me tell you something, Bernie. I know that you're upset, but I want you to think this thing out. For one thing, she's not your child, she's his, legally anyway, and for another, if he did take her, which I sincerely doubt, it's considered child stealing and not kidnap."

"What difference does that make?" Bernie didn't understand.

"Child stealing is a misdemeanor, and it is the removal of a child by a parent."

"In this case, it would not be 'removal,' but kidnap. The guy is a common criminal. Christ, he didn't even say two words to her when he picked her up. He just looked around the house and walked out, expecting her to follow, then he drove off in that rattrap car, and God knows where they are now." He felt hysterical just thinking about it, and he felt as though he had betrayed his promise to Liz. He knew he had. She had begged him not to let Chandler get his hands on Jane, and that was exactly what he had done.

Bernie called the police at ten o'clock, and they were sympathetic, but not overly worried. Like Bill, they felt sure that Chandler would eventually show up. "Maybe he had a few too many," they suggested. But at eleven o'clock, when he was near tears, they finally agreed to come and take a report from him, and by then Grossman was getting worried.

"You still haven't heard?" The police were still there.

"No, I haven't. Do you believe me now?"

"Christ, I hope not." He had been describing to the police what Jane had been wearing, and Nanny was quietly sitting in the living room with him in her dressing gown and slippers. She looked extremely proper and she had a calming effect on him, which was fortunate because half an hour later the police discovered that the license plate he'd taken down was of a car that had been stolen that morning. It was serious now. At least to Bernie. To the police it was exactly what Bill had predicted. Child stealing and no more, a misdemeanor and not a felony and they didn't even give a damn about the fact that he had a criminal record an arm long. They were more upset about the stolen car, and they put an APB out for it, but not for his daughter.

He called Grossman at midnight with that bit of news, and the moment he hung up, the phone rang. It was finally Chandler.

"Hi there, pal." Bernie almost got hysterical when he heard his voice. The police were gone, and here he was, alone. And Scott had his daughter.

"Where the hell are you?"

"Janie and I are just fine."

"I asked you where you were."

"Out of town for a spell. And she's just fine, aren't you, sweetheart?" He chucked her under the chin a little roughly as she stood shivering in the phone booth with him. She had only brought a sweater and it was November.

"What do you mean out of town?"

"I wanted to give you enough time to get the money together, pal."

"What money?"

"The five hundred thousand bucks you're going to give me to bring little Janie home. Right, sweetheart?" He looked down at her again, but he didn't really see her. "In fact, little Janie even thought you'd like to throw in that fancy watch you were wearing today, and I think that's a great idea. You might even want to throw in another one for my friend here."

"What friend?" Bernie was frantically thinking and getting nowhere.

"Never mind. Let's talk about the money. How soon can you get it?"

"Are you serious?" Bernie's heart was pounding.

"Very."

"Never. . . . My God, do you know how much money that is? It's a goddamn fortune. I can't get you that kind of money." There were suddenly tears in his eyes. He had not only lost Liz. He had lost Jane. Possibly forever. And God only knew where she was or what they would do to her.

"You'd better get me that money, Fine, or you're not going to be seeing Janie. I can wait a long, long time. And I figure you want her back eventually."

"You're a rotten sonofabitch."

"And you're a rich one."

"How do I find you?"

"I'll call you tomorrow. Stay off your phone and don't call the cops or I'll kill her." She stood staring at Scott with terrified interest as he said that but he didn't notice. He was concentrating on his conversation with Bernie.

"How do I know you haven't killed her already?" The thought terrified him, it was more than he could bear as he said the words. He felt as though there were a hand squeezing his heart.

At his end, Chandler Scott shoved the phone into her face. "Here, talk to your old man." She knew enough not to tell him where she was. She wasn't even sure herself. And she had seen their guns, and knew they meant business.

"Hi, Daddy." Her voice sounded so little and she started to cry the minute she got on the phone. "I love you. . . . I'm okay. . . ."

"I'm going to bring you home, sweetheart . . . whatever it takes . . . I promise . . ." But Chandler Scott didn't let her answer. He ripped the phone away and promptly hung up on Bernie.

He dialed Grossman with trembling hands. It was twelve-thirty by then. "He's got her."

"I know he's got her. Where is he?"

"He wouldn't tell me. And he wants half a million dollars." Bernie sounded breathless, as though he'd been running, and there was an endless silence.

"He kidnapped her?" Grossman sounded stunned.

"Yes, you asshole. Isn't that what I told you
. . . I'm sorry. What the hell do I do now? I don't
have that kind of money." He knew only one person who might, and he wasn't even sure he did,
and certainly not available in cash, but he would
try it.

"I'll call the police."

"I already did that."

"This is different." But it wasn't. They were no
more impressed than they had been an hour before. As far as they were concerned, it was a private matter, between two men, wrestling over one
child they both felt they owned, and the police
didn't want to get involved. He probably didn't
mean it about the money.

And all through the night, Nanny Pippin sat
there with Bernie, pouring tea, and eventually a
brandy. He needed it. He was as white as a sheet.
And at one point, between phone calls, she looked
him directly in the eye and spoke to him as she
would have a frightened child.

"We'll find them."

"How do you know that?"

"Because you're an intelligent man, and right is
on your side."

"I wish I were sure of that, Nanny." She patted
his hand, and he dialed Paul Berman in New York.
It was almost five o'clock in the morning, and
Berman said he didn't have the money. He was
aghast at what had happened. But he explained
that he didn't ever keep that much cash. He would
have to sell stocks, and he owned them all jointly

with his wife. He would need his wife's permission to sell and he would also lose a fortune if he sold because the market was rotten. He explained that it would take time if he could even do it. And Bernie knew he wasn't the answer.

"Did you call the police?"

"They don't give a damn. Apparently 'child stealing,' as they call it, is no big deal in this state. The child's natural father can do no wrong."

"They ought to kill him."

"I will if I find him."

"Let me know what I can do to help."

"Thanks, Paul." And he hung up.

He called Grossman again after that. "I can't get the money. Now what?"

"I have an idea. I know an investigator I've worked with."

"Can we call him now?"

There was only a fraction of a second of hesitation, but basically Bill Grossman was a decent guy, just a great deal too trusting. "I'll call him." He called back five minutes later and promised that the investigator would be there in half an hour. And so would Grossman.

It was three o'clock in the morning as the group assembled in Bernie's living room. Bill Grossman, Bernie, the investigator, who was a heavyset, ordinary man in his late thirties, a woman he had brought whom Bernie couldn't figure out, and Nanny in her dressing gown and slippers. She served tea and coffee to everyone. And she brought Bernie another brandy. She decided that the others didn't need one. They were going to have to stay sober, if they were going to find Jane for them.

The investigator's name was Jack Winters, his associate, the woman, was his wife and her name was Gertie. They were both ex-narcs, and after years of working underground for the San Francisco police, they had decided to open their own business. And Bill Grossman swore that they were terrific.

Bernie told them everything he knew about Chandler Scott's past, his relationship with Liz, his arrests, his time in prison, and his relationship, or lack of it, with Jane. And then he gave them the license plate of the stolen car, and sat back looking at them in terror.

"Can you find her?"

"Maybe." The investigator had a drooping mustache and a manner which suggested that he wasn't very bright, but his eyes were as sharp as any Bernie had ever seen. And the woman seemed to have the same interesting combination. She was plain but she wasn't stupid. "I suspect he went to Mexico or some place like that."

"Why?"

His eyes bore into Bernie's. "Just a feeling. Give me a few hours and I'll put some possibilities together for you. You don't have any pictures of him, do you?" Bernie shook his head, and he didn't think Liz had any either, and if she did, he had never seen them.

"What'll I tell him when he calls?"

"That you're getting the money together for him. Keep him busy . . . keep him waiting . . . and don't sound too scared. It'll make him think you've got the money."

Bernie looked worried. "I already told him I didn't."

"That's all right. He probably doesn't believe you."

They promised to contact him by the end of the day, and suggested he try to relax while he waited. But he had to ask them something before they left. He hated to ask the question, but he had to.

"Do you think . . . could he . . . do you think he might hurt her?" He couldn't say the word kill. It was too much for him by five o'clock that morning. And Gertie spoke to him in a soft voice, as she looked at him with wise eyes. She was a woman who had seen a lot, and he knew it.

"We hope not. We're going to do everything we can to find him before he does. Trust us."

He did, and they were back twelve hours later. It had been an interminable wait for Bernie. He had paced the floor, drunk more coffee, more brandy, more tea, and finally fallen into bed at ten o'clock the next morning, hysterical and exhausted. Nanny had never gone to bed at all but had taken care of Alexander all day, and was feeding him dinner when the doorbell rang and the investigators returned. Bernie didn't know how, but they had collected a fascinating portfolio of information, and they couldn't have had much sleep either.

They had all of Scott's mug shots and prison records. He had done time in seven states, always for theft or burglary or con games or bunko. He had lots of arrests for bad checks as well, but most of those had been dropped, maybe he had made up the money to the people involved, but they weren't sure and it didn't matter.

"The interesting pattern here is that everything this man does is for money. Not drugs, not sex, not passion . . . but money. You might say it's his hobby."

Bernie looked at them mournfully. "I wouldn't call half a million dollars a hobby."

Winters nodded. "Now he's hit the big time." They had checked with his parole officer, because he was an old friend of Jack's, it turned out, and they had hit on the right one the first time around, which was good luck on a Sunday, and they knew where Scott had been staying. He had checked out the day before, and he had said something to someone about going to Mexico. The stolen car had been located at the airport. And three stolen tickets had turned up on a flight to San Diego, and the threesome had been long gone by then, and the stewardess whom Gertie had talked to between flights that day thought she remembered a little girl, but she wasn't certain.

"My guess is that they've gone to Mexico. And they're going to sit on Jane till you come up with the money. And to tell you the truth, I feel better now looking at this guy's record. There's not a single act of violence here. That's something at least. If we're lucky, he won't hurt her."

"But how the hell do we find him?"

"We'll start looking today. If you want us to, we could be on our way down there tonight. I'd like to start from San Diego and see if I can pick up the trail there. They probably stole another car, or rented one they aren't going to return. They're not as smooth as you'd think. I think he knows he's in no real danger. He's not facing kidnapping charges here. We're talking child stealing—in the eyes of the law, that's peanuts." Bernie got angry just hearing it, but he knew it was true. And he was ready to do anything to find her.

"I want you to start right away." They both nodded. They had already made tentative arrangements, in case he said that. "What do I say when he calls me?" He still hadn't.

"Tell him you're working on getting the money. That it may take some time, a week or two. Give us some time to get down there and start looking. Two weeks ought to do it. We should have located them by then." It was an optimistic assessment but they also had a good description of his girl friend, who also had a record and was on parole and had been living with him at the hotel he had checked out of the previous morning.

"Do you really think you'll find him in two weeks?"

"We'll do our damnedest." And he believed they would.

"When are you leaving?"

"Maybe around ten o'clock tonight. We have to make a few more arrangements." They had three other jobs they were working on, but this was the biggest and they had other operatives to take over on the others. "Speaking of which—" He mentioned their fee, and it was a big one, but Bernie wasn't going to quibble. He'd come up with it somehow. He had to.

"That's fine. Where can I reach you if he calls me?"

They gave him a number where they'd be until they left, and twenty minutes after they left he got another call from Chandler.

"How's it going, old pal?"

"Fine. I'm working on getting the money."

"Good. Glad to hear it. When do you think you'll have it?"

He had a sudden flash of genius. "Probably not for a week or two. I've got to go to New York to get it."

"Shit, man." Scott sounded pissed and Bernie could hear him confer with his friend for a long time, and then finally he came back on the phone. They had bought the story. "All right. But two weeks is it. I'll call you two weeks from tonight. Be there. Or I'll kill her." And with that, he hung up, without even letting him talk to Jane. He was panicked but he dialed Winters' number.

"Why'd you tell him you were going to New York?" Winters was puzzled.

"Because I want to come with you." There was a brief silence.

"Are you sure? It may be rough. And he'll recognize you if you get close."

"I want to be close to Jane, if she needs me, when you get there. I'm all she's got left now. And I couldn't stand sitting here waiting." Bernie didn't see Nanny standing in the doorway, listening to him, and she quietly disappeared. She approved of his idea of going to Mexico to help find her. "Can I come? I'll still pay you the same fee."

"I'm not worried about that. I'm thinking about you. Wouldn't you be better off staying here, trying to continue your normal life?"

"My life stopped being normal at seven o'clock last night, and it won't be normal again until you find my daughter."

"We'll pick you up in an hour. Travel light."

"See you then." He hung up, feeling better. He called Grossman, who promised to report the entire disaster to the court the following morning. And he called Paul Berman in New York and his assistant at the store. And then he called his mother.

"Mom, I've got bad news for you." His voice trembled at the prospect of telling her. But he had to say something. Thanksgiving had just been all shot to hell, and maybe even Christmas and New Year's . . . and the rest of her life. . . .

"Something happened to the baby?" Her heart stopped.

"No. It's Jane." He took a deep breath and plunged in. "I don't have time to explain it all to you now. But Liz' ex-husband appeared a while back, he's a real sonofabitch and he's spent most of the last ten years in and out of jail. Anyway, he tried to blackmail me out of some money, and I wouldn't pay him. So he kidnapped Jane. He's holding her for half a million dollars ransom."

"Oh my God." She sounded as though she had just died and he felt it. "Oh my God . . . Bernie . . ." She couldn't believe it. What kind of person did something like that? What kind of lunatic was he? "Is she all right? Do you know?"

"We think so. And the police won't really get involved because his being the natural father makes it only child stealing, which is no big deal, and not kidnap. They're not real excited."

"Oh Bernie . . ." She started to cry.

"Don't, Mom, please. I can't take it. I'm calling because I'm leaving for Mexico tonight, to try to find her with two investigators I hired. They think she might be there . . . and Thanksgiving is off."

"Never mind Thanksgiving. Just find her. Oh my God . . ." For once in her life, she really thought she was going to have a heart attack, and Lou was out at some damn medical meeting. She didn't even remember where he was now.

"I'll call you if I can. The investigator thinks we might find her in two weeks . . ." To him, it sounded hopeful, to her it sounded like a nightmare, and she began sobbing into the phone.

"My God, Bernie . . ."

"I've got to go, Mom. I love you." He went to pack a small bag then, and put on a shirt, a warm ski sweater, blue jeans, a parka, and hiking boots. And as he turned to pick up his suitcase he saw Nanny Pippin standing in the doorway with the baby in her arms. And he told her what he was doing. He was leaving for Mexico at once, and he promised to call her as often as he could. And he wanted her to be careful of the baby. He was suddenly worried about everyone, after what had happened to Jane, but she assured him they'd be fine.

"Just bring Jane back soon." It sounded like an order and he smiled at the brogue as he kissed his son. "Be careful, Mr. Fine. We need you whole and hearty."

He hugged her silently and then walked to the doorway without looking back. There were too many people missing now . . . Jane and Liz . . . but he hurried down the stairs as Winters honked outside in an old station wagon that one of their operatives was driving.

Chapter 30

As they drove to the airport, Bernie couldn't help thinking how strange his life had become. Barely more than a year before, his life had been so normal. A wife he loved, a new baby, and the child she'd had before. Now suddenly Liz was gone, Jane had been kidnapped and was being held for ransom, and he was about to travel all over Mexico with two strangers he had hired to find her. And as he looked out the window, his thoughts of Jane rapidly overwhelmed him. He was terrified that Chandler Scott and his associates might do something to hurt her. And the thought of their molesting her had been on his mind all night. He mentioned it at the airport to Gertie, but she seemed sure that Scott's interest was purely the money, and Bernie let her convince him.

He called Grossman from the airport again and promised to let him know their progress. And it was a long night after that. They arrived in San

Diego at eleven-thirty, and rented a large car with four-wheel drive. Winters had arranged for it from San Francisco, and they set off in the car directly from the airport. They didn't want to waste time stopping at a hotel, and they crossed the border at Tijuana. They drove rapidly through Rosarito and Descanso, and were in Ensenada an hour later. Winters had a feeling that they would have gone there, and with only a fifty-dollar bill in hand, the border guard had remembered them in Tijuana.

It was after one o'clock by then, but the bars were still alive, and they spent an hour in Ensenada walking into a dozen bars, each one taking a cluster of them, ordering a beer, and then showing Scott's picture. Gertie came up with the gold this time, a bartender who even remembered the child. She was very fair, he said, and she seemed afraid of the couple with her. Scott's girl friend had asked him about the ferry to Guaymas at Cabo Haro.

Gertie hurried back to the car with the information, and they set out on the route the bartender had suggested, south through San Vicente, San Telmo, Rosario, and then east across Baja to El Marmol. It was nearly two hundred miles and the trip took them five hours on rough roads, despite the four-wheel drive. They stopped in El Marmol for gas at seven o'clock Monday morning, and at eight o'clock they stopped for something to eat as they drove down the east coast of Baja. They had two hundred miles to go to Santa Rosalia. And it was a long tiresome day before they got there shortly before three o'clock. And then they had to wait two hours for the ferry to Guaymas. But they hit gold again when the ferry operator who helped them load their car remembered Scott, the woman, and the child who sat between them.

"What do you think, Jack?" He and Bernie stood on the deck watching Baja disappear behind them, as Gertie stood some distance from them.

"So far so good, but don't expect it to stay that way. It doesn't work that way, as a rule. At least we're off to a good start so far."

"Maybe we'll get lucky fast." Bernie wanted to believe that, but Jack Winters knew it wasn't likely.

It was a hundred miles from Santa Rosalia to Empalme, and two hundred and fifty from Empalme to Espiritu Santo where the man on the boat thought Scott had gotten off. But in Espiritu Santo the men on the dock were sure he had gone to Mazatlan, which was another two hundred and fifty miles. And there the trail went cold. By Wednesday they knew nothing more than they had in San Francisco. It was another week before, with painstaking work covering almost every bar and restaurant and store and hotel in Mazatlan, the trail continued to Guadalajara. It was only three hundred and twenty-four miles from Mazatlan to Guadalajara and it had taken them eight days of painstaking work to follow Scott there.

In Guadalajara they knew he had stayed at a tiny hotel called Rosalba's on a back street, and they

knew very little more than that. Jack had a feeling
they would have gone inland, maybe to one of the
small towns on the way to Aguascalientes. It took
them another two days to follow that lead, and by
then it was Friday and Bernie's time had run out.
He had to be back in San Francisco in two days to
get Scott's phone call.

"What do we do now?" They had talked all
along of Bernie flying back to San Francisco from
Guadalajara, if they hadn't found her yet, so he
could take Scott's phone call, and the Winters
would stay in Mexico to hear from him. They were
calling Grossman daily, and Bernie was calling
Nanny and Alexander. All was well with them, and
he missed his son terribly. But by Friday, his
thoughts were filled with Jane, and the bastard
holding her hostage.

"I think you'd better go back tomorrow." Winters was thinking as he spoke, and they were both
drinking a cerveza back at their hotel. "I think you
ought to tell him that you've got the money."
Winters' eyes narrowed, formulating a plan, but
Bernie didn't like it.

"Five hundred thousand dollars? And what do I
do when I'm supposed to give it to him? Tell him
it was all a joke?"

"Just arrange a meeting place with him. We'll
worry about it after that. It'll tell us a lot if he
wants to meet us somewhere down here. You can
explain that it will take you a day or two to get
down here, and by then, with luck, we'll have
him."

Winters was thinking all the time. But so was Bernie. "You don't think they're back in the States by now?"

"Not a chance of it." Winters was sure of that. "He's too scared of the cops, if he has any brains. They won't do much to him for this, but with his record, that stolen car is going to wind him right back in jail, on a parole violation, if nothing else."

"Amazing, isn't it?" Bernie looked at him bitterly. "He steals a child, threatens her, maybe causes her untold emotional damage for the rest of her life, and they worry about a beat-up old car. Nice, our system, isn't it? It's enough to make you a goddamn Communist. I'd like to see the bastard hanged for this!"

"You won't." Winters was philosophical. He had seen a lot of this kind of thing, and worse. Enough to make him never want a kid, and his wife agreed with him. They didn't even have a dog anymore, after their last one was stolen and poisoned and dropped on their doorstep by someone they'd once gotten arrested.

They discovered nothing more the next day, and he left on Saturday night for San Francisco. He was home in San Francisco by nine o'clock that night, and he hurried back to the house, suddenly desperately anxious to see the baby. Now he was all he had left. Not only was Liz gone, but Jane was too, and what he wondered was if he'd ever hear her voice again, echoing down the hall as she came running to him, shouting "Hi, Daddy!" The thought of it was too much for him, and after he set down the bags in Nanny's room, he walked out quietly and went to sit in the living room, his face in his hands as he cried silently. It was too much to lose both of them, and Jane like this. He felt as though he had failed Liz in the only way that had ever mattered to her.

"Mr. Fine?" Nanny had seen the look on his face, and she had left Alexander asleep in his crib to find his father. She walked quietly into the darkened living room, knowing what a terrible two weeks it had been for him . . . a terrible fourteen months in fact. . . . He was such a decent man, and she was so sorry for him. Only her faith in God kept her certain that they would find Jane and bring her home again and she tried to tell him that from the doorway, but at first he didn't answer. "She'll be home again. God will give us the wisdom we need to find her." But instead, he found himself thinking of the Lindbergh kidnapping years before, and the heartbreak those people must have gone through.

"What if we never find them?" He sounded like a child, convinced that all was lost, but she refused to believe that. And slowly he raised his head to look at her, with the light shining behind her in the doorway. "Nanny, I couldn't face that."

"With the grace of God, you won't have to." She came over and patted his shoulder and turned on the light. And a few minutes later she brought him a mug of steaming tea and a sandwich. "You should go to bed early tonight. You'll think better in the morning, Mr. Fine." But what was there to think about? How to pretend he had half a million dollars he didn't? He was very, very frightened, and he hardly slept at all that night, tossing and turning, and thinking.

And in the morning Bill Grossman came to see him. They talked endlessly about where they'd been and what they'd found and how the trail went cold in Guadalajara. Winters called them that morning to report in and there was nothing new since the day before except a suggestion Gertie had made.

"She thinks we ought to try Puerto Vallarta." They had talked about it before, but decided he'd be too visible there, and would be more likely to go inland. "Maybe she's right. Maybe he's cocky enough to try something like that. And we know he likes the good life. Maybe he's trying on a yacht for size." But Bernie didn't think it very likely.

"Give it a shot." He was staying home all day, in case Scott called earlier than he said he would. He was terrified to miss him. And Grossman sat keeping him company till the late afternoon. He had already told him that morning that the court had proclaimed themselves "distressed" over Mr. Scott's "poor judgment." "Distressed?" Bernie had shouted. *"Distressed?* Are they out of their goddamn minds? My kid is God knows where right now, thanks to their stupidity, and they're *distressed?* How touching." Grossman knew how upset he was, and he had a right to be. He didn't tell him that the social worker assigned to the case had said it was probably because Mr. Scott was anxious to make up for lost time and get to know his daughter. There was a good chance that if Grossman had told Bernie that, he would have gone to City Hall and killed her. Not quite, but close. And his nerves were badly frayed when the phone rang at five o'clock. Bernie was sure that it was Scott, and he took a breath before he picked up the phone. "Yes?"

It wasn't Scott. It was Winters. "We've got something for you. Did he call yet?" It was just like playing cops and robbers, except what they'd stolen was his heart . . . his baby . . .

"No. I'm still waiting. What's up?"

"I'm not sure yet . . . but we may have found him. Gertie was right. He's been all over Puerto Vallarta."

"Is Jane with him?" Oh God . . . please God . . . don't let them have killed her. . . . He had been thinking more and more of the parents in cases like this who never saw their children again. Thousands of them every year . . . the figures were something terrible like a hundred thousand. . . .

"I'm not sure. He's been spending a lot of time at a place called Carlos O'Brien's." And so did everyone in Vallarta. It was the most popular bar in town, and Scott was a fool to have gone there. But no one seemed to remember the child or the woman. He had probably left them at a hotel. "See if you can get something out of him when he calls. Maybe you can chat for a while. . . . Play it friendly." Bernie felt his palm sweat on the phone at the thought.

"I'll try."

"And make a date with him. Pretend you've got the money."

"Yeah."

Bernie was a nervous wreck when he hung up, and explained to Grossman. And the phone rang again less than five minutes later. This time it was Scott, with a very poor long-distance connection.

"How you doing, pal?" He sounded happy and relaxed and Bernie wished that he could get his hands on him and throttle him till he choked.

"Fine. I've got good news for you." He tried to sound relaxed and in control and unconcerned as he shouted over the static.

"What kind of news?"

"Half a million dollars' worth." Bernie played his part well. "How's Jane?"

"That's great news!" Scott sounded delighted, but not as much as Bernie would have liked.

"I said, 'How's Jane?'" His hand clenched on the phone as he waited and Grossman watched him.

"She's fine. But I've got bad news for you." Bernie's heart stopped. "The price has gone up. She's such a cute little thing, I just figure she's worth a lot more than I originally thought."

"Oh really?"

"Yep. I think she's worth a million now, don't you?" Jesus Christ.

"That's not going to be easy." He scribbled the

amount down on a piece of paper for Grossman. But it might give them more time. "I'll have to go back to my sources again."

"You got the five hundred thou now?"

"Yes," he lied.

"Then why don't we do it in installments?"

"Do I get Jane back after the first installment?"

Scott laughed at him. "Not likely, old buddy." Sonofabitch. Bernie had never hated anyone so much, or had so much good reason. "You get her back when we get the whole million."

"Fine, then you don't get it in installments."

Scott's voice hardened in the phone. "I'll give you a week to get the other half, Fine. And if I don't get it . . ." He was the greediest bastard alive. But now they had another week to find Jane. With luck, in Puerto Vallarta.

"I want to talk to her." Bernie's voice matched Scott's.

"She's not here."

"Where is she?"

"She's safe. Don't you worry."

"I want to make one thing very clear to you, Scott. If you hurt one hair on her head, I'm going to kill you. You got that? And you're not getting one thin dime until I see her alive and healthy."

"She'll be fine." He laughed. "Hell, she even has a suntan." Puerto Vallarta.

"Where is she?"

"Never mind. She can tell you all about it when she comes home. I'll call you one week from to-night, and you better have the money, Fine."

"I will. You better have Jane."

"You got yourself a deal." He laughed. "For one million dollars." And on those words he hung up, as Bernie sat back breathlessly. There was a film of sweat on his forehead, and when he looked at Grossman, the lawyer was shaking.

"Nice guy." Grossman felt sick.

"Isn't he?" Bernie sounded bitter. He felt as though he would never recover from this, even if they did get her back.

The phone rang again half an hour later. It was Winters. He didn't mince words. "We got him."

"Oh my God. Are you serious? I just talked to him." Bernie's hand shook on the phone, and his voice trembled.

"I mean we know where he is. A waitress at Carlos O'Brien's has been babysitting for Jane. I had to pay her a thousand dollars to keep her mouth shut, but it was worth it. She says she's fine. She told the girl that Scott isn't really her dad, but he 'used to be,' he was married to her mom once, but he told her that if she ran away or tried to get help, he'd kill you and the baby. Apparently the girl friend got tired of babysitting at night while Scott goes out to play, so they hired this waitress."

"Christ! How could he tell her a thing like that?"

"That's not unusual. Usually they tell them their parents are dead or don't want to see them anymore. It's amazing what kids will believe when they're scared."

"Why didn't the girl go to the police?"

"She says she didn't want to get involved, you never know if kids are telling the truth. And anyway, he was paying her. We just paid her more. And she may be sleeping with him, but I don't think that holds much weight with her." She had offered Winters a blow job for another hundred dollars. But he hadn't put it on the expense account, and he'd laughed when he told Gertie. She was slightly less amused than he was. "What did he say on the phone?" Winters was worried they were going to make a move that night, after the conversation, and it might be hard to follow him without being spotted.

"He wants a million now. And he gave me a week to get it."

"Great. That means he'll relax. I want to grab the kid tonight. Okay by you? For another thousand bucks, the girl will help me. She's supposed to babysit for Jane tonight. I want to grab her then." Bernie's heart turned over at the thought. Please God keep her safe. "We can't get a plane out of here tonight, but we'll drive like hell for Mazatlan and catch a plane out in the morning." He sounded every inch a professional, and he was. But Bernie would have preferred to be there. He knew how frightening it would be for Jane. And Jack and his wife were just two more strangers. But it would be easier for them to move fast than it would have been with him, and Nanny and the baby. "With luck, you'll have her home tomorrow."

"Keep me posted."

"You should hear from us by midnight." It was the longest night of his life, and Grossman went home around seven and told him to call if he heard anything, no matter how late it was. Bernie thought of calling his mother too, and then decided to wait until he had more to tell her.

He didn't have as long to wait as Winters had thought. Shortly after ten o'clock he got a collect call from Valle de Banderas in Jalisco.

"Do you essept de charges?" the operator asked, and he instantly said yes. For once Nanny Pippin had gone to bed, and he was alone in the kitchen. He had been making a fresh pot of coffee.

"Jack?"

"We got her. She's fine. She's asleep in the car with Gertie. She's exhausted. I'm sorry to say it, but we scared the hell out of her. The girl let us in and we grabbed her. She's going to tell Scott that the cops grabbed the kid. You may not even hear from him for a while. Anyway, we've got reservations on a nine A.M. flight out of Mazatlan and we're staying at the Holiday Inn when we get there. And no one's going to touch her now." Bernie knew they were armed. There were tears streaming down his cheeks as he held the phone, and all he could say to the man who'd saved Jane was "Thank you," as he hung up the phone, sat down at the kitchen table, laid his head on his arms, and sobbed with relief and regret and pent-up terror. His baby was coming home. . . . If only Liz had been coming with her . . .

Chapter 31

The plane landed at eleven o'clock local time and Bernie was waiting at the airport with Nanny and Grossman and the baby. Jane was holding Gertie's hand as she walked off the plane, and Bernie lunged forward and swept her off the ground, holding her close to him as he sobbed openly. And for once even Nanny didn't retain her composure. There were tears streaming from her blue eyes as she kissed the child, and even Bill Grossman kissed her.

"Oh baby . . . I'm so sorry . . ." Bernie could barely speak, and Jane couldn't stop crying and laughing as she kissed him and the baby and Nanny.

"They said that if I said anything or tried to run away . . ." She started crying again. She couldn't say the words, but he knew it from Winters. "They said they had someone following you all the time."

"It was a lie, sweetheart. Like everything else they told you."

"He's a terrible man. I don't know why Mommy ever married him. And he's *not* handsome, he's ugly, and his friend was horrible . . ." But Gertie said that from talking to her alone, she was positive that the child hadn't been molested. They were strictly interested in the money, and they must have been mad as hell when they found that she was gone when they got back from Carlos O'Brien's.

When they got back to the house, Jane looked around as though she thought she had gone to heaven. It was exactly sixteen days since she'd left home and the nightmare had begun for all of them. Sixteen days and forty thousand dollars to find her. His parents had sold stock to help him pay Winters' fees, but it was worth every penny. And they called them now, so Jane could talk with Grandma Ruth herself, but his mother could only sob into the phone and finally had to pass it on to Lou. She had been sure that they would kill her. She had remembered the Lindbergh kidnapping too. She had been a young woman when it happened and it had impressed her all her life.

Bernie held Jane in his arms for hours that day, and they reported to the police that she'd been found, but no one sounded very excited, and the court was notified too. They proclaimed themselves pleased to hear it, and Bernie was bitter against everyone except Jack Winters. He had Winters line up bodyguards for him. Jane and

Alexander were not to leave the house without an armed guard, and Bernie wanted one at home with her whenever he was out. And then he called Paul Berman and told him he'd be back in the store by morning. He had only taken two weeks off, but it felt like a lifetime.

"Is she all right?" Berman was still horrified at what had happened. Those poor people had had one nightmare after another, with Liz dying and now this. He felt desperately sorry for Bernie and he had already begun the search for someone to replace him in California. Even Berman realized now that it wasn't fair to leave him in San Francisco any longer. The guy had been through enough, although he knew it might take months, or even a year, to find a replacement to run the San Francisco store. But at least the search had started.

"Jane's fine."

"We all prayed for her, Bernie."

"Thanks, Paul."

He hung up, feeling grateful that they had found her. He thought again about the people who never saw their children again, fathers and mothers who spent a lifetime wondering if their children were alive, and cherishing photographs of five-year-olds who by then were in their twenties or thirties, and maybe didn't even know their parents were alive, after the lies the kidnappers had told them. To Bernie, child stealing seemed almost as awful as murder.

The phone rang that night while they were having dinner. Nanny had made steak and asparagus hollandaise, because it was Jane's favorite. And she had made a huge chocolate cake for dessert, which Alexander was eyeing with lust, as Bernie stood up and went to answer the phone. The phone had rung all afternoon and all evening with calls from well-wishers, thrilled and relieved that their horror was over. Tracy had even called from Philadelphia. She had called earlier. Nanny had told her what had happened.

"Hello?" Bernie was smiling at Jane. They hadn't taken their eyes off each other all day, and she had fallen asleep on his lap for a while just before dinner.

There was static on the line, and a familiar voice. Bernie couldn't believe it. But he switched on the recording device Grossman had given him the day before. He had also recorded the request for the million dollars in ransom. "Got your baby back, eh?" Scott did not sound pleased, as Bernie listened, and watched the machine record him. "I gather the cops helped you grab her." The girl had told Scott just what she was supposed to and Bernie was pleased.

"I don't have much to say to you."

"I'm sure you'll find something to say in court." It was a joke. He knew Scott wouldn't dare take him to court again.

"I'm not real worried about that, Scott, and if you ever lay a hand on her again, I'll have you arrested. In fact, I might have you arrested anyway."

"On what grounds? Child stealing is a misde-meanor anyway. They'd put me in jail overnight, if they did that much."

"I'm not so sure kidnap for ransom is so popu-lar with the local courts."

"Try to prove it, buddy. You never got anything in writing from me, and if you were dumb enough to tape our conversations, it won't do you any good anyway. Recordings are inadmissible in court." The guy certainly knew what he was do-ing. "You haven't seen the last of me yet, Fine. There are more ways to skin a cat than one." But with that, Bernie hung up on him and stopped the recording device. He called Grossman after din-ner, and Bill confirmed to him what Chandler Scott had said. Recordings were inadmissible.

"Then why the hell did you have me bother to do that?" The law was definitely not on his side in this instance, and they had done nothing to help since the beginning.

"Because even if it can't be used as evidence, the people at Family Court can still listen to it, and hear what you were up against." But when Bill gave them the recordings they were less than sym-pathetic, and declared that Scott had probably been joking, or perhaps under some terrible strain after not seeing his daughter for so long, and hearing that his ex-wife had died of cancer.

"Are they crazy, or are they just kidding?" Bernie had stared at him. "The guy is a criminal and he kidnapped her for a million dollars ran-som, and he held her hostage in Mexico for sixteen days and they think he was 'joking'?" Bernie couldn't believe it. First the police didn't give a damn when Scott took her, and now the court didn't give a damn about the request for ransom.

But the worst news came the following week when they received a notification from the court that Scott wanted a custody hearing.

"A *custody* hearing?" Bernie almost ripped the phone out of the wall when Bill told him. "Custody of what?"

"His daughter. He is claiming to the court that the only reason he took her is that he loves her so desperately, and he wants her with him, where she belongs."

"Where? In jail? Do they take kids in San Quentin? That's where the sonofabitch belongs." Bernie was hysterical in his office, and at that very moment Jane was at the park with Nanny Pippin and the baby and a black bodyguard who had played tackle for the Redskins ten years before and was six feet five inches tall and weighed two hundred and ninety pounds. Bernie was praying that Scott would annoy him.

"Calm down. He doesn't have custody yet. He's just asking."

"Why? Why is he doing this to me?"

"You want to know why?" It was the worst case Grossman had ever had, and he was beginning to hate Scott as much as Bernie did, but that wouldn't get them anywhere. They had to be rational about it. "He's doing this because if he gets custody, God forbid, or even visitation, he's going to sell her back to you. If he can't do it by kidnapping her, he'll do it legally. Because the rights are his, he's her natural father, but you have the money, and that's what he wants."

"So let's give it to him. Why fool around going through the courts and playing games? He wants money, let's offer it to him now." It seemed very simple to Bernie. Scott didn't have to torture him to get what he wanted.

"It's not as simple as that. It's against the law for you to offer him any money."

"Oh. I see," Bernie said angrily. "But it's okay for him to kidnap the kid and ask for a million dollars ransom, that's okay, but my trying to buy the sonofabitch off isn't. Jesus Christ"—he slammed a hand on his desk and knocked the phone to the floor, still holding onto the receiver as the rest dangled crazily—"what's wrong with this country??!"

"Take it easy, Bernie!" Grossman tried to soothe him but it was useless.

"Don't tell me to take it easy. He wants custody of my kid and now you want me to take it easy? Three weeks ago he kidnapped her and I jack-assed all around Mexico thinking she was dead, and I should take it easy?! Are you goddamn crazy too?" He was standing on his feet and yelling at the top of his lungs in his office, and then he slammed down the phone and sat down at his desk and cried. It was all *her* goddamn fault anyway. If she hadn't died, none of it would have happened. But the thought of that only made him cry harder. He was so lonely for Liz, that every breath he took was painful, and even being with the children made it harder. Nothing was the way it had been before . . . nothing . . . not the house . . . not the kids . . . not the food they ate . . . or the way their laundry was folded. . . . Nothing was familiar anymore, and nothing was ever going to be the same again. He had never felt so bereft in his life, and he sat at his desk and cried. And for the first time, he realized that Liz was never coming back again. Never.

Chapter 32

The new hearing was set for December twenty-first, and it was given priority because it was a custody hearing. Apparently the matter of the stolen car had been dropped. And as a result, there could be no parole violation. The owners of the car didn't want to press charges because, according to Winters, they were dealing drugs, and Chandler Scott came back into the country without a problem.

He looked respectable and subdued as he walked into the courtroom with his attorney. And Bernie walked into the court in a dark blue suit and a white shirt, with Bill Grossman. The black bodyguard was at home with Nanny Pippin and the children. Bernie had chuckled to himself only that morning at the portrait they presented, she so tiny and white and British with her flashing blue eyes and sensible shoes, he so enormous and black and ominous-looking until he smiled his startling ivory smile and tossed Alexander into the air, or played jumprope with Jane. And once he even tossed Nanny into the air as she and the children laughed. The reasons for needing him were unfortunate, but his presence was a real blessing. His name was Robert Blake, and Bernie was grateful to have him.

But as he walked into the courtroom, Bernie was thinking only of Chandler Scott and how much he hated him. They had the same judge they had had before, the only one available to them, the domestic relations judge, as he was called. He was a sleepy-looking man with white hair and a friendly smile, and he seemed to think that everyone loved everyone, or could be taught to, with a little effort.

He chided Scott for being "overenthusiastic about being alone with his daughter prematurely," and Grossman had to grip Bernie's arm to keep him in his chair. And then he turned to Bernie and urged him to understand how strong a natural father's impulses were to be with his only child. And that time Bill was unable to restrain him.

"His natural impulses have not manifested themselves for nine years, Your Honor. And his strongest natural impulse was to try to extort a million dollars out of me for the safe return of my daughter when he . . . ."

The judge smiled at Bernie benevolently. "I'm sure he was only joking, Mr. Fine. Please be seated." Bernie wanted to cry as he listened to the proceedings. He had called his mother the night before, to bring them up to date, and she was convinced that they were persecuting him because he was Jewish. He knew that wasn't the case. But they were persecuting him because he wasn't Jane's natural father, as though that made a difference. Chandler Scott's only claim to fame was to have slept with Jane's mother and have gotten her pregnant. That had been his only contribution to Jane's life and well-being, whereas for half of her life, Bernie had been everything to her. And Grossman did everything he could to get the point across.

"My client feels very strongly that Mr. Scott is not emotionally or financially prepared to take on the responsibility of a child at this time. Perhaps at some later date, Your Honor . . ." Bernie lurched forward again, and Bill stared him into silence. "Mr. Scott has had several encounters with the law, and has not had regular employment for several years, from what we've been able to determine. And at the moment he is living in a transient hotel in East Oakland." Scott squirmed in his seat but only slightly.

"Is that true, Mr. Scott?" The judge smiled at him, anxious for a truth that would make Scott a good father in his eyes, and Scott was anxious to help him.

"Not exactly, Your Honor. I've been living on a trust my family left me a while ago." The aura of the country club again, but Grossman was quick to challenge it.

"Can you prove that, Mr. Scott?" he interjected.

"Of course . . . that money is gone now, I'm afraid. But I'm going to start work with the Atlas Bank this week."

"With his record?" Bernie whispered to Grossman.

"Never mind. We'll force him to prove it."

"And I rented an apartment in the city yesterday." He looked triumphantly at Grossman and Bernie, and the judge nodded. "Of course, I don't have as much money as Mr. Fine, but I hope Jane won't mind that very much."

The judge nodded again, anxious to please Chandler. "Material goods are not what's important here, and of course I'm sure you'll be happy to agree to a visitation schedule for Mr. Fine to see Jane."

Bernie suddenly looked at Grossman in terror, and leaned over to speak to him in a whisper. "What's he talking about? What does he mean a 'visitation schedule' for me? Is he crazy?"

Grossman waited a moment and then questioned the judge as to his intention, and he asked Bill to wait a moment, but then explained it to all parties concerned. "There is no question here but that Mr. Fine loves his stepdaughter, and that is not the issue here, but the fact remains that a natural father belongs with his child, in the absence of the natural mother. With the unfortunate death of Mrs. Fine, Jane must revert to living with her father. The court fully understands how painful this is for Mr. Fine, and we will remain open to discussion as we see how the new arrangement works out." He smiled benignly at Scott, as Bernie sat shaking in his seat. He had failed her. He had failed Liz completely. And now he was going to lose Jane. It was like hearing that they were going to tear off his arm. And actually he would have preferred it. Given the choice, he would gladly have given up any limb and kept the child, but they didn't offer him that option. The judge looked at both men, their attorneys, and finished his pronouncement. "Custody is hereby being given to Chandler Scott, with a satisfactory visiting schedule to be given to Bernard Fine, perhaps a biweekly visit," he suggested as Bernie gaped from his seat. "The child is to be turned over to Mr. Scott in forty-eight hours, at her domicile, at twelve noon on December twenty-third. I feel that the unfortunate little mishap in Mexico is only an indication of how anxious Mr. Scott is to begin a normal life with his daughter, and the court would like to see him do that as quickly as possible." For the first time in his adult life, Bernie thought he was going to faint as the judge rapped the gavel. He was as white as a sheet and he was staring down at the table when Bill Grossman looked at him. The room was spinning in front of his eyes, and he felt as though Liz had just died again. He could almost hear her voice in his ears . . . swear to me, Bernie . . . swear to me you'll never let him near her. . . .

"Are you all right?" Grossman was frightened

as he looked at him. He was leaning over him and he signaled to the clerk for a glass of water. They handed Bernie a soggy paper cup filled with luke-warm water, and a sip of it helped bring him to his senses. He silently got to his feet and followed Bill Grossman out of the courtroom.

"Do I have any recourse? Can I appeal this?" He looked badly shaken.

"You can ask for another hearing, but you have to give up the child in the meantime." He spoke in a matter-of-fact way, hoping to defuse the emotions, but there was no way to do that. Bernie was staring at him with open hatred. Hatred of Scott and the judge and the system, and he wasn't entirely sure Bernie didn't hate him too. And he wasn't sure he would have blamed him. It was a travesty of justice, but they were helpless.

"What if I don't give her up to him on the twenty-third?" he asked in an undertone outside the courtroom.

"They'll put you in jail sooner or later. But he'll have to come back with a deputy sheriff to do it."

"Good." Bernie's mouth set in a thin line, and he looked at his attorney. "And you better get ready to bail me out of jail, because I'm not giving Jane to him. And I'm going to offer to buy him off when he comes. He wants to sell me the kid? Great. Name the price. I'm buying."

"Bernie, things might go more smoothly if you turn Jane over to him and then try to deal with him. The court will take a dim view of it if . . ."

"To hell with the court," Bernie spat at him.

"And to hell with you too. Not one of you bastards gives a damn about my kid. You just want to keep each other happy and not rock the goddamn boat. Well, you're not talking about a boat, you're talking about my daughter, and I know what's good for her and what isn't. One of these days that bastard is going to kill my kid, and you're all going to tell me how sorry you are. I told you he was going to kidnap her, and you thought I was crazy. Well, I was right. And this time I'm telling you that I'm not giving her up to him on Thursday. And if you don't like it, Grossman, you can get off the goddamn case for all I care." Grossman felt desperately sorry for him. It was a rotten situation.

"I'm just trying to explain to you how the court feels about these situations."

"The court has its head up its ass, and it doesn't have any feelings. 'The court,' as you call it, is a fat little old man who sits in that chair up there and never made it as an attorney, so now he's spending his time lousing up people's lives and feeling important. He didn't even give a damn that Scott kidnapped Jane, and he probably wouldn't give a damn if he had raped her."

"I'm not sure of that, Bernie." He had to defend the system he worked for and believed in, but too much of what Bernie said made sense. It was very depressing.

"You're not sure, Bill? Well, I am." Bernie was livid, and he started walking down the hall to the elevator as Bill followed. They went down to the main floor in silence and Bernie looked at him as

they walked outside. "I just want you to understand. I'm not giving Jane to him when he comes
on Thursday. Blake and I are going to be standing
in the doorway and I'm going to tell him to go
screw himself, after I ask him pointblank what his
price is. I'm not going to play this game with him
any longer. And this time he's going to have to
sign his life away when I pay him. Not like the last
time. And if I wind up in jail, I'll expect you to bail
me out, or hire me another lawyer. Got that?"
Grossman nodded and Bernie walked off without
another word to his attorney.

He called his parents that night, and his mother
cried on the phone. It seemed like they hadn't had
a happy conversation in over a year now. First
there had been the agonies and hushed reports
over Liz' illness, and now there was this mess with
Chandler Scott. He told her what he was going to
do, and that he might end up in jail and she
sobbed openly at the other end of the phone, half
thinking about the grandchild she might never see
again, and half thinking about her son as a
jailbird.

They had been planning to come out that Friday but Bernie thought they should wait. Everything was just too much up in the air with the mess
Scott was making. But when he hung up, Mrs.
Pippin disagreed with him.

"Let the grandmother come, Mr. Fine. The
children need to see her, and so do you. It will do
everyone good."

"What if I'm in jail?" She giggled at the prospect and then shrugged philosophically.

"I'll just carve the turkey myself, I suppose." He loved her burr and her good humor. There seemed to be nothing she couldn't face. Flood, plague, or famine.

But that night, when he tucked Jane into bed, he realized how deeply frightened she was of his turning her over to Scott again. He had tried to explain that to the woman at Family Court but she refused to believe him, and she had only talked to Jane for five or ten minutes herself, and thought she just felt "shy" about her natural father. In truth, she was terrified of him, and the nightmares she had that night were the worst she'd ever had. He and Mrs. Pippin met in her bedroom at four o'clock in the morning as she screamed in terror and he finally took her into his own bed, and let her sleep there beside him, clutching his hand with her smaller one, as she slept with a troubled look on her face. Only Alexander seemed unaffected by the tragedies that had befallen them ever since his arrival. He was a happy sunny little child, and he was beginning to talk now. He was the only thing that cheered Bernie amidst the anguish of worrying about losing Jane. And he talked to Jack Winters again on Thursday morning.

"The apartment's for real. He moved in a few days ago, and he's sharing it with a friend. But I can't figure out the job at the Atlas Bank. They say they hired him as part of some new program they've got to give ex-cons a chance. I don't think it's much of a job, and he hasn't started yet anyway. I think it's just a PR thing they started to show how liberal they are. We're checking it out some more, and I'll let you know what I find out." Bernie didn't like the sound of him sharing his apartment. He was sure they were going to disappear with Jane again, if they got the chance. But Blake was going to see to it that that didn't happen. Bob had been sitting in the kitchen since that morning, with his jacket off and a large .38 in a shoulder holster that Alexander kept pointing at and saying "Bang!" as Nanny frowned in disapproval. But Bernie wanted him wearing it, and he wanted Scott to see it when he showed up at noon, and they refused to let him have Jane. Bernie wasn't playing parlor games with him anymore. Now they were in earnest.

And just as he had done before, he was late picking Jane up. She was hiding in her bedroom, and Nanny was trying to distract her.

At one o'clock Scott wasn't there, and at two o'clock he hadn't come either. Unable to stand the tension any longer, Bill Grossman called them, and Bernie told him that there had been no news. At two-thirty Jane came tiptoeing out of her bedroom, but Bernie and Bob Blake were still sitting in the living room, waiting, as the clock ticked, and Nanny baked cookies in the kitchen with Alexander.

"There's no sign of him," Bernie told Grossman when he called again, unable to figure it out. "He can't have forgotten."

"Maybe he got drunk at lunch. It's almost Christmas after all . . . maybe he went to an office party." At five o'clock Nanny started dinner and Bernie debated about sending Bob home, but Bob insisted on staying until they heard something. He didn't want Scott showing up ten minutes after he left. And Bernie agreed but he went to fix them both a drink, and Jane flicked on the TV to see if there were any cartoons or good shows on, but there was nothing but news. And then suddenly she saw him.

They were showing his picture on the screen. First in slow motion, and then a freeze frame, as he stood holding a gun on a whole lobbyful of people at the Atlas Bank. The film continued then and he looked tall and blond and handsome on the screen, and he was smiling at someone as he pulled the trigger and shattered a lamp next to where someone was standing and then he laughed some more. Jane was so terrified she couldn't even cry or call Bernie. She just pointed as Bernie and Bob came back with their drinks in their hands, and Bernie stared as he saw him. It was Chandler Scott. Holding up the Atlas Bank, in broad daylight.

"The gunman, who was unidentified at the time, walked into the Atlas Bank at Sutter and Mason shortly before eleven o'clock this morning. He had a female accomplice who wore a stocking mask, and they handed a teller a note, demanding five hundred thousand dollars." That seemed to be his magic number. "When she told them she didn't have it, he told her to give him all the money she had." The voice droned on as they ran the bank's film and suddenly saw him start shooting. Eventually, as the police surrounded the bank, because the teller had pressed a panic button, he and his accomplice held everyone hostage. None of the hostages had been injured despite what the anchorman called a little "playful shooting on the part of the gunman and his accomplice. He told them to hurry up, because he had a date at noon. But by lunchtime it was obvious that they were not going to get out of the bank without giving themselves up or injuring a hostage. They attempted to shoot their way out finally, and both of them had been killed before they ever reached the curb. The tall blond was a previously convicted felon named Chandler Anthony Scott, aka Charlie Antonio Schiavo, and the woman was Anne Stewart." Jane stared at the screen in amazement.

"Daddy, that's the lady who went to Mexico with us. . . . Her name was Annie!" She was staring wide-eyed as they showed Scott and the woman, lying facedown on the sidewalk in a pool of blood after the shoot-out, and then the ambulance taking away the bodies, and the hostages fleeing from the bank, as you heard Christmas carols in the background. "Daddy, they killed him." Her eyes were wide and she sat staring at Bernie, who looked at her and then Robert Blake.

They were all in shock, and for a moment he wondered if it could have been a different Chandler Scott, but it couldn't. It just seemed so remarkable . . . and now it was all over. He reached over and pulled Jane into his arms and held her there, signaling to Bob to turn off the television.

"I'm sorry you ever had to go through all that, baby . . . but it's all over now."

"He was such a terrible man." She looked so little and she said it so sadly, and then she looked up at him with enormous eyes. "I'm glad Mommy never knew. She would have been very angry."

Bernie smiled at the choice of words. "Yes, she would have. But it's all over now, baby . . . all over . . ." It was amazing, and he still couldn't believe it, as the reality sank in slowly. Scott was out of their lives. Forever.

They called Grandma Ruth a little while later, and told them to take the next plane they could get. He explained everything before Jane got on, but she gave her grandmother all the gory details herself. "And he was lying in this enormous pool of blood, Grandma . . . honest . . . right on the sidewalk . . . it was really, really yucky." But she looked so relieved. She suddenly looked like a little girl again. He told Grossman as well, and Nanny invited Bob Blake to join them for dinner, but he was anxious to get home to his wife. They were going to a Christmas party. And Bernie and Jane and Nanny and Alexander sat down to dinner. And Jane looked up at him, remembering the candles they had lit with Grampa on Friday nights, before her mother had died. She wanted to do it again, and suddenly there was time for everything. They had a whole life to look forward to. Together.

"Daddy, tomorrow can we light the candles?"

"What candles?" He had been helping her to some meat and then suddenly he understood, and felt guilty that he wasn't more observant of some of the traditions he'd grown up with. "Sure, sweetheart." And then he leaned over and kissed her, as Nanny smiled, and Alexander dug his fingers into the mashed potatoes. It was almost as though life was normal. And maybe one day it might be.

Chapter 33

It almost made Bernie shudder to go back to the same courtroom, but it was something that meant a great deal to both of them. And his parents had flown out again especially to be present. And Grossman had asked the judge if he would do it in chambers. They had come to City Hall for Jane's adoption.

The papers were waiting for them, and the judge Jane had never seen before smiled down at her and then glanced up at the family who had come with her. There was Bernie, of course, and his parents, and Nanny in her best blue uniform with the white collar. She never took a day off, and she never wore anything except the immaculate starched uniforms she ordered from England. And she had brought Alexander in a little blue velvet suit, and he was muttering happily as he took all of the judge's books off one of the lower shelves and stacked them up so he could stand on them to reach the next ones. Bernie went to scoop him up and held him as the judge looked at them solemnly and explained why they were there.

"It is my understanding"—he looked at Jane—"that you wish to be adopted, and that Mr. Fine wishes to adopt you as well."

"He's my father," she explained quietly, and the judge looked briefly confused and then glanced at his papers again. Bernie would have preferred to have someone else do the adoption, he still remembered him only too well from the fiasco in December when he had given custody to Chandler Scott, but no one mentioned that now as they went on.

"Yes, well . . . let's see." He examined the adoption papers, and asked Bernie to sign, then Grossman to witness it. And Bernie asked his parents to witness it as well.

"Can I sign too?" Jane asked, wanting to be part of it, and the judge hesitated. No one had ever asked him that before.

"There's no need for you to sign anything . . . er . . . uh . . . Jane. . . . But I suppose you could sign the papers too, if you'd like to."

She smiled up at Bernie and then back at the judge again. "I'd like to do that, if it's okay."

He nodded, and passed one of the documents to her, and she looked at it solemnly and signed her name. And then the judge looked at all of them. "I hereby declare, by the power vested in me by the State of California, that Jane Elizabeth Fine is now the lawful daughter of Bernard Fine,

adopted on this twenty-eighth day of January."
He rapped a small gavel he kept on his desk, and
stood up and smiled at all of them, and in spite of
the terrible thing he'd done to Bernie before, he
shook Bernie's hand. And then Bernie scooped
Jane up in his arms, just as he had when she was a
much smaller girl, and he kissed her and then set
her down again.

"I love you, Daddy," she whispered.

"I love you too." He smiled down at her, wishing that Liz could have been there. And wishing
also that he had done it all a long time ago. If he
had, he would have saved all of them a great deal
of pain. Chandler Scott wouldn't have had a leg to
stand on. But it was too late to worry about that. It
was all over now. And a new life had begun for
them. She was truly his daughter now, and
Grandma Ruth was crying as she kissed her, and
Grampa shook Bernie's hand.

"Congratulations, son." It was like getting married all over again, and they went to Trader Vic's
for lunch, except for Nanny and Alexander. And
while everyone was ordering lunch, Bernie
slipped his hand into Jane's and smiled down at
her. And without saying anything to her, he
slipped a little gold ring on her finger. It was a
delicate braid of gold with a single pearl. She
looked down at it with wide eyes, and then looked
up at him again.

"Daddy, it's beautiful." It was like being engaged to him. And now she knew no one could
ever take her away from him. No one. Ever again.

"You're beautiful, sweetheart. And you're a very, very brave girl." They were both thinking of the days in Mexico, but all of that was over now. They looked at each other, both thinking of Liz, and Bernie smiled at her, feeling in his heart of hearts that Jane Elizabeth Fine was truly his child now.

Chapter 34

For the first time in two years, Bernie took over the import lines again, and it was painful to go back to Paris and Rome and Milan without Liz. He remembered the first time he had taken Liz to Europe with him, and how excited she had been about the clothes she'd bought, the museums they'd visited, the lunches at Fouquet's and dinners at Lipp's and Maxim's, and it was all so different now. But this was also his bailiwick, and he fell rapidly back into step again. He felt as though he had been out of the mainstream for a long, long time. He felt more alive again after he had seen all the new ready-to-wear lines and spoken to his favorite couturiers. He knew exactly what was right for Wolff's that year, and when he stopped in New York on the way back, he and Paul Berman had a long quiet lunch at Le Veau d'Or and discussed all of Bernie's plans. He admired the way Bernie had handled everything, and he was looking forward to having him come home. No one suitable had turned up to take over for him at the San Francisco store, but he assumed that by year end Bernie would be back in New York.

"How does that fit in with your plans, Bernard?"

"All right, I suppose." He didn't seem to care quite so much anymore and he had just sold his old apartment. It would have been too small for him now anyway. And the tenant he'd had for years had wanted to buy it. "I'll have to think about schools for Jane before we come back, but there's time for that." He was no longer in a hurry. There was nothing to rush home for, and only the children and Nanny to bring with him.

"I'll let you know as soon as we have someone in mind." It wasn't easy to find the right person for the job. He had spoken to two women and a man so far, but all of them were too limited. They didn't have Bernard's experience, or his sophisticated eye. And he didn't want the San Francisco branch turning into some dull provincial store. In Bernie's hands it was their biggest moneymaker, after the New York store, and Paul Berman liked that. And better than that, so did the Board of Directors.

He saw his parents briefly before he went back, and his mother wanted him to send the children to stay with her for the summer.

"You don't have time to be with them all day long, and there's nothing for them to do in town." She had known without his saying it that they wouldn't be going back to Stinson Beach again. It would have been much too painful for him, but he didn't know where else to go. He had gone there with Liz since he had first moved out to California, and now he couldn't think of anything else without her.

"I'll give it some thought when I get back."

"Maybe Jane would like to go to camp this year." She was more than nine but he wasn't ready to let her go. They had both been through too much. It was only nine months since Liz had died. And the thing that shocked him most of all was his mother telling him that Mrs. Rosenthal's daughter had just gotten divorced and was living in Los Angeles, as though she expected him to do something about it.

"Why don't you look her up sometime?" He had stared at her as though she had suggested he walk down the street in his underwear, but he was also angry at her. She had no right to interfere in his life, or to start pushing women at him.

"Why the hell would I do that?"

"Because she's a very nice girl."

"So what?" He was furious. The world was full of nice girls, not one of them as nice as Liz, and he didn't want to know them.

"Bernie"—she took a deep breath and plunged in. She had wanted to say it to him since the last time they'd gone out to visit in San Francisco— "you have to get out sometime."

"I get out all I need to."

"That's not what I mean. I mean out with girls."

He wanted to tell her to mind her own goddamn business. She was digging into open wounds, and he couldn't take it.

"I'm thirty-nine years old. I'm not interested in 'girls.'"

"You know what I mean, sweetheart." She was nagging him, and he didn't want to hear any of it. Liz' clothes were still hanging in the closet as they always had, only the perfume was fading now. He went in there now and then, just to remind himself, and the smell of her perfume would overwhelm him . . . it brought back floodtides of memories, and sometimes late at night, he would still lie on his bed and cry. "You're a young man. It's time to think of yourself." No, he wanted to scream. No! It was still time to think of her. If he didn't, he would lose her forever. And he wasn't ready to let go of her yet. He was never going to. He was going to keep her clothes in the closet forever. He had their children and his memories. He didn't want more than that. And Ruth knew it.

"I don't want to discuss this with you."

"You have to start thinking about it." Her voice was gentle, but he hated her for feeling sorry for him and for pushing him.

"I don't have to think about a goddamn thing if I don't want to," he snapped at her.

"What'll I tell Mrs. Rosenthal? I promised you'd call Evelyne when you got back to the west coast."

"Tell her I couldn't find the number."

"Don't be smart about it . . . the poor girl doesn't know anyone out there."

"Then why did she move to Los Angeles?"

"She didn't know where else to go."

"What was wrong with New York?"

"She wanted a career in Hollywood . . . she's a very pretty girl, you know. She was a model for Ohrbach's before she got married. You know . . ."

"Mother! No!" His voice was louder than it had to be, and he was sorry to have been so rough with her, but he wasn't ready for that. He didn't think he ever would be. He didn't want to date anyone. Ever. Again.

They celebrated Alexander's second birthday when they got home to San Francisco. Nanny had arranged a little party with all his friends from the park, and she had baked him a cake herself, which he dug into with glee, getting most of it all over his face and hands, and a fair amount of it in his mouth, too, as he gave Bernie a big chocolate grin for the camera. But when he put the camera away again, Bernie felt profoundly sad, thinking that Liz should have been there to see him . . . and suddenly Bernie was overwhelmed with the memories of the day she'd given birth to him only two years before. He had been there to watch life bestowed on them, and then again to watch life taken from them. It was difficult to absorb it all, as he kissed Alexander good night that night, and went back to his own room, even lonelier than he had been before, and without thinking, he walked into her closet. It was almost like a physical blow as he closed his eyes and inhaled her perfume again.

That weekend, not knowing what else to do, he took the children for a drive, with Jane in the front seat next to him, and Nanny contentedly chatting with Alexander strapped into his car seat. They took a different direction than usual, when they went on rides. Generally, they roamed around Marin when they did things like that, and went to Paradise Cove in Tiburon, or wandered around Belvedere, or went to Sausalito and bought ice cream cones. But this time, Bernie drove north into the wine country, and everything was rich and lush and green and beautiful. And Nanny began telling them about life on a farm in Scotland when she was a child.

"It looked a great deal like this, actually," she observed as they passed an enormous dairy, and the trees were majestic as Bernie drove under them, and Jane smiled every time they saw horses or sheep or cows, and Alexander squealed and pointed, making all the appropriate "mooh" and "baah" noises, which made them all laugh, even Bernie, as he drove. It looked like God's country around them.

"It's pretty here, isn't it, Daddy?" She consulted him about everything. And the miseries they'd been through at Chandler Scott's hands had only brought them closer than before. "I like it a lot." She seemed older than her years sometimes, and their eyes met as he smiled at her. He liked it too.

The wineries had solidity, the little Victorian houses they passed along the way had charm. And suddenly he began wondering if this was a place where they could go in the summer, which was fast approaching. It was so different from Stinson Beach that it would be fun for them. He looked down at Jane then with a smile.

"What do you say we spend a weekend up here sometime and check it out?" He consulted her about everything, much as he would have her mother.

She was excited at the prospect of it, and Nanny chirped at them from the backseat as Alexander shouted "More . . . more cow! . . . Mooo!!" They were passing a whole herd of them, and the following weekend they came back and stayed at a hotel in Yountville. It was perfect for them. The weather was balmy and warm, it didn't even get the coastal fog that kept Stinson socked in some-times, the grass was lush, the trees were huge, the vineyards were beautiful, and on their second day there they found the perfect summer house in Oakville. It was an adorable Victorian, just off Highway 29, on a narrow winding road, it had been recently redone by a family that had moved to France, and they were looking to rent it for a few months, furnished, until they decided whether or not they wanted to come back to the Napa Valley. The owner of the bed-and-breakfast inn where they stayed pointed it out to them, and

Jane was clapping her hands excitedly, while Nanny proclaimed it the perfect place to keep a cow.

"And can we have chickens, Daddy? And a goat?" Jane was beside herself with excitement as Bernie laughed at them.

"Now wait a minute, guys, we're not starting Old MacDonald's farm, we're just looking for a summer house." It was just right for them. He called the realtor handling it before they went back to the city that night, and the price sounded right to him. He could have the house from the first of June till Labor Day. Bernie agreed to all their terms, signed the lease, wrote a check, and when they went back to the city, they had a summer house, which pleased him. He hadn't wanted to send the children to his mother. He wanted them close to him. And he could commute from Napa, just as he had from Stinson. It was a longer drive, but only by very little.

"I guess that takes care of camp," he laughed as he smiled at Jane.

"Good." She seemed pleased. "I didn't want to go to camp anyway. Do you think Grandma and Grampa will come out here to visit us?" They had room for them. There was a room for each of them, and a spare room for guests.

"I'm sure they will." But Ruth thought the whole project a mistake from the first. It was inland, probably too hot, undoubtedly there were rattlesnakes, and the children would have been much better in Scarsdale with her, she said.

"Mom, they're excited about this. And it really is a cute house."

"What'll you do about work?"

"I'll commute. It's only about an hour from here."

"More mishegoss. Just what you need. When are you going to get sensible?" She wanted to ask him about calling Evelyne Rosenthal again but she decided to wait awhile. Poor Evelyne was so lonely in Los Angeles she was thinking of going back to New York again and she would have been a nice girl for him. Not as nice as Liz maybe, but nice. And good for the kids. She even had two of her own, a boy and a girl. And thinking about it, she foolishly decided to mention it to Bernie after all. "You know, I talked to Linda Rosenthal today, and her daughter is still in Los Angeles."

He couldn't believe she was doing this to him. After pretending to be so fond of Liz, it infuriated him. How could she? "I told you. I'm not interested." His voice was tight, and it gave him a pain in his chest just thinking about other women.

"Why not? She's a lovely girl. She's . . ."

He cut her off, with fury in his voice. "I'm hanging up now." It was a dangerous subject with Bernie, and as always, Ruth was sorry for him.

"I'm sorry. I just thought . . ."

"Don't."

"I guess the time's not right." She sighed, and he sounded even angrier.

"It never will be, Mom. I'll never find someone like her." There were suddenly tears in his eyes, and his mother felt tears sting her eyes too as she listened in Scarsdale.

"You can't think like that." Her voice was gentle and sad as the tears rolled slowly down her cheeks for the pain she knew he lived with constantly, and it hurt her to know that.

"Yes, I can think like that. She was everything I wanted. I could never find someone like her again." His voice was barely audible as he thought of her.

"You could find someone different, whom you might love as much, differently." She tried to be very tactful with him now, knowing how sensitive he was. But after ten months she thought it was time, and he didn't. "At least go out a little bit." He stayed home with the children all the time, from what Mrs. Pippin said, and that wasn't good for him.

"I'm not interested, Mom. I'd rather be home with the kids."

"They'll grow up one day. You did." They both smiled, but she still had Lou, and for an instant she felt guilty.

"I've got about another sixteen years before that happens. I'm not going to worry about that now." She didn't want to press it any further for the moment, and instead they talked about the house he had rented in Napa.

"Jane wants you to come out and visit us this summer, Mom."

"All right, all right . . . I'll come." And when she did, she loved it. It was the kind of place to let down your hair, walk in the grass, lie in the hammock under giant shade trees, looking up at the sky. There was even a little brook on the back of the property, where they could walk along the rocks and get their feet wet, as he had in the Catskills when he was a child. In some ways, Napa reminded him of that, and it reminded Ruth of that too. She watched the children playing in the grass and the look on Bernie's face as he watched them, and she felt better about him than she had in a long time. It really was the perfect spot for them, Ruth conceded before she left. Bernie looked happier than he had in a long time, and so did the children.

And when Ruth left, she flew down to Los Angeles to meet Lou at a medical convention in Hollywood. And from there they were going to Hawaii with friends. She reminded Bernie of Evelyne Rosenthal, who was still in Los Angeles and available, and this time he laughed at her. He was in much better spirits, although he still wasn't interested in her. But at least he didn't bark at her about it.

"You never give up, do you, Mom?"

She had grinned at him. "All right, all right." She kissed him hard at the airport and took a last look at him. He was still her tall, handsome son, but there was more gray in his hair than he had had the year before, the lines were deeper around his eyes, and he still looked sad. Liz had been gone almost a year now, and he was still mourning. But at least the anger was gone now. He wasn't angry at her anymore for leaving him. He was just so damn lonely without her. Aside from losing his lover and his wife, he had lost his best friend. "Take care of yourself, sweetheart," Ruth whispered to him at the airport.

"You too, Mom." He had hugged her again and waved as she boarded the plane. They had grown much closer in the last year or two, but at what expense. It was hard to imagine how much had happened to them. And as he drove back to Napa that night, he thought about it all . . . and about Liz. . . . It was still hard to believe she was gone . . . that she hadn't gone away and would be back one day. Forever was so impossible to understand. And he was still thinking about her when he got to the house in Oakville and put the car away, but Nanny was waiting up for him. It was after ten o'clock and the house was peaceful and quiet. Jane had fallen asleep in her bed reading *Black Beauty*.

"I don't think Alexander is well, Mr. Fine."

Bernie frowned. The children were everything to him. "What's wrong with him?" He was only two years old after all, still a baby practically, and more so, in Bernie's eyes, because he didn't have a mother. In Bernie's eyes, he would be a baby forever.

Nanny looked as though she felt guilty as she confessed. "I think I let him stay in the pool too long. He was complaining about his ear when he went to bed. I put some warm oil in it, but it didn't seem to help. We may have to go to the doctor in town tomorrow if it doesn't improve by morning."

"Don't worry about it." He smiled at her. She was so incredibly conscientious, sometimes it was hard to imagine it, and he thanked his lucky stars that he had found her when he had. He still shuddered when he thought of the sadistic Swiss nurse or the filthy Norwegian au pair who kept taking Liz' clothes. "He'll be all right, Nanny. Get to bed."

"Would you like some warm milk to help you sleep?"

He shook his head. "I'll be all right." But she had noticed for weeks that he was up late at night, unable to sleep, prowling around. The anniversary of Liz' death had been only a few days before, and she knew it had been hard on him. At least Jane didn't have nightmares anymore. But that night it was little Alexander who awoke howling at four A.M. Bernie had just gone to bed, and he quickly pulled on a dressing gown and went to the baby's room, where Nanny was rocking him and trying to comfort him, to no avail. "His ear?" She nodded, singing to the child as loudly as she could. "Do you want me to call the doctor?"

She shook her head. "I'm afraid you'll have to take him to the hospital. It's too bad to make him wait anymore. Poor little man." She kissed his forehead and his cheek and the top of his head and he clung to her miserably as Bernie knelt down on the rug and looked at the baby that warmed his heart and broke it all at the same time, all because he looked so much like his mother.

"Feeling rotten, huh, big boy?" Alex nodded at his daddy and stopped crying but not for long. "Come to Dad." He held out his arms and the child went to him. He had a raging fever, and couldn't tolerate even the softest touch on the right side of his head, and Bernie knew that Nanny was right. He had to take him to the hospital. His pediatrician had given him someone's name up there in case either of the children had an accident or got sick. He handed Alexander back to Nanny, and went to get dressed and look for the card in his desk drawer. Dr. M. Jones, it said, with the phone number. He called the exchange and got the answering service. He explained what was wrong and asked them to ring through to Dr. Jones, but the operator came back on the line and explained that Dr. Jones was at the hospital on an emergency call already.

"Could he see us there? My son's in an awful lot of pain." He'd had problems with his ears before, and a shot of penicillin had always helped him. That and a lot of loving from Jane and Daddy and Nanny.

"I'll check." The operator was back on the line almost instantly. "That'll be fine." She gave him directions to the hospital, and he went to get Alexander, and gently put him in the car seat he still used. Nanny had to stay home with Jane, so Bernie was going alone, and Nanny almost wrung her hands as she covered Alex with a blanket and handed him his teddy bear as he cried woefully. She hated to let him go without her.

"I hate to let you go alone, Mr. Fine." Her burr was always stronger late at night when she was tired, and he loved the sound of it. "But I canna leave Jane, you know. She'd be frightened if she woke up." They both knew that she had been more easily frightened since her abduction.

"I know, Nanny. He'll be fine. We'll be back as soon as we can." It was four-thirty in the morning by then, and he drove to the hospital as quickly as he could. But it was ten to five before they arrived. It was a long way from Oakville to the city of Napa, and Alexander was still crying when Bernie carried him inside and gently set him down on the table in the emergency room. The lights were so bright they hurt his eyes, and Bernie sat on the table and held him on his lap, shielding him, as a tall dark-haired young woman came in wearing a turtleneck and jeans. She was almost as tall as he, and she had an easy smile, and her hair was so black it was almost blue. Almost like an Indian, he thought to himself with a tired look. But her eyes were blue, like Jane . . . and Liz. . . . He forced the thought from his mind and explained that he was waiting for Dr. Jones. He wasn't sure who the woman was, and assumed that she was a clerk at the emergency room.

"I'm Dr. Jones." She smiled at him. She had a warm, husky voice, and cool strong hands when she shook his, and despite her height and obvious competence, there was something very warm and gentle about her. And the way she moved was at the same time motherly and sexy. She gently took Alexander from him and examined the ear that pained him, talking to Alexander the entire time, telling him little stories, chatting, entertaining him, and glancing up at Bernie from time to time to reassure him too. "He's got one very hot ear, I'm afraid, and the other one is pretty pink too." She checked his throat, his tonsils, his tummy to make sure there was no problem there, and then gave him a penicillin shot as fast as she could. He cried but not for too long and then she blew up a balloon for him, and with Bernie's permission offered him a lollipop, which was a big success even in his weakened state. He sat up on Bernie's lap and looked at her thoughtfully. And she smiled down at him, and then wrote a prescription for Bernie to have filled the next day. She put him on antibiotics to be on the safe side, and gave Bernie two small codeine pills to crush for him if the pain didn't abate before morning. "In fact"—she looked at Alex' trembling lower lip—"why don't we do that now? There's no point in his being miserable." She disappeared and returned with the pill crushed in a spoon, her dark hair swinging across her shoulders as she moved, and the medicine was down and gone before Alex could even object to it. She made it kind of a game with him. And then he settled back into his father's arms with a sigh, still sucking the lollipop, a moment later, as Bernie filled out some forms, Alexander fell asleep. Bernie smiled down at him, and then looked at her appreciatively. She had the warm eyes of a deeply caring woman.

"Thank you." Bernie smiled down at him and stroked his hair, and then looked up at Dr. Jones again. "You were wonderful with him." That mattered to him a great deal. His children meant everything to him.

"I came in for another earache just like that an hour ago." She smiled at him, thinking that it was nice the father had come and not the mother for once, looking exhausted and harassed with no one to help her. It was nice to see men give a damn and pitch in too. But she didn't say anything to him. Maybe he was divorced and had no choice. "Do you live in Oakville?" He had put down their summer address on the form.

"No, normally we live in town. We're just here for the summer." She nodded, and then smiled at him as she filled out her part of the form for his insurance.

"But you're from New York?"

He grinned. "How did you know that?"

"I'm from the east too. Boston. But I can still hear New York in your voice." And he could hear Boston in hers. "How long have you been out here?"

"Four years."

She nodded. "I came out to go to Stanford Med School and never went back. And that was fourteen years ago." She was thirty-six years old, and her credentials were good and he liked her style. She looked intelligent and kind, and there was a sparkle in her eyes that suggested a sense of humor. She was looking at him thoughtfully. She liked his eyes too. "This is a nice place to live. Napa, I mean. Anyway"—she put away the forms and looked down at Alex' angelic sleeping face—"why don't you bring him in to the office in a day or two? I have an office in Saint Helena, which is closer to you than this." She glanced at the antiseptic hospital around them. She didn't like seeing children there unless it was an emergency like this one.

"It's nice to know you're so close to us. With children, you never know when you're going to need a doctor."

"How many do you have?" Maybe that was why the wife hadn't come, she thought to herself. Maybe they had ten kids and she had to stay home with them. Somehow the thought amused her. She had one patient with eight children, and she loved them.

"I have two," Bernie supplied. "Alexander, and a nine-year-old little girl, Jane."

She smiled. He looked like a nice man. And his eyes lit up when he talked about his kids. Mostly, they were kind of sad, like a Saint Bernard, she thought, and then chided herself. He was actually a very nice-looking man. She liked the way he moved . . . the beard. . . . Cool it, she told herself as she gave him final instructions and he left, carrying Alex in his arms. And then she chuckled to the nurse as she got ready to leave herself.

"I'm going to have to stop taking these late calls. The fathers start looking good to me at this hour." They both laughed and she was only teasing of course. She was always serious about her patients and their parents. She waved good night to the nurses and walked outside to where she'd left her car. It was a little Austin Healy she'd had since med school. She drove back to Saint Helena with the top down, her hair flying in the wind, and she waved as she passed Bernie on the way, traveling more sedately. Bernie waved. There had been something he liked, about her and he wasn't sure what it was. And he felt happier than he had in a long time as he pulled into the driveway in Oakville as the sun came up over the mountains.

Chapter 35

Two days later, Bernie took Alexander back to see Dr. Jones. He went to her office this time. It was in a small sunny Victorian house at the edge of town. She shared the office space with another doctor, and she lived upstairs above the office. And Bernie was once again impressed with her manner with the child, and he liked her as much as he had before, maybe even more so. She was wearing a starched white coat over her jeans this time, but her manner was casual, her touch was gentle, and her eyes were warm as she laughed easily with Alexander and his father.

"His ears look a lot better this time." She smiled at Bernie, then at his son, sitting next to her. "But you'd better stay out of the swimming pool for a while, my friend." She ruffled Alex' hair, and for a moment she seemed more like a mother than a doctor, and it tugged at something in Bernie's heart which he was quick to deny to himself.

"Should I bring him back again?" She shook her head and he was almost sorry that she hadn't said yes. And then he was annoyed at himself. She was pleasant and intelligent, that was all, and she had taken good care of the child. And if Alex had to come back again, Nanny could bring him in next time. That was safer. He found himself staring at the shiny black hair and it annoyed him. And her blue eyes reminded him so much of Liz. . . .

"I don't think he'll need to be seen again. I should get some information on him though, for my files. How old is he again?" She smiled pleasantly at Bernard and he tried to appear indifferent, as though he were thinking of something else, as he avoided the familiar eyes. They were so blue . . . just like hers. . . . He forced his mind back to her question.

"He's two years and two months."

"General health all right?"

"Fine."

"Vaccinations up to date?"

"Yes."

"Pediatrician in town?" He gave her the name. It was easier talking of things like that. He didn't even have to look at her if he didn't want to.

"Names of the rest of his family?" She smiled again as she wrote it all down, and then looked up at him again. "You are Mr. Bernard Fine?" She thought that was what she remembered from the other night, and he almost smiled at her.

"Right. And he has a sister named Jane, who's nine years old."

"I remember that." She smiled at him again and then looked at him expectantly. "And?"

"That's it." He would have liked to have had another child or two with Liz, but they hadn't had time before they discovered that she had cancer.

"Your wife's name?" Something in his eyes suggested sharp pain and she instantly suspected an ugly divorce.

But he shook his head, the pain of her question staggering him, like a blow he hadn't seen before it hit him. "Uh . . . no . . . she's not."

The doctor looked surprised. It was an odd thing to say and he was looking at her strangely. "Not what?"

"Not alive." You could barely hear the words, and she suddenly realized the pain she must have caused him, and she felt desperately sorry for him. The pain of death was something she had never grown immune to.

"I'm so sorry . . ." Her voice trailed off as she looked down at the child. How terrible for all of them, especially the little girl. At least Alex was too young to understand. And the father looked so devastated as he spoke to her. "I'm sorry I asked."

"It's all right. You didn't know."

"How long has it been?" It couldn't have been too long if Alexander was just two years old. Her heart went out to all of them as her eyes met Bernie's and she felt tears in her own eyes.

"Last July." It was obviously too painful for him to say much more and she went on, feeling a rock in her heart as she thought of it, and after they were gone it troubled her again. He looked so heartbroken when he spoke of it. Poor man. She thought of him all day, and was surprised to see him in the supermarket later that week. Alexander was sitting in the cart, as he always did, and Bernie had brought Jane along. She was chattering rapidly and Alex was pointing at something and yelling "Gum, Daddy, gum!" at the top of his lungs as Dr. Jones almost ran into them, and she suddenly stopped and smiled. They didn't look nearly as sad as she'd imagined. In fact, they looked very happy.

"Well, hello there, how's our friend?" She glanced at Alex and found a warm welcome in Bernie's eyes when she looked at him.

"He's a lot better. I think the antibiotics helped."

"He's still taking them, isn't he?" She couldn't remember the length of the course she'd given him, but he should have been.

"Yes, he is. But he's his old self again." Bernie smiled and he looked normal and harassed and his legs looked nice in hiking shorts. She tried not to notice, but she couldn't help it. He was a good-looking man. And he was noticing the same things about her. She was wearing jeans again, and an oxford shirt and red espadrilles, and her hair was so clean it shone. She was not wearing her doctor coat, and Jane couldn't figure out who she was.

Bernie introduced them finally, and Jane held her hand out stingily, as though afraid to open up too far. She watched the woman suspiciously and didn't mention her again until they were back in the car.

"*Who* was *that?*"

"The doctor I took Alex to the other night." He spoke casually, but it was like being five years old and dealing with his mother all over again. In fact it made him laugh it was so similar. They were the same questions Ruth would have asked him.

"Why did you take him to *her?*" The inflections told him exactly what she thought, and he wondered why she disliked her so much. It never occurred to him that Jane was jealous.

"Doctor Wallaby gave me her number before we came up, in case one of you had an accident or got sick, like Alex the other night. I was very glad to find her actually. And she was very nice about meeting us at the hospital in the middle of the night. In fact, she was already there, seeing someone else, which says a lot for her." And he remembered that she had gone to Stanford.

Jane barely grunted that time, and didn't say anything more. But when they ran into her again a few weeks after that, Jane ignored her totally, and didn't even say hello. And when they went back to the car, Bernie scolded her.

"You were very rude to her, you know."

"Well, what's so great about her anyway?"

"What's great is that she's a doctor and you might need her sometime. Besides which, she hasn't done anything to you, for heaven's sake. There's no reason for you not to be polite to her." He was grateful that Alex liked her at least. He had let out a great squeal when he saw her in the supermarket and immediately said hello. He remembered her that time, and she made a great fuss over him, and had a lollipop in a pocket for him. She told him her name was Doctor Meg. But Jane had refused the lollipop she'd offered her, and Megan seemed to take it all in stride and not notice.

"Just don't be rude to her, sweetheart." She was so damn sensitive these days. He wondered if she was growing up, or if she still missed Liz as much. Nanny said it was probably a little of both, and he suspected she was right as usual. Nanny Pippin was the mainstay of their lives, and Bernie was devoted to her.

He didn't run into Megan again until a party he got talked into going to on Labor Day. He hadn't been to any parties in almost three years, not since Liz had gotten sick, and certainly not since she died. But the realtor who had gotten the house for him made such a point of including him in a barbecue they were giving that night that he felt rude not going at least for a little while. And he went feeling like the new kid in town, knowing absolutely not a soul, and feeling overdressed the instant he got out of the car. Everyone had worn T-shirts and jeans and cut-offs and halter tops, and he was wearing white slacks and a pale blue shirt. He looked more like Capri or Beverly Hills than the Napa Valley and it embarrassed him as his host handed him a beer and asked him where he was going afterwards.

Bernie just laughed and shrugged with a smile. "I guess I've just worked for a department store for too long." His friend took him aside then and asked if he would be interested in keeping the house for a while. The people who were renting to him were going to stay in Bordeaux for longer than they'd planned, and they were anxious to have him stay on there. "Actually, I might like that, Frank." The realtor was pleased with the news and suggested he keep it on a month-to-month basis, assuring him that the valley was even more beautiful in the fall, with all the leaves changing colors.

"The winters aren't even bad either. It might be nice for you to come up whenever you have a chance, and the rent is reasonable enough." He was ever the salesman, and Bernie smiled, anxious to leave the party.

"I think that would suit us just fine."

"Did Frank just sell you a winery?" a familiar voice asked. Her laugh had a tinkling sound, like silver bells, and Bernie turned and saw the shining black hair and the blue eyes that had startled him wherever they met. It was Megan Jones and she looked very pretty. He realized now how tan she was. Her skin was dark, in sharp contrast to her light blue eyes. And she had worn a white peasant skirt and white espadrilles with a bright red gypsy blouse. Suddenly she looked very beautiful and it made him uncomfortable. It was easier thinking of her in blue jeans and her starched white coat. This was much too accessible, and the silky smooth shoulders caught his eye, as he forced himself to look straight into her blue eyes. But that was no easier for him. Her eyes always made him think of Liz, and yet they were different. Bolder, older, wiser. She was a different kind of woman. And there was a compassion there which made her seem older than her years, and was useful in her profession. He tried to pull his eyes from her now, but was surprised to find that he couldn't.

"Frank just extended my lease for a while." He spoke quietly, and she noticed that no matter how much his mouth smiled, his eyes didn't. They were quiet and sad, and told people to keep their distance. His grief was still too fresh to be shared and she easily sensed that as she watched him, thinking of his children.

"Does that mean you're going to be staying up here?" She looked interested as she sipped at a glass of local white wine.

"Just on weekends, I guess. The kids love it here. And Frank says it's beautiful in the fall."

"It is. That's why I got stuck up here. It's the only place around here that gets some kind of autumn. The leaves turn just like they do back east, the whole valley turns red and yellow and it's really wonderful." He tried to concentrate on what she said, but all he saw were her bare shoulders and her blue eyes, and she seemed to be looking deep into his eyes, as though she wanted to say more to him. It made him curious about her. He had been since he first met her.

"What made you stay out here?"

She shrugged, and her perfect bronze flesh beckoned him as he reached for another beer and frowned, trying to deny the attraction he felt toward her. "I don't know. I couldn't imagine going back to Boston and being serious for the rest of my life." The mischief he had suspected danced in her eyes and he listened to the sound of her laughter.

"I suppose Boston can be that way. Very much so, in fact." He looked terribly handsome as he chatted with her and she decided to risk asking him something about himself, despite what she already knew about him.

"And why are you in San Francisco and not New York?"

"A quirk of fate. The store I work for sent me out here to open their new branch out here." He smiled thinking about it, and then his eyes clouded as he thought of why he'd stayed after that . . . because Liz was dying. "And then I got stuck here." Their eyes met and held, and she understood him perfectly.

"Are you here to stay then?"

He shook his head and smiled at her again. "I don't think I'll be here for too much longer. Sometime in the next year I'll probably be going back to New York." She looked instantly sorry, and in spite of himself it pleased him. And he was suddenly glad he had come to the party.

"How do the kids feel about moving back?"

"I don't know." He looked serious. "It might be hard on Jane. She's always lived out here, and it'll be hard on her going to a new school and making new friends."

"She'll adjust to it." Megan was looking at him searchingly, wishing she knew more. He was a man who made you want to know where he had come from, and where he was heading to. He was the kind of man one seldom met, warm and strong and real, but untouchable. And after seeing him in her office the last time, she knew why. She would have liked to draw him out, to really talk to him, but she wasn't sure how. "What store brought you out, by the way?"

"Wolff's." He said it modestly, as though it were an unimportant store, and she laughed with wide eyes. No wonder he looked like that. He had the instinctive style of a man who dealt daily with high fashion, yet in a very masculine, unselfconscious way that she liked. In fact there was a lot she liked about him.

She smiled warmly at Bernie then. "It's a wonderful store. I go there every few months just to stand on the escalator and drool at everything. Living up here doesn't give one much opportunity to think about things like that."

"I've thought about that this summer." He looked interested and pensive, as though sharing a secret project with her. "I've always wanted to have a store in a place like this. Kind of a small, simple country store, with everything from riding boots to evening wear, but really, really beautiful merchandise, the best quality. People up here don't have time to drive a hundred miles for a good-looking dress, and walking into an enormous store is inappropriate up here, but something small and simple and really good would be exciting here . . . wouldn't it?" He looked excited and so did she. It sounded like a terrific idea to both of them. "Only the best though," he went on, "and very little of it. Maybe take one of the Victorians and turn it into a store." He loved the idea the more he thought of it and then he laughed. "Pipe dreams. I guess once you're a merchant, it corrodes your thinking wherever you are."

He laughed and she smiled at him. She liked the look in his eyes when he talked about it.

"Why don't you do something like that? We have absolutely nowhere to shop, except a few miserable stores that aren't worth bothering with. And there's a lot of money up here, especially in the summer months, and with the wineries there's actually money here all year round now."

He narrowed his eyes, and then shook his head. He had afterthoughts of it, but to no avail. "I don't know where I'd find the time. And I'll be going back pretty soon. But it's fun to dream." He hadn't dreamt in a long, long time. Of anything. Or anyone. And she could sense that. She enjoyed chatting with him, and she liked his idea. But more than that, she liked him. He was an unusual man. Warm and strong and decent. And he had the gentleness of the very strong, and she liked that.

He noticed her beeper then hooked to the back of her belt and he asked her about it. Talking about the store seemed frivolous to him although it interested her more than he realized. "I'm on duty four nights a week, and have office hours six days a week. That keeps me on my toes, when I'm not yawning in someone's face from lack of sleep." They both laughed and he was impressed. It seemed conscientious of her to work that hard, and even have the beeper with her at a party. And he noticed that she had refused the wine after one glass. "We're short of doctors up here too, not just stores." She smiled. "My partner and I are the only pediatricians within twenty miles, which may not sound like much, but it gets awfully busy sometimes, like the night I saw you at the hospital. You were my third earache that night. I saw the first one at home, and the other one left the hospital just before you arrived. It doesn't make for a quiet home life." But she didn't seem unhappy about it. She looked content and satisfied and it was obvious that she enjoyed her work a great deal. She looked excited when she talked about it. And he had liked her style with Alexander.

"What made you go into medicine?" She had to be so dedicated, he had always been impressed by, but never attracted to, that life. And he had known since he was a child that he didn't want to follow in his father's footsteps.

"My father is a doctor," she explained. "He's in obstetrics and gynecology, which didn't appeal to me. But pediatrics did. And my brother is a psychiatrist. My mother wanted to be a nurse during the war, but she only made it as far as the Red Cross volunteers. I guess we all have the medical bug. Congenital," she pronounced and they both laughed. They had all gone to Harvard as well, which she didn't mention to him. She seldom did. She had gone to Radcliffe, and then Stanford Med School, and had graduated second in her class, a fact that mattered very little now. She was busy doing what she did, healing hot ears, and giving shots and setting bones, and curing coughs, and being there for the children she loved and took care of.

"My father is a doctor." Bernie looked pleased that they had something in common. "Ear, nose, and throat. Somehow it never seemed very exciting to me. Actually, I wanted to teach literature in a prep school in New England." It sounded silly now. The era of his passion for Russian literature seemed a thousand years ago and he laughed thinking of it. "I often suspect that Wolff's has saved me from a fate worse than death. I wanted to work for a small school in a sleepy town, as I thought of it, and thank God none of them wanted me, or I might have become an alcoholic by now." They both laughed at the thought. "Or hanged myself. It's a hell of a lot better selling shoes and fur coats and French bread than living in a place like that."

She laughed at the description he offered of Wolff's. "Is that how you see yourself?"

"More or less." Their eyes met and they felt a sudden inexplicable bond.

They were chatting easily about the store when her buzzer went off after that. She excused herself and went to the phone and came back to report that she had to meet someone at the hospital.

"Nothing terrible, I hope." Bernie looked worried, and she smiled. She was used to this. In fact, it was obvious that she loved it.

"Just a bump on the head, but I want to take a look at him, just in case." She was cautious, reasonable, and as good a doctor as he had suspected. "It was nice to see you again, Bernard." She held out a hand, and it was cool and firm in his own, and for the first time he noticed the perfume she wore as she stepped closer to him. It was sexy and feminine in the same way she was, yet not overpowering.

"Come and see me at the store next time you come in. I'll sell you some French bread myself to prove that I know where it is."

She laughed. "I still think you ought to open the store of your dreams here in Napa."

"I'd love that." But it was only a dream. And his time in California was almost over. Their eyes met then, and she left him regretfully, thanked their host, and was gone. He heard the Austin Healy roaring away, and saw her hair flying out behind a moment later. He left the party and went home, a short time afterwards, thinking of Megan, wondering if he'd see her again, and surprised by how much he liked her and how pretty she had looked in the gypsy blouse with the bare shoulders.

Chapter 36

A month later, on a rainy Saturday, Bernie was in Saint Helena doing some errands for Nanny, when he walked out of the hardware store and bumped into Megan again. She was wearing a long yellow slicker and red rubber boots, with a bright red scarf over her dark hair. And she looked startled as they collided, their arms full of packages, and she gave him a friendly smile. She had thought of him a number of times since they'd last met and she was obviously happy to see him.

"Well, hello again. How've you been?" Her eyes lit up like blue sapphires and he looked at her with pleasure as they stood there.

"Busy . . . fine . . . the usual . . . how are you?"

"Working too hard." But she looked happy. "How're your kids?" It was a question she asked everyone, but she actually gave a damn and it showed.

"They're fine." He smiled at her, feeling like a kid again himself and enjoying the feeling.

They were standing in the pouring rain, and he was wearing an old tweed hat and an English raincoat that had seen better days over his jeans and he suddenly squinted at her in the rain. "Can I buy you a cup of coffee or are you dashing off somewhere?" He remembered the beeper, and the bumped head she had run off to check on Labor Day when she left the party.

"Actually I'm through for the day, and I'd love it." She pointed to a coffee shop just down the street and he hurried after her, wondering why he had invited her. He always liked her when they met, and then was annoyed at himself because he was attracted to her, and that didn't seem right to him. He had no business being attracted to her. There was the usual awkwardness as they found a table and sat down. She ordered a hot chocolate, and he a cappuccino and then he sat back and looked at her. It was extraordinary, as unadorned as she was, she was beautiful. She was one of those women who look plain at first, and then slowly one realizes that there's a great deal more to them, their features are beautiful, their eyes remarkable, their skin exceptional, and all put together it makes someone very special. But it is not all hung with bright lights that catch one's eye at first. "What are you looking at?" She saw him staring at her and was sure she looked terrible, but he smiled and cocked his head to one side, smiling at her.

"I was thinking how pretty you look in your slicker and boots and red scarf on your black hair." He looked genuinely enraptured and she blushed furiously at the compliment and laughed at him.

"You must be blind, or drunk. I was probably the tallest girl in my class from kindergarten on. My brother said I had legs like lampposts and teeth like piano keys." And hair like silk . . . and eyes like pale sapphires and . . . Bernie forced the thoughts from his mind and forced himself to say something ordinary to her.

"I think brothers always say things like that, don't they? I'm not sure, having been an only child, but it seems to me that their appointed role in life is to torment their sisters as best they can."

She laughed at the memories he evoked. "Mine was good at it. Actually, I'm crazy about him. He's got six kids." She smiled thoughtfully. And Bernie laughed. Another Catholic. His mother would be thrilled at the news. And suddenly the thought amused him. This was definitely not Mrs. Rosenthal's daughter, the model from Ohrbach's. But she was a doctor. His mother would have liked that, and so would his father. If that mattered. And then he reminded himself that this was only hot chocolate and coffee on a rainy afternoon in Napa.

"Is your brother Catholic?" Irish Catholics would explain her black hair, but she shook her head and laughed at the question.

"No. He's Episcopalian. He just loves kids. His

wife says she wants twelve." And Megan looked as though she envied them, and so did Bernie.

"I've always thought big families were wonderful," he said as their hot drinks arrived. Hers covered with whipped cream and his coffee with steamed milk and nutmeg. He took a sip and glanced up at her, wondering who she was, where she had been, and if she had children of her own. He realized how little he knew of her. "You're not married, are you, Megan?" He didn't think she was anyway, but realized he didn't even know that for certain.

"Not much room for it, I'm afraid, with late night calls and eighteen-hour days." Her work was what she loved best of all and it didn't really explain her single state. And suddenly she decided to be honest with him. Like Liz long before, she saw a man in him that she could be open and honest with, and talk straight to.

"I was engaged to someone a long time ago. He was a doctor too." She smiled at Bernard and the openness he saw there caught him off guard like a physical blow. "After his residency, he was sent to Vietnam and killed just before I started my residency at UC."

"How awful for you." And he meant every word of it. He knew better than anyone the pain she must have gone through. But for her it had been a long time ago. She still missed Mark, but it wasn't the same anymore. It wasn't the same sharp pain Bernie was living with, barely more than a year after Liz had died. But he felt as though she understood him better now, and he felt a special kinship for her, which hadn't been there before.

"It was pretty rough. We'd already been engaged for four years, and he'd been waiting for me to graduate. He was at Harvard Med School when I was premed there. Anyway"—she averted her eyes and then looked back at him—"it was quite a blow, to say the least. I was going to take a year off and postpone my residency, but my parents talked me out of it. I even thought of giving up medicine completely, or going into research. I was pretty mixed up for a while. But my residency got me back on track again and then I came up here afterwards." She smiled quietly at him, as though to tell him that one could survive a loss, however painful. "It's hard to believe it but it's been ten years since he died. I suppose I really haven't had time for anyone in my life since then." She blushed and then laughed. "That's not to say I haven't gone out with anyone. But I've never gotten that serious with anyone again. Amazing, isn't it?" The fact that it had been ten years seemed remarkable to her. It seemed only yesterday since they'd left Boston together. She had gone to Stanford because of him, and she stayed out west afterwards because it was a way of staying closer to him. And now she couldn't imagine living in Boston again. "Sometimes I regret not getting married and having kids." She smiled and took a sip of her hot chocolate as Bernie looked at her admiringly. "It's almost too late now, but I have my patients to fulfill those needs. All that nurturing and mothering they need." She smiled but Bernie wasn't convinced that was enough for her.

"That can't be quite the same thing." He spoke quietly, watching her, intrigued by all that he saw in her.

"No, it's not the same thing, but it's very satisfying in its own way. And the right man has never come along again. Most men can't handle a woman with a serious career. There's no point in crying over what can't be. You have to make the best of it." He nodded. He was trying to, without Liz, but it was still so damn difficult for him, and he had finally found someone he could say that to, and who understood it.

"I feel that way about Liz . . . my wife . . . as though there will never again be anyone like her." His eyes were so sincere that it made her ache for him.

"There probably won't be. But there could be someone else if you're open to it."

He shook his head, feeling he had found a friend. "I'm not." She was the first person he had been able to say that to, and it was a relief to him to say it.

"Neither was I. But eventually you feel better about things."

"Then why didn't you marry someone else?" His words hit her like a fist and she looked at him seriously.

"I don't think I ever wanted to." She was totally honest with him. "I thought we were a perfect match. And I never found that again. But you know what? I think I may have been wrong." She had never admitted that to anyone, certainly not to her family. "I wanted someone who was just like him. And maybe someone different would have been just as good for me, if not better. Maybe the Right Man didn't have to be another pediatrician, just like me, who wanted a rural practice just like me. Maybe I could have married a lawyer or a carpenter or a schoolteacher and been just as happy and had six kids by now." She looked at Bernie questioningly, and his voice was deep and gentle when he answered her.

"It's not too late, you know."

She smiled and sat back in her chair again, feeling less intense, more relaxed, and happy to be talking to him. "I'm too set in my ways by now. An old maid to the core."

"And proud of it," he laughed, not believing her for a moment. "You know, what you said helps me. People have started pressuring me about going out, and I'm just not ready to do that." It was a way of excusing himself to her for what he wanted and didn't want, all at once, and mostly didn't understand as he looked at her and felt things that stirred old memories for him, memories that confused him as he watched her.

"Don't let anyone else tell you what to do, Bernard. You'll know when it's the right time. And it'll be easier for the kids, if you know what you want. How long has it been?" She meant since Liz had died, but he could handle the question now.

"A little over a year."

"Give yourself time."

Their eyes met, and he looked at her searchingly. "And then what? What happens after that, when you never find the same thing again?"

"You grow to love someone else." She reached out and touched his hand. She was the most giving woman he had met in a long, long time. "You have a right to that."

"And you? Why didn't you have a right to that too?"

"Maybe I didn't want it . . . maybe I wasn't brave enough to find it again." They were wise words, and they talked of other things then. Boston, New York, the house he was renting, the pediatrician she shared her practice with. He even told her about Nanny Pippin, and they chuckled over some of the adventures she'd had. It was a delightful afternoon and he was sorry when she said she had to go. She was driving to Calistoga to visit a friend for dinner that night and he was suddenly curious who it was, woman or man, friendship or romance. It reminded him of the things she'd said as he watched her drive off through the rain with a last wave at him . . . "Maybe I wasn't brave enough to find it again." . . . He wondered if he ever would be himself as he started his car, and drove back to the house where Nanny and the children were waiting for him.

Chapter 37

Bernie's mind was occupied with other things when his secretary came in the following week and told him that there was a lady there to see him.

"A lady?" He looked surprised, and couldn't imagine who it was. "What lady?"

"I don't know." His secretary looked as surprised as he did. Women did not generally come to see him, unless they were members of the press or wanted to plan fashion shows for the Junior League, or flew out from New York sent by Paul Berman. But in all of those instances, they had appointments, and this woman didn't. She was attractive in any case. His secretary had noticed that, but she didn't seem to fit into any of those categories. She didn't have the stereotyped look of the Junior League, with blond streaks in her hair, gold shrimp earrings she'd had for ten years, and shoes with little gold chains running across them. Nor did she have the look of the dowdy matron planning the charity event, or the shark-like air of the buyers from New York, or the press. She looked wholesome and clean, and yet well put together somehow, even though her clothes were neither exciting nor overly stylish. She was wearing a navy blue suit and a beige silk blouse, pearl earrings and high-heeled navy blue shoes. And she had very good legs, although she was tall. Almost as tall as Bernie.

He sat staring at his secretary then, unable to understand why she could not provide more information. "Did you ask her who she was?" The woman was generally not stupid, but she looked flustered this time.

"She just said she came to buy bread. . . . I told her this was the wrong department, Mr. Fine, that these were the executive offices, but she insisted that you told her . . ." And then suddenly, with a crack of laughter he was out of his chair, and walked to the door himself as the secretary watched him. He pulled it open, and there she was. Megan Jones, looking very chic, and not at all like a doctor. The white coat and jeans had disappeared, and she was smiling at him mischievously as he grinned at her from the doorway.

"You scared my secretary to death," he said in a soft voice. "What are you doing here? . . . I know . . . I know . . . buying bread." His secretary disappeared quietly through the other door, and he invited Megan into his office. She followed him in and looked around. He had all the accoutrements of an important man, and she looked suitably impressed as she sat on one of the large leather chairs and smiled at him, sitting on the corner of his desk. He looked very pleased to see her. "What brings you here, Doctor? . . . Other than bread, of course."

"An old friend from med school. She dropped out to get married and have babies. At the time I thought it was shocking . . . now I'm not so sure. She just had number five, and I promised to come and see her. I also figured I'd better buy myself some new clothes. I'm going home for the holidays, and my mother will cry if I show up in my Napa wardrobe. I have to remind myself that people don't look like that in Boston." She smiled sheepishly at him. "I have to start out looking proper at least. By the end of the third day, I've usually degenerated to jeans. But this time I thought I'd make an effort." She glanced down at her blue suit and then back at her friend. "I was practicing today. How do I look?" She looked momentarily unsure of herself and it touched him, coming from someone as capable as she was.

"You look lovely, very chic and very pretty."

"I feel naked without my blue jeans."

"And the white coat . . . somehow my mental image of you is either in the white coat, or your slicker." She smiled. She thought of herself that way too. And she always remembered him in the open blue shirt and the white pants he'd worn to the Labor Day party. He had looked so handsome, but he did in his business suit too. It was almost awesome . . . but not quite, because she knew him. "Do you want me to show you around the store?" She could see from the mountains of papers on his desk that he was busy, and she didn't want to interrupt him, but it had been nice to see him for a few minutes anyway.

"I can manage on my own. I just wanted to say hello."

"I'm glad you did." But he didn't want to let her go yet. "What time are you seeing your friend with the new baby?"

"I told her I'd come by around four, if I finish shopping by then."

"How about a drink after that?" He looked hopeful, and there were times when he felt like a small boy with her. He wanted to be her friend . . . and yet he wanted more . . . but he didn't. . . . He didn't know what he wanted from her, other than her friendship. But he didn't have to worry about it yet. They seemed to enjoy just being friends, and she wanted nothing more from him. She looked pleased at the invitation.

"I'd love that. I don't have to be back in Napa till eleven. Patrick is covering for me till then."

"And then you go back on duty?" Bernie looked horrified. "When do you sleep?"

"Never." She grinned. "I was up till five this morning, with a five-month-old baby with croup. You get used to it eventually."

He groaned. "I wouldn't have. That's why I work for Wolff's, and I'm not a doctor, the way my mother would have wanted. You now"—he grinned at Megan—"you're every Jewish mother's dream. If only you were my sister, my mother would be happy forever."

She laughed. "And my mother begged me not to go to med school. She kept telling me to be a nurse or a teacher, or even a secretary. Some nice job where I'd meet a man and get married."

Bernie smiled at the description. "I'll bet she's proud as hell of you now, isn't she?"

Megan shrugged modestly. "Sometimes. And at least she has grandchildren thanks to my brother, or she really would drive me crazy." She glanced at her watch then, and then smiled up at Bernie. "I'd better get going. Where should I meet you for drinks?"

"L'Étoile at six?" He said it without thinking, and then wondered if he should have. She was the first woman he had taken there since Liz, other than his mother, but he decided what the hell. It was a great place to have drinks, and she deserved the best. She had an element of quality about her that intrigued him. This was no ordinary girl he had met, and he knew it. She was a bright woman, a good friend, and a great doctor.

"I'll see you there." She smiled at him from his office doorway, and his day seemed better after she had been there. He left the office at five-thirty, and took his time getting to L'Étoile. He was in a good mood and he brought her a loaf of French bread, and a bottle of her favorite perfume, and she was startled when he handed them to her across the table. "Good heavens, what's all this?"

She looked delighted, and he could see in her eyes that it hadn't been a great day for her.

"Something wrong?" he asked her eventually, as they both sipped their kir. They discovered that they both loved it, and she had spent her junior year in Provence and spoke flawless French, which impressed him.

"I don't know . . ." She sighed and sat back in her chair. She was always honest with him, and he listened easily to her confession. "Something happened today when I looked at that baby." He waited to hear what she was going to tell him. "It was the first time I felt that terrible ache women talk about . . . that ache which makes you wonder if you've done the right thing with your life." She took a sip of the drink and then looked at him almost sadly. "It would be terrible never to have children, wouldn't it? And I've never felt that before. Maybe I'm just tired after last night with that sick baby."

"I don't think it's that. Having children has been the best thing that's ever happened to me. And you're smart enough to know that. You know what you're missing, most women don't."

"So now what? I run out and kidnap a baby . . . or get pregnant by my butcher at the market in Napa?" She smiled, but it was obvious that she was also troubled, and he smiled back, only partially sympathetic.

"I suspect there must be better volunteers than that." It was impossible to believe that there weren't, and she blushed faintly in the dim light of the room, as the piano played softly behind them.

"There might be, but I'm not anxious to have a child to raise without a father. I'm not even sure I'm anxious to have any child. But tonight"—her voice grew dreamy, and her eyes had a distant look—"when I held that baby . . . what a miracle children are." She looked up at him then, and shrugged. "It's stupid to wax poetic about it, isn't it? I have a good life like this."

He spoke for himself as well as her. "Maybe it could be better."

"Maybe." But she wasn't anxious to pursue it. Conversations like that always made her think of Mark, and that still hurt, even after all these years. There had never been anyone like him. "Anyway, think of the diapers I don't have to change. I can just run around waving my stethoscope, loving everyone else's babies." It sounded lonely to him. He couldn't imagine his life without Jane or Alexander, and he decided to tell her that.

"I was thirty-seven when Alex was born, and he's the best thing that's ever happened to me."

She smiled at him, touched by the confession. "And how old was your wife?"

"Almost twenty-nine. But I think she would have had him even if she'd been ten years older than that. She really wanted more children." It was a shame they hadn't had them. A shame she hadn't lived. A shame Mark hadn't either. But they hadn't. That was the reality of it. And Bernie and Megan had survived them.

"I see older mothers in my practice all the time. I think they're very brave. The good thing is they've done what they wanted to do, had their flings and freedom and established their careers, if that's what they want. Sometimes I think it makes them better parents."

"So?" He smiled, feeling like his own mother. "Go have a baby."

She laughed openly at that. "I'll tell my parents you said so."

"Tell them you have my blessing."

"I shall." They exchanged a warm smile, and she sat back, listening to the piano.

"What are they like?" He was always curious about her. He wanted to know more about her. He knew she was torn about having children, that she had gone to Radcliffe and Stanford, that her fiancé had been killed in Vietnam, that she came from Boston and lived in Napa, but he didn't know much more than that, except that he thought she was a damn fine woman, and he liked her. A lot. Maybe even too much, except that he didn't admit it. He pretended to like her a little. To himself at any rate.

"My parents?" She seemed surprised at his question, and he nodded. "Nice, I guess. My father works too hard, my mother adores him. My brother thinks they're both crazy. He says he wants to make a fortune and not stay up all night delivering babies, that's why he went into psychiatry instead of obstetrics. But I think he's serious about what he does"—she looked pensive and then smiled—"as serious as he ever is. My brother is practically crazy. He's tiny and blond and looks exactly like our mother." The thought of it amused Bernie.

"And you look like your father?"

"Exactly." But she didn't seem to regret it. "My brother calls me the giant. I call him the dwarf, and thus began a thousand wars when we were children." Bernie laughed at the images she created. "We grew up in a nice house that had been my grandfather's in Beacon Hill and some of my mother's relatives are very fancy. I don't think they ever completely approved of my father. I don't think being a doctor was aristocratic enough for them, but he loves what he does, and he's very good at it. I went to a number of deliveries with him while I was in med school, whenever I went home for the holidays, and I saw him save a number of babies who would never have lived otherwise, and one mother I know for certain wouldn't have, if it hadn't been for his skill. I almost went into O.B. because of that, but I'm really happier doing what I'm doing in pediatrics."

"Why didn't you want to stay in Boston?"

"Honestly?" She sighed with a gentle smile. "Too much pressure from all of them. I didn't want to follow in Dad's footsteps, I didn't want to do O.B., or be a devoted wife like my mother, just taking care of her husband and children. She thought I should let Mark be the doctor, and I should stay home and make life comfortable for him. There's nothing wrong with that, but I wanted something more. And I couldn't have stood all that gentle Episcopalian, puritanical prodding. Somehow, in the end, they would have wanted me to marry someone fancy, and live in a house just like theirs, and give little social teas for friends just like theirs." She looked frightened just thinking of it. "That wasn't me, Bernie. I needed more space and more freedom, and new people and my blue jeans. That life can be very restrictive."

"I'm sure it can. It's really not that different from the same pressures I would have hated in Scarsdale. Jewish, Catholic, Episcopalian, it's all the same thing in the end. It's what they are and what they want you to be. And sometimes you can, and sometimes you can't. I couldn't. If I could have, I'd be a Jewish doctor now, married to a nice Jewish girl, having her nails done at this very moment."

Megan laughed at his description. "My best friend at med school was Jewish, she's a psychiatrist in Los Angeles now, and making an absolute fortune, and I'll bet you she's never had her nails done."

"Believe me, she's an exception."

"Was your wife Jewish?" She was curious about her too, but he shook his head, and he didn't look upset at the mention of Liz, as he smiled at Megan.

"No. Her name was Elizabeth O'Reilly." He laughed suddenly, remembering a scene a thousand years before. "I actually thought I had given my mother a heart attack the first time I told her."

Megan laughed out loud and he told her the details of the story. "My parents acted that way when my brother introduced his wife to them. She's as wild as he is, and French. My mother was sure that French meant she had been posing for postcards." They both laughed at that, and continued telling stories of their parents' foibles, until Bernie glanced at his watch and realized it was eight o'clock. And he knew she had to be back in Napa by eleven.

"Do you want to eat here?" He had assumed they would be having dinner, or hoped so anyway, and he didn't care where they ate, just so they were together. "Or do you want Chinese, or something more exotic?"

She looked at him hesitantly, calculating the time. "I go on duty at eleven . . . which means I should leave town by nine-thirty." She smiled at him sheepishly. "Would you hate me if we went for a hamburger somewhere? It might be quicker. Patrick gets upset right now if I show up late to go on call for him. His wife is eight months pregnant and he's scared to death she's going to go into labor while I'm tied up somewhere. So I really have to get home on time tonight." Not that she wanted to. She would have liked to spend hours talking to Bernie.

"I wouldn't mind a hamburger. In fact"—he signaled for their check at L'Étoile and the waiter appeared at once, as Bernie pulled out his wallet

—"I know a fun place not far from here, if you don't mind a bit of a mixed crowd." There was everything from longshoremen to debutantes, but he liked the atmosphere there and suspected she would too. And he was right. As soon as they walked in, she loved it. They ate their hamburgers and apple pie at the longshoreman's bar on the wharf called Olive Oyl's, and she left him with regret at nine-thirty to drive back to Napa. She was afraid she'd be late, and he walked her quickly back to her Austin Healy after dinner.

"Will you make it home all right?" He was worried about her. It was late to be driving to Napa alone, but she smiled at him.

"Much as I detest the words referring to my size, I'm a big girl now." He laughed at her. She was sensitive about her height. "I had a wonderful time."

"So did I." And he really had. It was the most fun he had had in a long, long time. It was easy being with her, and comfortable sharing his most private thoughts and listening to hers.

"When are you coming back up to Napa again?" She looked hopeful.

"Not for a while. I have to go to Europe next week, and Nanny doesn't take the children up when I'm away. It's too much trouble packing up, schlepping everything around. I'll be back in less than three weeks. I'll call you when I get back, maybe we can have lunch up there." He looked at her with a smile, and then he thought of something. "When are you going home for the holi-days?"

"Christmas."

"So are we. To New York. But we thought we might have Thanksgiving in Napa this year." He didn't want to be in town for that, thinking of what was no more. "I'll call you when I get back from New York."

"Take care of yourself, and don't work too hard." He walked her out to her car, and smiled as she said that to him.

"Yes, Doctor. You too, and drive safely."

She waved and he looked at his watch as she drove away. It was exactly nine thirty-five. And he called her at eleven-fifteen, from his house. He asked her service to page her if that was possible. And she said she had just walked in the door and hung up her coat when she answered.

"I just wanted to make sure you got home all right. You drive too fast." He scolded her.

"You worry too much."

"It's in the genes." He laughed and in his case it was true. He had worried all his life, but it also made him good at things. He was a perfectionist about almost everything he touched, with excellent results at Wolff's at any rate.

"It's beautiful in Napa tonight, Bernie. The air is crisp and clear and the stars are all out." The city was swathed in fog, and he was happy in either place, although he would have enjoyed being with her again. The evening had ended too quickly. "Where are you going in Europe, by the way?"

She was curious about his life. It was so different from what she did.

"I'll be in Paris, London, Milan, Rome. I go twice a year for the store. I have to stop in New York afterwards for meetings."

"Sounds like fun."

"It is. Sometimes." It had been with Liz. And before that. Lately it was less so. Like everything else he did, it was lonely.

"I had a wonderful time tonight, Bernie, thank you."

He laughed, thinking of their dinner at Olive Oyl's on the wharf. "It certainly wasn't Maxim's."

"I loved it." And then her buzzer went off and she had to leave him.

He could still hear her voice in his ears after he hung up, and just to clear his head afterwards, he walked into his closet, and took a deep breath of the very faint scent of Liz' perfume still lingering there. One had to work harder now to catch it, and he closed the door softly, feeling guilty. He wasn't thinking of Liz tonight, but of Megan. It was suddenly her perfume he longed for.

Chapter 38

Bernie stayed in New York longer than he had planned. This was an important year for ready-to-wear, there were major changes happening in the trade, and Bernie wanted to be on top of things. But he was pleased with the way things had gone when he finally left for San Francisco again. And he didn't remember the scarf he'd bought for Megan at Hermès until they went to Napa. He suddenly remembered it, tucked into a corner of his briefcase, and went to look for it. He found it, and decided to deliver it to her himself. He drove the car into town, and stopped outside the Victorian where she lived, and where her offices were. Her partner said she was out and he left the small tan box for her, with a note that read only "To Megan, from Paris. Best, Bernie."

She called him that night to thank him for it, and he was pleased she liked it so much. It was navy and red and gold, and it had reminded him of her in her red boots and jeans and yellow slicker.

"I just got home and found it on my desk. Patrick must have left it there for me when you dropped it off. And it's beautiful, Bernie, I love it."

"I'm glad you like it. We're opening a boutique for them here in March."

"How fabulous. I love their things."

"So does everyone. That ought to be good for us." He told her about some of the other deals he'd made and she was impressed.

"All I did was diagnose three earaches, seven streps, a budding bronchitis, and a hot appendix in three weeks, not to mention a million cuts, splinters, bumps, and one broken thumb." She sounded disappointed in herself, and he wasn't.

"That sounds a lot more meaningful to me. No one's life depends on my Italian luggage boutique or a line of French shoes. What you do gives some meaning to life. It's important."

"I suppose it does." But she was feeling down again. Her partner's wife had had the baby that week, a girl, and she had had that same ache again. But she didn't tell Bernie. She didn't know him that well and he was going to start thinking she was neurotic about other people's babies. "Did they tell you when you're moving back to New York?"

"Not yet. And for once, we didn't even have time to talk about it. There's a lot happening at the store just now. At least it's interesting. Would you like to have lunch tomorrow?'' He was going to offer to meet her at the coffee shop in Saint Helena.

"I wish I could. Patrick's wife had the baby this week, and I have to cover for him. I could stop by the house on my way to the hospital to do rounds. Or would that upset Jane too much?'' She was being honest with him. She had felt how strong Jane's resistance was when they met before, and she didn't want to upset her.

"I don't see why it should.'' He didn't see what Megan did, or at least not as clearly.

"I don't think she's crazy about having ladies around.'' She meant around him, but she didn't say it.

"She's got nothing to worry about.''

She wasn't sure Bernie understood the nature of it. She was protecting her mother's memory, and it was understandable. Megan just didn't want to rock her boat too hard. There was no need for it. "I don't want to upset anyone.''

"You'll upset me if you don't stop by. Besides, it's time you met Nanny Pip. She's the best member of the family. What time were you thinking of coming by?''

"About nine. Is that all right or is it too early?''

"Perfect. We'll be having breakfast then.''

"See you tomorrow.'' And his heart raced at the thought of seeing her again. He told himself it was because she was such an interesting woman and he forced himself not to think of the shining black

hair or the sensation he got in the pit of his stomach when he thought of her.

Megan arrived the next morning at nine-fifteen,
after he had set another place for her. And as he
put the place mat down, Jane had looked up at
him questioningly.

"Who's that for?"

"Dr. Jones." He tried to look noncommittal as
he pretended to shuffle through *The New York
Times*. But Nanny was watching him. And so was
Jane. Like a vulture.

"Who's sick?" Jane pursued.

"No one. She just wanted to come by for coffee."

"Why? Who called her?"

Bernie turned to look at her. "Why don't you
relax, sweetheart? She's a nice woman. Now drink
your juice."

"I don't have juice." They were eating strawberries, and he looked up distractedly and
grinned.

"Drink it anyway."

She smiled, but she was suddenly suspicious of
him. She didn't want anyone in their life. They
had everything they needed now. Each other,
Alex, and Nanny Pip. It was Alex who had started
calling her Pip and the name had stuck immediately. Nanny Pippin was too much for him.

And then Megan arrived, with a big bunch of
yellow flowers and a sunny smile for everyone.
Bernie introduced her to Nanny Pip, and Nanny

pumped her hand with a radiant smile and it was obvious she was impressed with her from the first.

"A *doctor,* how wonderful! And Mr. Fine said you were kind to poor little Alex with his ear." Megan chatted pleasantly with her and Nanny made it clear that she approved of her, as a doctor, and a woman, by lavishing every possible attention on her. She poured her coffee, gave her muffins, eggs, bacon, sausages, and an enormous bowl of strawberries as Jane stared at her with barely veiled hatred. She was angry at her for coming by, angrier at her for making friends with Bernie.

"I don't know why Daddy asked you to come by," she said loudly, as Megan praised the delicious food and smiled at her. "No one's sick here." Bernie was stunned by her rudeness, as was Nanny, who growled at Jane, but Megan smiled at her pleasantly, looking undisturbed by the child's words.

"I like getting to know my patients when they're well too. Sometimes"—she explained patiently, looking undaunted by the black looks Jane was giving her openly—"it's actually easier to treat someone if you've known them a little bit when they're not ill."

"We go to a doctor in San Francisco anyway."

"Jane." It was a single warning word. Bernie wasn't pleased with her. He glanced at Megan apologetically, as Alexander sidled over to her and stood staring up at her.

"Lap," he announced. "I wanna sit on your

lap." His English still sounded like an awkward translation from the Greek, but Megan understood him perfectly, and plopped him on her knees, and handed him a strawberry which he shoved into his mouth in one piece as Megan smiled down at him. And as Bernie watched, he suddenly noticed that Megan was wearing the scarf he had dropped off to her the day before. It pleased him to see her wearing it, but almost at the same instant he noticed it, so did Jane. She had seen the box on his desk the day before and asked him what it was. He said it was a scarf for a friend, and Jane had rapidly figured it out. She remembered the Hermès scarves he had brought Liz. And this time he had also brought one for Nanny Pippin. A beautiful navy and white and gold that she could wear with her uniforms and navy coat and brogues, and the hat that made her look like Mary Poppins.

"Where did you get that scarf?" She acted as though Megan had stolen it, and the pretty young woman gave a start and then rapidly recovered. It had almost been Jane's point, but in the end, it was Megan's.

"Oh . . . that . . . I got it from a friend a long time ago. When I lived in France." She instantly knew what she had to do and Bernie was grateful to her. It was as though they had begun a conspiracy, without ever intending to, but now they were suddenly partners.

"You did?" Jane looked surprised. She thought

Bernie was the only person in the world who knew Hermès.

"Yes." She sounded totally credible, and calmer now. "I lived in Provence for a year. Have you been to Paris with your daddy, Jane?" she asked innocently, and Bernie concealed a smile. She was good with kids. Hell, she was great with them. And Alex was cuddling up to her happily with little warm noises and snuggles. And having eaten all her strawberries, he was now assisting her with her eggs, and gobbled a piece of her bacon.

"No, I haven't been to Paris. Not yet. But I've been to New York." She suddenly felt important.

"That's terrific. What do you like best there?"

"Radio City Music Hall!" Unwittingly, she was getting pulled into it. And then suddenly she looked suspiciously at Megan. She had just remembered that she didn't want to like her, and she refused to continue the conversation, answering only in monosyllables until Megan left.

Bernie apologized to her as he walked her to the car. "I feel terrible. She's never rude like that. It must be some kind of jealousy." He was genuinely upset and Megan shook her head and smiled at him. He was an innocent in matters she understood only too well. The heartaches and dilemmas of children.

"Stop worrying about it. It's perfectly normal. You and Alex are all she's got. She's defending her turf." Her voice was gentle, but she didn't want to cause him pain by being too blunt with him. He was still fragile too, and she knew it.

"She's defending her mother's memory. It's very hard for her to see a woman around you, even a nonthreatening one." She smiled. "Just don't take any sexy blondes home to her, or she'll poison them for you." They both laughed as he opened the car door for her.

"I'll remember that. You handled her beautifully, Meg."

"Don't forget that's my line of work, more or less. You sell bread. I know kids. Sometimes." He laughed and leaned toward her, suddenly wanting to kiss her, and then just as quickly backed off, horrified by his own reaction.

"I'll try to keep that in mind too. See you soon, I hope." And then he remembered what he'd wanted to ask her. Thanksgiving was only two weeks away, and they weren't coming back till then. "Do you want to have Thanksgiving dinner with us?" He had thought a lot about asking her, all the way home from New York in fact.

She looked at him thoughtfully. "Do you think Jane is ready for that? Don't push her too fast."

"What am I supposed to do? Sit alone in my room for the rest of my life?" He sounded like a disappointed child. "I have a right to friends, don't I?"

"Yes. But give her a chance to catch her breath. Why don't I just come for dessert? That might be a good compromise."

"Do you have other plans?" He wanted to know who she was seeing. She seemed so busy all the time, and he wondered with whom. It was hard to believe her work could keep her that busy and yet it seemed to.

"I told Patrick's wife, Jessica, I'd give her a hand. They have relatives coming from out of town, and she could use a hand cooking dinner. Why don't I get her on her feet and then come here?"

"Anything else you're planning to do? Give mouth-to-mouth to someone on the way?" He was amazed by her. She was constantly doing something for somebody. And rarely for herself.

"It's not as bad as that, is it?" She looked surprised. She never thought of it. It was just the way she was, and one of the things he liked best about her.

"Seems to me you're always doing things for everyone but yourself," Bernie said with concern in his eyes.

"I get what I need out of it, I suppose. I don't need much." Or at least she never had before. But lately she was wondering. There were things that seemed to be missing from her life. She knew it when Alexander stood looking up at her and pointing at her lap, and even when Jane stared at her so angrily. Suddenly she was tired of just looking into ears and down throats and testing reflexes.

"See you on Thanksgiving then. For dessert if nothing else." But he was still disappointed she wouldn't come for more, and he secretly blamed it on Jane, and was annoyed with her when he went back inside again. And even more so when she spoke up against Megan.

"Boy, is she ugly, isn't she, Daddy?" She was looking piercingly at him and he glared at her.

"I don't think so, Jane. I think she's a very good-looking girl." He was not going to let her get to him, no matter what.

"Girl? Yuck! She looks about four hundred years old."

He clenched his jaw and looked at her, trying to speak quietly. "Why do you hate her so much?"

"Because she's dumb."

"No." He shook his head. "She's not dumb. She's very smart. You don't get to be a doctor by being dumb."

"Well, I don't like her anyway." There were suddenly tears in her eyes, and a plate slipped from her hands and broke as she tried to help Nanny Pip clear away the dishes.

Bernie walked over to her quietly. "She's just a friend, sweetheart. That's all she is." Megan was right. Jane was frightened of a woman coming into his life. He could see that now. "I love you very much."

"Then don't let her come here anymore." She was crying now and Alexander was staring at her, worried but fascinated, with no idea of what they were talking about.

"Why not?"

"We don't need her here, that's why." And with that, she ran from the room and slammed her bedroom door, and Nanny Pip looked at him quietly and held up a hand as he made a move to follow her.

"Leave her alone for a little while, Mr. Fine. She'll be all right. She has to learn that things aren't always going to be this way." She smiled gently at him. "I hope not anyway, for your sake. And for Jane's. I like the doctor very much." She made "very" sound like "vera."

"So do I." Bernie was grateful for the encouragement. "She's a nice woman and a good friend. I wish Jane hadn't gotten so worked up about nothing."

"She's afraid of losing you." It was exactly what Megan had said.

"She'll never do that."

"Be sure you tell her so. Frequently. And for the rest, she'll just have to get used to it. Go slowly . . . and she'll come around." Go where? He wasn't going anywhere. With Megan or anyone. And he looked at Nanny solemnly.

"It's nothing like that, Nanny Pip. That's what I wanted Jane to understand."

"Don't be so sure of that." Nanny looked at him honestly. "You have a right to more than the life you're leading now. It wouldn't be healthy to live like this for the rest of your life." She knew exactly how celibate he was, and she also knew about the closet full of clothes that he and Jane still wandered into now and then, pretending to look for something else. She thought it was time to get rid of them, but she also knew he still wasn't ready.

Chapter 39

Megan was true to her word and came for dessert after Thanksgiving dinner with Patrick and Jessica, and the new baby, and she brought a mince pie she had made herself. Nanny said it was wonderful, but Jane said she'd had enough to eat, and Bernie had a piece, and was surprised at how good it was.

"You don't know how amazing it is." She looked pleased with herself, and was wearing a red dress she had bought at Wolff's the day she had drinks with him. "I am literally the worst cook in the world. I can barely boil an egg, and my coffee tastes like poison. My brother begs me never to walk into his kitchen."

"He sounds like a character."

"In this case he's right." Jane grinned in spite of herself, and Alex sidled up to her again, and this time climbed onto her lap without asking permission. She gave him a taste of the mince pie, but he spat it out. "See, Alexander knows. Right?" He nodded solemnly and everyone laughed at him.

"My mom was a terrific cook, wasn't she, Daddy?" The comparison was half obnoxious and half sad as Jane said it.

"Yes, she was, sweetheart."

"She used to bake a lot." She remembered the heart-shaped cookies on the last day of school and it almost made her cry as she stared unhappily at Megan.

"I admire that. I think it's nice to know those things."

Jane nodded. "She was real pretty too." Her eyes were sad and it was suddenly more a memory than a comparison, as Bernie listened. It hurt hearing it, but he knew she needed to say it. "She was blond and kind of skinny and little."

Megan smiled at him. There was certainly no question of his being attracted to her because she looked like his late wife. In fact, she was almost exactly the opposite, and in a way, she felt better about that. People so often tried to duplicate what they had lost, and it made everything so difficult. It was impossible to stand in someone's shadow as the sun moved on. And she looked at Jane gently now. "You won't believe this, but my mom is skinny and blond and little too. And so is my brother."

Jane laughed at the thought. "For real?"

"For real. My mom's about this high." She pointed to her shoulder and smiled. "I look just like my father." In either case, no loss. They were both handsome people.

"Is your brother short like your mom?" Jane was suddenly fascinated and Bernie smiled. Maybe there was some hope that Jane would calm down after all.

"Yes, he is. I always call him the dwarf."

"I'll bet he hates you for that." Jane giggled at the thought and Megan grinned.

"Yes, I guess he does. Maybe that's why he's a psychiatrist, so he can figure it out." They all laughed at that, and Nanny brought her a cup of tea, and the two women exchanged a knowing smile. She took Alexander away for his bath after that, and Megan helped Bernie and Jane clear the table. They threw things out, put food away, scraped, rinsed, and loaded the dishwasher, and when Nanny came back again, everything was done. She had been about to say that it was nice having a woman around the house and then thought better of it, and just thanked all of them for cleaning up, which was more diplomatic.

Megan stayed for another hour after that, chatting with all of them, sitting in front of the fire, and then her beeper went off, and she let Jane call the answering service for her, and she listened in while Megan took the call. Someone had choked on a turkey bone. They had gotten it out fortunately, but now the child's throat was badly scratched. And as she hung up, her beeper went off again. A little girl had cut her hand on the carving knife and needed to be stitched up.

"Urghk." Jane made a face. "That one sounded terrible."

"Some of them are. But I don't think that one will be too bad. No fingers lopped off or anything messy like that." She smiled at Bernie over her head. "Looks like I'm going to have to go."

"Do you want to come back again?" He was hoping she would, but she still wanted to be cautious about Jane.

"I think it might be late by then. Somehow you never finish as quickly as you think you will. You don't want me pounding on your door at ten o'clock tonight." He wasn't entirely sure of that, and they were all sorry when she left, even Jane, and Alex especially, who came looking for her after his bath, and cried when Jane told him she'd gone.

It reminded Bernie of what the children didn't have, and he wondered if Nanny Pip was right, that their lives wouldn't always be that way. But he couldn't imagine changing it now. Except of course that one day they'd move to New York, although he never thought about it anymore. He was content in California these days.

They went to New York for Christmas without seeing Megan again. They didn't have time to go back up, with all that Bernie had to do in the store, and there was plenty for the children to do in town. Nanny took them both to the *Nutcracker* and the children's show at the symphony. They went to see Santa Claus at Wolff's, of course. Alex was enthralled by him, and now that she was nearly ten, Jane didn't believe in him anymore, but she went anyway to humor Alex.

And Bernie called Megan once before they left. "Have a wonderful holiday," he wished her fervently. She deserved it, after all she did for everyone, all year round.

"You too. Give my love to Jane." She had sent her a warm pink scarf and hat for the trip to New York, but they hadn't arrived yet when Bernie talked to her. And she had sent Alex a cuddly Santa doll.

"I'm sorry we won't be seeing you before the holidays." Sorrier than she knew. He'd been thinking of her a lot in recent weeks.

"Maybe I'll see you in New York," she said thoughtfully.

"I thought you were going to Boston to see your family."

"I am. But my crazy brother and sister-in-law are going to New York and absolutely insisting that I come. One of our fancier cousins is getting married, with a great to-do at the Colony Club. I'm not sure I could stand an event like that, but they seem to want me to come along, and I said I'd think about it."

She had agreed so she could see him in New York, but now she felt foolish admitting it to him. But he was excited at the prospect of seeing her.

"Will you let me know if you're coming down?"

"Of course. I'll see what's on the agenda when I arrive, and I'll call you as soon as I know." He gave her the number in Scarsdale, and hoped she would call him.

And that night when he went home, he found the huge box of presents she had sent to them. The hat and scarf for Jane, the Santa doll for Alex, a Pringle sweater for Nanny Pip, which was exactly what she liked, and a beautiful leather-bound book for him. He saw immediately that the book was old, and discerned easily that it was also rare, and her note said that it had been her grandfather's and had brought her through hard times and she hoped it would do the same for him. She wished him happy things in the coming year, and a Merry Christmas to all of them. And as he read her note, he felt lonely for her. He was sorry they weren't spending the holidays in the same town, and that life had to be so complicated sometimes. Christmas was lonely for him. It reminded him of Liz, and their anniversary. And he was quiet on the flight east. Too quiet, Nanny thought. He was thinking of Liz, she could tell from the grief etched on his face. He was still so lonely for her.

And on her own flight, Megan was thinking of her old fiancé, and Bernard, and quietly comparing them. They were two very different men and she respected them both. But it was Bernie she missed now, and she called him that night just to talk to him. His mother was stunned when the phone rang, almost as soon as they got home, and Nanny was putting the children to bed. His mother handed the phone to him with a worried look. She had said she was Doctor Jones, and his mother continued to hover nearby until he waved her away nervously. She thought someone was sick, and Bernie almost laughed as he took the phone. He would have to explain to her afterwards, he knew. But he was anxious to talk to Megan first. He was dying to talk to her in fact.

"Megan?" His face lit up like a Christmas tree. "How was the trip?"

"Not bad." She sounded happy to hear him, too, and faintly embarrassed to have been the one to call. But she didn't give a damn. She had suddenly been so lonely for him once she arrived in Boston again, that she had had an irresistible urge to reach out to him. "It's always strange coming home again at first. It's as though they forget we're grown up, and they start ordering you around like a kid. I always forget that till I come home again." He laughed, he always felt the same way. And he still remembered how odd he and Liz had felt staying in his old room. It was like being fourteen years old again, and sex was taboo. He preferred staying at a hotel, but with the kids there was no point. And they had come to share the holidays with their grandparents. In some ways it was less lonely here, with them, than staying at a hotel, but he knew exactly what Megan meant.

"I know exactly what you mean. It's like taking a step back in time and proving they were right all along. You are fourteen years old, and you've come back to do it their way this time . . . except you don't. And eventually everyone gets pissed at you."

She laughed. In Boston, they already were. Her father had gone to do a delivery an hour after she arrived, and she hadn't wanted to go with him because she was tired, and he had left, obviously annoyed at her, while her mother had scolded her for not bringing boots that were warm enough, and folding everything in her suitcase wrong. And an hour after that, she had chided her for leaving her room a mess. It was difficult after eighteen years of living alone, to say the least. "My brother said he'd rescue me tonight. They're having a dinner party at their house."

"Will that be Boston sedate, or completely nuts?"

"Probably both, knowing them. He'll probably get completely drunk, and someone else will take off all their clothes, probably some Jungian analyst who gets gassed on his lethal punch. He loves doing things like that."

"Watch out he doesn't get you." It was strange thinking of her in that milieu, and lonely for him. He realized how much he missed her suddenly, and he wasn't sure if he could say that to her. It seemed inappropriate in their friendship somehow, and yet there was more to it than that, and there was a great deal to be explored. "Are you coming to that wedding down here?" He was counting on it, but didn't tell her so.

"It looks like they are anyway. I'm not sure what my parents will say about my going away when I'm supposed to be visiting them, but I thought I'd mention it and see what they say."

"I hope they let you come." He looked like a worried teenager, and suddenly they both laughed. It was the fourteen-year-old syndrome again.

"See what I mean!"

"Listen, just come for one night, it would be fun seeing you here."

She didn't disagree with him, and she wanted to see him very much. He had been on her mind for weeks, and she was sorry she hadn't seen him again before they both left for the east, but they both led busy lives, with a great many responsibilities. And maybe getting together in New York wasn't such a bad idea. "I'll see what I can do. It would be fun." And then she had a better idea. She sounded like a kid as she suggested it to him. "Do you want to come to the wedding with me?" She loved the idea the more she thought of it. "Did you bring a dinner jacket to New York?"

"No, but I know a great store." They both laughed. "Are you sure it's appropriate since I don't know the bride and groom?" A wedding at the Colony Club sounded like a very serious affair to him, and the very thought of it intimidated him, but Megan laughed at the thought.

"Everyone will be so drunk they won't give a damn who you are. And we can slip away early and go somewhere else . . . like the Carlyle to listen to Bobby Short." He fell silent as he listened to her words. That was one of his favorite things to do in New York, and Bobby was an old friend from his New York days. He had been following him for years.

"I'd love that." His voice sounded husky, as he thought of her, and he felt young again, as though life were beginning for him, and not as though it had already begun, and ended in tragedy less than two years before. "Try and come down, Meg."

"I will." There was an urgency between them now, and in a way it almost frightened her, and yet she wanted to see him while she was there. She didn't want to wait until they met in Napa again. "I'll do my best. And put the twenty-sixth on your calendar. I'll come in that morning, and stay at the Carlyle. My crazy brother always stays there."

"I'll pick up a dinner jacket at the store this week." It all sounded like fun, except the wedding itself, which he was dreading a little bit. It was only three days before his anniversary with Liz. It would have been four years. But he couldn't think of that now. He couldn't go on celebrating anniversaries that didn't exist, and suddenly he wanted to reach out to Megan, as though to force the memories from his head, and she heard something odd in his voice and was suddenly worried about him. It was as though she knew him better than she did. It was odd the communication they had. They had both noticed it.

"Are you all right?" Her voice was soft from her end, and he nodded with a tired smile.

"I'm okay. The ghosts get me sometimes . . . particularly at this time of year."

"It's hard for everyone." She had gone through it too, but it had been such a long time, and there had usually been some man or other in her life at this time of year. Either that or she was at the hospital, on call with sick kids. Either way, she suffered less than she knew he would. She hoped his family would be good to him. She knew how difficult the holidays would be for him, and the kids, or Jane anyway. "How's she?"

"Happy to be here. She and my mother are as thick as thieves. They've already got plans for the next three weeks, and Nanny is staying on here with them after I leave. I've got to be back in San Francisco for a meeting on the thirtieth, and Jane doesn't have to be back in school till the tenth, so that gives them two more weeks after I leave, and they're all looking forward to it." She wondered if he'd be lonely then.

"Will you come up to Napa while they're gone?"

"I might." There was a long silence as they shared the same thoughts and then shied away from them again, and she promised to call him by the end of the week, to tell him her plans. But the next time he called her. It was two days after they had arrived in New York, and it was Christmas Day, and her father answered the phone in a booming voice and called out to her, telling her to hurry up.

She came scurrying to the phone breathlessly, and Bernie smiled the moment he heard her voice. "Merry Christmas, Meg." He had fallen into calling her that, and she smiled. No one had called her that since her best friend when she was a child, and it warmed her heart when he did it.

"Merry Christmas to you too." She was happy to hear his voice, but there seemed to be a lot of noise in the background, and someone was calling her.

"Is this a bad time?"

"No. We were just leaving for church. Can I call you back?" And when she did, she announced herself to his mother as Doctor Jones again. They had a nice long chat, and when he hung up the phone, his mother eyed him curiously. The children were in their room, playing with some of their presents with Nanny Pip. They had gotten most of their gifts for Chanukah, but Grandma Ruth couldn't forgo Christmas entirely. She didn't want to disappoint Alex and Jane, so Santa Claus now came to their house too, which made Bernie laugh. If he had wanted to celebrate Christmas as a child, they would have been horrified. But for their grandchildren, even that was all right. They had mellowed a lot over the years. But not totally.

"Who was that?" His mother attempted unsuccessfully to look naive, after his call from Meg.

"Just a friend." It was a game that was familiar to him, although he hadn't played it with her in a long, long time, and he was secretly amused by it.

"Anyone I know?"

"I don't think so, Mom."

"What's her name?"

He used to balk at that, but he didn't care anymore. He had nothing to hide, even from her. "Megan Jones." She looked at him, half pleased that someone had called, half angry because her name wasn't Rachel Schwartz.

"Another one of those again." But secretly she was pleased. There was a woman calling him. He was alive again. And there was something in his eyes which almost gave her hope. She had said as much to Lou the night he arrived, but Lou said he didn't see anything different in him. He never did. But Ruth did. And she saw it now. "How come you never meet Jewish girls?" It was a question as much as a complaint and this time he grinned at her.

"I guess 'cause I don't go to temple anymore."

She nodded, and then wondered if he was angry at God because of Liz, but she didn't want to ask him that, which was just as well. "What kind is this?" There were long pauses between her questions and Bernie smiled at her.

"Episcopalian." He remembered the scene at Côte Basque and so did she.

"Oy." But it was a small unedited word, more of a statement of fact than a warning of collapse. "An Episcopalian. Is it serious?"

He was quick to shake his head and she wondered about that. "No, it's not. She's just a friend."

"She calls you a lot."

"That makes twice." And she knew he had called her too, but she didn't say that to him.

"Is she nice? Does she like the kids?" A double-barreled question this time, and he decided to say something on Meg's behalf, to assure her of his mother's respect at least.

"She's a pediatrician, if that makes any difference." And of course he knew it did. The jackpot for Megan Jones! He smiled to himself, watching the look on his mother's face.

"A doctor? . . . Of course . . . *Doctor* Jones . . . Why didn't you tell me that before?"

"You didn't ask." They were the same old words to the same game. Like a song they'd been singing to each other for years. It was almost a lullaby by now.

"What was her name again?" Now he knew she'd have his father check her out.

"Megan Jones. She went to Harvard undergraduate, med school at Stanford, and did her residency at UC. That way Dad won't have to look her up. His eyes aren't so great these days."

"Don't be fresh." She pretended to be annoyed, but in truth she was impressed. She would have liked it better if he had been the doctor and she worked at Wolff's, but what the hell, you couldn't have it all in one life. They all knew that by now. "What does she look like?"

"She has warts and buck teeth."

And this time his mother laughed. After almost forty years, she finally laughed with him.

"Will I meet her sometime, this beauty with the warts and buck teeth, and the fancy degrees?"

"You might, if she sticks around."

"Is it serious?" She narrowed her eyes as she asked him again, and he backed off. It was all right to play with her, but he wasn't ready to talk seriously yet. For the moment they were just friends, no matter how often she called, or he called her.

"No."

She had learned something else over the years. She knew when to back off, and when she saw the look on his face she did. And she didn't say another word when Megan called him again that night to tell him what time she'd be at the Carlyle the next day. She was coming in to go to the wedding with him. He had already brought the dinner jacket home, and it fit him impeccably. His mother had been stunned when she saw him going out the next night. And she was even more impressed when she saw the long black limousine waiting outside for him.

"Is that her car?" Her eyes were wide and she spoke in hushed tones. What kind of a doctor was this? After forty years with a good practice on Park Avenue in New York, Lou still couldn't afford a limousine. Not that she wanted one, but still . . .

Bernie smiled. "No, Mom, it's mine. I rented it."

"Oh." It deflated her a little bit, but not much. She was very proud of him, and she watched from behind the curtain as he got into the car and disappeared. And she sighed to herself as she stepped back into the living room and saw Nanny Pippin watching her. "I just . . . I wanted to make sure he was all right. . . . It's icy out to-night." As though she needed an excuse.

"He's a good man, Mrs. Fine." Nanny Pippin sounded as though she were proud of him too, and her words touched Ruth's heart.

Ruth Fine glanced around to see if anyone was listening to them, and then advanced cautiously on Nanny Pip. They had established a tenuous friendship over the past year, but Ruth respected her, and Nanny liked her in return. And Ruth figured that Nanny knew everything that went on in his life. "What's the doctor like?" She spoke in a voice so low that Nanny could barely hear, but she smiled.

"She's a good woman. And very intelligent."

"Is she beautiful?"

"She's a handsome girl." They'd have made a fine pair, but Nanny didn't want to encourage her too much, there was no reason to think anything serious would happen between them, although she would have liked to see something like that. Megan would have been perfect for him. "She's a good girl, Mrs. Fine. Perhaps something will come of it one day." But she offered no promises, and Ruth only nodded her head, thinking of her only son riding into town in a rented limousine. What a handsome boy he was . . . and a good man. . . . Nanny was right. She wiped away a stray tear as she turned off the living room lights and got ready to go to bed, and wished good things for him.

Chapter 40

The drive into town took longer than usual because of the snow, and he sat in the back seat thinking of her. It seemed forever since he had seen her in Napa. And he was excited to be seeing her again, especially in this setting. It was new and different and exciting. He liked the quiet, simple life she led, working hard at what she did, with love and dedication. And yet there was more to her than that, her family in Boston, the "crazy" brother she described so fondly, and the fancy relatives she spoke of with amusement, like the cousins getting married that night. But more than that, there was what he felt for her. The respect and the admiration and the growing affection. And there was more than that. There was a physical attraction he could barely deny now, no matter how guilty it made him feel. It was still there, growing more powerful day by day. And he was thinking of how lovely she was as the limousine sped up Madison Avenue on the salt-strewn street, and turned east on Seventy-sixth Street.

Bernie got out of the car and went inside the elegant lobby to ask for her. An assistant manager at the front desk, wearing a morning coat and a white carnation, checked the register and nodded to him solemnly.

"Dr. Jones is in four-twelve."

He took the elevator to the fourth floor, and turned right as they told him to. And he held his breath as he pressed the bell. He suddenly couldn't wait to see her again, and when she opened the door in a navy satin evening gown, she took his breath away with her shining black hair and her blue eyes, and a stunning sapphire necklace with matching earrings. They had been her grandmother's but it wasn't her jewelry which took his breath away, it was her face and her eyes, and he reached out and gave her a warm hug that felt like coming home to both of them. It was incredible how much they had missed each other in such a short time, but they barely had time to say anything before her brother came bounding into the room, singing a filthy song in French, and looking precisely as she had described him. Samuel Jones looked like a very handsome, aristocratic blond jockey. He had gotten all their mother's elegant, delicate looks, and everything about him was tiny, except his mouth and his voice and his sense of humor and according to him his sex drive. He pumped Bernie's hand, warned him never to eat his sister's cooking or let her dance with him, and he poured Bernie a double Scotch on the rocks, as Bernie attempted to catch his breath and say a few words to Megan. But a moment later, her sister-in-law appeared in a flurry of green satin and red hair and giggles and squeals in French and a lot of very large emeralds. Being around them was like being in a whirlwind and it was only when they were alone in the limousine on the way to the church that he could sit back quietly and look at her. Sam and his wife had gone in their own car.

"You look absolutely spectacular, Megan."

"So do you." Black tie suited him to perfection. And it was a long way from their jeans and her slicker.

And then he decided to tell her what he'd been feeling. "I've missed you. It was almost disorienting coming back here this time. I keep wanting to be in Napa talking to you, or going for a walk somewhere . . . or at Olive Oyl's eating a hamburger."

"Instead of all this grandeur?" she teased as she smiled at him, indicating their elegant garb and the limo.

"I think I prefer the simple life in the Napa Valley." He smiled, thinking of their life there. "Maybe you were right to leave Boston." He was almost sorry he was coming back to New York now. It didn't appeal to him as it once had. All he wanted was to go back to California, where the weather was gentle and the people were more polite, and where he knew he would see Meg in her jeans and her starched white doctor's coat. In a funny way, he was homesick.

"I always feel like that here." She understood perfectly. She could hardly wait to go back in four more days. She was going home to spend New Year's Eve in the Napa Valley, on call for Patrick, who was on call for Christmas, and they both agreed that they needed a third doctor in their practice. But that was a long way away tonight, and Bernie held Megan's hand as they got out at Saint James' Church on Madison and Seventy-first. She had never looked lovelier and he was proud to be with her. There was a regal quality about her, a quiet elegance and strength. She looked like someone one could turn to and he stood beside her at the wedding, proud to be with her. He met her cousins afterwards, and chatted with her brother and his wife for a little while, and was surprised at how much he liked them. He found himself thinking of how different she was from Liz. She had strong family ties and a family she loved deeply, unlike poor Liz, who had been so alone in the world, except for him and Jane and Alexander.

He danced with Meg's sister-in-law, but more importantly, he danced with Meg. He danced with her until two o'clock in the morning, and then they sat at the Bemelmans Bar at the Carlyle till four-thirty, spilling stories, sharing confidences, and making discoveries about each other. It was almost six in the morning when he got back to Scarsdale in the limo. And he met her for lunch the next day. He had been in meetings at the store since nine, and he was exhausted from the night before. But at the same time he felt exhilarated and happy, and she looked pretty in a bright red wool coat when he picked her up and took her to "21" for lunch. They ran into her brother there, pretending to pick his wife up at the bar, and claiming that he was horribly hung over. He still had his hand on his wife's behind when he ordered lunch, and Bernie couldn't help laughing at him. He was boyish and shocking and outrageous, forty-one going on nine, as Megan said, but he was also very handsome. And eventually he and Marie-Ange went upstairs and left Megan and Bernie alone. He had already told Megan that morning over Bloody Marys and steak tartare that he hoped she was lucky enough to catch Bernie. He thought he was terrific and just what she needed: style, brains, and balls, as he described it, but he had forgotten the best part. A heart the size of a mountain. It was that that Megan loved so much about him. And she looked at him over lunch at "21," and they talked about the Napa Valley. They could both hardly wait to get back there.

"Why don't you do your store there, Bernie?" She still loved the idea and the way his eyes sparkled when they talked about it.

"How can I, Meg? That's a full-time project."

"Not if you know the right people to help you run it. You could run it from San Francisco, or even New York, once it really got started."

He shook his head, smiling at her innocence. There was an enormous amount of work involved which she didn't understand. "I don't think so."

"Why not do it anyway? Try it." She had always encouraged him and he felt a spark of interest ignite in him again.

"I'll think about it." But he was more excited about their plans for New Year's Eve. They had decided to spend it together, even if she was on call. He didn't mind that, and he had promised to drive to Oakville after his meetings in town on the thirtieth. It made it less painful to leave her that afternoon. She had to pick up her things at the Carlyle after lunch and fly back to Boston. And he had to go to a meeting with Paul Berman. He had two days left with his parents and the children and they flew by. And two days later, he was back on the plane to San Francisco and excited to see Megan again. He could hardly wait till the following night when he was planning to drive to Oakville. She had flown from Boston the day before, but when he'd called her she had been in the emergency room with a child with a hot appendix. And it was when he was alone in the house again that he realized how empty his house and his life and his heart were without her. He wasn't sure if he missed her, or Liz, and he felt guilty about his own confusion. And it was a relief when the phone rang at eleven that night. He was in the bedroom packing for Napa. It was Megan, and he was so happy to hear her voice he could have cried, but he didn't.

"Are you okay, Bernie?" She asked him that a lot and it touched him profoundly.

"I am now." He was honest with her. "The house is so empty without Jane and Alex." . . . and Liz . . . and you . . . and . . . he forced himself to think only of Megan, no matter how guilty it made him.

She told him about the medical journals on her desk, and it made him smile thinking of his father. And he told her about the meetings he was running the next day, and she brought up the Napa idea again. She insisted that she had a friend who could run a store for him to perfection.

"Her name is Phillippa Winterturn. And you'll love her." She sounded so excited he smiled. He loved her enthusiasm. She was always full of new ideas bubbling over.

"Good God, Meg, what a name."

Megan laughed. "I know. But it suits her perfectly. She's got prematurely gray hair, green eyes, and more style than anyone I know and I ran into her in Yountville today. Bernie, she'd be just perfect. She used to work for *Women's Wear*, and for Bendel's in New York a long time ago. She's fabulous, and she's free now. If you want, I'll introduce you to her." She wanted him to do the store. She sensed how much he would love it.

"All right, all right. I'll give it some thought." But he had other things on his mind now. New Year's Eve among them.

They had decided to make dinner together at his house, the following evening. She was going to buy the groceries and they were going to cook together, and with luck she wouldn't get called out before midnight. He could hardly wait to see her. And when they hung up the phone, he stood staring at Liz' closet but this time he didn't touch the door. He didn't open it, he didn't walk in. He didn't want to go near it. He was leaving her inch by inch. He knew he had to. No matter how much it hurt him.

Chapter 41

He got to Napa at six o'clock the next night, and stopped at his place to change. He wanted to get out of his city clothes, and he put on comfortable flannel slacks and a plaid shirt, and over it he put a heavy Irish sweater. He didn't need more than that when he picked her up, and when he got to her office, he could feel his heart pound, he was so excited to see her. She pulled open the door, and without thinking he pulled her into his arms and spun her around as he hugged her.

"A little decorum here, please, Dr. Jones," her partner teased as he watched them. He knew Megan had been happy lately, and now he knew why. He also suspected they'd seen each other in New York, although she hadn't said so.

The three of them left the office together, and Bernie carried the groceries to his car, as she told him about her day, and he teased her that she wasn't working hard enough. She had seen forty-one patients.

They went back to his place and made steaks and a Caesar salad, and just as they finished the steaks, her beeper went off and she looked at Bernie apologetically.

"I'm sorry. I knew that would happen."

"So did I. Remember me? I'm your friend. It's okay." He put the coffee on while she went to the phone and she was back a moment later with a frown.

"One of my teenagers got drunk and locked himself in the bathroom." She sat down with a sigh, grateful for the mug of coffee he handed her with a smile.

"Shouldn't they call the fire department instead?"

"They did. He passed out and hit his head, and they want me to make sure he doesn't have a concussion. And they think his nose might be broken."

"Oh Lord." He smiled at her. "How about letting me play chauffeur tonight." He didn't want her driving on New Year's Eve, and she was touched by his thoughtfulness.

"I'd like that, Bernie."

"Finish your coffee while I dump this stuff in the sink."

She did and they left a few minutes later in the BMW as they headed for the town of Napa. "It's nice and toasty in here," she murmured happily. And they enjoyed the music on the way down. There was a festive air to the evening even if she was working. "I'm always glad my roof leaks on the Austin. It's so cold and drafty that it keeps me awake at night coming back from the hospital at all hours, otherwise I might wind up wrapped around a tree sometime. But there's no chance of that freezing my ass off." He didn't like thinking of her in danger or uncomfortable, and he was glad he had driven her tonight with all the drunks on the road. And afterwards they were planning to go back to his place for dessert and more coffee. She didn't want to drink champagne while she was on duty.

"Dr. Jones . . . Dr. Jones to the emergency room . . ." They were paging her at the hospital when she got there, and Bernie settled down in the emergency room with a stack of magazines. She promised to be back as soon as she could, and she was back exactly half an hour later.

"All done?" She looked businesslike in her white coat as she nodded, and she took it off and threw it over her arm as they walked out the door.

"That was easy. Poor thing was practically out cold, and he did not break his nose, or have a concussion. But he had a hell of a bump, and he's going to feel awful tomorrow. He drank a pint of rum before his parents found him."

"Ouch. I did that in college once. Actually rum and tequila. I thought I had a brain tumor when I woke up."

She laughed at him. "I did it with margaritas when I was at Harvard. Someone had some damn Mexican party, and all of a sudden I couldn't stand up. It was my second year there and I never lived it down. Apparently I did everything except run up and down the street naked and barking." She laughed at the memory, as did Bernie. "Sometimes I feel a hundred years old when I think of things like that." They exchanged a warm look and his eyes were gentle on hers.

"One nice thing, you don't look it." She barely looked thirty, let alone six years older. And it still amazed him to realize he'd be forty on his next birthday. Sometimes he couldn't help wondering where the time went.

They pulled into his driveway an hour and a half after they'd left his house, and he went into the living room to start a fire while she put on water for coffee. He found her in the kitchen a few minutes later and smiled at her. It was an odd way to spend New Year's Eve but they were both happy. And he brought her a steaming mug of coffee as she sat in front of the fire with her legs crossed, looking comfortable and relaxed. She looked at him happily. "I'm glad you came up this weekend, Bernie. I needed to see you."

It was a nice thing to say, and he felt the same way about her. "Me too. It was so damn lonely in the house in the city, and this is a nice way to spend New Year's Eve. With someone you care about." He was cautious about the words and she understood that.

"I was thinking of staying up here this week while the kids are gone. I don't mind the commute." Her face lit up as he said it.

"That sounds wonderful." She looked enthused as her beeper went off again, but this time it was only a five-year-old with a mild fever and she didn't have to go anywhere. She just gave standard instructions and told them she wanted to see the child in the morning, and to call her back if the little girl's fever went over a hundred and four.

"How do you do that night after night? It must be exhausting." But he knew how much she loved it. "You give so much of yourself, Meg." That never ceased to impress him.

"I have no one else to give it to, why not?" But she didn't look sad as she said it. It was something they had talked about before. In a way, she was married to her practice. But as she looked at him something strange happened. He suddenly couldn't keep within the boundaries he had set for himself before. Just hugging her had opened doors of desire he could no longer close. And as though it were the most natural thing in the world, he took her in his arms and kissed her. He kissed her for a long, long time, as though remembering how as he went along and liking it more and more as he did it. And when he stopped, they were both breathless. "Bernie? . . ." She wasn't sure what they were doing, or why. She was only sure of one thing. That she loved him.

"Should I tell you I'm sorry?" He searched her eyes but saw only tenderness there and he kissed her again without waiting for her answer.

"Sorry for what?" She was dizzy now and he kissed her again as he smiled at her, and then held her tight. He couldn't stop anymore. He had wanted her for too long without even knowing he had, and now he wanted her more than he could control. He pulled away from her suddenly, and stood up, embarrassed to have her see the huge bulge in his pants. He had an uncontrollable, enormous erection.

"I'm sorry, Meg." He took a deep breath, and walked to the window, trying to remember Liz, but he found he couldn't, and that panicked him. He turned to Megan with the look of a lost child and she was standing just behind him.

"It's okay, Bernie . . . no one's going to hurt you." And as she said it, he took her in his arms again and began to cry as this time she held him, and he kept her close to him, as though needing to feel her warmth next to him, and then he looked into her eyes, his lashes damp, his face serious and strong.

"I don't know what else I feel, Meg . . . but I know that I love you."

"I love you too . . . and I'm your friend. . . ." He knew it was true, and he reached out and cupped her breasts with his hands, and then slid them over the lean flat stomach, and into her jeans and his breath caught he wanted her so much. He unzipped her jeans, and touched her softly, as her eyes closed and she moaned softly. And then without a word of protest from her, he carried her to the couch, and they lay there, in front of the fire, discovering each other's bodies. Her body was pale and her flesh was a delicate white, like slivers of moonlight, and her breasts were small and high as he touched them and they hardened, and she gently opened his pants, and reached inside to find him. He sprang into her hands with hunger, and he pushed the rest of their clothes away as he pressed himself against her, and then inside her as she gave a sharp cry of desire, and suddenly they were both crying out, in desperation, in anguish, in passion, in joy, and she clung to him as she came, and he felt as though his whole life had ended as they soared through the sky and fell back to earth together.

They lay a long time in silence, he with his eyes closed, stroking her gently, and she staring into the fire, thinking of how much she loved him.

"Thank you." The words were a whisper from him as he lay there. He knew how much she had given him, and how desperately he needed it. More than he had ever known. He needed her love and her warmth and her help now. He was letting go of Liz, and it was almost as painful as when she died, more perhaps because this was forever.

"Don't say that. . . . I love you."

He opened his eyes, and when he saw her face he believed her. "I never thought I'd say that again." He felt a relief he had never felt before. Relief and peace and safety just being with her. "I love you." He whispered again.

She smiled and held him close to her, like a lost child, and he fell asleep as she held him.

Chapter 42

They were both stiff when they woke up the next day, and Megan was cold, but they looked at each other anxiously, and when they saw that they had nothing to fear, they looked happy. It was New Year's Day, and Bernie teased her about the way they had spent New Year's Eve as she giggled.

He went to put the coffee on, and she found an old bathrobe of his and put it on and followed him into the kitchen. Her long, thick black hair was disheveled and she looked beautiful as she sat down and cupped her chin in her hands as she leaned her elbows on the counter. "You're a beautiful man, you know." He was the sexiest man she had ever slept with, and she had never felt for anyone what she did for him. But she knew it could be dangerous for her. He was an invitation to a broken heart. He hadn't gotten over his wife, and he was moving back to New York in a few months. He had told her so himself. And she was old enough to know that sometimes it was the honest ones who really hurt you.

"What are you thinking about? You look awfully serious, pretty lady."

"I'm thinking how sorry I'm going to be when you go back to New York." She was going to be honest with him too. She had to. She had survived her own tragedies over the years, and she had scars that could not be forgotten.

"It's funny. I'm not looking forward to going back anymore. The first couple of years here, that was all I wanted." He shrugged and handed her a mug of steaming black coffee, which was how she took it. "Now I wish I didn't have to. Why don't we not think about it for a while?"

"It's going to hurt either way." She smiled at him philosophically. "But I figure that for you, it's worth it."

"That's a nice thing to say." He would have paid any price for her too. He was surprised by how much he loved her.

"I thought you were terrific the night you came to the hospital with Alex. I told the nurse . . . but I thought you were married. I gave myself a good lecture on the way home about not getting heated up about my patients' fathers." He laughed and she smiled. "I did. Honestly."

"Some speech. I wouldn't have called you cool last night." She blushed and he came to sit next to her, wanting her again, wanting more than he could have . . . wanting her forever. They were living in a fairyland of love for the moment. But as he looked at her, he wanted more, and he gently opened the robe she had tied so carefully only moments before, and it fell to the floor as he led her to his room and they made love on his bed this time, and again before she finally took a shower and insisted that she had to get dressed and do rounds at the hospital with Patrick.

"I'll come with you." His eyes were happier than they had been in two years, and hers were warm as she turned to him, still wet from the shower.

"Do you really want to come with me again?" She loved it, loved having him near her and sharing her life with him. But she also knew that that was dangerous. Sooner or later, he would have to leave her.

"I can't stay away from you, Meg." It was honest. And it was as though having lost one woman he loved, he couldn't bear to lose another, even if it was only for an hour.

"Okay."

They were inseparable for the entire weekend, eating and sleeping and walking and running and laughing together, and making love three and four times a day. He was like a man who had been starved for love and sex and affection and couldn't get enough of her to make up for it. And for the entire week, he came back from the city early every day, and went to meet her at her office, bringing little presents and treasures and things to eat. It was like the early days with Liz, only it was different. They both knew it wouldn't last.

One day he would go back to New York and it would be over. Only that was still a long time off, as long as Paul Berman didn't find anyone to replace him.

And on their last night together before the children came home, he opened a bottle of Louis Roederer champagne and they drank it and she made dinner for him. Patrick was on call for her that night and they had a peaceful but passionate night in each other's arms until morning.

He was taking the day off to be with her too, but they were due in at six o'clock, and at four he had to head for the city.

"I hate to leave you." They had barely been apart for ten days, and it depressed him to think of leaving her now. Things wouldn't be the same with the children around, especially Jane. She was too old and too observant to be fooled by lies, and they couldn't sleep together openly, without upsetting her terribly and violating the proprieties they both believed in. They would have to go away somewhere if they wanted to do that, or he would have to sleep at her house and leave at six in the morning to slip back before the children got up. "I'm going to miss you so damn much, Meg." He almost felt like crying and she kissed him as he said it.

"I'm not going anywhere. I'll be right here. Waiting for you." The way she said it touched him. But he had filled a spot in her soul that had been empty for a long, long time. She knew just how deeply she loved him, maybe more than she could ever tell him, and she knew she had to love him with open arms. She had no right to cling to him, and she had promised herself not to. "I'll see you this weekend, my love." But it wouldn't be the same now. They both knew it, and he promised to call that night once the children were in bed. But as he stood waiting for them at the airport, he felt as though he had lost something very dear to him, and he wanted to run back to her and make sure it was still there. But it was only when he went back to the house, with Nanny Pip and the children, that it hit him.

He was honestly looking for something this time. A box that Jane swore he had, with some old photographs of Grandma and Grampa. She wanted to make an album for them as a present, and he opened Liz' closet, and suddenly it was as though she were standing there, reproaching him for what he'd done with Megan. He felt as though he had cheated on her and he slammed the door, and felt breathless as he left the room without the photographs Jane wanted. He could no longer face Liz' closet.

"I don't have them." His face was pale beneath the beard. What had he done? What had he done to Liz? Had he forgotten her? Was that it? He had sinned. He had sinned awfully. And he was sure that God would punish him. He had betrayed her.

"Yes, you do have those pictures," Jane persisted. "Grandma said so."

"No, I don't!" he shouted and then walked into

the kitchen looking tense. "She doesn't know what she's talking about."

"What's wrong?" Jane was confused but she knew him well.

"Nothing."

"Yes, there is. Don't you feel well, Daddy?" He turned to face her and she saw that his eyes were brimming with tears and she ran to him and threw her arms around him, frightened.

"I'm sorry, baby. I just missed you so much I went crazy." He wasn't sure if he was apologizing to her or to Liz, but once the children were in bed, he called Megan anyway, and his desire for her was so overpowering that he wanted to be with her as soon as he could. He felt as though he were going crazy without her.

"Are you okay, sweetheart?" She had heard something strange in his voice and she thought she understood it. She knew that going back to the house he had shared with Liz would be painful. Especially now. Especially the way he was. She knew he was feeling guilty.

"I'm fine." But he didn't sound it.

"It's okay, if you aren't." She already knew him well and he sighed. It was a relief in some ways, annoying in others. He was embarrassed at the confusion he felt, and the guilt, but it was real and he couldn't help it.

"You sound like my mother."

"Oh oh." She smiled and he laughed. But she didn't press him.

"Okay, okay." He decided to make a clean

breast of it, and in the end, it brought them closer. "I feel so damn guilty. I opened the closet and it was as though I still felt her there . . ." He didn't know what else to say but Megan understood it.

"You still have her clothes there?"

That was embarrassing too in a way. "Yeah. I guess . . ."

"It's okay. You don't have to apologize, Bernie. That's your life. You have a right to all that." She was the first person who had said that to him and he loved her all the more for it.

"I love you. You're the best thing that's happened to me in a long time, and I hope I don't drive you crazy."

"You do. But not the way you mean." She blushed faintly. "In a nice way."

He smiled. He felt lucky again. He hadn't felt lucky in a long, long time. "How are we going to get together this weekend?"

They devised a plan where he would spend the night with her on Friday, and go home early the next morning. And it worked. It worked on Saturday too. And he went up the following Wednesday night too, and told Jane he had to go to Los Angeles on business.

He started telling them that every week, and one week he went for two nights. Only Nanny Pip knew the truth. He wanted her to know where he was, in case something happened to one of the children. He didn't tell her who it was. He just gave her the number and told her only to use it in an emergency. It embarrassed him. But she never said a word. And she never seemed shocked about it. It was as though she thought it was normal. He suspected she knew who it was. She always sent him on his way when he was going up there with a little smile and a pat on the shoulders.

And on the weekends they went to Napa, and Megan dropped by. She taught Jane how to make a nest for a little bird that fell out of a tree near the house, and she helped her set his leg when they discovered it was broken. She took Alex on errands with her and he squealed with delight now whenever he saw her coming. And Jane was slowly relenting.

"How come you like her so much, Daddy?" she questioned him one day as they were putting the dishes in the sink for Nanny.

"Because she's a nice woman. She's intelligent and kind and loving. That's not an easy combination to find." And he had. Twice. He was a lucky man after all. He would be lucky this time until he had to move back to New York from California. But more and more lately he was questioning that decision.

"Do you love her?"

He held his breath, not sure what to say to her. He wanted to be honest but he didn't want to push her. "Maybe." Jane looked stunned.

"You do? As much as you loved Mommy?" She looked shocked and suddenly angry.

"No. Not yet. I haven't known her for as long." Jane nodded. It was serious then. But try as she might, she couldn't go on hating Megan. She was too easy to like, and too kind to the children, and when he had to go to Europe in April, Jane asked if they could stay with her on weekends. It was a major breakthrough, and Bernie almost cried with gratitude and relief when she said it.

"Do you really want them up there?" He had promised Jane he would at least ask her. "I could send Nanny with them."

"I'd love it." Her house was tiny, but if she slept on the couch, and she insisted she wanted to, she could give Nanny her room, and the children her study. And they loved it. They went up on weekends after school finished on Friday. And Bernie came back in time for Alexander's third birthday. They celebrated it all together, and afterwards Bernie went out for a long walk with Megan.

"Did something happen in New York?" She looked worried. "You seem quiet."

"Berman thinks he's getting closer to finding someone to replace me. There's a woman he wants to hire away from another store. And they're haggling over the money. But he usually wins those kinds of battles. What'll I do, Meg?" There was a look of anguish in his eyes that touched her deeply. "I don't want to leave you." He had missed her desperately while he was in Europe, more than he had ever thought he would.

"We'll face it when we have to." And they made love that night as though there never would be a tomorrow. And two weeks later, he came out from the city especially to tell her the news. Berman had lost his replacement. She had signed a new contract with her old store for almost twice the money. It was a relief and yet Bernie knew he couldn't keep depending on the fates to save him.

"Hallelujah!" He had brought her champagne and they went out to dinner to celebrate that night at the Auberge du Soleil, and they had a wonderful evening. He was going to drive back to the city at eight o'clock the next morning, but she insisted that there was something she wanted to show him first. She led the way in her Austin Healy. It was a perfect little Victorian house, nestled between some vineyards off the highway.

"It's beautiful. Whose is it?" He looked at it casually, as one would someone else's wife, with admiration but no urge for possession, but she was smiling at him, as though she had something up her sleeve now.

"It's an estate. It belonged to old Mrs. Moses and she died while you were in Europe. She was ninety-one years old and the house is in perfect condition."

"Are you buying it?" He was intrigued and she seemed to know a lot about it.

"No. But I have a better idea."

"What's that?" He glanced at his watch. He had to get to the store for a meeting.

"How about opening your store now. I didn't want to say anything until you knew if you were leaving or not. But even if you only stay for a few months, Bernie, it could be a fantastic investment." She was so excited she looked almost girlish, and he looked at her, touched, but he knew he couldn't do it. He had no idea how soon he'd be leaving.

"Oh Meg . . . I can't."

"Why not? At least let me introduce you to Phillippa."

"Baby . . ." He hated to disappoint her, but she had no idea how much effort went into starting a store. "I don't just need a manager, I'd need an architect, a buyer, a . . ." He faltered.

"Why? You know all that stuff. And there are a dozen architects up here. Come on, Bernie, at least think about it." She looked at him and his eyes danced a little, but not enough, and she was disappointed.

"I'll think about it, but I gotta go now. I'll be back on Saturday." It was two days away. Their whole life was built on the days they spent together.

"Will you have lunch with Phillippa?"

"Okay, okay." He laughed and pinched her bottom and got in his car, waving as he drove away. And she smiled to herself as she drove to the hospital, hoping it would do the trick. It was something she knew he wanted to do, and there was no reason why he couldn't do it. And she was going to do everything she could to help him. He had a right to his dream, and maybe, with luck . . . he would stay in California.

Chapter 43

Phillippa Winterturn had one of the funniest names and the prettiest faces Bernie had ever seen. She was a pretty white-haired woman in her early fifties and she had done everything from run a store in Palm Beach, to run a chain of them on Long Island, to work for *Women's Wear Daily* and *Vogue* and design clothes for children. She had had her finger in every aspect of the retailing pie for the past thirty years and she had even graduated from Parsons.

And Megan listened to them talk, barely able to suppress a smile. She didn't even care when she had to go back to the office to set a broken wrist for an eight-year-old. When she came back they were still talking. And by the end of lunch, Bernie's eyes were in flames. Phillippa knew exactly what she wanted to do, and she was dying to do it with him. She didn't have the money to make the investment, but Bernie felt sure that he could handle that himself, with a loan from the bank and maybe even a little help from his parents.

The trouble was, it just didn't make sense for him to undertake a project like the one they discussed. He still had to go back to New York sooner or later. But the idea preyed on his mind after his lunch with Phillippa.

He drove past the house Megan had shown him several times. It gnawed at him, but there was no point in his buying property in California except maybe as an investment.

But whenever Paul called now, Bernie sounded distant and distracted. He was suddenly haunted by old ghosts again. Liz seemed to come to mind far too often and it made him testy with Megan.

Bernie spent the entire summer with the San Francisco store, in body anyway. But his heart and his mind and his soul seemed to be somewhere else. In Napa with Megan, and the house he wished he were buying, and the store he wished he were starting. He felt guilty about his mixed emotions, and Megan sensed what was happening to him. She was very calm and quiet and supportive and she asked him no questions about his plans, and he was grateful to her for that. She was a remarkable woman. But he worried about that too now.

They had been living on borrowed time for seven months, and sooner or later they'd have to face the music. And he didn't like it. He loved being with Megan, going for long walks, talking late at night, even going to the hospital with her when she had a late-night call and she was so wonderful with the children. Alexander was crazy about her, and now so was Jane, and so was Nanny Pippin. She seemed to be the perfect woman for him . . . except there was still Liz' memory to contend with. He tried not to compare them to each other, they were two entirely different women, and whenever Jane tried to, Megan would always stop her.

"Your mommy was very, very special." It was impossible to disagree with her and it was comforting to Jane when she said that. She seemed to know the children so well, and Bernie even more so. He didn't even like staying in the city anymore, and there was something about their house there that depressed him. The memories there didn't seem happy anymore, and all he could think of now was when Liz had been sick and dying, and trying so desperately to hang on, dragging herself to school, cooking dinner for them, and weakening hourly. He hated thinking about it now. It was two years since she'd left them, and he preferred thinking of other things. But it was hard to think of her at all, without thinking of her dying.

In August his parents came out to visit the children. Bernie and the children were living in Napa for the summer, and they settled in as they had the year before, and his parents took Jane on a trip as they had before. And when they brought her back, he introduced them to Megan. It was obvious who she was from the earlier description he had given them. And his mother looked her over carefully with a knowing look, but she didn't disapprove of her. She even liked her. It would have been impossible not to, even for his mother.

"So you're the doctor." She said it almost proudly, and there were tears in Megan's eyes when she kissed her. She drove them around Napa the next day, when she was off call and Bernie was at work, and she showed them all the sights. Bernie's father could only stay for a few days. He was going to San Diego for a medical convention. And Ruth opted to stay in Napa with the children. But she was still deeply troubled about her son. She sensed that, in spite of his involvement with Megan, he was still grieving for Liz. And they talked about it over lunch at the Saint George in Saint Helena. Ruth felt that she could be open with this young woman she liked so much.

"He's not the same as he used to be." She said it sadly, wondering if he ever would be again. In some ways he was better, more sensitive, more mature, but he had lost some of his joie de vivre after Liz died.

"It takes time, Mrs. Fine." It had already been two years and he was only beginning to recover. And it was the decisions he had to make that were weighing on him now. The choices that were so painful. Megan or Liz' memory, San Francisco or New York, a store of his own or his loyalty to Wolff's and Paul Berman. He felt torn in every direction, and Megan knew it.

"He seems so quiet right now." Ruth spoke to

her like an old friend and Megan smiled gently. It was the smile that comforted hurt fingers and aching ears and painful tummies, and it comforted Ruth too. She felt that in this woman's hands her son would be happy.

"This is a hard time for him. I think he's trying to decide if he wants to let go. That's scary for anyone."

"Let go of what?" Ruth looked puzzled.

"His wife's memory, the delusion that she'll come back again. It's not unlike what Jane has gone through. As long as she rejects me, she can pretend that her mother might come back one day."

"That's not healthy," Ruth said, and she frowned.

"But it's normal." She didn't tell her of Bernie's dreams of his own store in the Napa Valley. That would just have upset her further. "I think Bernie's on the verge of making some decisions that are difficult for him, Mrs. Fine. He'll feel better when he gets them behind him."

"I hope so." She didn't ask if one of those decisions was whether or not to marry Megan. But they chatted on through lunch and she felt better when Megan dropped her off at the house after lunch and waved as she drove off. "I like that girl," she told Bernie that night. "She's intelligent and sensitive and kind." She took a short breath. "And she loves you." For the first time in Bernie's memory, his mother looked frightened to annoy him, and he smiled at her.

"She's a terrific woman."

He agreed.

"Why don't you do something about it?"

There was a long silence as he met his mother's eyes, and then he sighed. "She can't move her practice to New York, and Wolff's isn't going to keep me out here forever, Mom." He looked as torn as he felt and his mother felt sorry for him.

"You can't marry a store, Bernard." Her voice was soft and low. She was operating against her own interests, but for her son's and it was worth it.

"I've thought of that."

"So?"

He sighed again. "I owe a lot to Paul Berman."

For an instant, Ruth looked angry. "Not enough to give your life up for him, or your happiness, or the happiness of your children. As I see it, he owes you more than you owe him, after all you've done for that store."

"It's not as simple as all that, Mother." Bernie looked exhausted and she hurt for him.

"Maybe it should be, sweetheart. Maybe you should think about that."

"I will." He smiled at last and kissed her cheek, and then he whispered, "Thank you."

Three days later she joined Lou in San Diego, and Bernie was genuinely sorry to see her go. She had become his friend over the years, and even Megan missed her.

"She's a wonderful woman, Bernie."

He grinned at the woman he was so desperately in love with. It was their first night alone since his mother left, and it felt good to be lying side by side in her bed again. "She said the same thing about you, Meg."

"I have a lot of respect for her. And she loves you a lot." He smiled. He was glad that they liked each other. And she was happy just being with him. She never tired of his company, they spent hours together whenever they could, talking and hugging and making love. Sometimes they stayed awake all night just to be together.

"I feel like I haven't seen you in weeks," he whispered as he nuzzled into Megan's neck. He was hungry for her body and the feel of her skin next to his own, as they lay side by side and made love, until the phone rang in the distance.

It always amazed them how hungry they were for each other. Their desire for each other hadn't abated in the eight months since they'd begun making love, and they were still breathless as she pulled away apologetically to reach for the phone. But she was on call for Patrick.

He lay closer to her, and fondled her nipple, not wanting to let her leave him.

"Baby, I have to . . ."

"Just this once . . . if they don't find you, they'll call Patrick."

"They may not be able to find him." She loved him, but she was always conscientious. She had already pulled herself away from him regretfully, and grabbed the phone on the fourth ring, with the perfume of his loving still hanging over her, as he followed her and held her bottom. "This is Dr.

Jones." It was her official voice, followed by the usual silence. "Where? . . . How long? . . . How many? . . . How often? Get her to intensive care . . . and call Fortgang." She was already grabbing her jeans, their loving forgotten, and this time she looked worried. "And get me an anesthesiologist, a good one. I'll be right over." She hung up the phone and turned to look at him. There was no time to mince words. She had to tell him.

"What was that?"

Oh God . . . it was the worst thing she had ever had to do to anyone. . . . "Baby . . . Bernie . . ." She started to cry, hating herself for the tears that sprang from her eyes, and instantly he knew that something terrible had happened to someone he loved. "It's Jane." His guts shrank at the words. "She was riding her bicycle, and she was hit by a car." She was dressing while she talked to him, and he stood staring at her, as she reached out her hands and touched his face. He looked as though he didn't understand her. He did, but he couldn't believe it. He couldn't believe that God would be that terrible. Not twice in a lifetime.

"What happened? Goddammit, Megan, tell me!" He was shouting at her and she wanted to leave. She had to get to the hospital to see her.

"I don't know yet. She has a head injury, and they're getting an orthopedic surgeon in. . . ."

"What's broken?"

She had to tell him quickly. Time was wasting.

"Her leg, arm, and hip are badly broken, and there could be some damage to her spine as well. They're not sure yet."

"Oh my God . . ." He covered his face with his hands and she handed him his jeans and ran to get their shoes. She helped him put them on, as she put hers on.

"You can't let go now. You can't. We have to get to her. It may not be as bad as it sounds." But it sounded awful, even to her, as a doctor. It was possible that Jane would never walk again. And if there was brain damage from the head injury, it would be disastrous.

He grabbed her arm. "Or it could be worse, couldn't it? She could die . . . or be crippled or be a vegetable for the rest of her life."

"No." She wiped her eyes and pulled him toward the door. "No . . . I won't believe that. . . . Come on . . ." But as she started her car and shot into reverse, pulling onto the highway almost without warning, he stared straight ahead, and she tried to keep him talking. "Bernie, talk to me."

"Do you know why this happened?" He looked as though he had just died, and that was how he felt inside.

"Why?" It was something to say at least. She was going over ninety and praying the cops would come to give her an escort. The nurse at the emergency room had told her what Jane's blood pressure was. She was as close to dead as she could get, and they had a life support machine standing by for her.

"It happened because we were in bed with each other. God was punishing me."

She felt tears sting her eyes, and pushed the accelerator down harder. "We were making love. And God isn't punishing you."

"Yes, he was. I had no right to betray Liz . . . and . . ." He started to sob and his words cut her to the quick, but she kept talking to him all the way to the hospital, to keep him from snapping completely.

As they pulled into the parking lot, she warned him. "I'm going to jump out of the car as soon as we stop. You park it, and come inside. I'll tell you what's happening as soon as I know. I swear." The car stopped and she looked at him. "Pray for her, Bernie. Just pray for her. I love you." And with that she was gone and she came back to him twenty minutes later in a green surgical suit and a cap and mask, with paper slippers over her loafers.

"The orthopedic man is working with her now. He's trying to see how bad the damage is. And there are two pediatric surgeons coming in by helicopter from San Francisco." She had called for them and he knew what it meant when she told him.

"She's not going to make it, is she, Meg?" His voice was half dead. He had called to tell Nanny and he was sobbing so hard she could hardly understand him. She ordered him to pull himself together and told him she'd be waiting by the phone for word. She didn't want to frighten Alexander by bringing him to the hospital. She wasn't even going to tell him. "Is she . . . ?" Bernie was pressing her, and she could see in his eyes how guilty he felt. She wanted to tell him again that it wasn't his fault, that he wasn't being punished for betraying Liz with her, but this wasn't the place for that. She would have to tell him later.

"She's going to make it and if we're very, very lucky, she's going to walk again. Just hang onto that." But what if she didn't? He couldn't get the thought out of his mind as Megan disappeared again. And he sank back into the chair like a rag doll, as a nurse brought him a glass of water, but he didn't want it. It reminded him of Johanssen telling him that Liz had cancer.

The helicopters landed twenty minutes later, and the two surgeons came in at a dead run. Everything was prepared for them and the local orthopedic man assisted, and so did Megan. They had brought a neurosurgeon along too, just in case, but the head injury was not as bad as they had first feared. The real damage was to her hip and the base of her spine. That was the real terror for them now. The leg and the arm were clean breaks. And in one sense, she had been lucky. If the crack in her spine had been two millimeters deeper than it was, she would have been paralyzed from the waist down forever.

The surgery took four hours, and Bernie was almost hysterical when Megan came out to him again, but at least it was over, and she held him in her arms while he sobbed.

"She's all right, baby . . . she's all right . . ." And by the next afternoon they knew she would walk again. It would take time and a great deal of therapy, but she would run and play and walk and dance and Bernie sobbed openly when they told him. He looked down at Jane's sleeping form and he could not stop crying. And the next time she woke up again, she smiled up at him, and then glanced at Megan.

"How're we doing, love?" Megan asked softly.

"I still hurt," she complained.

"You will for a while. But you'll be out playing again in no time."

Jane smiled wanly, looking at Megan as though she was counting on her to help her. And Bernie held Meg's hand openly with one hand as he held Jane's with the other.

Megan and Bernie called his parents together, and it was a shock for them. But Megan gave Bernie's father the details and he was as reassured as they were.

"She was very lucky," he said with awe and relief, and Megan agreed. "It sounds like you did everything right too."

"Thank you, sir." It was a compliment she treasured. And she and Bernie went out for a hamburger after that to discuss the mechanics of the next few months. Jane would be in the hospital for at least six weeks and a wheelchair for months after that. There was no way she could manage the stairs of their San Francisco house in a wheelchair, nor could Nanny. They would have to stay in Napa, and he didn't hate the idea for entirely other reasons.

"Why don't you stay out here? You don't have stairs to worry about out here. She can't go to school anyway, and you could get her a tutor." Megan looked at him thoughtfully and he smiled. A lot was suddenly coming clear to him now, and then suddenly as he looked at her he remembered what he had said to her when it happened.

"I owe you an apology, Megan." He was looking at her tenderly across the dinner table, seeing her as though for the first time. "I felt so guilty . . . I have for a long time, and I was wrong. I know that."

"It's all right." She whispered at him. She understood it.

"Sometimes I feel guilty about how much I love you . . . as though I'm not supposed to do that . . . as though I'm still supposed to be faithful to her. . . . But she's gone . . . and I love you."

"I know you do. And I know you feel guilty. But you don't have to. One day it'll stop."

But the funny thing he suddenly realized was that it had. Sometime in the last day or two. Suddenly he no longer felt guilty for loving Megan. And no matter how long he had left Liz' clothes in the closet, or how much he had loved her. She was gone now.

Chapter 44

The police checked out the accident, and they had even given the driver a blood test within the hour, but there was no question, it was an accident, and the woman who had struck her said she would never recover. The real fault was Jane's, but that was no consolation as she lay in the hospital, recovering from surgery and facing months in a wheelchair, and months of therapy after that.

"Why can't we go back to San Francisco?" She was disappointed to be missing school, and not to be seeing her friends. And Alexander had been scheduled to start nursery school, but all their plans were up in the air now.

"Because you can't manage the stairs, sweetheart. And neither can Nanny, with a wheelchair. This way at least you can go out. And we'll get you a tutor." She looked bitterly disappointed. It had ruined her whole summer, she said. It had almost ruined her life, and Bernie was grateful it hadn't.

"Will Grandma Ruth come back out?"

"She said she would, if you want her." Everything was on hold for the moment.

That brought a small smile, and Megan was spending most of her off-duty hours with her, and they had long thoughtful conversations that brought them closer than they'd been before. The fight seemed to have gone out of her around the same time the guilt had gone out of Bernie. He seemed more peaceful than he had in a while, but he was stunned by the call that came the next day. It was from Paul Berman.

"Congratulations, Bernard." There was an ominous pause, and Bernie held his breath. He sensed that something earthshaking was coming. "I have an announcement to make to you. Three of them, in fact." He didn't waste a moment. "I'm retiring in a month and the board just voted you into my shoes. And we just hired Joan Madison from Saks to fill your shoes in San Francisco. She'll be there in two weeks. Can you get everything wrapped up in San Francisco by then?" Bernie's heart stopped. Two weeks? Two weeks to say goodbye to Megan? How could he? And Jane couldn't be moved for months, but that wasn't the point now. The point was something entirely different and he had to tell him. There was no point putting it off any longer.

"Paul." He felt his chest tighten and wondered if he would have a heart attack. That would certainly simplify everything. But it wasn't what he wanted. He didn't want an easy out now. He knew exactly what he wanted. "I should have told you a long time ago. And if I'd known you were planning to retire, I would have. I can't take the job."

"Can't take it?" Paul Berman sounded horrified. "What do you mean? You've invested almost twenty years of your life preparing for it."

"I know I have. But a lot of things changed for me when Liz died. I don't want to leave California." Or Megan . . . or a dream that she had spawned. . . .

Berman was suddenly frightened. "Has someone else offered you a job? Neiman-Marcus? . . . I. Magnin? . . ." He couldn't imagine that Bernie would defect to another store, but maybe they had made him a remarkable offer. But Bernie was quick to reassure him.

"I wouldn't do something like that to you, Paul. You know my loyalty to the store, and to you. This is just based on a lot of other decisions I had to make in my life. There are some things I want to do here that I couldn't do anywhere else in the country."

"I can't imagine what, for heaven's sake. New York is the lifeline of our business."

"I want to start my own business, Paul." There was stunned silence on the other end, and Bernie smiled to himself as he said it.

"What kind of business?"

"A store. A small specialty store, in the Napa Valley." He felt like a free man just saying the words and he could feel the tension of the last months just flowing out of his body. "It won't be competition for you, but I want to do something very special."

"Have you done anything about starting it yet?"

"No. I had to make a decision about Wolff's first."

"Why not do both?" Berman was desperate and Bernie could sense it. "Open a store out there and get someone else to manage it for you. Then you can come back here and take the place you've earned for yourself at Wolff's."

"Paul, it's something I've dreamed of for years, but it's not right for me anymore. I have to stay here. It's the right decision for me. I know it."

"This is going to be a terrible shock to the board."

"I'm sorry, Paul. I didn't mean to embarrass you, or put you in an awkward position." And then he smiled. "Looks like you can't retire yet then. You're too young to do a foolish thing like that anyway."

"My body doesn't agree with you, especially this morning."

"I'm sorry, Paul." And he was, but he was also very happy. He sat in peaceful silence in his office for a long time after the call. His replacement was coming in two weeks. After years with Wolff's, he was going to be free in two weeks . . . free to start a store of his own . . . but there were other things he had to do first. And he left the store in a hurry at lunchtime.

The house was deathly quiet as he turned the

key in the lock, and the silence which greeted him was as painful as it had been ever since she died. He still expected to find her there, to see her pretty smiling face as she emerged from the kitchen, tossing her long blond hair over her shoulder and wiping her hands on her apron. But there was no one. Nothing. There hadn't been in two years. It was all over, along with the dreams that had gone with it. It was time for new dreams, a new life, and with his heart in his mouth, he dragged the boxes into the front hall, and then into their bedroom. He sat down on their bed for a moment, and then stood up quickly. He had to do it before he started to remember her again, before he inhaled the perfume of the distant past too deeply.

He didn't even take the clothes off the hangers, he just lifted them off the racks in bunches, like the boys in their stockrooms, and dumped them into the boxes along with armloads of shoes and sweaters and handbags. He kept only the beautiful opera gown and her wedding dress, thinking that one day Jane would like to have them. But an hour later, everything else stood in the front hall in six enormous boxes. It took him another half hour to get them all down to his car and stowed inside, and then he walked back into the house for a last time. He was going to sell the house, but without Liz, there was nothing in it he cared about now anyway. It held no charm for him. She had been the charm of their entire existence.

He gently closed the closet door. There was

nothing in it now except the two dresses he had saved in their plastic cases from Wolff's. The rest was empty. She needed no clothes now. She rested in a peaceful place in his heart, where he could always find her. And with a last look around the silent house, he walked quietly to the door, and then outside into the sunshine.

It was a short drive to the thrift shop he knew she had used before for Jane's cast-off clothes. She always felt that nothing should go to waste, and someone could use the things they no longer needed. The woman at the desk was pleasant and chatty and she insisted on giving Bernie a receipt for his "generous donation," but he didn't want it. He only smiled sadly at her and walked out the door, back to the car, and went quietly back to the office.

And the store looked different to him now as he rode up the escalator to the fifth floor. Somehow Wolff's wasn't his now. It belonged to someone else. To Paul Berman and a board in New York. And he knew it would be painful to leave, but he was ready.

Chapter 45

Bernie left the store early that afternoon. There were a number of things he had to do. And he felt exhilarated as he stopped on his errand, and then headed for the Golden Gate Bridge. He had made an appointment with the real estate broker for six o'clock, and he had to drive like crazy to make it. He was twenty minutes late when he arrived, thanks to traffic in San Rafael, but the woman was still waiting for him. And so was the house Megan had shown him months before. The price had even dropped, and it had cleared probate in the meantime.

"Will you be living here with your family?" the woman inquired as she filled out the preliminary papers. Bernie had written her a check as a deposit, and was anxious to get to work to raise the rest of the money.

"Not exactly." He had to get permission to use the house commercially and he was not yet ready to explain anything to this woman.

"It'll make a wonderful rental property with a little work."

"I think so too." He smiled. Their business was concluded at seven o'clock. And he went to a pay phone and dialed Megan's exchange, hoping she was on duty and not Patrick.

When a voice answered a moment later, he asked for Doctor Jones, and the officious voice at the other end informed him that she was in the emergency room but they could page her, if he would give them his name, his child's name and age, and the problem. He claimed to be a Mr. Smith with a little boy called George, who was nine years old and had a broken arm.

"Couldn't I just meet her at the emergency room? He's in a lot of pain." He felt rotten using a ruse like that, but it was for a good cause, and the operator agreed to warn Dr. Jones that they were coming. "Thank you." He hid the smile in his voice and hurried back to his car to drive to the hospital to meet her. And he saw her standing at the desk with her back to him as he walked in, and his whole body smiled at the sight of her. The bright shiny dark hair and the tall, graceful body were just exactly what he had longed to see all day. He walked up behind her and gently patted her behind as she jumped and then grinned, attempting unsuccessfully to look reproachful.

"Hi there. I was just waiting for a patient."

"I'll bet I can guess who."

"No, you can't. He's a new patient. I haven't even met him myself."

Bernie leaned toward her and whispered in her ear. "Mr. Smith?"

"Yes . . . I . . . how did . . ." And then she blushed. "Bernie! Were you playing tricks on me?" She looked stunned but not really angry. It was the first time he had ever done that.

"You mean little George and the broken arm?"

"Bernie!" She wagged a finger at him, and he pulled her gently into an examining room, while she scolded him. "That's a terrible thing to do. Remember the boy who cried wolf."

"That was Wolff's and I don't work there anymore."

"What?" She looked truly stunned and stared at him in amazement. *"What?"*

"I quit today." He looked delighted as he grinned at her, looking far more boyish than the imaginary George ever could have.

"Why? Did something happen?"

"Yes." He laughed. "Paul Berman offered me his job. He wanted to retire."

"Are you serious? Why didn't you take it? That's what you've worked for all your life."

"That's what he said." He was fishing for something in his pocket and he looked extremely happy as she continued to stare at him in amazement.

"But why? Why didn't you . . ."

He looked her straight in the eye. "I told him I was opening my own store. In the Napa Valley."

If it was possible, she looked even more stunned as he beamed proudly at her. "Are you serious or crazy, Bernie Fine?"

"Both. But more about that later. First, there's something I want to show you." And he still had to tell her about the house he had just bought, to house their store. But there was something else he wanted to show her first. He had picked it out with enormous care and thought after he left the office. He handed her a small gift-wrapped box, which she eyed with more than a little suspicion.

"What's that?"

"A very, very small black widow spider. Be careful when you open the box." He was laughing like a boy and her hands trembled as she fought with the wrapping and then found herself holding a black velvet box from a well-known international jeweler.

"Bernie, what is this?"

He stood very close to her and gently touched her silky black hair and spoke so softly that only she could have heard him. "This, my love, is the beginning of a lifetime." He snapped the box open for her and she gasped as she saw the handsome emerald ring surrounded by small diamond baguettes. It was a beautiful ring, a beautiful stone, and the emerald had seemed just right for her. He hadn't wanted to get her a ring like the one he'd bought Liz. This was a whole new life. And now he was ready for it. And when he looked at her, there were tears sliding slowly down her cheeks, and she cried as he put it on and then kissed her. "I love you. Will you marry me, Meg?"

"Why are you doing all this? Quitting your job . . . proposing . . . deciding to open a store

. . . you can't make decisions like that in one afternoon. That's crazy."

"I've been making them for months, and you know it. I just took a long time before I did anything about it, and now it's time."

She looked up into his eyes with joy and a little fear. He was a man well worth waiting for, but it hadn't been simple. "What about Jane?"

"What about her?" Bernie looked startled.

"Don't you think we should ask her first?"

He looked suddenly frightened but Megan insisted.

"She has to adjust to what we want."

"I think we have to tell her before it's a fait accompli," and after a ten-minute discussion, Bernie agreed to go upstairs and discuss it with her, but he was afraid that she wasn't ready.

"Hi." He smiled at her nervously and she sensed something strange about him instantly as they walked into the room, and she could still see the tears on Megan's eyelashes.

"Something wrong?" She looked worried but Megan was quick to shake her head.

"Nope. We want your advice about something." She was concealing her left hand in the pocket of her white coat, so Jane didn't see the ring first.

"Like what?" Jane looked intrigued and as though she suddenly felt very important. And she was. To both of them.

Megan looked at Bernie and he moved closer to Jane and reached for her hand as he stood next to the bed. "Megan and I want to get married, sweetheart, and we want to know how you feel about it." There was a long, pregnant silence in the room as Bernie held his breath and Jane looked at both of them and then smiled slowly as she lay back against her pillows.

"And you asked me first?" They both nodded and she grinned. This was terrific. "Wow. That's really something." Even her mother hadn't done that, but she didn't tell Bernie.

"Well, what do you think?"

"I think it's okay . . ." She smiled at Megan. "No . . . I think it would be pretty nice really." All three of them grinned and Jane started to giggle. "Are you gonna give her a ring, Daddy?"

"I just did." He fished Megan's hand out of her pocket. "But she wouldn't say yes, till you did." Jane shot a glance at Megan that said they were friends forever for that one.

"Are we gonna have a big wedding?" Jane inquired and Megan laughed.

"I haven't even thought of that. So much happened today."

"You can say that again." He told Jane about leaving Wolff's, and then he told them both about the house he was buying to open his store in. They both stared at him in amazement.

"You're really going to do it, Daddy? Open the store, and we'll move to Napa and everything?" Jane clapped her hands in excitement.

"I sure am." He grinned at both his ladies and sat down on one of the chairs provided for visitors. "I even thought of a name for it on the drive up here."

Both of his ladies waited expectantly. "I was thinking about both of you, and Alexander, and all the good things that have happened lately . . . the fine moments in my life, and then it came to me." Megan slipped her hand into his, and he could feel the emerald on her finger and it pleased him as he smiled at her and then at his daughter. "I'm going to call it 'Fine Things.' What do you think of that?"

"I love it." Megan smiled happily at him and Jane squealed with delight. She didn't even mind being stuck in the hospital now, so many good things were happening to them.

"Can I be a bridesmaid at the wedding, Meg? Or flower girl or something?" There were tears in Megan's eyes as she smiled at her and nodded, and then Bernie leaned over and kissed his bride.

"I love you, Megan Jones."

"I love all three of you," she whispered, glancing from father to daughter, and including Alexander. "And Fine Things is a beautiful name. . . . Fine Things . . ." It was a fitting description of all that had happened to him since he'd met her.